THE
THREAD
THAT BINDS

CEDAR McCLOUD

Printed in the United States of America

Third printing.

ISBN-13: 978-0-9995449-2-1

Published by Numinous Spirit Press
numinousspiritpress.com

A Note About Pronouns

Most of the characters in this book use the English neo-pronoun set e/em/eir(s), as they live in a culture that doesn't traditionally have a concept of gender—though there are characters from other countries that do.

Neo-pronouns can take some getting used to, it's true! I encourage you to keep reading even if they feel a little strange or clunky. One of the best ways we can get comfortable with new language is to use it a bunch. Real life people use neo-pronouns, including e/em, which I did not invent. If we can normalize new language like this, it will make the world easier for so many folks!

How to pronounce and use e/em/eir(s):

I saw **him** walking to the store with **his** friend. **He's** picking up the food **he** ordered. That box is **his**.

I saw **em** walking to the store with **eir** friend. **E's** picking up the food **e** ordered. That box is **eirs**.

e – pronounced like the "e" in "he"
em – pronounced like the "em" in "them"
eir(s) – pronounced like the "eir(s)" in "their(s)"

You may see a few other neo-pronoun sets like ze/hir in the book, but they are very rare. Otherwise, sometimes characters use singular they/them for someone whose pronouns they don't know. Characters with binary genders use she/her and he/him. **Please be respectful of a character's pronouns when writing reviews. If you're not sure, contact me!**

Thank you!
(signed, your nonbinary author who goes by they/them)

Glossary

Some terms you may want to become familiar with that appear over the course of the book:

Ren, Renna – gender neutral term equivalent to "Mom" or Dad," from "paRENt"

Grandren, Great-Grandren – same as above but for a grandparent or great-grandparent

Nibling – gender neutral form of niece/nephew

Entie - gender neutral form of aunt/uncle

Priestex – gender neutral form of priest(ess)

Prx. – abbreviation for Priestex, used as an honorific

Goddex - gender neutral form of god(dess)

Abbex - gender neutral form of abbot/abbess

Nun – is used in a gender-neutral fashion instead of "monk" to counteract the way masculine forms of address are often used as the "neutral."

Mx. – gender neutral honorific to replace Ms./Mr.

Mgx. – short for "Magistrix," an honorific for those who work in highly skilled magical fields like Illumination

Poppy beetle/bug – a ladybug (I had to take out the word lady, you see)

I did not invent all of these and/or others have invented the same words concurrently to me, so please feel free to use them in your own work or use them in real life!

Heat Level

Low to nonexistent. Someone makes a joke about masturbating.

Content Warnings

Please be advised that the following appear in *The Thread That Binds*, and though I've done my best to handle them with care, may be triggering to some:

- **emotional abuse, manipulation, and gaslighting by parents to an adult child, and by a mentor/boss to an employee**
- **discussion of past emotional child abuse and its effects**
- a nightmare concerning past emotional child abuse
- mention and brief threat of domestic violence
- minor character death/death of a mentor (off page, peaceful, assisted death)
- mention of terminal brain cancer diagnosis (not explored further beyond one line)
- characters attend a memorial service/funeral
- discussion of toxic friendships
- descriptions of anxiety, panic attack, and PTSD symptoms, including dissociation
- use of spiritual/religious beliefs to manipulate people and accrue power
- weight loss due to illness
- historical figures who were victims of murder or were murderers
- expressions of grief

Bold = major theme

If you would like elaboration or clarification on any of these warnings, including what chapter they occur in, please go to **numinousspiritpress.com/t3b-cw** for more info. Please note that this page contains many major spoilers.

Part One: Stories
Summer 4018

TABBY

Stars twinkle overhead. There are no constellations a waking mind would recognize, but I know them as I know my own heart. They shift on a whim, shaped by thought and emotion—seasons of the spirit, rather than of nature.

I make my way through a thicket of tall grasses, glancing upwards every fifty feet or so. The path can change quickly, and one wrong step could whisk me far away from my destination. The easiest way to travel in the dreamscape is to stay still and conjure the place you want to visit with a memory or wish. But some places are hidden too deeply in the subconscious. You have to make the journey on foot.

Creatures shuffle through the grass around me unseen. They might be spirits, or they might be figments of my subconscious. I keep my mind clear in case it's the latter, not wanting an encounter to slow me from reaching the garden. I abandoned it years ago, so it isn't surprising to find the way so overgrown and unkempt.

After the grasses, a briar thicket. The canes range from hairlike tendrils to poles as thick as my wrist. The red thorns on them are long, sharp daggers, protection against unwanted visitors. I gaze through the looping briars for the secret tunnel and find it immediately. After all these years, some part of me still remembers.

I get down on my hands and knees, imagining myself smaller, younger. The last time I came here, I was thirteen, big for my age and already six feet tall. It had been difficult then. I imagine myself at nine, soft and round and looking for an escape. My spirit body shifts, and the briars grow larger. The thorns aren't quite as menacing now, but magical and inviting.

I start crawling. The ground beneath my hands is covered in leaf litter and dotted with glowing blue mushrooms. The sky overhead deepens first, then grows light as I crawl on; it was always daytime in the garden. I'd been afraid of the dark as a child. Nighttime had always come with shouting matches and breaking dishes.

By the end of the tunnel, it's nearly dawn. The round portal of sky before me, edged with thorns, is the color of a ripe peach. Pink rosebuds line the briar canes, gathering energy to bloom. My heart pounds. This is it. This is the edge of the garden I created all those years ago, the one I—

Tabby!

Oh, no. Not yet.

"Taaaabby!"

The dreamscape fades. I open my eyes, staring at the gauzy canopy above in confusion. I was just on my knees. How did I get on my back? I blink and roll over. Something is making an annoying chiming noise.

I pull aside the curtain and fumble for my phone on the nightstand to silence the alarm. It says it's been going off for a while, but that's not what woke me up.

"Ah, there you are," Rhiannon says from the doorway. "Sorry, but your alarm was going off for like, ten minutes."

"You can hear it out there?"

My voice is still groggy with sleep. Rhiannon smiles and leans against the doorframe, still wearing pajamas emself. My platonic partner is thin and lanky, with brown skin and green eyes. Eir long purple hair floats around em in frizzy wisps. Bedhead.

"I mean, I can hear it when I walk by your door, and normally I wouldn't wake you up until it's been going for like, twenty, but today's kind of important," Rhiannon says, "right?"

"Oh!" A different kind of alarm goes off inside me. Psychic test day at the Eternal Library is finally here. "Yes, right! Thank you, Rhee."

I jump out of bed and start searching the closet for an appropriate outfit. Today… something floral. I pick a white dress covered in pink roses. Comfortable, but professional enough with the right shoes. I want to look presentable and friendly.

"You're welcome," Rhiannon says, arms crossed. "I'ma go get breakfast going, kay?"

I smile with the dress halfway on, still over my head. Rhee is usually too lazy to make anything but cereal on work days, but today is special. Today, I'm taking a giant step towards getting my dream job.

The smell of batter and butter fills the apartment as I continue getting ready, making sure my face is washed and my hair brushed. It's easy for me to accidentally skip ordinary tasks when I'm nervous, but Rhiannon posted a checklist by the mirror. I nearly put hand soap on my toothbrush, but otherwise, it keeps me in order.

By the time I join em in the living area, the table has been set not only with pancakes and jam, but tea as well. Our fanciest teapot, the glass one with a compartment for gem infusions, is steeping fresh rosemary and sage. An amethyst crystal sits in a little glass bubble in the bottom of the teapot, close enough to infuse the tea with its energy without actually touching the liquid. Amethyst isn't toxic when dropped in water, but a lot of crystals are.

"All this for me?" I ask. Warmth spreads through my chest, smothering my nerves.

"I know you're gonna pass these tests and blow the competition outta the water," Rhiannon says, shaking a spatula at me, "but what kinda partner would I be if I didn't? Sit. Eat."

Rhiannon and I have been together for six years now, but it's still a surprise when someone wants to take care of me. Usually I'm the one doing the caretaking. I do my share in our relationship, but that's just it—it's shared. Equal. Thinking about that as I eat makes the pancakes and apricot preserves taste extra sweet.

Once e dumps the dishes in the sink, Rhiannon plops down at the table and starts shoveling food into eir mouth. E grabs a thick tome from the other end of the table and lays it open gently beside eir plate. Rhiannon would never crack a book's spine, but to me, there's something magical about an obviously well-loved book. I should probably take more care if I'm going to work at the Library. Rhiannon might forgive my rough handling, but I'm not sure they would.

I pour the steaming tea into our cups and hope all my preparations are going to pay off.

***

The Eternal Library is only a short train ride away. We picked our apartment so that Rhiannon—and I, with any luck—could be close to work. The station platform bustles with librarians, conservationists, researchers, and patrons, but Rhiannon marches confidently through the chaos towards campus, as e has for years now. I follow easily, Rhee's purple hair a beacon in the crowd. I wonder if anyone we pass is also hoping for an apprenticeship, if they feel as terrified and excited as I do. I wonder where they've come from, and why they're here, and if they might be better suited for the job than me.

When we step outside of the station, all of those wonders fall away. This side of campus hosts the oldest surviving buildings (*The oldest* above-ground *buildings,* I hear Rhee correct me in my mind): a trio of sandstone structures shaped like seashells. Abalone, whelk, snail. They glow in the morning golden light, round windows gleaming like portholes into another world.

But that's nothing compared to what's inside.

"You want me to come in the front with you, Tabs? Normally I use a side door," Rhiannon says as we approach.

I nod. I could use the company.

I've been in the Library many times, but today feels different. The smell of ink and paper hits me harder than usual with waves of relief and nostalgia. It feels like home. Or what home should be. The polished black granite floor glitters under our feet as we walk through the lobby and past the three enormous statues of the Founders.

Light pours into the atrium from the dome high overhead, making the statues appear to glow. Amethyst for Isylwyn, rose quartz for Daryn, and white quartz for Eirlys. Small pockets of geodes glitter in their otherwise smooth sides. One thousand years ago, they founded the art of Illumination: the creation of magical, immortal illustrated manuscripts. Books that will never crumble with age, and last until the end of time, should they be kept safe from fire and water. They then founded the Eternal Library to house all the world's written knowledge—something it still strives to do to this day.

I touch the statue of Eirlys as we pass. For luck. The stone is warm and makes my fingers tingle.

Rhiannon leads me through a maze of bookshelves, taking what must be the most efficient route even if it zigzags unpredictably. On any other day I'd mosey through the stacks, pick up anything that looked interesting and bring it to a cozy nook to read. Today there's no time for that. We leave the books to themselves.

Eventually, we reach a long hall full of meeting rooms. One of them has the doors propped open, with a sign that says "Bindery Psychic Testing." There are already people inside, and my nerves skyrocket. My arms and legs feel ghostly, my heart fluttering in my chest like a hummingbird.

Rhiannon peers at me over eir glasses. They're oversized and round, with clear red rims. Definitely the look of a Librarian.

"You're gonna do awesome, Tabs," e says.

"You don't know that," I say.

"Sure I do. I know you."

"But what if there's someone better than me?"

"Then I'll tie them up," Rhiannon says, "and put them on a train going out of town—"

"*Rhee.*"

Rhiannon shrugs. "Just sayin'. Anyway, in that case, it doesn't mean you're *not good enough*, okay?"

I hesitate, but Rhiannon raises eir eyebrows and peers further over eir glasses in a funny way.

"Okay, okay," I say, a laugh escaping me.

We hug, and Rhiannon heads off towards the Archives. I head inside the doors.

CHAPTER TWO
RHIANNON

I head down the steps to the Archives, nerves zinging with excitement for Tabby. The bright light from the windows fades, replaced by dim crystal lamps. My body relaxes a little. I've always liked the lighting down here better. There aren't any windows, just stone walls worn smooth by the passage of time and thousands of Librarians. The carpets beneath my feet are soft and faded. Newer parts of the Archives are made from concrete, but the main hub—if it can even be called that, in the labyrinth of tunnels down here—is hundreds of years old and carved into the bedrock of the mountains, sealed off from water and weather with ancient mixtures of pitch and sap. It smells like dirt and old paper. What could be better?

The average person wouldn't look at the Archives and think "library." There are a few public-facing stacks, the shelves locked and covered by glass-fronted doors. Most objects down here are stored out of sight and reach of patrons in giant metal flat files, rolling cabinets with airtight drawers, or stone reliquaries with impossibly heavy lids. Millions of books, pamphlets, codices, manuscripts, scrolls, tapestries, photographs, drawings, maps; a vast hoard of knowledge and history unlike any other in the world.

If only everything down here was so neatly filed away. I weave my way through corridors filled with piles of yellowing paperbacks, in various states of disrepair. There haven't always been enough Librarians to handle a collection that strives to include *every book in the world ever written*. Especially when earthquakes and fires have rolled through the area every few decades. What do you do with the books when the above-ground structures fail? Shove them in the basement!

It's a mess, but I love it.

The main office area is, to my chagrin, a shared space. A naturally formed cavern that was sculpted to include shelves in the stone, and quartz veins enchanted to light it. Our desks and workstations are spaced evenly throughout, except for the Head Archivist's office at the northern end.

I eye the heavy metal door as I plop my bag down beside my desk. It's closed, but there's light shining through the little porthole window. Great, Mairead is here. Not that e's ever *not* here. From the half-eaten breakfast on the desk closest to the office, Camille's here, too. They must be having a meeting.

I edge up to the door, listening. I'm a nosy bastard by nature, but down here it pays to get the drop on the latest gossip before it gets the drop on *you*. The heavy door and stone walls muffle their conversation, but it sounds like—

The door flies open and nearly hits me in the face. I jump back, not wanting to lose my glasses or my teeth, and watch Camille storm out, auburn hair frazzled and fists clenched. Her pale skin is flushed, a scowl distorting her usually amiable middle-aged face.

"I can't take this," Camille huffs. "I know how I feel, and I know what happened, and you can't tell me otherwise anymore."

Mairead steps out of the office behind Camille. E looks calm, but then, Mairead always looks calm. Mairead is in eir early sixties, olive-skinned with salt and pepper hair cut into a neat bob. Tiny little round glasses perch on an equally tiny nose. E's slender and shorter than me, a Librarian in a dancer's body. The only indication that e's been arguing with Camille is a wrinkle between eir thick black eyebrows.

"I was just trying to make sure you understood my intentions," Mairead says.

Camille stops beside the studio doors and crosses her arms. She throws a glare over her shoulder at Mairead.

"I understand them *just fine,*" Camille says.

"Then why are you reacting this way?" says Mairead. "There was never any intended harm. Just a lot of misunderstandings, it seems."

Camille makes an exasperated noise and draws her arms tighter around herself, hunching over. "You always make it sound so reasonable," she mutters under her breath.

"I'm sorry you feel upset about it."

Slowly, Camille turns to face Mairead, eyes blazing. "This is exactly what I'm talking about. *You're* sorry that *I* feel upset." She puts her hands on her hips, brow furrowed as if bracing herself for impact. "I'm going up to HR. Expect a letter of resignation under your door later today. I'm transferring to Restoration like I should have moons ago," she says.

The line between Mairead's brows deepens, and e starts to say something, but Camille is already gone, the doors to the studio swinging behind her. If I hadn't come in early to take Tabby to the testing room, I probably wouldn't have witnessed that. I'd have come in to an office buzzing with rumor and hearsay, each person's overheard version of events a step farther from the truth.

Mairead's head suddenly swivels in my direction. Eir gray eyes bore into me, and I take a step back.

"Rhiannon," e says slowly. Thoughtfully.

"Uh, mornin'," I say.

Mairead's sharp stare melts into something kinder. E glides across the space between us, hands pressed together in an apologetic gesture. Despite the dustiness of the Archives and the amount of ink we handle, Mairead's clothes are always spotless. Today it's a crisp gray suit that matches eir eyes.

"I'm sorry you had to see that," e says. "I try my best, but sometimes Camille can have a bit of a temper. Seems it got the best of her, finally."

That strikes me as odd. Camille is strict sometimes about rules, but I've never seen her yell at anyone. Except Mairead, I guess.

"So, Camille's gone?" I ask.

"Yes, it seems that way. She has a lot going on at home, and I think she's been taking some of that out on me without realizing. Poor dear."

It seems funny to call someone in their forties "poor dear," but I guess Camille is twenty years younger than Mairead. What does that make me, the youngest employee in the Archives by a generation? The other archivists treat me like one of their grandkids or niblings, even though I'm twenty-seven. Some of them are sweet about it. Others, not so much.

"That's too bad," I say. I don't know anything about either of their home lives, just that their work arguments have been escalating for weeks. It was only a matter of time before Camille quit or got fired, like all the other Head Assistant Archivists.

Mairead sighs and puts a hand on my shoulder. I stiffen. Most of my coworkers know I don't like to be touched unexpectedly, but Mairead has trouble remembering. I don't say anything, because I know e'll make a big deal out of apologizing and explaining, for the hundredth time, that e can't help being so touchy-feely. It's how e expresses emself.

Using eir grip on my shoulder, Mairead steers me over to the lounge where we keep the tea and couches. E fills a teapot from the water cooler and sets it to steep, while I sit down. The floral print couches are as ancient as anything down here; they may as well be carved from stone, too. What do you expect from people who do everything they can to preserve the past?

"You've been here for some time now, haven't you?" Mairead asks.

"Here this morning, or here in general?"

"I do like your sense of humor," e says. "I meant in general, how long you've been working at the Library."

"Eight years," I say.

Mairead taps one finger against eir chin. "Has it been that long already? I remember when you first got here. We hadn't gotten any new, young blood in a very, very long time, and you were *very* young. Everyone was so excited."

Of course they were. I was nineteen, but I had a master's degree in Cultural Resource Management and ancient Casporan languages already. "Child genius." A prodigy with an unusual talent for psychometry, in that I can touch objects—like books or photographs—and receive visions of their pasts. They had me demonstrate for them, to test whether what I saw in my scrying bowl of ink was accurate. They were so excited by the results that they kept handing me new objects until I nearly passed out from exhaustion. I was hired on the spot.

I shrug. The timer beeps, and Mairead fills two cups with tea. The scent of lavender fills the nook. Not my choice of early morning brew, but it does soothe my nerves. I'm not sure where this conversation is going. The news about Camille quitting is buzzing around inside me like a giant wasp.

Mairead sets the teapot on the coffee table, along with two cups. The table is a huge slab from an old fallen redwood, inlaid with a pre-Revolutionary map of Caspora City. It's probably worth a mint, or it would be if we didn't constantly spill tea on it. The cups are bone china that's translucent at the rims and decorated with gold leaf. I researched the maker's stamp on the bottom once, and they're at least fifty years old. As I said, nothing new down here. Except me.

"It's good, you being young. Someone has to carry on the traditions down here," Mairead says. "Much as I'd like to, I won't be here forever."

"None of us will," I say. "That's death for you."

Mairead sits down beside me, a little too close. I scoot away, and e notices, by the flicker of eir eyes. E doesn't question it, though, just snorts at my words.

"There's that sense of humor again. If you're lucky, though, you have a lot longer before death comes for you than I do," e says. E picks up a teacup and sips at it delicately, eying me from the side. "Have you thought much about the future of your Library career?"

I smother a jolt of surprise and excitement. There's an obvious reason why Mairead would ask that question, but I won't believe it until I hear it. It's too good to be true.

"Well, you know, a bit," I say, even though being head of the Archives has been my dream since I was twelve.

"Surely someone as promising as you doesn't plan to translate photo captions and update that Astranet database for the rest of your life," Mairead says. "I feel like we haven't been putting your talents to their full use."

I shrug, but my nerves are zinging again. There's a ball of electricity sitting in my chest, humming and zapping me every few seconds. I try to keep my feet still. My hands are twitchy inside the pockets of my slacks.

A slow smile spreads across Mairead's face. "Rhiannon, how would *you* like to be my new assistant?"

CHAPTER THREE
AMANE

I still can't believe I'm here. Here! On the other side of the world, in Caspora City, in the Eternal Library, in a room where I'll test for an apprenticeship with one of the best Illuminators alive today. I actually *made it*, and I'm here.

The room is an amphitheater-style lecture hall, big enough to house a hundred. Floor-to-ceiling windows drench the mural on the opposite wall with light, making the gold halo around Daryn Sunseeker's head glow. In Gildea, the Founders of Illumination and the Library are legendary, but here they're deities. The mural paints Daryn's lovely, round form with reverence, a shining bottle of ink held in each soft brown hand. The Founder's kind green eyes gaze down at me as if e were alive.

As if eir spirit were in the room with us. I shiver a little. The Library is *brimming* with spirits, and they all want my attention. Many of them are ghosts. Others are mysterious denizens of the astral, the spiritual plane which overlaps with ours. Overwhelming them all are the books, a vast ocean of whispers constantly beneath the surface of the physical world. Their words flutter like paper against my spirit body, felt rather than heard.

I thought about putting on extra wards this morning to turn down the volume, but I didn't want it to interfere with the testing. So, I'll just have to deal with it.

There are a dozen of us here. I was the first one to arrive, half an hour early (as planned), waiting until a staff member came to unlock the doors. I sat myself in the center front row seat and watched the other eleven bookbinding Illumination candidates trickle in (also as planned, to scope out the competition). They're of all different ages and appearances, possibly from all over the world. Although, it's true they could have been born here. Caspora City has been a neutral zone during times of war for centuries and a hub of learning for longer, always welcoming to immigrants—myself included.

About half the group are indigenous Casporans, with warm, medium brown skin and black hair, their eyes in shades of green and brown. One of them is covered in tattoos that I swear move out of the corner of my eye. An older Noxian person with broad shoulders is wearing several pounds of amber jewelry. A few people are frowning, focused on journals full of notes, while others are sitting meditatively, their eyes closed and faces relaxed. One very tall, large white person with blonde hair looks like they're about to fall asleep on their desk.

I just sit and watch. I'm ready. I've *been* ready.

One minute to start time, the actual Illuminators come in. I sit up straighter, my heart pounding as I recognize my idol, my inspiration, in the flesh for the first time.

Juniper Stargrove, age sixty-four, Senior Illuminator and Librarian, is of average height and build. Eir face is pale and freckled, with deep laugh lines around eir eyes and mouth. Several inches of gray roots fade into brilliant red hair that falls around eir shoulders in fluffy waves, and e's wearing loose linen clothing the colors of the sea. Everything about em is buoyant and calm.

E's smiling now as e helps a much older Librarian navigate eir electric wheelchair up a ramp and onto the lecture stage. This person must be in eir eighties at least, even shorter than me— and I'm just over five feet tall. Absolutely tiny, with wrinkled brown skin and wispy snow white hair in a pixie cut. Eir green eyes are sharp, flickering from the stage to all of us seated in the first two rows. I feel eir gaze go over me like an x-ray scan.

Behind the two of them is another person about Juniper's age, an extremely tall indigenous Casporan with elegant posture. E's leanly muscled and wearing a sleek black dress with voluminous sleeves rolled up at the elbow. Eir silver and white hair is pulled up into a bun, but a few loose curls have escaped. Gold glints on eir ears, fingers, wrists, and in eir eyes; they're that peculiar yellow-gold color that I'd never seen before I moved to Caspora. Eir lips are painted bright red and pressed into a stern line.

The tall Illuminator sits on a chair farther back from the edge, where Juniper is standing beside the tiny Librarian in the wheelchair. The latter gazes out at all of us with eir x-ray eyes again. I shiver, feeling pinned to my seat. The room is quiet in tense anticipation.

"Good morning," the Librarian says, eir voice soft but clear, "welcome to the Eternal Library. Doubtless most of you have been here before, but if this is your first visit, then welcome all the more. I'm Catrina Rosefall, Head Illuminator and Head Librarian, soon to be retired from both. But while I'm still here, I welcome your shining auras and faces."

The Head Librarian. *Of course.* Catrina Rosefall has been in the position for nearly forty years, and will stay there until e dies. The oath of the Head Librarian is for life. I wonder what e means then, talking about retirement. I didn't think that was technically possible.

"You can call me Rose," e continues, "none of this 'Your Honor' nonsense. With me are the Magistrixes Stargrove, whom you can call by their first names so as not to confuse them. You should keep the honorific, though, to be polite."

Juniper clears eir throat and waves cheerily at us.

"Hello! Yes, I'm June, and I'm the one you're all looking for an apprenticeship with, if you didn't know what I looked like already," e says. E gestures at the tall Illuminator behind em. "This is my spouse Aeronwy, who also works in the Bindery. E's here to help with the testing."

Aeronwy nods respectfully in our direction. I hope my surprise doesn't show too clearly on my face. I knew Juniper—June, I guess e prefers—was married to another Illuminator, but I hadn't thought to do research on em as well, and I'm not familiar with eir work. They look like complete opposites.

"Oh, and all of us use e/em pronouns!" June adds.

"Ah, yes, thank you, June," Rose says. "We train only a handful of Illuminators a decade. It is a profession that requires an enormous amount of knowledge, creativity, and psychic ability. Those of you here have passed the technical requirements for those first two things with the sample work and resumes you sent in. Today we're here to make sure you have the third element.

"Especially," e continues, leaning forward, "because this apprenticeship is for a permanent spot on our own team. Most Illuminators trained here will leave to work at other libraries, other binderies, but whichever one of you is chosen will, if you complete your apprenticeship, get to work here, where the craft originated. I understand this is very desirable to all of you."

That's an understatement. I wouldn't have come halfway around the world if this wasn't the thing I wanted most in my whole entire life. I could've learned Illumination in Gildea and worked in a bindery there, sure. But it wouldn't have been the *same*. This is the birthplace of Illumination, the largest library in the world, with the most resources and prestige. On top of that, I'd get to learn it all from June, whose work inspired me to take this life path in the first place.

There's total silence among the candidates. I steal a glance around and see that everyone is absolutely entranced. The ambient psychic energy in the room was high already, and rises still as everyone turns on and tunes in. They're going to be tough competition.

Rose pats June's arm, and June bends down to take several rectangular cloth-wrapped objects from the bags hanging on the back of the wheelchair. They look like books. They have to be books. Why would they be anything else? Still, I'm curious. And surprised. I figured psychic testing would involve testing our specific clair-abilities with cards and crystal balls and silver mirrors and all that.

Aeronwy and June carefully take the wrapped packages and deposit one on each candidate's desk. I'm the fourth to receive mine, from June, who flashes me an encouraging smile. I could just about die of happiness… but first I have to ace this test.

The cloths are all different colors, and mine is a soft, mottled red. It looks hand-dyed, maybe with madder. Some people are touching theirs, but we haven't been instructed to do anything yet, so I keep my hands in my lap.

"Unwrap your books, please," Rose says.

Chapter Three

I do as e asks. Under the layers of cotton is a slim hand-bound tome with a cloth cover the color of rust. The title, embossed in gold, is *Beginner's Knot Magic*. Curlicues and flourishes of turquoise are inlaid around it in a beautiful pattern that all comes together at the bottom in an intricate knot. I run my fingers over it lightly and the book's spirit stirs like rough rope against my skin. Every book has a spirit, but Illuminated books are stronger and more powerful. They'd have to be, in order to last forever.

The Stargroves pass out paper and pencils next. As if I didn't bring my own. If anyone in this room didn't come prepared at that most basic level, they shouldn't be here. But I'll use the materials provided since that seems to be the official approach.

There's a low murmur of conversation going now as people compare what they got. The older candidate next to me with all the amber jewelry has a big green book with a hand-illustrated cover and decorative stab binding. The thread stitching the spine together is designed to look like leaves going down the left-hand side of the cover. I've never seen a stab binding that intricate, and I wish I had that book instead. Maybe they'll let us trade off afterwards.

"This test is simple," Rose says, bringing us back to attention. "Ask your books about themselves. What they're about, what they're made of, who they were made by, et cetera. Tell us things you couldn't know from reading it or examining its physical form. Use whatever methods of divination or psychic ability you like."

Everyone starts moving at once. I open my purse and take out one of the oracle decks I always carry with me. I only own about two hundred of the things, and rotate them accordingly—except for my Great-Grandmother's Threadbound Oracle, which never leaves my side.

Maybe because Great-Grandma herself is still attached to it. I feel her presence within the cards like a warm, leathery hand holding mine. The deck is old and worn, perfectly fit to my small hands. Even though I brought other decks, I can't imagine using any but this for something so important.

I plant my feet firmly on the floor and take a deep breath, grounding and centering myself. The extra spirit chatter isn't making this easy, but I've worked in noisy places before. Eyes closed, I put my hands on the book and invite its spirit to talk with me. I sense the rough rope feeling against my palms again, and a general air of assent. Good. I let my hands linger to get a better connection, then pick up the deck and start shuffling.

The noise of the cards slapping against one another is loud in the lecture hall, and more than one person turns to look at me, including June and Rose. I feel the heat rising in my face, but I don't stop. This is how I get the clearest messages, short of actual possession (which would be too intense, here among strangers). I won't be embarrassed by it. I'm not the only person who's pulled out a divination tool: I see pendulums and rune stones and bones on people's desks, but they've got soft cloths to cast onto. Theirs don't make much noise.

I lay out a row of three cards and flip them over quickly. Three of Thread, The Weaver, The End. The first two cards are expected for a book about knot magic, but the third one is interesting. It shows a rainbow skein of threads about to be snipped by a pair of golden scissors, floating on a hard black background.

I write my findings down and pull a few more cards, pausing to touch the book a few more times to keep the connection going and ask questions. The author of the book wanted the information to be as simple and distilled as possible, hence the slim size. It's not just about making magical connections, but shearing them, too, when they've gone bad. I think the book wanted to be made out of the same materials used for threads and twines and ropes. The paper is made of hemp, the cover cloth cotton.

Does that mean the Illuminator asked the book how it should be made? Is that how this works? Illumination is an initiatory tradition, the specifics of the craft kept secret from the outside world. I know it involves forging a deep connection with the book spirits, but that's about all.

After half an hour, I feel like I've written plenty. I take a moment to stretch and rest my mind before proofreading. I glance around the room. Everyone is bent over their books and papers, focused on absolutely nothing else. Everyone but the sleepy blonde candidate, who appears to be taking a *nap* with their head on their book. What in the world? The person stirs suddenly and opens their eyes, catching me staring.

I look away quickly, but not before noticing the adorably surprised look on their face. Surprised to find me watching, or surprised that they fell asleep? I bury my nose in my book, pretending to read it while my cheeks burn with embarrassment. Eventually the heat leaves my face, and I read a few pages about wind knots until I get curious again.

Placing the book carefully on the desk, I lean back casually in my chair and do a sweeping glance around the room. All but four of the candidates look like they've finished and are waiting for instructions. The candidate who was sleeping is writing quickly now, a dreamy smile on their face. Was the nap… intentional? They have dimples. It's very cute.

Rose and June watch everyone from the stage. I wonder what they're looking for, if anything. Rose and June pay equal amounts of attention to everyone, but Aeronwy has a notebook open on eir lap—no, a sketchbook. There's a languid look in eir eyes, as if e's not seeing the paper in front of em. But e's definitely sketching something. Bored doodles of us, maybe?

Aeronwy glances up at me as if e can read my thoughts, pencil stilling on the paper. One perfectly manicured eyebrow goes up. This time I don't look away; I feel like I'm being examined. I will myself not to blink and hold Aeronwy's gaze until e smirks and starts drawing again. I feel like I passed a different test just now.

I go back to reading the knot magic book until the hour is up. Rose claps eir hands to get everyone's attention.

"Your test is now over. Bring up your responses and books as we call your names, and then you're free to go. It will take us some time to read everything, but in a week or two you will hear whether we'd like to request an individual interview with you or not. Typically, only a third of testing candidates will get an interview. Among that third, only one will be chosen for the apprenticeship with June. If you have any questions, we're happy to answer them for you now or over email later," e says.

"Good luck! We're looking forward to meeting you!" June adds. E pulls out a piece of paper and adjusts eir glasses, which have stylishly clear blue rims. "First… Amane Sol?"

I wrap my book back in its cloth and gather my papers as quickly as possible. I have *so* much to ask.

CHAPTER FOUR
TABBY

"This place is really fancy, Rhee, are you sure we can afford it?"

"Hey, I'm getting a promotion—which comes with a raise—and you're getting a new job with an even higher pay grade! We can totes afford it," Rhiannon says, snapping out a white cloth napkin and laying it in eir lap.

"I don't have the job yet," I say, "I have an interview."

Rhiannon shrugs and leans eir elbows on the table. "Which you're going to ace, obviously."

I want to protest, but Rhiannon's confidence warms my heart. I lay my own napkin in my lap and pick up the leather-bound menu, which is printed in silver ink. The prices are alarming, but this *is* a special occasion.

Sweet/Salt is a tiny but well regarded seafood restaurant in the heart of the harbor. We're seated on the outdoor balcony, which has a beautiful view of the Seafoam Sound. The water sparkles under the high summer sun, which won't set until after nine. Far out on the peninsula, the Spiral Mountains shadow the horizon, their high peaks capped with white all year round.

The water has such a pleasing hypnotic quality to it. The waves ripple, light and shadow forming and breaking on the surface in an eternal, abstract pattern. My eyes start to close.

"Should we go all the way and get appetizers?" Rhiannon's voice snaps me back to reality. "Because there's some real wild shit on here. Like damn. What even is a 'green tomato glaze' or 'kombu honey' or 'cranberry bean boullion?'"

I take a deep breath and tear my eyes away from the water. I almost drifted off. What would be more embarrassing than falling asleep on the table of a very fancy restaurant? And who knows where on the dreamscape I would have ended up, being so near to the water. There are some strange, deep places there I'd rather not visit. I focus on the menu instead, skimming the names and origins of twelve different kinds of oysters.

"We can find out," I say.

The wait staff comes back and takes our orders. I sip on the bubbly mineral water e left with us, which has cucumbers and mint in it. Rhiannon raises eir glass for a toast and I clink mine against it.

"To dream jobs!" e says.

"Is it really your dream job to work directly under Mairead?" I ask. Rhiannon deserves a promotion, and I'm happy for em, but I don't like what I've heard of the Head Archivist. Namely, that no one lasts long in the Assistant Head Archivist position because of em. There have been three in the last eight years, an unheard of turnover rate for such a position.

"No," Rhiannon says with a scowl of disgust, "but it *does* put me first in line to be Head Archivist when Mairead retires, or, more likely, kicks the bucket. E's *definitely* a lifer."

"That could be twenty years from now," I say. 'Lifers' are Librarians at the Eternal Library who work through their old age all the way until death. They're in love with their work, and the system is very accommodating to them. Beyond even the cushy hours, pay, and benefits everyone shares.

"Eh. You do what you gotta do," Rhiannon says. E shrugs and downs the rest of the bubbly water.

"I'm sorry, I really am excited for you! Just concerned."

"You know I appreciate that about you, Tabs. Always lookin' out for me."

E smiles wryly, but I know e means it. When we first met, Rhiannon was twenty-one and struggling to adjust to life on eir own. Growing up in a family with thirteen kids and four parents meant there was always someone else to share the burden or lend a hand. I was only twenty-four, but I had far more practical life experience. As an only child, I had to take care of myself… and often my parents as well.

"Well, anyway, will you get to handle older, more interesting documents now?" I ask.

"Hell yeah, I will! Probably some Illuminated books, even."

Rhiannon's eyes are sparkling, and e shifts around with a nervous, excited energy. It's been a long time since I've seen em like this. For all the snark and dark humor, Rhee has a bright spark of passion within em. I think it's amazing how far e's come in the Archives in so little time, from such a young age. Especially in a department with such a stark generational divide. All that history down there, waiting…

The twisting halls of the Archives rise in my mind's eye. Dim corridors filled with yellowing pages, the air musty and cool. The floors are inlaid with chipped mosaics that glint in the crystal light, their patterns shifting like the waves on the sound. Ghostly figures drift between the stacks, wearing clothes from all different eras across time. There are Scriptivist nuns in their purple robes, ink witches with their fingers stained black, revolutionaries with yellow scarves who ousted the Authorist theocracy. Their emotions stain the hall with curiosity and grief and determination.

The halls shift and lengthen as I walk down them. Here are the oldest books now, the magical ones handwritten by Illuminators hundreds and hundreds of years ago, trapped behind glass. Illuminated books last forever, but their readers don't. They ask me to let them out. They want to be read. I put my hand on the glass doors of the bookcase—

Rhiannon snaps eir fingers in front of my face, and I wake up. The cool breeze from the Sound whips my hair across my face, which thankfully isn't laid flat against the table. I fell asleep sitting up.

"You wandered off," Rhiannon says.

Wandered off is our code word for my sleep attacks. Or should they be called dream attacks? They've been occasionally triggered by stress since I was a teenager, but recently they've gotten worse. Now any strong emotion or desire can send me immediately into REM.

"I'm sorry," I say. My face heats up, undoubtedly red for all the other diners to see.

"You don't have to apologize. And I don't think anyone noticed," Rhiannon says.

Rhiannon's spark has dimmed for the moment, eir thick eyebrows furrowed in concern. E starts to say something, but our appetizers arrive, interrupting the moment.

I poke at mine, steamed baby clams in saffron broth and a crispy house-made baguette smeared with truffle butter. It looks delicious, but I lose my appetite when I'm worried. And then I worry that my worrying will cause another sleep attack. And then sometimes it does. It's a vicious cycle, and I feel it starting with the squeezing in my stomach.

Rhiannon reaches across the table and lays a hand on mine.

"Hey. We're celebrating tonight," e says. A crooked, reassuring grin spreads across eir face. "You wandering off a little isn't gonna ruin that. Big things are about to happen for us, Tabs. Really big things."

***

They've invited us to Rose's office for the interviews. The Head Librarian works in the Spire, one of the oldest and most beautiful buildings in the Library. It's the one shaped like a whelk shell on the outside. When you step through the doors, you find yourself staring up all the way to the tip. The floors are one continuous spiral around the outside edge of the building, with a central column in the middle like a spindle. Walkways branch off from it in curved white spokes, making you feel like you really are inside of a seashell.

If that weren't enough, this is where most of the Illuminated books are kept. The ones that have been made by hand by Illuminators for centuries, each unique and according to the spirit's wishes. The air is heavy with magical energy, despite the giant obsidian mirrors built into the wall to absorb it. I feel like I could walk straight onto the dreamscape, physical body and all. I resist the urge to try.

Rose's office is at the bottom of the central column. The tall double doors are made of gleaming redwood and carved with bookbinding motifs. Awls, scissors, curling pages, curved needles, spools of thread, swirling text. Rhiannon said they're four hundred years old, cut from a felled tree five times that age.

Another person approaches the doors at the same time I do, startling me out of my thoughts. They look up from their book, eyes going wide with recognition. They're the one I caught watching me during the testing.

"I remember seeing you during the psychic testing! Did you get an interview, too?" they ask in a light Gildean accent, consonants soft and vowels elongated. "My interview's not for a few hours, but I had to make sure I knew where the office was. My name's Amane. She/her pronouns, please."

The words burst from her like bubbles. She holds out her hand for me to shake, which I take cautiously. Her palm is a little sweaty; she must be nervous.

She's also cute. Her skin is deep brown and smooth, save for a few dark beauty marks. She has a heart-shaped face and enormous brown eyes with cat-eye eyeliner so sharp she must use a ruler to do it. Her black hair is pulled up on top of her head in a huge spray of tiny curls that add six inches to her height. The loudly patterned dress of violet and lime ruffles she's wearing hugs all her big curves perfectly.

You know she's your competition, right, Rhiannon's voice says in my head. Right. Well, that doesn't mean I can't be civil. Friendly, even. As if I could be anything else, even to my own worst enemy. If I had enemies.

"Nice to meet you. I'm Tabby," I say. "E/em pronouns are fine. I think I'm next, actually."

"Are you nervous? Excited?" Her eyes shine with emotion.

"Both, definitely."

Amane puts one finger to her lips in thought. She's wearing purple lipstick to match her dress, as if it weren't bold enough on its own. It's the same shade as Rhiannon's hair.

"Can I ask you something? Why were you sleeping during the test? Was that… intentional?" she says, plowing through to her question before I can even respond to the first.

I've heard this sort of thing before. I may be actively exploring the dreamscape, but all outsiders see is my sleeping face. They don't realize I'm doing something magical. I rub the back of my head.

"Well, yes, it was intentional. I'm a dream witch," I explain.

Her well-groomed eyebrows shoot up. "Oh! I see! That makes sense. Can you fall asleep really fast, then? Like on command?"

"Pretty much," I say. Usually explaining my witchcraft to strangers is a chore, but she's so genuinely interested. It's kind of nice to get that kind of attention for once. "When I—"

The doors to the Head Librarian's office open, interrupting me. One of the other candidates, an older Noxian draped in beads, strolls out with a sigh of relief. There's a sheen of sweat on their dark forehead, which they wipe off with a patterned handkerchief. Their arms jangle with silver bangles, giant hoops on their ears flashing as they notice us staring.

"Good luck to whoever's next," they say in a low voice. "It's all three of them in there. Very intimidating."

"Ohhh," says Amane.

She looks at me. So does the other candidate. I wring my hands, not sure what they're waiting for until—

Right. It's my turn. I look at my watch and see that it's exactly two minutes until my interview is scheduled. I shoot to my feet and hurry past them to the doors, waving goodbye to Amane and flashing the other candidate a reassuring smile. I can't help it. I want to soothe anyone in obvious distress, even if it might benefit me to let them suffer.

The Head Librarian's office is utterly dreamy. The room is round, its gently curved walls lined with books arranged, of all things, by color. I love the look of a rainbow bookcase, but I'd never expect to see one in a library. Air plants hang from the ceiling in glass baubles, lit by the world's longest skylight above. In the center of the room is an enormous redwood desk with dozens of drawers and tiny compartments, their knobs sparkling crystals. A set of stylishly mod chairs are lined up before the desk: bright primary red, yellow, and blue.

Behind the desk sits Rose, elevated by eir wheelchair and draped with a thick blanket, even though it's Blackberry Moon and the days are hot. The blanket is neon pink and blue, an eyeful ready to compete with Amane's dress. June and Aeronwy are seated on either side, the former looking comfortable in emerald green linen and the latter intimidating in a sleek black turtleneck. They're all staring at me expectantly. The colors on the wall behind them begin to drip…

No. No, I won't drift off. Not here, not now. I take a few steps forward and hover beside the chairs, smiling through the urge to run off into a dream.

Rose glances down at a clipboard on eir desk. "Tabitha Fairweaver?"

"Yes, that's me," I say.

Rose gestures at the chairs. "Have a seat, please. Thank you for joining us."

I sink down into the central yellow chair and fold my hands in my lap. I didn't bring anything with me. Was I supposed to? Will they judge me for not having any references prepared, notes readied, anything to make it clear how much I want this apprenticeship? I've never been great at being organized. It's easier for me to try my best in the present moment.

Rose leans forward on the desk and smiles. The expression is genuine and meant to be reassuring. I relax.

"First of all, congratulations on making it this far through the selection process," Rose says. "It certainly isn't easy."

I nod and smile. "Thank you. I'm so honored to be here."

"Are you from here, Tabitha?"

"I grew up in Standing Stone, but I've been living in Caspora City since I was eighteen and came here to go to university. It's home."

"And how old are you now?"

"Thirty."

June crosses eir legs and regards me with a pleasantly curious expression. Even with the gray roots and wrinkles that give away eir age, there's something youthful about eir face. E's not holding a clipboard or papers, unlike the other two Illuminators. Eir posture is completely at ease, and there's a mischievous twinkle in eir blue eyes.

"Your application said that you're a dream witch, which made your, ah, approach to the psy-testing much clearer. I was a bit worried before I realized what you were doing. What drew you to oneiromancy?" e asks.

I bite my tongue. I should have expected them to ask a question like that. Should I give them the real answer, or the sanitized one? Going into too much detail might trigger a sleep attack, but I don't want to be dishonest.

"I had a difficult childhood. Dreaming was a way for me to cope with it. Lucid dreaming, and then dreamwalking, was something I learned over time, naturally. When I got older, I did more study on it," I say, keeping my voice even, "but my skill is largely from direct experience."

June nods in understanding. Rose writes something down on eir clipboard. Aeronwy, who was lounging gracefully in eir chair, sits up straighter and watches me.

"Do books dream?" e asks.

June claps eir hands together in delight and leans over to look at Aeronwy. "Ooh, that's a good question. I like that question."

Aeronwy nods in June's direction, but eir eyes don't leave mine.

"They—some books—it's more like, books *are* dreams," I stammer. It feels strange for three of the world's top experts on magical books to ask me such a question. As if they don't know the answer far better than I ever could.

"*Yes*," says Rose, pointing eir pencil at me, "that sounds exactly right."

"Dreams made manifest, dreams of ink and paper," June muses. "Is that what's drawn you to this apprenticeship? This career?"

The accuracy of the observation floors me. No one's ever made that connection before. Usually when I try to explain it, people don't understand. They think I'm talking about wanting to write down the contents of a dream and bind it. They think I want to write a novel inspired by a dream. I've done both of those things, but neither satisfies the desire in my heart.

"Yes… I… Outside of dreams, books were my other method of comfort as I was growing up. They still are. Sometimes I'd fall asleep with a book in bed with me and end up in its world, exploring it in a way that imagination alone could never match. I'd dream things I hadn't gotten to read yet, meet characters before they were introduced on the page… It made me question whether it was my mind making up visions or if what was written exists somewhere on the astral. I thought that if I could make a book from start to finish, I might find out. I—" I hesitate. "Sorry, I started rambling there."

June shakes eir head. E has a smile that lights up eir face, eyes nearly crinkled shut.

"No, no, by all means go on," June says. "I like what you're saying."

"Don't you have more questions to get to?"

E shrugs. "Not necessarily. We want to get to know *you* a little, and why you're here."

"O-okay." This isn't exactly how I thought this interview would go. I'm fine speaking to my credentials, my schooling, my work history, but to talk about myself?

Rose gestures at the papers on eir clipboard. "We know what you're capable of with regards to your work," e says, as if reading my mind. "Your mind and body are ready. But, are *you*? Is your spirit? *That* is what we want to know."

RHIANNON

News of my appointment to the Assistant Head position has spread like wildfire through the Archives, causing a stark divide between those who think I deserve it, and those who don't. Mairead's clique of archivists who attend the Authorist temple e leads are upset because they think one of *them* should have been chosen. The rest, who I'd consider my work friends, are all smiles and congratulations—and joke warnings about how no one has lasted more than three years in the position since Mairead became Head Archivist.

Neither reaction leaves me with particularly warm feelings.

An email pings in my inbox, an automated request to bring an item upstairs to one of the private reading rooms. Normally I hate venturing out of the basement, but I could use a break from this tension. I memorize the call number and scurry off into the stacks before anyone notices.

The requested book is kept in a locked vault embedded with black tourmaline, which means a) it's Illuminated, b) it's super old, and c) super valuable. The book itself is housed in a wooden box carved with a seven-pointed star, a roll of paper, an ink bottle, and a spool of thread: the symbols of the Library. The carvings nearest the edge are worn, presumably by the opening and closing by hundreds of hands. I clutch the key to the vault in hand, doubts about my new promotion fading. Whatever the others think, it's worth it to have direct access to treasures like this.

The box is incredibly heavy, and something like five hundred years old. I heft it gently onto a cloth-lined cart and head upstairs. What mysterious patron requested this? I'm almost as curious to know as I am to crack open the box itself.

The reading room is small, but airy. The walls are lavender with pale wooden shelves built in, on which are dozens of low-light, air filtering plants. Long spiky spider plants dangling their offshoots, twining philodendron vines, giant monstera leaves with holes like viewports. The one window in the room is round and faces towards the front gardens. An ancient computer in the corner is the only thing out of place, although honestly, I find it kinda charming.

Two people are seated at the table in the middle: one is a work friend of mine, the other a stranger. They both have deep brown skin and black hair, but that's where the similarities end. Bosede works as a Librarian in the Spire, where the modern Illuminated are housed. She's thirty-five, slender and tall with braids that fall to her lower back. Her earth-toned cardigan and corduroy slacks reflect her quiet, easygoing nature.

The stranger looks about ten years younger and is wearing a ruffled purple and lime green dress. They jump from their seat and bounce across the room when I enter, hovering over the cart with excitement. They're short and heavy, and their purple lipstick matches their dress.

"Room service, ding ding," I joke, tapping the metal cart with my fingernail. "Someone ordered the original Illuminated copy of *The Guide to the Threadbound Oracle* by Calliope Everberry?"

"Oh, my goddess, is that really it?" the stranger exclaims in Gildean, turning back to Bosede.

"This is it," I say, and they look at me with an embarrassed smile.

"Sorry, I wasn't expecting you to speak Gildean, too," they said. "Most people here don't."

"No worries. Although, in the Library, I'd always assume someone within earshot can understand the language you're speaking," I say. Our patrons and Librarians are from all over the world. Makes it difficult to have secret gossip sessions without being overheard.

Bosede laughs and gets up from the table. "I'll leave you with Rhiannon now, if that's all right. I need to get back to my department."

"Oh, of course! Thank you so much for your help!" the stranger says earnestly. She speaks Casporan with a moderate accent, which suggests she was born in Gildea, unlike Bosede, whose grandparents were immigrants.

"My pleasure," Bosede says as she slips out the door.

I turn back to the stranger, who's watching me expectantly. Their hands are clasped primly behind their back, but there's mischief in their eyes. Their gaze darts back and forth between me and the cart.

"Soooo," I say, acutely aware of how little experience I have interacting with patrons, "introductions, right. I'm Rhiannon Rivergreen-Haybloom, Assistant Head Archivist."

"I'm Amane Sol, she/her pronouns, please," the stranger says.

Ah. Traditionally, the Casporan language only has one pronoun set: e/em/eir. Casporan culture doesn't include a concept of gender, so that's all we needed. But since language is a living, breathing thing, it's come to reflect our diverse immigrant population, too. Some people who come from cultures with genders, like Amane, have come up with their own Casporan pronouns to help them feel more at home. As a polyglot, I think it's fascinating. I just wish I understood what the hell gender actually is. No one can explain it to my satisfaction.

"Cool, e/em for me," I say.

"It's such a pleasure to meet you, Mx—or, is it Magistrix?" Amane says.

I shake my head as I drape a velvet cloth over the reading table. "Oh, no, no, no, just Rhiannon is fine. My boss isn't here. I feel weird getting all formal and shit. Damn, I'm not supposed to curse, though," I say, and pause when I realize I've done it twice.

Amane laughs. "I don't mind. I need someone to teach me the more obscure Casporan curses. You can only learn so much on the Astranet," she says.

I think I like her. "Good place to start, though."

Gingerly, I pick up the carved wooden box and set it on the table. The polished wood gleams: I hear Amane's breath catch. Honestly, same. I undo the clasp, a combined crescent moon and sun motif which separates with a *click*. Inside, the box is lined with a gorgeous marbled paper in faded red, yellow, and blue.

The book itself looks as new as the day it was bound. That's the magic of Illumination; though they can be destroyed by fire, water, beetles, and the human hand, the ravages of time will never touch these pages.

"It feels *alive*," Amane breathes. She turns to me, her eyes alight. "Can you *feel* that?"

I shake my head. "I actually can't sense magical energy or spirits. Was born that way, and no amount of training has helped."

Her perfectly manicured eyebrows shoot up. "Does that make it hard to do your work here? The Library is—" Wrinkling her nose, she spreads her arms out wide and gestures emphatically at our surroundings. Now it's my turn to laugh.

"Yeah, I know. Or rather, I've heard how intense it can get. Sometimes I think I'm better off, especially since I have other psychic talents," I say. "Anyway, what do you say we open this baby up? Unfortunately, I can't let you touch it, so just let me know when you want a page turned."

Amane sticks her arms down by her sides and turns back to the table, standing on her tiptoes to get a closer look.

The Guide to the Threadbound Oracle is bound in thick ivory leather over wooden boards, customary for its time and the weight of the volume. The title is embossed with shining gold leaf, and below it, a hand painted wreath of forget-me-nots. I'm not normally good at recognizing flowers, but Tabby grows them in our garden. Inside the wreath are three spools of red thread, which unfurl towards a knot in the center.

"Are you a cartomancer?" I ask Amane as I gently open the book to its flyleaf. The endpapers are handmade and hand-printed with the same symbols as the box: seven-pointed star, roll of paper, ink bottle, thread spool.

"Yes," she says. Her eyes never leave the book. "The Threadbound Oracle is my favorite. I have dozens of different versions, and I have mundane translations of this book in modern Casporan and Gildean. I never thought I'd see the *original*."

"So I'm sure you already know the author and original creator of the deck, Calliope Everberry, was an Illuminator here at the Library about five hundred years ago. It's funny, I've done a good bit of research on em, but not about the Oracle," I say.

It's a damn shame, too, because this book is *gorgeous*. Calliope's familiar handwriting and distinctive illustrations make the pages of my heart flutter. Narrative archetypes like The Protagonist and The Healer are depicted in vibrant botanical inks, their symbolism explained in poetic ancient language that I can just about get the gist of without my translation resources. Paper, ink, and thread make up a set of number suit cards. I particularly like the illustration for a card called The Seer, which feels like a kindred spirit. The figure's prominent Casporan nose reminds me of my own, and the ink blots representing divination are cool.

"Calliope Everberry also wrote a book about how the Library was founded. Is that what you were researching?" Amane asks, drawing my attention away from the book.

"Yeah, I'm surprised you know that," I say.

"I do my *own* research," she says proudly.

My regard for her rises. "Have you read any translations of *The Founding*? I hear there's a new one from Bloddwen Whitefeather coming out soon—"

Amane's grin stretches from ear to ear. Her gold jewelry glints in the sunbeam from the window. "I got to read an ARC of that recently. My family's company is publishing it in Gildea."

Her name clicks into place: Sol, as in Sol Publishing House, one of the largest publishers on the planet and *the* largest in Gildea. I nod respectfully at her, not wanting to make a big deal of it. The same way she didn't make a big deal out of someone my age being Assistant Head Archivist. Amane nods back, cementing our new bond.

She eyes me conspiratorially. "Have you seen the *original* Illuminated copy of *The Founding*?"

"No," I say with a bitter sigh. "It's been missing since the big fire that happened in 3986. We lost *so many* books in that damn fire. Either because they, you know, *burned*, or because they got shoved somewhere in the basement caverns in the chaos afterward. I would know. It's been my job for the last eight years to catalog all that shit, and my specialty is ancient Library history."

Amane pouts, which looks ridiculous with her purple lipstick. Then she gives herself a shake and turns back to *The Guide to the Threadbound Oracle* reverently. "At least there's *this*. Would you mind if I… tried something?" she asks.

"Like what?"

"I'm a medium," she says, "and in addition to regular readings, I also use my cards to communicate with spirits. I want to talk to the spirit of this book—or maybe even to Calliope emself."

She reaches into her gigantic purse and pulls out a silk bag decorated with silver stars. From that, she pulls an ancient-looking copy of the Threadbound Oracle. I'm not well versed on the subject, but its age alone has me interested. The spools of thread on the back look like they were printed by hand.

"My Great-Grandren made this deck herself," Amane says.

"Shit, that's amazing."

"I know! So, can I?"

"You seem like someone who knows what she's doing. Go ahead," I say, eager to satisfy my own curiosity. I've never been able to talk with spirits, and the cards intrigue me.

Pleased, Amane pulls up a chair and seats herself at the table. I scoot the book back so that she'll have room to lay out her cards, and she beams at me. I beam back; I may be a cantankerous old fool, but I have a soft spot for cheerful folk. I take a step back to give her some room.

Amane closes her eyes and takes a deep breath. She places the cards on the table, and plants her palms on either side. She continues to breathe deeply, eyelashes fluttering as she connects with the invisible spirit plane that coexists with ours. After a moment, she picks up the cards and shuffles them, brows knitted in concentration. The soft sound of paper on paper fills the small room.

Suddenly, she bolts upright and opens her eyes. Working quickly, she cuts the deck and lays three cards on the table in front of her. I scoot in for a closer look as she flips them over.

The Protagonist, The Gardens, the Seven of Ink. The first one shows a young Gildean person not unlike Amane standing between shelves of rainbow books, a determined look on their face. The second shows a lush garden late at night, a tiny couple silhouetted against the moonlight. The third shows seven diamond-like ink bottles in a circle, spilling rainbows onto a field of crocuses.

Amane's face softens as her gaze flickers over the cards.

"Can I ask you what those mean? Did you get in touch with the book's spirit?" I ask.

"I definitely did, it was so easy with a spirit that's so powerful and in this place where everything's so *close—*"

Amane's voice cuts out as if someone pressed a mute button on a remote. Her body goes rigid, and her eyes roll up until only the whites are visible. Her lips move as if trying to form words, but still no sound emerges. With a jerky motion, she reaches out and grabs the deck of cards. A few go flying across the table and land on top of *The Guide to the Threadbound Oracle.*

For once, I'm not worried about the book. I'm worried about Amane. My first thought was that she's having a seizure, but the more likely answer is that she's *possessed.* I rack my brain for the proper response; I must need to renew my magical first aid training, because it's *deep* in there.

Since I can't sense magical energy, all I can do is go through the motions and hope I'm doing it right. It's like singing with headphones on; you have no idea whether you sound amazing or downright terrible until someone else tells you.

Step one, place your hands over the third eye and heart center of the afflicted person. I do so, hovering my hands above her skin since I don't like touching strangers, and I can't ask for her consent.

Step two, envision a bright golden light flowing from your hands to envelop the afflicted person's spirit. Easy enough. *Step three, ask the possessing spirit to leave the body. If you know the spirit's name, use it.*

I have no idea who's possessing Amane right now. I don't think books can possess people, and there are so many ghosts in this place.

"Whoever you are, please leave Amane Sol's body now. You weren't fucking invited," I say.

I'm not prepared for this to work, but I'm *also* not prepared for Amane to grab my wrist tightly with one hand and look up at me with the whites of her eyes. Her lips pull into a concerned frown. I don't move. I can't move. My body is frozen.

"This is for you," Amane says, although it takes my brain a minute to translate because she's speaking in Old Casporan, a language she *definitely* doesn't know.

With her free hand, she picks four cards from the deck and holds them up. The Seer, The Author, The Book, The End.

"Who are you? I don't know what that means," I say.

The spirit nods towards *The Guide to the Threadbound Oracle*, still open on the table. Understanding lances through me like lightning.

"Ask the books," says Calliope Everberry in Amane's voice.

Then Amane's eyes snap shut, and she slumps backward in her chair. After a moment of stillness, she comes to, blinking and rubbing her forehead in confusion. She looks at the four cards still clasped in her hand.

"Well, *that* was interesting," she says.

CHAPTER SIX
AMANE

After taking *The Guide to the Threadbound Oracle* back to the Archives, Rhiannon shows me to the cafeteria. Possession is exhausting, even when it lasts a few minutes. At first e insisted on taking me to the infirmary, but e pivoted when I insisted that all I needed was something sweet and a cold drink.

I'd watched the whole scene from above, my spirit floating in the ether while Calliope used my body. I didn't understand the words that came out of my mouth, but Rhiannon did. I feel guilty for worrying someone so cool and interesting. We have a lot in common, and I could use a friend in this brand-new place.

The cafeteria smells *amazing,* especially the baked goods section. Everything in Caspora has berries in it; the cakes and muffins are filled with blueberries, cherries, blackberries, raspberries, and others I've never even heard of. I pick muffins with huckleberry and salmonberry jam inside because they're new to me. The tart flavor is refreshing compared to our sweets made with dates and figs at home.

There are a lot of people in the cafeteria. We squeeze through them towards the windows, where there's an open-air patio and tables with big gold umbrellas. I feel better as soon as I sit down. My body aches, and my head feels fuzzy. Rhiannon takes a seat across from me, munching on a scone.

"So, you get possessed often?" e says through a mouthful of crumbs.

"Not often, but it's not the first time," I explain. "It can happen in places where there are a lot of spirits and I'm not strong enough to keep them all out. It also happens if there's a spirit who desperately wants to get a message to someone around me. It was both this time—I'm so sorry, I should have been better prepared. I'll cast stronger wards next time."

Rhiannon shrugs. "It's no big deal. I just wanna know that you're okay. The Library's a thousand years old and contains thousands of magical texts. The ambient psychic temperature here is off the charts."

I try to hide my embarrassment with a smile, but some of it must show through.

"You know what," Rhiannon says, "when I first got here, the first time I did a scrying ritual, I got blasted out of time and space and had visions for like twelve hours. When I came back, I kept running up to everyone like, 'What year is this?!'"

E holds eir arms out to the air as if shaking an invisible person, eyes wide in an exaggerated expression of confusion. A laugh bursts out of me, and my head feels clearer.

I take a sip of my boba tea, chewing on a tapioca pearl thoughtfully. "I wonder why Calliope needed to speak with you so badly."

"Hey, you're the cartomancer," says Rhiannon, "you tell *me* what that message was about."

"It's mysterious to me, too. You said that you do scrying?"

"Yeah, I'm hella retrocognitive and really good at psychometry. Maybe to make up for the whole not-sensing-energy-or-spirits thing," Rhiannon says.

"The Seer card probably represents you, then. Other than that… I could tell you what the cards mean in general? After being possessed, I guess I'm too tired to do a proper reading," I say, trying not to be too disappointed in myself. Most of the time, when I look at the cards, the story comes together like beautiful pieces to a puzzle. Once in a while, I get nothing but static.

"That's okay. We could meet up again when you feel better and talk about it, if that's cool." Rhiannon leans back in eir seat and props eir feet up on the table, arms crossed to disguise eir interest in my answer.

I bounce to my feet and slap my hands on the table. "I'd love to!" I say, before a wave of dizziness overtakes me and I have to sit down again.

While we're exchanging phone numbers and following each other on social media, Rhiannon's phone vibrates with a text message. A silly grin lights up eir face when e reads it.

"Hey, is it cool if my partner joins us for lunch?" e asks.

"Sure! Work partner, or partner-partner?"

"Partner-partner. Platonic," Rhiannon says. "I'm aroace. We've been together for like six years or something now. I think you'll like em. Everyone does."

I have to speak in Gildean to do so, but I tell Rhiannon that I'm pansexual and what that means in my culture, which e seems fascinated by. The conversation goes on for a while about the intersection of gender and language while we relax in the warm summer sun. Summer in Caspora City is like winter in Aquanea, comfortable with bright blue skies and not a hint of humidity. I didn't realize how out of place I felt without a friend to talk to. At least, I hope Rhiannon will be my friend.

Then Rhiannon's phone vibrates again, and e stands up to wave at an approaching figure. It looks like the pretty dreamwalker I met earlier, who's also a Bindery candidate, but that can't be right.

My heart jumps up into my throat as I realize it's not a mistake, and Tabby walks up to us, tea and sandwich in hand. E's smiling widely, a dimple in each round cheek that I find adorable even though we're rivals, and I shouldn't form crushes on *my rivals*. Rhiannon jumps up and Tabby pulls em into a tight hug, enveloping Rhiannon's stick-thin body with eir own large softness.

I shouldn't be jealous of a hug. But I am. A little.

"Rhee! I think everything went really well!" Tabby exclaims.

"I told you it would. Now I gotta hear all about it." Rhee turns back to face me. "Amane, this is my partner, Tabby. Tabs, this is Amane. She just got possessed."

Tabby notices me and the smile turns into an *o* of surprise. The excitement falls out of eir body, and e tenses up. Still sipping on my drink, I choke on a boba and nearly spit tea everywhere, my mouth full of gummy pearls.

"What's wrong with you two? Have you met?" Rhiannon says, watching us with a frown.

"Amane is one of the other Illumination candidates," Tabby says in a much quieter voice than the one e greeted Rhiannon with. Hands folded in front of em, e smiles again, nervously this time. No dimples.

"What? Seriously?" Rhiannon pushes eir glasses farther up eir nose, looking at me incredulously.

"Yes, I am," I say. I bite my lip to hold back a torrent of apologies, questions, and explanations. The dizzy, fuzzy feeling in my head returns. Everything was going so *well*.

Rhiannon shoves eir hands in eir pockets, distressed. Eir eyes dart between me and Tabby. I was sure e feels the same connection I do, the same *click* that happens when you meet a potential best friend. Now what?

"Ugh, this is so awkward," Rhiannon groans.

"It doesn't have to be," says Tabby uncertainly. "Um, is it okay if I sit down?"

I nod, and Tabby slides into the seat beside Rhiannon. Above, the sun moves behind a cloud, casting a shadow over the patio.

Everyone is quiet while we eat our food. Then Rhiannon breaks the silence with, "Amane, earlier you said you'd just *moved* here from Gildea, but did you mean you just *arrived*, on a visit? While you're waiting for the results of the Bindery job testing?"

I pause, second muffin halfway to my mouth. "No, I moved here. Permanently."

Tabby's thick blonde eyebrows go up. "Even though you haven't gotten the apprenticeship yet? You're not just on a visit until you know for sure?"

I've heard this question—often more of an accusation—so many times in the past year. From my friends, from my parents, from professors, and the government officials who helped me fill out the reams and reams of paperwork. I have a practiced answer to it at this point: *I've worked my whole life for this. I know I'm going to get the job. I'm the perfect candidate and I'm leaving no other options. It's in the cards for me.*

Literally, I read my own cards on the topic a million times. I paid others to read for me. I don't usually like fortune telling with oracle cards, since the future is always shifting, but I couldn't help myself. All the readings were extremely positive, encouraging, so *definite* sounding, even with how subjective an art divination is.

But I can't say that to Tabby. It feels mean.

"I'm… very confident in my abilities," is what I end up saying, without much confidence at all.

"Lots of Illumination candidates who don't make it get other jobs in the Library and try again when a spot opens up," Rhiannon says. "Is that your plan?"

E gives me a pleading look. E wants to support both me and Tabby, even though one of us succeeding means the other fails. I can't even think about the third option, where neither of us gets the apprenticeship.

The truth is that I don't have a backup plan. In every other area of my life, I research and plan and organize every possible outcome, but in this one, I felt it would be bad luck. That in some superstitious way, if I only acknowledge one possibility, it's the only one the universe will offer me.

"That's the smart thing to do, isn't it?" I say, to avoid revealing my foolishness.

They nod. Rhiannon takes another huge bite of scone. Tabby wrings eir hands together and gives me a reassuring smile. Cheeks flushed pink, shoulders curled inward, as if to make emself smaller and less threatening. Eir brown eyes are kind, which isn't fair. It'd be so much easier if e was snobby or jealous. I love cute, shy people. I want to take them under my extroverted wing, make them smile, and maybe smooch them.

Rivals, rivals, rivals.

I can't do this right now. I check my phone, the time, slurp down my tea, and stuff the rest of my muffin into my purse.

"Um, I've actually got to go to the restroom and check my makeup and stuff before the interview, so I'm gonna go do that," I say, getting up from the table.

"Aw, okay," Rhiannon says, disappointed but relieved.

"Good luck," says Tabby. E gives me a little wave.

"Thank you," I say, feeling my face flush. "I'll talk to you later, Rhiannon?"

Rhiannon brightens. "Yeah! Of course! And you can call me Rhee if you want. All my friends do. It's shorter and all that."

"Great! Great, yeah, I'll text you later."

I scurry off to the bathroom, to make sure I don't look possessed. My lipstick is smeared. I reapply and practice my smile in the mirror, trying to brighten up. What were the chances that I'd make my first new friend in Caspora, only to find out that eir partner is my competition? Fierce competition, to have reached this stage. Tabby's interview probably did go well. E must have stopped talking about it to avoid hurting my feelings. Even though it would have been great emotional warfare before my own interview.

I guess it worked anyway. I have to pull myself together. I stop outside the doors to the Head Librarian's office and adjust my posture, put a determined smile on, slap my own face a little to get the blood flowing again. I can do this. I've worked half my life for this. I can always make new friends. Or maybe Rhiannon and Tabby will be understanding. I can always hope.

Here we go. I open the doors and step inside.

***

Rose's office is beautiful, but I pull my gaze away from the rainbow of books and focus on the three Illuminators. June smiles when I sit down, but Rose has eir head tilted back in eir wheelchair, eyes closed. Aeronwy glances at me and then back at the sketchbook in eir hands. It's the same one e was drawing in during the psy-testing.

"Last one for the day," e says. E has a low, smooth voice with a dry edge to it. "Miss Amane Sol?"

"Yes, it's her. I recognize her aura from the testing day, when she asked us a hundred questions," Rose says, eyes still closed. "I can see it through my eyelids. It's exceedingly bright."

I sit up taller and uncross my legs. Aside from being Head Librarian, Catrina Rosefall is also a famous artist and author on the Second Sight. I recognize the abstract painting hanging above the desk as one of eir own. Alcohol-based inks poured over paper in huge puddles, like iridescent oil slicks of black and pink and yellow and cyan. It's much more impressive in person.

Just like Rose emself. The painting is a self-portrait.

"What does my aura look like?" I ask.

Rose opens eir eyes and stares down eir nose at me, contemplating. There are deep shadows under eir eyes, and eir posture, even wrapped up under a thick blanket, is tired.

"Like someone cut open a prickly pear and spilled the juice all around you, and then poured gold glitter into it," e says, amused. "You're very charismatic and confident, aren't you? I got that much from your testing results, as well."

"They were impressively detailed," June adds, which makes my heart skip a little beat. A compliment! From em!

"Thank you so much," I gush, leaning forward in my chair. "I just wrote what the spirit told me. I hope it was the information you wanted."

"Oh, it was. That's the real test, you know. It's not just whether you can communicate with the book spirits or not, although that's important. It's about finding the person who understands what and how to ask them," June says.

I nod to show I understand. "Listening and respecting their wishes is important. Too many people think they can *demand* energy or help or answers from spirits, or even force them to do things, but that's not right."

"Exactly our thoughts," Rose says. "I can't let people into the Bindery who will distress the books, or I'd be breaking my oath."

"How do you communicate with them? With *all* of them?" I ask.

They're interviewing me, so they should ask the questions, but I can't help it. My Moms say I was born with my eyes open, a sign that I'd want to know and see everything about the world. They were right. And now I'm seated in front of someone who speaks on behalf of several million book spirits when the Library makes important decisions.

I wonder suddenly if Rose is here so the *books* can judge me.

A crooked grin spreads across Rose's wrinkled face. "One at a time," e says, and chuckles. The laugh fades a little early, as if e's out of breath. "Through astral travel. The astral plane is close here, and vibrant, which makes it easier to access."

"Though that means it can be overwhelming to those who are sensitive," Aeronwy says, pointedly. "Such as mediums."

"I have it under control," I say, smoothing down my skirt.

I push today's possession from my mind. I put extra wards on in the bathroom, but this room is like a bubble in a churning sea. I don't feel anything. Even the books on the shelves are quiet.

Aeronwy nods and plows on to another pointed question. "When we reviewed your initial application, your surname struck a familiar chord. Are you at all related to the Sol family of Sol Publishing House?"

"My parents currently own and run it," I reply proudly. "I've been around books and book people all my life. It's in my blood."

June and Rose give me nodding smiles, but Aeronwy frowns.

"Do you or have you worked for them at all? The Eternal Library, of course, has contracts with Sol Publishing regarding its collections. We wouldn't want any complications to arise because of your employment here," e says.

I swallow a pang of fear and shake my head. "I don't currently and never have worked for my family's company. I've known since I was young that I wanted to work here, and spent all my time working for that goal, instead. My older siblings are the ones who will inherit the company, not me."

This seems to satisfy Aeronwy. For now. E leans back, hands clasped.

June looks at me and says, "I'm curious to know about your connection to cartomancy. How long have you been reading cards, and how did you get into it?"

"Since I was thirteen," I say, "so, about twelve and a half years, now! It's a family tradition. My Great-Grandren was also a medium and a reader. She taught me everything before she passed away while I was in college."

"That's wonderful you got to learn from family. I'm sorry for your loss," June says.

I shake my head. "Thank you, but, it's okay. Her spirit is still with me, and it was her time to go. She was ready."

Rose tilts eir head at me curiously. "Now *I* have a question for you, Miss Sol, if you'll indulge me."

"Of course," I say.

"Would you do an oracle card reading for me? Assuming you have a deck on you," Rose says. "I hope it isn't lost on you that the verb we use for performing divination, like with your cards, is *reading*. Just as one reads a book, you read your cards. The way a diviner reads can tell you much about them."

I fumble with my purse and pull out my Threadbound Oracle. I scoot my chair closer to the desk, so I'll be able to shuffle on it, and set the deck face-down. Rose eyes the ragged edges and faded backs, which used to be bright red but have faded over time. The gold paint on the spools of thread is scratched. But its spirit radiates intense psychic energy.

June watches me closely. "You have a strong bond with your cards," e says.

"Y-yes," I say.

That's June's specialty. Etheric cords, spiritual bonds, the thread of life. I wonder what e's Hearing. I've read all of June's books, and e mostly works through clairaudience. That means e just *listens* for what the books need, no tools necessary. I wonder how e gets by in the chaotic etheric landscape of the Library. I'll have to ask.

I put my palms flat on the table, then slowly turn them upwards and look at Rose. Even though e's clearly tired, eir gaze doesn't waver. Like e can See into the secret places of my soul.

"If I'm reading for a person, I like to hold their hands for a moment before shuffling, to get a better lock on your energies,"

I say. I'm bold in my words, but this is the scariest thing I've ever asked.

"Certainly," says Rose, and puts eir hands in mine.

My heart pounds as I close my fingers and open my psychic senses. Rose's spirit is enormous, as striking as the painting hanging above eir head. E feels like paint drying on your skin and the static air around a lightning strike that makes your hair stand on end. E smiles knowingly at me when I open my eyes and pull away.

I pick up the deck and center myself. I feel my nerves soothed away, the rhythm and slap of the cards lulling me into a meditative state. I wait for the tug from my gut to tell me I'm finished shuffling, and then put the deck back on the desk in front of Rose.

"If you could cut the deck, please."

Rose does so, separating the cards into two piles and putting the bottom one back on top. I take the deck and lay out three cards. A fourth one falls out of the deck as I'm dealing, so I add it to the spread. I can feel all three Illuminators' eyes on me as I flip them over. This is the most important reading I've ever done in my life.

"The Threadbound Oracle," June comments, "a wonderful choice here in the Library, where it originated. You should check out our collections on the topic when you get the chance. They're really something."

I look at the cards, because I can't look Rose in the eye again until I know what I'm going to say. A knot forms in my throat. I think about how Rose said e was retiring soon, even though the Head Librarian position is for *life*.

The Five of Thread: Needle: a black background, on which a delicate white and red flower is being pierced by five needles attached to threads. The Train: the interior of a train car, filled with passengers reading, decorated with celestial motifs, only white beyond the windows. The Waters: a sun and shade dappled ravine, through which a waterfall flows into a clear, serene pool. The End: another black background, a skein of glowing rainbow threads looping across it, about to be cut in half by a pair of golden scissors.

The room is so silent.

"You can say it," Rose says, gently.

My head snaps up. Green eyes bore into mine.

"Are you dying?"

Aeronwy and June exchange a devastated look over Rose's head. Not surprised, but unhappy to be reminded; they already knew.

"Yes," Rose says plainly. "This is not public knowledge yet, but you already have the information right in front of you. The cancer I thought I had beaten twenty years ago has returned. It's everywhere, including my brain. The doctors can't do anything."

"I'm so sorry," I say, because what else is there? But I glance at the cards. There is more.

"I'm eighty-five. I've lived a wonderful, long life. I don't want to suffer," Rose continues. "So, I've hired a death doula, and am having an assisted death. The date is one week from now."

That explains The Waters card, which is about relief, coming *before* The End card, rather than after. The Five of Thread is about pain and surprise. The Train is a card of transition—waiting to die. The End is self-explanatory. Experts say the card almost never heralds literal death, soothing the worries of reader and querent alike. In twelve years, this is the first time I've seen it happen.

June's head is bowed, glasses pushed onto eir forehead with one hand. Aeronwy gets up and stands behind June, leaning over to murmur in eir ear and rub eir shoulders. The sharp look in eir gold eyes is now misty and far-away. The way they so clearly love Rose sends an arrow straight through my heart.

"I hope it's everything you want it to be," I tell Rose.

Rose smiles and presses a tiny hand to eir heart. "Thank you, Amane. I believe it will."

CHAPTER SEVEN
TABBY

Rose's memorial service is beautiful. Everyone is asked to wear bright, joyful colors instead of mourning gray. The crowd in the Library gardens is a rainbow sea, dotted with a few clouds who stuck to tradition. Tents from various temples line the cobbled paths, offering refreshments and areas for prayer. You'd think we were at a festival if it weren't for the soft murmur of condolences and blessings. Rhee and I hold hands as we weave through them.

The gardens are a patchwork of green and gold, speckled by late summer wildflowers and berries. Soon the rains will be back, bringing with them the steady gray winter Caspora is famous for. But for now, the sky is clear, cloudless blue.

We find the ceremony centered around a perfectly circular pool which reflects the sky like a mirror. Rose's family are seated to the side of the pool to receive offerings. The funeral and gravesite were private, so people wishing to throw wildflower seeds or sow sprouts for Rose's body can leave them here. There are enough seed packets and seedlings on the table behind the family to cover a mountainside.

According to eir obituary, Rose is survived by two adult children, four grandchildren, and one great-grandchild. Eir partner passed away some time before. These must be the three generations of people seated around the pool—one of them only an infant in eir parents' arms.

Aeronwy and June are seated with them. They're smiling, but it doesn't quite reach their eyes. The mood is bittersweet.

"Rhee? Tabby?"

We turn to find Amane standing behind us. Her face is solemn, but her outfit is a riot of color. A sundress patterned in magenta, yellow, and cyan triangles, over which she's wearing a bolero covered in shimmering black sequins. They look like iridescent drops of oil, and like—like the painting Rose had hung in the Head Librarian's office. Her thoughtfulness is touching.

"Can I join you?" she asks.

Her eyes dart between me and Rhiannon, questioning. The official decision about the apprenticeship is being withheld until the mourning period for Rose is over: one full moon cycle from the day of eir death. Until we know the results, there's still tension between us.

Rhiannon squeezes my hand. I squeeze back.

"Yeah, of course," Rhiannon says. The tension drops out of Amane's shoulders.

"Thanks. I don't know anyone here, and I've never had to observe Casporan funeral customs," she says. "I tried to read up on it for the last two weeks, but some of this seems… non-traditional, maybe? I don't want to offend anyone by accident."

"The last *two* weeks?" Rhiannon says what I'm thinking, as e often does. Rose only died a week ago.

Amane looks stricken and claps a hand over her mouth. "I—well, you see—" She pauses to take a deep breath and collect herself. "In my interview, I did an oracle reading for Rose. It said… and then Rose said… what was going to happen."

If Rose had trusted Amane with that information, e must have connected with her. Maybe even favored her over the other candidates. I put a pin in those thoughts; now's not the time. I mentally apologize to Rose's spirit for being disrespectful.

"Shit, that's some heavy news to hold onto," Rhiannon says. "You okay?"

"I'm fine," Amane says. "I deal with death and loss a lot, as a medium. Most of the spirits I channel for people are loved ones who've passed on. Rose seemed at peace with going."

"Does that mean you could channel Rose?" Rhiannon asks, voicing my thoughts again.

"Yes, but I would only do it if a family member or friend asked me to," says Amane, "and not so soon. I barely knew em. There's no reason for me to bother eir spirit at this time."

In my mind, I see Amane in the Bindery with June and Aeronwy, relaying Rose's messages through her cards for them. *They* were Rose's family. Maybe they'll decide it's a plus to having her as June's next apprentice. I push the image away, ashamed again.

"Makes sense," says Rhiannon. "We were gonna pay our respects and drop off some offerings. Wanna get in line with us?"

We join the line in front of Rose's family, which is filled with mourners of all ages. Many of them work at the Library, but I think just as many are patrons. They love the Library, and so they love Rose as well. A few people stand before the pool with a microphone in hand, telling stories from Rose's life. Apparently, Rose was known for hiding under desks or curling up in the bottoms of bookshelves when e didn't want to be found. Quick to anger, but also quick to defend those who needed it most.

I lean towards Amane. She's nearly as short as Rose was and only comes up to my shoulder.

"I like your outfit choice," I say quietly. "That was my favorite painting of Rose's."

Amane brightens, smoothing down the sequins on her bolero. "You noticed! I wasn't sure if anyone would. It's my favorite, too."

"That and the one hanging in the lobby of the Sunseeker Building, where they keep the art books. The one that's ten feet tall and looks like swirling pink clouds at sunset," I say.

Amane clasps a hand to her chest. "*Soft as Mountains*," she says, naming the piece. "I didn't know that was on display here. I'll have to go see it eventually, I had no idea it's that *big*!"

"Everything Rose painted was big," I say.

"Everything Rose *did* was big," Rhiannon interjects from in front of us. "Whoever's Head Librarian next has some fuckin' shoes to fill. Do you know how much the collection expanded under Rose's care? How many new community outreach programs were launched? E found so many ways to twist the foundational laws of the Library, since we can't change them without the Charter Book. Rose was a damn visionary."

Amane starts asking Rhiannon questions about how to greet Rose's family, when and where to hand over the offerings, all the little things that make up the ritual for the deceased. Rhiannon answers patiently and directly: tell them your name, express your condolences, hand the offering to the youngest relative, don't hold up the line too much. If you feel called, go up to the mike and tell a story. If you'd rather write it down, there would be a booth where you could do so. The stories will all be published as a volume freely available to the public.

Soon enough it's our turn. We bow our heads and shake hands with Rose's family, wishing them healing in the time to come. The youngest relative, Rose's great-grandchild, is too young to take offerings, so we hand them to eir Ren: poppy seeds from Amane, a bottle of cider from Rhiannon's family's farm, yellow flag iris bulbs from me.

As we're doing this, I notice June and Aeronwy watching us. Aeronwy whispers in June's ear as we move down the line to greet them. June smiles widely at our group, spreading eir arms in welcome before shaking each of our hands. E's wearing an emerald jumpsuit that shimmers in the sun, and there are bluebells woven into eir braided hair.

"I'm so glad to see you here," e says to me and Amane. "Amane, Aeronwy says you're dressed like the painting in Rose's office. I admit, you do look a lot like it. Was that intentional?"

Amane beams so brightly she could be a second sun. Her wide eyes and smile are so sweet and eager as she clasps June's hands and nods.

"A fitting tribute," June says, beaming back.

Their expressions mirror one another's. They have the same energy, vibrate on the same wavelength. Even at an event like this. My heart plummets.

And my phone rings.

Heat floods my face as I fumble to fish it out of my pocket to silence it. Everyone in line, all of Rose's relatives, are looking at me. The screen says it's Lilja, my Ren, and my heart rockets back up into my throat, hammering as I swipe the cancel button.

She won't like that I'm not answering, but I really can't. I put it on vibrate.

"I'm so sorry, I didn't realize it was on," I say.

"It's no problem," June says, "happens to me all the time. I love all this modern technology, but I can't say I'm terribly good with it."

"That's not true," Aeronwy interjects.

"Honey, just because you barely know how to use your phone *at all*..."

My phone buzzes in my pocket again while they're talking. Stops. Buzzes again. Something must be wrong. Or Lilja thinks something's wrong with me and is panicking about it. But I haven't gotten a chance to say anything about Rose to Aeronwy and June, and it would be extra rude not to now, even if there *is* an emergency. It's always an emergency with my parents.

I swallow and my mouth and throat are dry. The colors around me shift. The bluebells in June's hair sprout new stalks and bloom, creating a halo of blossoms around eir head. I can hear them chiming. Aeronwy's crimson scarf curls into a pair of flames that flicker against eir broad chest. I look away, trying to clear my vision of dreams, and my eyes fix on the mirror pool. It's so perfect, like a portal to another world.

And it is. The ground tilts. My world shifts, and I'm falling through its surface into a blue void.

***

Once in a while, I have an ordinary dream. One where I'm not dreamwalking. Sometimes I know it's a dream, but I can't control what happens, only go along with the narrative. They're usually nightmares. This one promises to be.

I am small. And alone. Curled up in the safest hiding spot I could find and still fit into at nine years old: my closet, beneath my hanging clothes and surrounded by piles of books that won't fit on the shelf. I can hear hurled insults and accusations in the hallway. Dreamspace warps the sound; the words don't make sense, but I know what's happening. I know why they're angry.

Not again, I think, *how is this happening again? I thought I left this place.*

Doors slam. Boot heels clack down the hallway, towards my room. I curl up tighter, waiting to hear the bedroom door creak open, waiting for light to spill into the closet, waiting for admonishments and shouting. Waiting to be asked for support I don't know how to give.

But when it does, a less familiar voice only says, "Tabby?"

Someone tall crouches down beside me. I know they're tall even though I haven't seen them yet. The dream logic tells me.

"Tabby, it's all right. Come with me."

I open my eyes and lift my head enough to peer over my arms. Aeronwy is kneeling in front of me, offering a hand. A flickering flame emerges from eir chest, lighting the closet with a warm glow.

In the dream logic, there's no reason for me to find Aeronwy's presence strange. I feel an immense sense of relief as I take eir hand and let em lead me out of the closet. It leads not into my childhood bedroom, but into a garden. My garden, the one I dreamed so long ago and have been trying to find again. Every inch of it is on fire. I cling closer to Aeronwy.

"It's all right," e says again, leading us through the wildfire without pause. "You're safe now. I promise."

I wake up.

Gasping, my eyes open to the real world once more. I'm on my back, on a cot. Above me, a pink canvas tent ripples in the breeze. Rhiannon is leaning over me with a worried expression that softens when e sees I'm awake.

"*There* you are. Author, that was a bad one," e sighs.

"What—where—"

Another voice answers me from behind my head. "You're in the magical first aid tent. When no one could wake you, they brought you here to see if I could help."

I tilt my head back. A stout, older person wearing the pink robes of a Caoimhen nun is seated behind me. E has a strong face wrinkled with laugh lines, and a luxurious black-and-silver beard that's braided and decorated with beads. Eir head is covered in a floral-patterned scarf, piled up high in a way that suggests a mountain of hair underneath. E pulls eir hands away from my head and holds them up.

"I'm Siobhan Heartseeker. I was administering some energy healing to try to bring you out of your dream," e says. "Your partner said it would be all right, since I couldn't ask you to consent. But I didn't touch you physically."

"Oh. Thank you," I say. "I think it worked. I woke up faster than usual."

"You seem to be awake and aware of your surroundings now," Siobhan says. "How are you feeling?"

Slowly, I sit up. My vision grays as all the blood rushes from my head. The space I'm in is small, partitioned off from the rest of the tent by hanging curtains. Despite being a temporary, outdoor setup, it's lush with pillows and blankets in calming colors. A cone of cedar incense smolders in the corner.

I feel fine, if embarrassed by the strange dream I had. The nightmare about my parents, that's normal. But I don't even know Aeronwy. Where had that come from?

"How did I get here?" I ask Rhiannon, who's perched on the side of my cot. "I didn't—I didn't actually fall into the pool, did I?"

Rhiannon smiles dryly. "Well, no, or else you'd be soaking wet right now. You just missed it when you fell. When I couldn't wake you up, Aeronwy and Amane and I carried you here. Thank the fucking gods it wasn't far, and Aeronwy's strong for an old person."

"Hey, I'm an old person. Some of us *do* have muscle," Siobhan says, chuckling.

"Obviously, I guess."

I sigh inwardly in relief. So that's it. Any one of the people who helped carry me could have appeared outside the closet, my brain just picked the oddest one. Ordinary dreams are strange like that.

Something else that Rhiannon said strikes me.

"Did you say Amane helped?" I ask, embarrassed for other reasons now. I raise a hand to my face, which I'm sure is turning red.

"Yeah. We both took your feet 'cuz I wasn't strong enough on my own," Rhiannon says.

E turns and slaps the curtain a few times. Amane pokes her head in, eyes widening when she sees I'm awake. My face burns hotter. Am I embarrassed because I think she's cute, or because I've revealed my vulnerability to a competitor? Likely both.

"You're okay!" she says. "Can I come in now?"

"Let me out first, there's not enough space," says Siobhan. E turns to me. "Will you be okay? I can give your spirit body another check and clear out any blockages, if you like."

I shake my head. "I'm okay. Thank you so much for your help."

Siobhan smiles, brightly painted lips parting to show wide, white teeth. "That's what I'm here for. There's no shame in getting overwhelmed at a time like this; Caoimhe is our goddex of love *and* loss for a reason. If you need anything else, just let us know. Feel free to rest as long as you like."

E grabs a set of canes from against the tent wall, the kind with arm rests, and makes eir way out of the tiny room. Amane edges into the space left over and sits on one of the pillows.

"I was worried when I saw you faint like that, but Rhee says it's a thing that happens and you were just dreaming," she says, looking directly at me. "I could feel it when we picked up your feet. Your spirit was far away. What were you dreaming about?"

Rhiannon makes a *yikes* face because e knows better than to ask me that question. I'd rather volunteer that information on my own, if I feel comfortable—even when you have control of your dreams like I do, they're such personal things. Being asked puts pressure on me to share. People don't always understand when I say I don't want to. They assume I dreamed about something shameful.

"That's kind of a private thing," Rhiannon stage whispers to her. Bless Rhiannon, always coming to my rescue.

Amane bites her lip. "Sorry. I know I ask a lot of questions. They just kind of come out. You never have to answer anything you don't want to. I won't mind."

A flicker of warmth spreads through my chest. "Thanks. That's refreshing to hear," I say. "It was… some old memories. It happens sometimes when I'm stressed…"

I remember suddenly what I was feeling stressed about. I pat my pockets down for my phone, my anxiety rising when I can't find it. Rhiannon notices and pulls it from eir own pocket. E hands it over.

"It was one of your parents calling, wasn't it," e says in a flat voice. Rhiannon doesn't like my parents. Which is okay because they don't like Rhiannon, either. It only took one family meal to figure that out.

I turn on the screen. Eight missed calls, all from Lilja except one, from Oran, who left a voicemail. Lilja must have called em when e couldn't get a hold of me, to see if e knew anything. They think that if I'm 'ignoring' one of them, it must be because the other parent told me to.

Rhiannon puts a hand over the screen. "Don't call them now and get worked up again. Just send a text saying you're at Rose's memorial service and you'll talk later," e says.

I take several deep breaths, fighting the urge to call anyway and get it over with. It'll eat away at the back of my mind the longer I put it off. Oran will be mad if I wait. But e's probably already mad that I didn't answer in the first place.

"I'm going to at least listen to the voicemail to make sure nothing's wrong," I say.

Rhiannon rolls eir eyes, knowing how my parents are, but nods.

Beside em, Amane fidgets uncomfortably. "I can leave if you want," she says.

"No," I say, "It's okay. And thank you for helping, you really didn't have to do that."

"I wanted to," she says, glancing away.

She knew about Rose's death ahead of time. Is it possible she knows who they're going to pick for the apprenticeship? Maybe she's knows she's been chosen, but they haven't made the announcement public yet. Maybe she feels sorry for me and wants to make up for it. Disappointment settles in my chest. It'll be easier to face reality if I start preparing for the worst now.

But the deepest part of my heart hopes I still have a chance.

RHIANNON

I walk into the Archive lounge and everyone stops chatting. Three pairs of eyes track me from behind thick glasses as I fix myself a cup of tea. I allow the silence to drag on, ignoring the heat on my back until my tea has finished steeping. All I hear is the soft clink of spoons and the shuffling of slacks on the ancient couch.

"'Sup?" I say, turning around and taking a sip of my tea. It's way too hot, even with milk in it, but I need a prop for effect.

Caerwyn, Elísabet, and Yan stare back at me over their own teacups. Mairead's three most devoted followers are known in the Archives as the Three Old Crones, after an old folk legend of the same name. They're in their late seventies and have worked at the Library for decades. They are, in the grand scheme of things, mostly harmless.

Mostly.

Caerwyn peers over eir trifocals at me. A tiny smile touches the wrinkles at the corners of eir mouth. With eir weathered brown skin and long gray beard, e could be part of the collection emself. Caerwyn is an expert on Casporan temple architecture and standing stone circles.

"We just wanted to give you a belated congratulations on your promotion to Assistant Head," e says.

"Please, forgive us for our initial shock," adds Yan. Yan is from Yijun and speaks five languages. Hir fingertips are stained black with ink, but I've never seen hir leave a single print anywhere. Ze handles our acquisitions from eastern countries.

Elísabet's family is from Hrafnland, and everything about her is as pale as new paper. She has a high, warbling voice and specializes in Reclamation-era herbariums. She waves a delicate hand at me and says, "High Priestex Mairead explained everything."

"Oh yeah?" I say.

I lean an elbow on the water cooler, feigning an air of indifference. All three of them attend Mairead's Authorist temple regularly. As a result, they refuse to refer to em as anything but High Priestex.

"It was obvious as soon as e said you're a Protagonist," Elísabet continues.

It takes all my willpower not to spit out my tea. I may have been raised a Scriptivist, but I'm not super religious. We were a Readerist household, and generally took the view that the whole 'the Universe is a Book' thing is a pleasant metaphor. Not… literal reality. I'd much rather interpret the world the way a reader would a text than believe my life has been written for me beforehand. Predestination sucks.

Plus, the Authorist branch of Scriptivism was created by Library Founder Isylwyn Moonscryer, who was a Casporan monarch, alleged murderer, and definite narcissist. Anyone claiming to be "the Supreme Author's Own Self-Insert in the Story of the Universe" is suspect in my book. Others, unfortunately, believe the hype and disbelieve the part about the murder.

My disapproval must show on my face, because Caerwyn says, "We know you don't believe in that sort of thing, but then, it doesn't really matter, does it? The Author's Narrative will guide you, regardless."

"Protagonists usually have humble beginnings. The world is set against them. And then they rise up using their special gifts that set them apart from the rest. We'd never considered your psychic talents and youth in that light before, but as Elí said, it just makes sense," says Yan.

"What we mean to say is that we support you." Caerwyn sets eir teacup down and places one hand over eir heart. "We're your supporting cast."

"…thanks," I say, because I don't know how to tell them that their whole character-based caste system freaks me out. I understand why they accept that they're 'supporting' characters instead of 'protagonists' in the story of the world: it comforts them to have a defined role and purpose, one without a ton of responsibility. But I don't get why you'd *want* that to be true.

"High Priestex Mairead has very high hopes for you," says Elísabet. "Much higher than e had when Camille was hired, e confided in us."

"She turned out to be a real red herring," Yan smirks, and they laugh. Ha-ha, right, because Camille has red hair. I roll my eyes. Then Yan's face falls and e says, "That poor dear."

The three of them sigh and glance away sorrowfully, which I find suspicious. They were friendly towards Camille until about three moons ago, when they suddenly turned passive-aggressive and started ignoring her. Camille never knew what it was she did to piss them all off. I wonder if it had anything to do with the fight I witnessed between her and Mairead.

"I'm sure she'll be fine over in Conservation," I say.

Caerwyn's thin gray eyebrows shoot up. "You didn't hear?"

"Hear what?" I say, frowning in anticipation of the latest gossip.

"Camille's in the hospital. She collapsed last week, and the doctors don't know what's wrong with her."

They shake their heads and cluck their tongues in pity. I freeze in place, hands locked around the heat of my mug. The hospital? Camille and I weren't friends outside of work, but my stomach clenches in worry. Why didn't anyone tell me?

The Three Old Crones suddenly brighten and sit up straight. I follow their gaze to the doorway, where Mairead has appeared. E smiles warmly at the Crones.

"Good morning Caerwyn, Yan, Elísabet," Mairead says cheerfully, and turning to me, "Rhiannon. If you don't mind coming with me, we have a lot of work to do today. Best that we get started immediately."

I clear my throat. "What kind of work?"

"The kind you've been waiting all your life to do."

***

Mairead slips through the twisted corridors like a cat, prowling around stacks of old books with practiced steps. The lights in the sub-sub-basement are practically nonexistent, but Mairead didn't bother to bring a lantern. I've got my phone flashlight on to avoid the worst stones sticking out of the floor, the loose books scattered by tremors or critters. I guess if you spend forty years down here, you learn your way around.

E won't tell me where we're going, but it's *deep* in the abandoned section of the Archives. These tunnels started off as natural caves, a dry place to store books in a rainy climate. Over the centuries, they were expanded many times by many different people, leaving behind a huge labyrinth. For the last eight years I've been leading efforts to recover and re-catalog what's down here, a never-ending task that's satisfying, nonetheless. You never know what you're going to discover.

There's no sound but our footsteps down here. *My* footsteps, since Mairead glides as silently as ever. In eir flowing white blouse and slacks, e could be a ghost. A wisp leading me to my doom. No one would find my body for months or even years.

I shake off the morbid thought and take a deep breath of stale, dusty air.

"Are we looking for something?" I ask.

"Perceptive as always," Mairead says. "Ah, here we are."

We stop in front of a stone bookshelf covered in dusty old novels. Their bindings are broken, their cloth frayed. The gilding on the spines has all but disappeared. Looking at them makes me sad.

Mairead reaches for a thick tome that appears to be in better shape than the others. It has no title, only a series of silver eyes which stare at us in the gloom. Mairead licks a fingertip and runs it down the length of the spine. The book shivers, and then the wall begins to move.

"It took me ages to reconfigure the spell to allow me in this room," Mairead says while I stand by, open-mouthed. "I'll add you, as well. I'll just need some of your hair and your signature in the book."

E gestures for me to enter first, but I'm already stepping past the threshold. The room beyond the secret door is lit by a soft purple glow—veins of amethyst run through the stone walls, enchanted to hold ley line energy before the invention of electricity. On the far wall, a geode the size of my head sparkles with crystal points. The floor is inscribed with sigils and protective circles, in the center of which stands a desk.

I approach the desk slowly. Smooth black stone, polished to a shine. Small indentations hold ink bottles of indeterminable colors, and a moth-eaten quill stands upright beside them. In the middle of the desk, where you'd expect a flat writing surface, a shallow bowl has been carved.

I turn to Mairead, jumping back when I find em much closer than expected. My thighs bump against the desk.

"What *is* this place?"

"Isn't it amazing?" Mairead says, spreading eir arms wide. The room isn't much larger than a storage closet, and I wish e would learn more about personal space. I step around to the other side of the desk, placing it between us.

"It's incredible. How did you find it?"

Mairead's eyes narrow. "It was shown to me," e says, smiling.

I start to ask by whom, but I already know. Mairead talks all the time about how e receives messages from the spirit of Isylwyn Moonscryer, one of the Library's Founders and the founder of Authorism, on a regular basis. I've grudgingly collected Mairead's stories on the topic for my own research and determined that they're genuine.

"Why?" I ask.

Mairead laughs. "This is why I like you, Rhiannon. You won't accept anything at face-value. Earlier, you asked if we were looking for something. *That* is the purpose of this room: to find what we're looking for."

That was obvious the moment I saw the desk, which is made for ink scrying. The amethyst in the walls act as a natural psychic amplifier, and the thick stone walls keep the room dark, cool, and quiet. There are probably wards in the inscriptions to keep out spirits and stray magical energy, though I can't sense them.

"I hate to break it to you, but I don't do object location," I say. Although, in a room like this, who knows what I'd be capable of? I might be able to scry the whole damn history of the universe, right back to the Big Bang.

Mairead crosses eir arms and gives me a look. "I know that. But you *can* search for an object in *time*, can't you?"

"That depends," I say, "on a *whole* lotta factors. Why don't you just give it to me straight?"

"You're ruining my dramatic reveal," Mairead pouts.

I stare at em without responding, and e sighs.

"If there was *one* lost book you wish you could find more than any other, what would it be?"

"The Charter Book," I answer immediately. No one has seen the Illuminated manuscript the Founders wrote to lay the magical foundation of the Library in five hundred years. Only the Head Librarian can edit the law inside. Since its disappearance, the murder rate for Head Librarians decreased significantly. Years in office skyrocketed.

Mairead purses eir lips. "Other than that."

"Uh, the original Illuminated copy of *The Founding*, I guess," I say, remembering my conversation with Amane a few weeks ago.

Mairead lights up and points a finger at me. "Exactly."

From the pocket of eir dress, e pulls an old, yellowed slip of paper. I squint in the dim, purple light, leaning over the scrying table to see it better. It's an old catalog card, from before we started digitizing everything. It's for *The Founding,* last signed out by Catrina Rosefall in 3983 and never recorded as returned.

"I'm the one who brought Catrina *The Founding* thirty-five years ago, so that e could make an Illuminated translation for the National Library of Hrafnland. This is my handwriting on the card," Mairead says, tapping it with one finger. "We lost huge parts of the catalog in the '86 fire, but somehow this survived. It was given to me as a sign from Isylwyn that the book still exists, and we should find it."

It annoys me that Mairead refers to Rose as Catrina, even though everyone knows e hated being called that. I start to say something, but now Mairead is on a roll.

"There's an exhibition on fashion in the Reclamation period coming up at the Casporan History Museum, which I'm on the research committee for. Just *imagine* if we could lend them the original copy of *The Founding* for the collection! Calliope Everberry was an important Reclamation figure. Eir work deserves to be on display," e says. "When Isylwyn revealed this room to me, I knew that you would be the one to help me find the book. We'll even put your name on the caption in the museum."

That *would* be pretty damn cool. Exceedingly cool, actually. I imagine taking Tabby to the museum (if there's one thing Tabby and I both love, it's museums) and pointing to the plaque with my name on it. *Recovered by Rhiannon Rivergreen-Haybloom, Assistant Head Archivist of the Eternal Library.* I imagine the proud look on eir face. Shit, I imagine just getting the chance to *look* at the original copy of *The Founding,* what it would lend to my research on the Founding mythology. I could finally publish my book.

Still—

"So, let me get this straight. You want me to use this old catalog card to scry through the book's history and figure out where it got put, instead of being returned? You *do* realize that book is five hundred years old and without the object itself, I can't control what period from that time my visions show me? It could take weeks or even moons for me to find what you want," I say.

Mairead leans across the desk to touch my arm. "You know, if you're going to fit into this new Assistant Head position, you're going to have to challenge yourself. You aren't even thirty yet, and you've done so many amazing things. I'd hate for you to find out you've already hit your peak, and things are only downhill from here."

A jolt of pure fear shoots through my chest. It's every child genius's worst nightmare.

"I haven't peaked yet," I say, my voice squeaking awkwardly. "Also, don't touch me unless I say you can."

Mairead throws eir hands up in a warding off gesture. "I meant no harm. I didn't say you *have* peaked. I simply want to make sure that's not what happens to you. You'll only grow by pushing yourself into uncomfortable territory."

"I mean, yeah, I guess," I say, crossing my arms.

"Don't you *want* to see the original copy of *The Founding*?" Mairead's gray eyes sparkle behind eir glasses. They're lavender in this light.

"Of course I do."

"I've seen it, briefly. It's utterly entrancing. Absolutely incredible," says Mairead. "The reproductions don't come close to capturing the original's beauty."

The look of rapture on eir face says e's not kidding. I plop down on the cold stone chair that sits in front of the scrying desk. I imagine filling the basin with spring water, adding the drops of ink so that they swirl and curl and dance until they've completely spread out. The surface of the water would become a smooth mirror. Classic black vine ink would work well for this. I would place a hand on either side of the basin and peer inside…

I look up at Mairead. "You *swear* it'll be my name on the museum caption, and not yours?"

Mairead places a hand over eir heart and says, "I swear."

AMANE

One moon and one day after Rose's death, I'm riding the elevator up through the Spire to the Bindery. *The* Bindery. In the Eternal Library. My body is filled head to toe with joy, and I can't stop smiling, even while trapped in a cramped metal box. I hate elevators, but this one is delivering me to my dreams. Just like it will tomorrow, and the next day, and so many days after that. I can even ignore the strange clanking noises and the way it doesn't line up with the floor when the doors open at the top. It's all worth it.

The email I got yesterday was vague, but there can only be one reason why I'm here: I got the apprenticeship. Why else would I get a personal invitation to the place where the magic happens? I step confidently out of the elevator, my heels clacking on the worn wood floor. To my right is a glass door leading to a balcony, beyond which the Sound glitters under the sun. The Spire sits on the foothills of the Bell Mountains, and the view of the city as it slopes down to the water is breathtaking.

To my left is the Bindery. I pass a bathroom and storage closet before emerging into a large octagonal room. A communal area, with a long yellow couch and plush blue armchairs in the center. There's a stunning circular rug underneath depicting the constellations of the northern hemisphere.

The walls are a warm peach color that glows in the light filtering down from the domed glass ceiling. Paper charms and knot spells for a happy home are strung from the exposed rafters, the beads on their ends glittering. There aren't any windows on the walls because each wall contains an ornately carved door depicting plants used to make paper, ink, and thread. Matching stained glass windows arch over each one, some lit from within and others dark.

Copper plaques adorn each door. Press Room, Paper Room, Supply Room, Kitchen, and then names: Catrina Rosefall, Aeronwy Stargrove, and Juniper Stargrove. One door is missing its plaque.

I wander slowly, taking it all in. It's so vibrant and cozy and *awesome*. In the true sense of the word.

I know I'm early. I'm always early—being on time is being late, in my book. Maybe I'll sit on the couch and wait. Someone will come out eventually. That would probably be the polite thing to do. Or will it be awkward that I didn't simply announce myself? The door to June's studio is partly open. I have way too much energy (and coffee) buzzing through my veins to be patient.

"Hello?" I call out, "Anyone around? I just wanted to let you know I'm here!"

I hear ruffling papers and then footsteps from June's studio. E emerges and smiles brightly when e catches sight of me. Eir hair is pulled back into a loose braid, wisps of gray and red floating around eir cheerful face. E's dressed casually in jeans and a sleeveless gray button-up with leaves embroidered on the collar. I wonder if e did that emself; June is an accomplished fiber artist.

"Amane! Good to see you made it up here," June says, crossing the room to join my side.

"Sorry that I'm a bit early."

June waves my apology away. "Ah, we don't keep strict hours up here, it's no matter. The nature of the craft can have you working at all odd hours of the day and night. Easier to come and go as needed. Why don't you have a seat?"

I sit down on the yellow couch, which is softer than it looks. June walks over to the door with Aeronwy's name on it and knocks once, then pokes eir head inside.

"My love, Amane is—are you still napping?" June sighs and turns back towards me. "Just a moment. Aery is hard to wake."

June disappears into Aeronwy's studio. This couch would be good for a nap, but I've never been the type. Too many things to do. If I could get away with not sleeping for the rest of my life, I would. Thinking of how much more I could get done with another six to eight hours frustrates me to no end.

I can hear murmurs of conversation from the studio. I wonder how long it takes Aeronwy to wake up. I guess I'll find out if I'm working here. The thought brings the grin back to my face, the ear-to-ear one I know from photos makes me look a little rabid.

The elevator dings. Who could that be? I have a clear view of the elevator; Tabby steps out and then walks down the hall. E stops at the edge of the room and on seeing me, looks confused. My smile falters.

"Hi," e says.

"Um, hi," I say.

Tabby gazes around the room the way I must have when I first entered, mouth slightly open and eyes shining. Eir blonde hair is freshly trimmed by the ears, and e's wearing a cute white top patterned with cacti. E sits down in one of the armchairs, clasping a brown messenger bag in eir lap. The scent of lavender washes over me.

"This place is so beautiful, don't you think?" e says, watching me uncertainly.

E doesn't ask what I'm doing here. I thought I knew, but now I'm not so sure. The vagueness of the email returns to haunt me. Is there a *third* test? One to narrow things down even further? Are more people going to show up? Or is it between Tabby and I now?

"It's really something," I reply, and I can hear how stiff I sound. Ugh.

Thankfully, the door to Aeronwy's studio opens, saving me from further awkward conversation. June and Aeronwy join us in the communal area. June is smiling fondly and Aeronwy is yawning, running both hands through eir hair. The long silver and white curls are gone, what's left swept back in short, stylish waves. E catches sight of us staring, and our confusion must show on our faces because one corner of eir mouth twitches upward.

"I told you we ought to have explained it to them in the email," e says to June, inclining eir head towards us.

June notices Tabby and gives a little start. E presses a hand to eir chest and chuckles. "Tabitha! Good to have you with us, too! Of course you'd come in the moment I was out of the room," e says.

"You can call me Tabby. Please." Tabby's voice is so soft I can barely hear em.

"Alright, then, yes, Tabby," says June. E chuckles. "Tabby Fairweaver. Did your parents do that on purpose?"

"Sorry?" says Tabby, looking even more confused.

"I guess not. That's even more delightful. The most basic weaving pattern is called 'tabby' or 'tabby weaving.' Your name is a pun," June explains, chuckling some more.

Tabby just stares. So do I. I'm not in the mood for puns right now.

"I had no idea," Tabby says faintly.

June plops down into the other armchair while Aeronwy leans on the back of it. E's wearing a lacy white blouse tucked into a high-waisted black skirt and black boots with pointy toes. It looks as if e walked out of a designer catalogue. Coral lipstick to top it off. I like it.

June opens eir mouth to speak, then closes it, looks thoughtful, opens it again, and stops a second time.

"Hmm, I didn't quite think through how to start this."

"You might start with congratulations," says Aeronwy, amused.

"But before we say that, they have to accept our offer," says June, tilting eir head up at Aeronwy.

"Offer?" I blurt out, and they both look at me.

"Yes. I guess I should get straight to it. You see, originally there was only one apprenticeship spot available, with me, which you both applied for," June says. "However, things have been changing quite a lot up here in the past few moons, and so, now there are two."

Tabby and I exchange a glance. My hopes rise, and I can see the same happening in Tabby's eyes.

June sighs and adjusts eir glasses. "The first spot opened up when Mayumi announced eir retirement a year ago. That's when the application process started, you'll recall. Then Rose got sick, and," e pauses to clear eir throat. E'd been cheerful at Rose's memorial, but now e seems distraught. Aeronwy rubs eir shoulders, and e continues, "We weren't planning on filling that spot for a while."

"But… you are now?" I ask. I bounce one of my legs nervously.

"Yes. The catch is that one of you would be training with me, instead," Aeronwy says.

At that, I look harder at em, past the fancy clothes. Aeronwy is tall, with broad shoulders and ruler-straight posture. Elegant and stern. I don't know if that's the kind of person I want to be my mentor.

"We thought we'd let the two of you decide. I know you both initially signed up to apprentice with me, and the match between mentor and student does matter very much. If one of you would like to wait until the other has finished, I'd be happy to take you on later. You're both wonderful candidates," says June.

I bounce both legs now. I need to apprentice with June. That's what I came here for. What I moved to an entirely different hemisphere of the planet for. I don't want to wait. What would I do in the meantime? What would my family think? They're so proud that I'm carrying on the Sol tradition of excellence and never settling for anything but the best. I can't let them down. I can't let *myself* down.

I sneak a glance at Tabby. To my surprise, e's the least anxious person in the room. Posture relaxed, hands folded calmly in eir lap, Tabby is watching Aeronwy like e's just seen the solution to a difficult puzzle.

"Um, how long do we have to decide?" I say.

"How long do you need?"

"Not long," Tabby says, before I can answer. "Can I talk to Amane in private for a few minutes?"

"Of course. Let us step out, then. Knock when you need us," says June.

E gets up and the two of them go into June's studio, closing the door behind them. I turn to Tabby immediately, hands raised in defense.

"Tabby, I think you're really nice, and I think we could be friends, and I want to keep being friends with Rhee without it being awkward between you and me, I don't want to mess all that up, but I really, really, *really* need this apprenticeship with June in particular, e's my inspiration and the whole reason I started—"

"That's fine," says Tabby simply. E doesn't seem bothered or upset at all.

"Are you *sure*? You're not just…" I tuck my hands under my arms and stare down at my lap. I want to be the one who apprentices with June, but I don't want Tabby to agree just to avoid conflict. I don't want to foster resentment down the line. "You won't regret it?"

"No. I'd *prefer* to apprentice with Aeronwy instead," Tabby says. There's a little surprise in eir voice, as if e wasn't expecting this, either.

"Why?" I have to ask. I always have to ask.

Tabby's face turns red. E reaches up with both hands, tucking strands of hair behind eir ears. "I had a dream," e murmurs.

"What kind of—" I say, and then stop, remembering what Rhiannon said about that particular question. My mouth snaps shut.

It must have been personal, because Tabby doesn't explain further. That only makes me want to know more. *Maybe one day e'll be comfortable enough to tell you,* says a voice in the back of my head. *E's not your competition anymore, e's your coworker.*

Understanding dawns on me. Tabby wants to apprentice with Aeronwy. I want to apprentice with June. They're giving us the opportunity to do exactly that. We'll be working together. Apprenticeships are three to five years, and then if we're successful, we could both be here for the rest of our careers.

Most Illuminators practice their craft for life. For once my tongue feels tied in knots. Tabby could well become someone important in my life.

"So, everything's fine? That works for you?" Tabby asks.

I nod. We sit in silence for a minute before I get antsy and go knock on June's studio door. I'm still processing all these new developments. Things are going far differently than I planned, but it's not going *wrong*. It's hard to wrap my mind around. Part of me sees any deviation from the dream as failure, but this… isn't?

"That was quick," June says as e and Aeronwy come back to their seats. "You've decided?"

"Yes," says Tabby, taking the initiative again. My impression of Tabby so far is that e's quiet, shy, timid even. E must really trust in the dream e had. "Amane would like to stay with you, June, and I'll apprentice with Aeronwy. If that's okay. We agreed."

"You're certain?" Aeronwy says. E stands very still.

"We're certain," I say. Tabby nods.

Aeronwy relaxes, nodding. June slides down in the armchair with a huge sigh of relief, arms and legs flopped in odd directions. "Oh, thank the Author, that's good. I don't know how we would have decided who would go first if you both wanted to apprentice with me," e says.

"Flip a coin?" suggests Aeronwy in a wry voice. The very idea makes me shudder.

"I really couldn't decide between the two of you," June says. "Usually the candidacy process is so clear. It was a nightmare until Aery offered to take one of you on."

"Everything fell into place," says Aeronwy. E pats June on the head reassuringly.

June straightens back up, smiling again. That seems to be eir default expression. I liked eir sparkling energy when watching lecture videos on the Astranet. In person, I can *feel* the optimism and joy radiating from em, and it's magical.

"Yes, it did! And *now* I can say congratulations: you've both been accepted as Illumination apprentices here at the Eternal Library."

Part Two: Paper
Fall 4018

CHAPTER TEN
TABBY

Every time I get close to my old dream garden, I wake up. Whatever time of night or day, wherever I am in my sleep cycle, it happens. Once I reach the end of the thorns, my eyes snap open. Someone or something doesn't want me to gain access to it. That someone might be me.

In the waking world, summer turns to fall. Temperatures drop into the sixties and gray clouds roll across the sky on a crisp, wet breeze. In the dreaming, I wander through fields and deserts, beneath mountains, through halls I've never seen before, but which feel so familiar. The night before the autumn equinox, the day Amane and I will take our oaths as Librarians, I decide to visit the Library's dreamscape.

It would be easier if I were sleeping in one of the buildings, but I find my way there well enough. I call up a pathway from my memories. The darkness shifts around me, pinpricks of light popping up in the distance like lanterns leading down a long hallway. I follow them until I reach a pair of towering doors made from open books. I press my hand against its surface and ask permission to enter; the pages of the books shiver, and part to let me through.

Inside, bookshelves twist and double and rise to heights that by all the laws of physics shouldn't be possible. Stories spill from ruffled pages, altering the landscape. Futuristic cities, tiny rural villages, blooming meadows, grimy alleyways, bustling shops appear and disappear as I pass the book they're written in. Characters haunt the rows, acting out their dialogue or having conversations their authors never wrote, but perhaps imagined.

Chapter Ten

At least that's what I think they're doing. They could be coming up with things all on their own, but does that mean they're beings in their own right? Or are they just figments of imagination? Some characters are more solid than others. Their words are clearer, louder, make more sense. They have more readers. More minds conjuring them into existence, loving or hating them into being. I turn myself invisible, just a shimmer on the wind, and drift past a congregation of murderers in the mystery section.

I walk through the nonfiction stacks, the natural history section. I'm tempted to pick up one of the books. Open any of these books and you'll find yourself in a slide show of swirling narration. Facts drift in through the dream logic, and suddenly you just Know Things. At least while you have the book in your hands. I've never been able to study successfully in the dreamscape. The knowledge slides out of my mind once I wake up.

I continue to the Illuminated books. Thousands of illustrated manuscripts, each one crafted by hand by a single artisan. These books contain dreams. If I open one here, I can walk into its world entirely and experience hours and hours of immersive story or information.

The ghosts of Librarians past seem drawn to this section of the Library dreamscape, because I see clusters of them everywhere, drawn by the concentrated source of magic. These are people who can't or won't reincarnate yet, or ever, in some cases. They had traumatic deaths, or are waiting for loved ones to join them, or they simply don't want to start all over again.

I understand that. The idea of having to be a child again makes the dreamscape ripple around me with dread. At least as an adult, I have some control over my life. As a child I had none.

I need to distract myself before I start drawing nightmares. I think about Rose. It's been over a moon since e died now, enough time for eir spirit to materialize. It's also enough time to have reincarnated already, but something in me doubts Rose would move on from the Library so quickly. I wonder how the Head Librarian's oath impacts their dreamscape. That would be a worthy area of study.

And that makes me wonder: does the *Library* have a heartscape? I pause between the spectral stacks and place my forehead against the twisted wood, searching for a pulse. It takes a while, but once I lock onto it—

Brilliantly colored words burst before my eyes, streaming through my spirit body and filling me up with song. I stumble back and fall to the floor. The Library's heartscape must be huge and powerful, to have a pulse like that. There's no way I could listen to it long enough to triangulate its location.

I stand and shake snippets of strange music from my head. I'll just have to look for it the old fashioned way: by dreaming.

***

When I arrive at the Library's main ritual room that morning, in the flesh, I find myself horribly underdressed. I'm wearing tan slacks and a white blouse, my idea of formal wear, but Amane and Aeronwy have gone all out.

Amane is wearing another one of her vibrant, curve-hugging dresses; this one goes all the way to the floor and has a huge peplum at the waist. Her hair is hidden in a tall head wrap of the same fabric. She looks absolutely beautiful, and my heart beats a little faster. Aeronwy is dressed entirely in crimson silk, a blazer with padded shoulders cut sharp over a sheer tunic and wide-legged pants. E's accessorized with sleek gold jewelry in every place possible.

They examine each other's fashion choices, which I admit looks very funny. Amane only comes up to the middle of Aeronwy's chest and has to crane her head all the way back to look em in the eye. Aeronwy stares down eir nose at her.

"Where do you *get* these things?" she says, gesturing at Aeronwy's clothes. "It looks like it just came off this year's runway! Maybe *next* year's!"

Aeronwy crosses eir arms. "I have my sources."

"Are you friends with the designers, or what?"

Aeronwy catches sight of me as e turns away from her and gives a nod of recognition. Amane abruptly stops talking to smile and wave. Her friendliness brings a smile to my face. I'm glad we're not competing anymore.

June appears at my side, similarly underdressed and looking harried. "Good morning, everyone! I hope you're ready to take your oaths," e says, fiddling with eir glasses. E looks at me, then at Amane and Aeronwy, and then back to me. "I'm glad I'm not the only one who's more casual today, eh, Tabby?"

The solidarity makes me feel better about my fashion choices. "Comfort is key," I agree.

June nods and then looks at Aeronwy. "There's… a slight problem. Maybe not a problem. But I thought you should know. I only just found out."

Aeronwy frowns. "What is it?"

Amane and I glance at one another. June isn't addressing us, so maybe it's not something we need to worry about. But she looks wide-eyed, and my stomach gives a squeeze.

"Ah, good morning, future of the Library! So glad to see new apprentices stepping into the magic circle!"

An unfamiliar voice rings out through the high-ceilinged room. Unfamiliar to me, at least, because June winces and Aeronwy drops eir arms in an ungraceful, exasperated motion. The frown on eir face deepens into a scowl.

The hairs on the back of my neck prickle, and suddenly there's someone standing between Amane and I. A slim Librarian in a lavender pantsuit, with tiny round glasses and a ballerina's posture. E's a little shorter than June, but probably about the same age. E's wearing an ornate crown of quartz crystals over eir short gray hair with an open, golden book as the centerpiece.

"Thank you! I'm so excited to be here!" Amane says to em, oblivious to June and Aeronwy's reactions. Or the energy in the room.

The Librarian pats her on the shoulder and smiles. "Wonderful, wonderful. I hope you're prepared for—"

"Mairead, what are you doing here?" Aeronwy interrupts, dragging a hand down eir face.

Mairead? As in, Rhiannon's boss, Mairead? The Head Archivist? It must be. The description fits. Alarm bells go off in my head and heart. I've never been able to put my finger on why, but I don't like what I've heard of em. Something always felt off while listening to Rhee's stories. This is the first time

I've met Mairead in person, though, so I'll have to form my own opinions. I try to give everyone the benefit of the doubt.

Mairead glances at Aéronwy, but doesn't look em in the eyes. "I'm Acting Head of Library Ritual while Cailean is on sabbatical. Anyone on the ritual committee can do the Charter Oath, but few members know the apprentice-mentor binding now that Rose and Mayumi are gone. So, I'm here," e says, very matter-of-factly.

"Be that as it may, it's an incredibly personal ritual, and I don't want *you* performing it," Aéronwy says. Every word sounds forced. The look in eir gold eyes is steely.

Mairead laughs as if e's said something ridiculous. "You're still doing this? Come on now, haven't we let bygones be bygones?"

Beside me, June mutters, "You know we prefer someone else facilitate our apprenticeship bindings. That hasn't changed."

Mairead ignores em. E puts eir hands on eir hips and glances between Amane and I with a wry smile. "Your first taste of Library politics. Hopefully, you make less enemies than I do in your time here," e says, laughing again.

Amane's big brown eyes flicker back and forth, looking for clues on how to respond. I'm at a loss, too. I've heard enough about Library politics from Rhiannon to know I don't want to get involved with someone else's drama if I can help it.

"Isn't there someone else who can do it?" Aéronwy asks.

"No," says Mairead, and suddenly eir casual, friendly demeanor is gone. E pierces Aéronwy with a look. "Either I do it today, or we postpone for the vernal equinox and you wait a half a year to start your apprenticeships. This binding can only be done two days out of the year, you know that and should have checked in with who was available if it matters so much."

Amane's panic becomes more apparent. I can't see her wanting to wait another week to start the job, much less *half a year*. I'm not thrilled about it either, honestly. I flash her a reassuring glance that says I understand, and she settles down.

Aéronwy and June look at one another. They don't speak, but after a moment June nods and Aéronwy shrugs.

"You can do mine, but I'll do Aeronwy's," June says, turning to face Mairead.

Mairead looks offended, but quickly covers the expression with a placating grin. "You're not on the ritual committee. You can't do that."

"I can. I've seen it at least a dozen times. I know the whole ritual by heart. Besides, it's thread magic," June says calmly.

"But—"

"You still get to do one," Aeronwy says. "We won't have to wait until spring. Can't you accept a compromise for *once*?"

Mairead is smiling, but I sense the anger simmering beneath the surface. A reaction I'm awfully familiar with, thanks to my parents. My instincts scream at me to mediate, an edge of panic creeping into my veins. I push it down and bite my tongue.

"You can administer their Charter Oaths, then my bond with Amane, and that way you don't have to wait around while I do Aeronwy's," June says to Mairead, "if Amane's all right with that."

"Yes! That's perfectly fine!" Amane says, looking relieved.

Mairead ignores June and pats Amane on the shoulder again.

The main ritual room is a circular hall with auditorium seating around the outside edge. The stands are empty, but the room is full of animosity. Amane and I remove our shoes and step into the circle inscribed in the center of the room. A seven-pointed star fills its bounds, etched deeply into the stage. The floor is made of smooth, cold stone without tiles or seams. I know from Rhiannon's research that this room was built right into the bedrock of the mountain.

June and Aeronwy wait in the wings, while Mairead administers the Charter Oath. The ritual is simple, ancient, and powerful. Mairead cleanses both of us with ringing bells, asks our full names and places of birth, and invites our ancestors and deities to be present. E moves through the ritual with ease and a flair for the dramatic, raising the energy in the circle to swirling heights.

Amane exhales deeply when the spirits are called, as if a great weight has settled on her. Her eyes are closed, face tense. I don't envy her mediumship abilities in a place like this. I reach over and take her hand to comfort her. Her palm is sweaty. She shoots me a grateful look, and I hold on until Mairead asks me to step forward on my own.

Before me sits a reproduction of the Charter Book on a pedestal. Though the original tome created by the Founders is lost, we still swear to uphold the law within. To recognize that we are the ones in service here, to the Library, to the community, to patrons, to the books. We must always bear that in mind, and work in their best interests over our own.

Mairead opens the book to the central signature, where there's an empty circle drawn across two pages. I place my writing hand on it, as instructed.

"Do you swear by the Sun, Moon, Stars, and any deities in your worship, to uphold the Charter and its values, and become a Librarian of the Eternal Library?" Mairead asks in a grave voice. The light rising from the activated circle beneath our feet makes em look mysterious and foreboding

"I do swear."

Rhiannon told me what would happen, but I'm still not prepared for the way the words double and then lift off the page, spiraling up my arm and pressing into my skin like firm, hot fingers. They glow blindingly white and then fade, sinking through my body and into my spirit. My hair stands on end for another minute, then settles. I can feel the oath like a thread tied around my wrist.

Amane watches with fascination, then takes her turn. The tension in her face melts away as the words disappear into her dark skin. She takes her hand from the pages and looks at it wondrously, face glowing with pride.

With that, Mairead closes the book and the ceremony, but not the magic circle. It's time for our individual rituals. Legs shaking, I walk over to where June and Aeronwy are sitting in the stands. June joins Amane in the circle, and I sink into a chair gratefully. I wasn't expecting to feel so drained. My eyelids droop, heavy with fatigue. I need to put my head down, just for a moment.

Eyes closed, I slip into the dreamscape and find myself in a forest of towering redwoods. These trees are like nothing I've seen in the waking world, with trunks the size of houses and canopies that disappear far above. There's no underbrush, only a thick carpet of red-gold needles and cones the size of thimbles. The air is thick and still. Somewhere, a bird is singing.

I walk through the grove slowly, enjoying the rejuvenating scent of living wood. Is this part of the Library's dreamscape? Do the books remember being trees, once? We switched mostly to hemp for paper production two hundred years ago, but much of the Eternal Library's collection is older than that.

Dappled sunlight filters through the canopy high above. In the waking world, redwood canopies are full of life, harboring entire ecosystems in their middle and upper branches. I gaze skyward, wondering. What could be up there?

Before I can explore further, I wake up. Someone has said my name.

"Tabby, it's our turn."

Beside me, Aeronwy closes the sketchbook on eir lap and stands. But not before I catch a glimpse of the sketch inside: towering redwood trees, a tiny figure no more than a scribble at their base.

I walk back to the magic circle with em, mind tumbling over questions like rocks in a stream. Did e pick up on my dream, or did my dreaming pick up on the drawing? Is there a difference? What does it mean? What does it have to do with the *other* dream, from Rose's memorial service?

I'd assumed Aeronwy'd appeared there because e had helped carry me to the first aid tent. When Amane and I were invited to the Bindery and presented with the new apprenticeship offer, I realized it had been a premonition. An omen. The contents of the dream itself are still confusing, but I knew right away what I should do about the apprenticeship.

Now this.

Aeronwy and I join June in the center of the room. The harried look from earlier is gone, replaced by a beatific smile. I catch the tail end of Mairead's lavender pant leg as e slips out the door, duties finished for the day. Aeronwy's mood lightens considerably. I'll have to ask Rhiannon if e's heard anything about that. I don't know the older Illuminators well enough yet to ask them personal questions.

Aeronwy and I turn to face one another. I'm used to looking down at people, but Aeronwy is a few inches taller than me. Looking up at someone feels odd. Aeronwy has the yellow-gold eye color that comes from the valleys. It's even more striking against eir brown skin than Rhiannon's green. Despite the severe cheekbones and stern expression, eir eyes are filled with a quieter light. Like twin candle flames. Comforting and steady.

June recites the words to the ritual without stumbling, eir soothing voice flowing over and around us as the energy in the circle grows once more. E hands Aeronwy a crystal goblet filled with water and a drop of sacred red ink, from which e drinks before handing it to me. I take a sip; it tastes sweet and makes my tongue tingle.

"So, the cup is passed as knowledge shall be, from one generation to another, master to apprentice, handed down through the ages from the Founding of the Library and the Founder, Eirlys Starsower emself. For all Illuminators may trace their lineage back to em, our guiding light in the darkness," June sings the words, clearly enjoying emself.

June takes the cup back and sets it aside for a small lacquered box with moonstone inlaid on the lid. Inside, resting on black velvet, is a golden spool wrapped with bright red thread and a tiny pair of golden scissors. The handles are shaped to look like a crescent moon and sun that fit together when the blades are closed.

Aeronwy holds out a hand. I take it, and e curls eir long, ring-heavy fingers around my stubby ones with the nails bitten down to the quick. Eir touch is unusually hot, as if e has a fever. June takes the thread from the box and ties the end around Aeronwy's wrist, nudging aside a gold bangle, then twines it around our hands and ties it off on my wrist. The thread is waxy and stiff, the kind you'd use to bind a book. E snips the end with the celestial scissors.

June places both of eir hands over ours. My chest tightens with an unfamiliar emotion. Longing? Sorrow? Joy? All three? Perhaps it's the magic of the ceremony.

"Aeronwy Stargrove, do you pledge yourself to the sacred role of the teacher, to impart knowledge, to offer support, to protect and guide the mind, heart, and spirit of your apprentice in ways that are compassionate and effective?" June recites.

"I do pledge," Aeronwy says.

The thread hums against my skin. The smell of smoke fills my nose and lungs, and the scent of sticky printmaking ink, the sense of charcoal being dragged across rough paper. Spirit sense. A warmth in my chest that flickers and flutters, lightning quickening in my blood and ready to jump out at the slightest spark. It feels dangerous and comforting at the same time.

June turns to me. "Tabitha Fairweaver, do you pledge yourself to the sacred role of the apprentice, to listen, to learn, to open your mind, heart, and spirit to the knowledge given to you by your teacher, in ways that challenge you to grow?" June asks.

"I do pledge," I say.

My tongue tingles so much I'm afraid I won't get the words out, but when I do, I can taste the power in them. The thread hums again; it will hold me to my oath. I wonder what my spirit feels like to Aeronwy, what dreams drift across this new bond forged between us. I can't tell from the quiet expression on eir face. We're only holding hands, but the moment feels incredibly intimate.

"Then it is done," says June. "So it is, so it will be."

E holds up the golden scissors again and cuts the thread with the final word.

CHAPTER ELEVEN
RHIANNON

I am being created. Calliope etches the words into my pages, pen dancing along ligatures and flourishes. The face looking down at me is soft and round, with brown eyes and brown skin. Black hair falls in waves around eir shoulders, sometimes brushing up against me. There are hints of wrinkles at the corners of eir mouth, perhaps from frowning in concentration. This is the face of my creator—my Author.

My vessel is made of leaf and earth and seed and skin. My words come from Calliope's mind, my pictures from eir paintbrush. Sometimes e snips off locks of that long black hair and uses it to paint my illustrations. I watch as e grinds pigments for my ink, whispering encouragement beneath moon and sun and stars.

The celestial bodies appear often within my text. They are the symbols of my characters, a trio of legends long past. Slowly, I understand myself to be a story of love and betrayal and loss. My name is The Founding. *To build, first the ground must be broken. First the trees must be cut, the stones hewn, the nails hammered in the forge. Eirlys Starsower, Isylwyn Moonscryer, and Daryn Sunseeker knew this when they created* Illumination *and the Eternal Library. It is their tale I tell.*

Calliope must know love and loss as well, for sometimes when e writes, tears fall from eir eyes.

There is much shouting in the Bindery during my birth. Calliope protects me with eir body, hiding me from being torn apart in the search. Something valuable, something powerful, has been misplaced, and they cannot find it. Calliope does not want them to find it. I understand it to be a fellow book.

The book belongs in the hands of the Head Librarian, the searcher says. The searcher is the Head Librarian. E didn't used to be, Calliope whispers to me later. The Head Librarian used to be Calliope's mentor, a wonderful Illuminator named Llewella Golddancer. Apparently, Llewella Golddancer is now dead.

I comfort Calliope the best I can, inviting em to get lost in the detailed borders, the decorative drop caps, the perfectly flowing script. As the time passes, the shake in Calliope's hand steadies. Eir breath slows. But the fire in eir eyes never dims.

When e writes the dedication page at my front, e inscribes: For Llewella. May what happened to you never happen again.

The new Head Librarian comes to me in a dream. My dream? Theirs? Do I dream, or am I one? Eir name is Ciarán Stonefeather, and eir conscience is heavy with death. Llewella Golddancer's death. E seeks refuge in the books, trying to escape the memory in our pages, to lose emself in our worlds. In my pages, Ciarán sees eir own story reflected back at em. Isylwyn Moonscryer, second Head Librarian of the Eternal Library, also allegedly killed eir predecessor to possess the power of the missing Charter Book.

The past we are doomed to repeat, Ciarán says, and wonders if perhaps it is a good thing the Charter Book is lost.

Ciarán reads my story more times than any other. I can't tell if this is for comfort, or for penance. E has much work to do, and it is all so much harder without the Charter Book. The Library in this time is fractured, its Librarians divided along lines the other books do not understand. But I do. For the first crack was laid long ago, in the very foundation of our world.

The images in the ink fade to black. Slowly, I come back to my senses, back to my body, back to the present. My neck is stiff. My back groans when I sit up. Time means nothing to me, memories swirling vividly through my mind as if they happened minutes ago, though it's been years. What was I even *doing*? Where *am* I?

Someone shoves a small bottle in my hand. Habit takes over, and I hold the bottle up to my nose, inhaling the sharp scent of rosemary. My brain fog dissipates.

"What did you See this time?" Mairead asks excitedly.

I lean my elbows on the stone scrying desk and put my head in my hands. I'm going to have *such* a migraine later. "I was the book again," I say, "it's so weird. Usually I just see the book from an observer's position. I've never *been* the book before."

"Did you see Calliope again? Or was it more recent?"

I look up blearily. Mairead is sitting on the edge of the desk, biting eir lip in anticipation. "I saw Ciarán Stonefeather. Seems like maybe e regretted being a murderer. I wonder if e would have felt that way if the Charter Book hadn't been lost. Shit was wack back then," I say.

Mairead snorts. Reclamation-era politics and religion (when your country is a theocracy, they're the same thing) are eir specialty. The fact that we still use the term Reclamation to describe the period irks me. The Library was founded on values from *both* religious sects. They weren't reclaiming shit. I don't say that to Mairead, though. I already know we disagree on the subject.

At the time, a wave of immigrants from war-torn Glykiági had divided Casporans, mostly along Authorist/Readerist lines. The world was quickly expanding at the time, and the Readerist-majority Library wanted to welcome the immigrants, to share our cultures with one another, and send scholars out into other lands to help end the war.

Many Authorists found this abhorrent, as they preferred to protect their collected knowledge and preserve tradition. They wanted to wait and watch when it came to war, to write the history books from afar. They wanted the newcomers to assimilate. The wave of immigration was the catalyst for what they named the Reclamation, insisting that the Library—and thus the whole country—was founded on Authorist values.

Ciarán Stonefeather, noted Authorist leader, had poisoned staunch Readerist Llewella Golddancer and ran for Head Librarian unopposed. The poisoning wasn't proven until later, but Llewella wasn't the first to die over the power of the Charter Book. People *knew*.

Calliope knew.

"It's incredible that you can See that far back. I've never met anyone who can go back farther than a couple hundred years," Mairead says, handing me a bottle of water. "You have a really incredible gift, and even better, you know how to use it."

"Thanks," I say, both for the water and the compliment. Since we started this project, Mairead has been friendlier than usual. I'm starting to enjoy eir company down here in the depths.

I place a board over the scrying bowl, so I can write down what I Saw. The ballpoint pen confuses me, my time-addled brain expecting a quill with a nib. I shake my head to clear the sensation. I was only visiting the past. I'm not *from* then.

"The fact that you're receiving these visions means the book still exists somewhere, and didn't burn in the '86 fire," Mairead muses. "Though it seems it might take a long time for your visions to catch up with the present. Even so, we're gathering such a wealth of knowledge in the process."

"I know, right? If you want to use any of this for your research, you can always cite me in your bibliography," I say.

"I may have to take you up on that," Mairead says with a laugh.

E hops down from the table, black skirts billowing. I watch em from the corner of my eye as I write. E paces slowly around the room, trailing eir fingers along the glowing veins of amethyst.

"You're a much better Assistant Head than Camille thus far," e says. "A pity I didn't realize your potential earlier. But then, everything happens exactly when it's supposed to. This project appeared just before the position became available for you to take. I should know by now that when Isylwyn sends me a message, it heralds tremendous changes."

"E is one of the Founders after all," I say, feeling both proud of and uncomfortable with the comparison to Camille. I can't help it. I like being the top of the class.

Mairead turns on eir heel, face lit with purple stars from the glowing geode. "Do you want to see?"

"See what?"

Mairead perches on the arm of the stone chair and holds a hand out to me. "I've seen you work your magic. Do you want to see how I do mine? I'll show you my memory of when I found the catalog card. I know you can't control what you See, but if I focus on sending it to you, it should work. I've done it before with others."

"Um," I say, because, again, I don't care for touching people I'm not close to. Diving into a living person's memories in the scrying bowl is fraught with ethical considerations. But Mairead is so excited, and e's given me permission. "Sure, why not."

I add a few more drops of ink to the bowl, violet this time to see the more recent past and attune with Mairead's energy. The ink is iridescent, shimmering and swirling through the black water in mysterious currents. I take Mairead's hand, which is dainty and cool, and then peer into the bowl.

I blink. We're in the Library's new Authorist temple. There are tiny temples on campus for just about every deity and faith, but this one is huge. Big enough to house a few hundred worshipers. It fell into disuse after the Revolution, but Mairead's worked tirelessly to restore it to its former glory.

More and more Librarians, and even a few staff from the kitchens and housekeeping, are coming to the services. They like that it feels like storytime. They like that they are each given a role to fill, so they can stop questioning their life's purpose. No more wandering about, confused. Every piece in its place. The main ritual space has smooth wood floors etched with magical circles and domed skylights above to let in the moonlight. Circular pews ring the center space, gleaming with polish.

The moon is at its zenith now, full and flooding the sanctuary with pale white light. There are no other lights in the room. Mairead kneels on the center stage, dressed in eir ceremonial garb: a flowing cotton dress the color of paper, crystal diadem, and belt with a Priestex's tools attached. Ink, quill, book, and thread.

A classical cello piece plays on the overhead speakers. It starts with slow, long, deep notes. Mairead rises from the floor in time with the music, lithe body swaying. Arms raised, e glides gracefully across the sanctuary in a dance to call the spirits. One spirit in particular: Isylwyn Moonscryer, the Author's own insert, who understood the Book That Is the Universe better than anyone.

The music picks up, the cellist drawing the bow sharply across the instrument now. Mairead's movements quicken. The look on eir face is one of absolute joy.

Dust in the moonlight stirs. The old Temple building groans. The groaning grows louder, over the sound of the music. A shadow, a flicker, no more, and suddenly the bookshelf on the nearest wall collapses. It's two stories tall, overladen, perhaps, and smashes across the sanctuary floor with a thunderous boom, paper rustling and tumbling as if in a gale. The edge of the heavy redwood shelf lies inches from Mairead's startled form, a weight that would have surely killed em. The shock keeps em kneeling in place.

A sharp prickle runs down eir spine as a piece of paper flutters to the floor and lands in the moonlight before Mairead's feet. Hand shaking, e reaches for it. It looks like an old catalog card, the type they used when Mairead was much younger.

The Founding, *Calliope Everberry, original Illumination by Calliope Everberry, publication date Opal Moon 28, 3018. Call no. 1111.333 EVER. Property of the Eternal Library.*

The knowledge fills Mairead's head, quick and fast and strong. Isylwyn's message is clear: search for what was lost, and you will find more than you ever imagined.

Mairead stands, surveying the damaged bookshelf. An omen. The toppling of a false institution. The shaking of the very foundation of the Library. Secrets, revealed. Mairead knows e's past the age of a proper Protagonist—e already had that adventure as a much younger Librarian, discovered e was living in a tragedy, and accepted eir fate—but now e has the chance to play the role of the hero again.

Holding the catalog card tightly, e whispers a promise to the moonlight: "This is my story. I will find the book."

***

I should know better. I was already past my limit before Mairead showed me eir memory, and that night I'm taken prisoner by the worst migraine I've had in years. It lasts three whole fucking days. I know it's three days because Tabby and I mark them off on the calendar each morning, to help me return to the present. Going so far back in time with the card from *The Founding* has screwed with my biological clock something fierce. When you become unmoored in time, you start to see how fake the concept really is. Then existential dread hits you in the face like a cast-iron skillet.

On the morning of the fourth day, Amane texts me.

> **AMANE:** Heeeey, how are you feeling today? Any better?

> **ME:** meh, maybe

> **AMANE:** aww
> **AMANE:** I'm off work today, do you want me to come by and help cheer you up? maybe go out somewhere, get some fresh air?

> **ME:** i dunno, schedule seems kinda full, let's see
> **ME:** oh yes
> **ME:** i was planning on spending the next twelve hours face down on my bed, contemplating the meaninglessness of the universe

> **AMANE:** can you contemplate the meaninglessness of the universe and go clothes shopping at the same time?

> **AMANE:** because I definitely don't have enough warm clothes for this climate. It got so chilly all of a sudden!!!
>
> **ME:** well
> **ME:** i def don't want you to freeze
> **ME:** this is only the beginning
> **ME:** the Big Gray is coming. Also the rain. ALL THE RAIN
> **ME:** what kind of friend would I be if I didn't help you acclimate to the climate, hmmmm?
>
> **AMANE:** YAY
> **AMANE:** So where do you want to go?

I meet Amane in the harbor district downtown, where there are boutiques in little rowhouses all squashed together with outdoor markets, their stalls colorful and cheap. The sky is full of puffy white clouds, blocking out the sun save for the occasional glimpse. The breeze blowing off the Sound is brisk, making Amane shiver in her bright orange short-sleeved shirt and matching pants.

"Yeah, see, this won't do, we need to get you some *layers*," I say, tugging at her sleeve. "C'mon."

"*You* look nice. I wasn't sure if you cared about clothes," Amane says as we head for the boutiques.

I've been wearing nothing but pajamas for the last few days, so it felt good to pick out something stylish to wear downtown. Big denim jacket with mismatched colored patches, olive parachute pants, a button-up with *Fuck Off* embroidered in cursive on the collar. I feel more myself while advertising I want people to stay away from me.

"That's the idea. I strive to look good without looking like I'm *trying* to look good."

Amane laughs. "The ultimate goal!"

As we move through the shops, it becomes clear we don't have the same style *whatsoever*. That doesn't stop us from handing each other things to try on. Amane makes a beeline straight for the brightest colors and wackiest prints on the rack, especially when there's a combination of those two things. She makes me try on shirts that scream *PAY ATTENTION TO ME PLEASE,* pairing them with equally eye-catching bottoms. There are a lot of sequins involved.

I get back at her with anything baggy or slouchy or oversize, which she complains hides her figure. Our bodies are different, too: I'm stick straight and on the tall side, while she's short and fat. I start taking this into consideration and handing her things that will hug her hips or show off her cleavage (of which there is no shortage). She stops handing me dresses, which I've never liked, and starts picking out shoes. You can do a lot with a good pair of shoes.

We take about a million selfies and post them to Astragram. Tabby comments on every single one with encouragement and rainbow hearts, even though e's supposed to be reading for work. I browsed a few of those books in the huge stack Tabby brought home from the Library, and some of them were dry as fuck, so I don't blame em for taking a break.

After lunch, we wander into the pricier part of the market district, where the artsy designers strut their stuff. These are bespoke garments, made from the best materials by master seamstresses, so the prices make sense. I'm just mad they're out of my range.

Not Amane's, though. She's got a trust fund squirreled away from her rich and illustrious publishing family. I drag my feet when she spots a shop called House of Inyene, squeals loudly in delight, and insists we go inside. I'm not fancy enough to browse the stuff in there, which from the window display appears to be elegant, silky things with sharp profiles and sharper prices. Still, it's kind of cool to see stuff in person you'd normally only see on a Fashion Week runway livestream.

"Just puff yourself up and *act* important," Amane advises me. "It's not about the money, it's about your attitude."

"But I like slouching."

"Then add some swagger to your slouch," she giggles. "Look bored and then glare at people if they stare."

"Oh, I can do *that.*"

She gathers herself up, all five-foot-one-plus-six-inches-of-hair, and marches through the door with her nose held high. I slink in after her, wearing my best I-don't-give-a-shit face, hands shoved in my jacket pockets. At least with all these bags on our arms, we look like we might buy something. Hells, maybe Amane will.

The clerk, a tall Gildean person with the biggest gold hoops in their ears I've ever seen, rounds on us immediately and starts asking questions. Amane handles him expertly, turning on the full force of her charm and namedropping her family. She's clearly done this before. I watch with admiration, giving snooty nods of approval or disapproval when asked.

As we're admiring Amane in a stunning sapphire jumpsuit, two people step out from the back room, and she gasps loudly. The smug socialite look drops from her face and she stares at them, open-mouthed. The clerk, who was adjusting the jumpsuit with pins for her, inclines his head respectfully.

"Mister Polaris, Magistrix Stargrove," he says.

But I recognize them, too. Inyene Polaris isn't just a fashion designer, but also a celebrity and judge on several reality television shows. Which I watch. Ironically. He's about my height, with narrow shoulders and broad hips. His skin is a deep, bluish-brown, and glowing despite his age. Mid-sixties, I think. He's dyed his close-cropped hair and beard a brilliant yellow. His suit is the same color. It's like looking at the sun; now I know where Amane gets her fashion inspiration from.

Beside him is another striking figure, who I've seen in the halls of the Library. Aeronwy Stargrove is taller than Inyene, slender but powerful. Eir white and silver hair is swept back from eir face save one perfectly curled swoosh in the front. E's wearing a black dress with the back draped like a cape, and a bright gold belt cinched at the waist. Also, knee-high black boots with a gold heel. Are you even *allowed* to wear heels when you already tower over everyone else?

"You!" Amane squeaks.

Aeronwy and Inyene stop their conversation and look at her. Inyene looks bemused, but Aeronwy's gaze sharpens immediately.

"Amane," e says, "good afternoon."

"Friend of yours?" Inyene asks. His Gildean accent is much deeper than Amane's, and I like it.

Aeronwy inclines eir head and gestures towards Amane with a flourish. "June's newest apprentice, Amane Sol, also of the Sol Publishing House family."

Amane smiles nervously and bows, wincing when, presumably, some of the pins stick her in sensitive areas.

Inyene crosses the distance between them and takes her hand, bowing his own head.

"An incredible pleasure to meet you then," he says in Gildean. "You look lovely in that color, what do you think of it?"

Amane giggles and fans herself with her free hand, clearly star-struck. I've never understood that kind of reaction. I know who Inyene is, too, and I like his clothes, but he's just another person like the rest of us. I watch the two of them chat and flirt with fascination. Inyene is a perfect picture of charm, his voice rich and warm, and Amane is all fluttery and grinning like a fool.

"You," says a voice to my left. Not Amane this time. Not an exclamation, but slow and pondering.

I turn to face Aeronwy, who is scrutinizing me closely. We've never been formally introduced. After all, e works on the highest floor in the whole Library campus, the shining white tower of the Spire. I work in the basement of basements.

"Me?" I squint up at em, returning the challenge.

"You work in the Library, too," e says. E gestures at my hair with the swirl of one finger. "This is very recognizable."

That I can't deny. I flick a lengthy purple strand over my shoulder. "Yeah. I do work there. I know who you are."

From behind us, Amane pipes up, "Aeronwy, this is my friend Rhiannon! Who's also Tabby's partner! E's the Assistant Head Archivist."

Aeronwy's gaze darkens noticeably. "Assistant Head?"

I don't like eir tone of voice. "Yeah, something wrong with that?"

E shoots me a cold look. Ice cold. "Of course not. There simply aren't many younger folks working down there, especially in high positions. It's unusual."

I shrug. I resist the urge to shoot back a, *Well,* you're *unusual!* Sometimes I think going to college when everyone else was in middle school stunted my emotional maturity.

"Always a pleasure to meet more Librarians. We should be going off to lunch though, I'm starving," Inyene says, oblivious to the tension. He kisses Amane's hand chivalrously and then retreats to take Aeronwy's arm. "Shall we?"

"Yes. I will see you both at work, presumably. Amane, you ought to try the ivory jumpsuit instead. It suits your coloring better. Good day," Aeronwy says to us.

As they're leaving, Inyene turns towards me, winking and shooting finger guns. "I like your glasses, by the way," he says. He adjusts his own pair, which are the same oversized round frames as mine, but pink instead of red.

Then they're gone.

The shop is silent in their wake, save for the ringing of the little bell on the door. Aeronwy's reaction simmers in the forefront of my mind, looming larger than Inyene's compliment. Amane is cupping her cheek with one hand and staring dreamily into the distance. Even the clerk seems dazed, though he quickly puts his customer service smile back on for us. It seems more genuine than it was earlier, maybe because we're friends of a friend of the designer.

"Would you like to try on the ivory one?" he asks Amane.

Amane buys the blue jumpsuit in the end. We take the train home, watching clips of our favorite Inyene reality tv reactions on our phones. The autumn chill deepens as the clouds thicken and cover the sky in a smooth gray blanket. Amane pops on one of her new sweaters and looks contented, watching out the window as we speed through the city.

I have a vague idea why Aeronwy reacted the way e did to the news that I work in the Archives: Mairead. Tabby told me how unhappy the Stargroves were when Mairead showed up to do their Charter Oath and Binding ceremonies. Beef between coworkers in the Library is common. There are as many deep-seated grudges between the stacks as there are books in them.

Aeronwy must think I'm one of Mairead's lackeys. I don't blame em for giving me the stink-eye. I *have* been spending a lot of time around my boss, lately. I was starting to think e might not be as bad as everyone says e is, but Aeronwy's reaction makes me wonder.

***

Tabby is cooking dinner when I get home. The apartment smells like ginger and lemongrass, two scents that make my mouth water. I drop my bags on the table and hover behind Tabby's shoulder at the stove, peeking around to see what e's making.

"Is that what I think it is?" I press the side of my face against Tabby's arm.

"Your favorite rice noodle soup? I thought you could use it after the week you've had," Tabby says, stirring the broth with a ladle. "Did you have fun with Amane?"

"Sure did. I'm glad you two can be friends now. She's pretty cool," I say. When Tabby puts the ladle down, I scoop it up to take a taste. Salty, sour, and sweet, just the way I like it. In two more pans, Tabby stir-fries batches of chicken and tofu. I grew up on a farm and am chill with eating animals, but Tabby gets emotional about it and is vegetarian. We've learned how to compromise with meals over the years.

"'Pretty cool' coming from you is a big compliment," Tabby laughs.

"Yeah, well."

"I'm glad. I like her, too. Actually," Tabby says, hesitating, "I think I have a little bit of a crush on her."

I blink in surprise. We don't usually talk about Tabby's romantic crushes unless e's thinking of pursuing someone. "You gonna ask her out on a date?"

"Oh, I don't know. Being coworkers makes it a little more complicated," says Tabby. Eir face is red, but e's smiling.

"You and I are coworkers now."

"But we don't work in the same department."

"Hey, I support whatever you end up doing," I say. "Speaking of coworkers, we ran into Aeronwy when we were out shopping," I say.

Tabby's thick eyebrows go up. "You did? I've told em about you. Did e know who you were?"

I pull a chair out from the kitchen table and sit down. "Yeah. I hope you only told em good stuff. I think e's suspicious of me because I work with Mairead," I say.

"Oh," says Tabby, eyes widening. "Did you ever find out why the two of them don't like each other?"

"No, I haven't had the chance to ask yet. Most of the time I'm working with Mairead these days, I'm either scrying or out of my mind *from* scrying. It takes forever to write all that shit down. Why don't you ask Aeronwy about it?" I say, propping my feet up on the table. They ache from all the walking we did today.

Tabby playfully pushes my feet off the table. "Don't do that right before we eat," e says.

Egg, our big fluffy white cat, runs in from the hallway and leaps into my lap. E yowls at me until I pet em, then walks in circles on my thighs and curls into a ball.

"Eggsy missed you today," says Tabby, ladling soup into bowls and placing them on the table. E leans over to pet the cat, scratching em behind the ears. Egg purrs loudly and drools on my pants.

"Getting spoiled with me home so many days in a row."

Tabby sits down and I spin around in my chair, dumping an annoyed Egg onto the floor. E slinks over to the food bowl by the refrigerator and chows down moodily. I immediately slurp up my noodles, even though they're way too hot. Tabby stares thoughtfully into space while I huff and puff over my bowl.

"Back to your question, Aeronwy's still a bit... intimidating... I don't know if I could ask em a personal question like that yet," e says.

"It's not personal, it's business. They're coworkers. The Stargroves were always Rose's biggest allies in introducing liberal, Readerist programs. June especially, spearheading the whole digitization process," I say. Mairead hates etheric-books even more than e hates etheric mail. I love the smell of ink and paper as much as anyone, but I love e-mail and my e-reader, too. They're handy and accessible. "Maybe it's just that."

"Maybe," says Tabby. "I just have... a feeling."

Tabby's feelings are always on point, so I say, "I'll ask Mairead. Put it on my to-do list." I point to the tattoo on my left forearm, which is an unfurled scroll with "To Do" inked at the top. I write on it with markers whenever I need to remember something.

"Thanks," Tabby says, brightening.

We're quiet for a while as we dig into our dinner. Comfortable quiet, settled into the routine of our shared life. I've always appreciated that we can do this: just be with each other. Tabby smoothes down my sharp edges. When you have twelve siblings, you get poked, prodded, and teased a lot. That's just how kids are. You develop armor. I like that Tabby lures my squishy, emotional snail-self out of its shell of sarcasm.

After a while I break the silence with, "How's things at work, anyway?"

"It's wonderful. I'm already learning so much just from watching Aeronwy in the studio," Tabby says. "E wasn't expecting to have another apprentice so soon, so e's finishing up a project while I watch and read. Once e's done, we'll work on a new book together."

"What's e like?" I ask, thinking of the cold look I got at Inyene's shop. Tabby is a sensitive person. The thought of someone looking at em like that makes me angry.

"Quiet. Serious. Methodical," Tabby says. "There's something warm underneath, though. I don't really know how to describe it. I feel—it feels safe when I'm there."

I don't know what I was expecting, but it wasn't that.

"That's good."

Tabby takes a long drink of lemonade and then squirts more hot sauce into eir soup. "I wish I could tell you all the things I'm learning about Illumination," e says, cheeks reddening from the spice. "It's all so fascinating! Some of these techniques have been used for hundreds of years, even thousands. You'd love it."

Unfortunately, Illumination is an initiatory practice, and Tabby is oathbound not to spill its secrets to anyone outside the trade. At least they no longer require you to become a Scriptivist nun, although Tabby has the personality for it.

"Just promise me you'll make an Illuminated edition of my book when it finally comes out," I say, "with a steep family discount." Given that it takes an Illuminator anywhere from half a year to half a decade to complete a book, they're not cheap. If you have a publisher or a grant, they'll help pay for it, but it's still thousands of reams out of your own pocket.

Tabby nods enthusiastically, mouth too full of noodles to talk. Once e swallows, e teases me with, "You'll have to finish writing it first. Also, which one? Don't you have a dozen planned by now?"

Egg snakes around my legs beneath the table, tail twitching for treats. I slip em a piece of chicken. "You *wound* me," I say dramatically. "I'll write them all eventually. Then me and you will be the biggest power couple at the Library. You, up in the Spire, immortalizing worthy stories. Me, down in the basements, churning out books on ancient slang and marginalia like nobody's business."

"Sounds good to me," says Tabby.

CHAPTER TWELVE

AMANE

June's studio is a daydream come to life. The walls are a sunny lemon yellow, colorful tapestries hung between the shelves. Every tool, book, inkwell, and glue bottle is clearly organized. One large wall rack holds a rainbow of yarn, each skein neatly hung on a wooden peg. In addition to bookbinding equipment, there's a large tapestry loom in the far window corner. A floral loveseat draped with blankets and pillows sitting opposite looks like the world's coziest reading nook. I want to curl up in it immediately.

There are books in various states of finish on the counters, in the presses, with sticky notes taped to them. The sticky notes are everywhere, scribbled with teeny, tiny handwriting in different colored pens. I sneak a glance at one on the door, but it's in Fenian. I know from our initial chats that June was born in Caspora to Fenian immigrants. A devastating earthquake sent the family back to Fenia when e was a teenager, but e returned to Caspora after college.

"Let's see, let's see," June sings to emself, rifling through piles of papers. "What did I want to start with today? What would *you* like to do, Amane?"

"Me?" I say, taken aback. "*You're* the teacher."

"Sure, but the teacher serves the student," June says with a chuckle.

"I wouldn't know where to begin."

I gaze around the room. I know how to bind books. I know what all the tools and equipment are for. I have a passing knowledge of printmaking, drawing, calligraphy, gilding, dyeing. What I *don't* know is how all those things are brought together to make a book that will last until the end of time.

June pulls a stool up beside the loveseat and gestures for me to sit, so I do. I sink into the cushions deeply, my feet lifted off the floor as I'm enveloped in a world of softness. I can't believe I'm here, sitting across from Juniper Stargrove emself. If this loveseat weren't so comfy, I'd jump right back up and pace in excitement.

June waits patiently. I pull a large pillow into my lap and lean forward on my elbows. My voice comes out in an urgent whisper, even though we're the only two in the room.

"What makes it work? What's the secret?"

"I thought you might ask that. Do you have an oracle deck with you?" e asks.

"I have several!" I rummage around inside my purse for one. I come out with my great-grandmother's Threadbound Oracle, and June nods in approval.

"Let's ask your cards how it works. I'm curious what they'll say," June says.

"Um, okay. I need a flat surface of some kind."

June pulls a small side table into the space between us. I settle in, take a breath, and center myself. I split the deck and shuffle the cards against the glass table, falling into the rhythm while focusing on the question in my mind. My intuition gives a little tug when it's time to deal. I lay out three cards to start and flip them over.

The Weaver: an older, wise-looking figure standing before a bookcase, with glowing rainbow threads twined between outstretched hands: connections, patterns, diplomacy. The Three of Thread, the Knot: a circle of forget-me-nots and three red spools of thread, which are tied into a bow at the center: promises, bonds, memories. The Book: an ancient-looking tome resting on an elaborate plinth carved with the sun, moon, and stars, giant redwood trees rising around it and glowing rainbow threads leading off into the distance: soul, story, essence.

I look up at June to see if this is somehow correct, but eir expression is carefully blank, eyes flickering across the cards before rising to meet mine.

"Well, what do you think?"

I'm not used to being asked so many open questions. Not before I've already been given the answers. Much of my schooling was one long series of tests, each one carefully designed on the preceding material. I went out of my way to get it right. Put in the extra hours. Read the extra booklists. Turned in the extra credit. Stayed after class to ask more questions and get more answers. To be prepared.

I look down at the cards. I want, more than anything, to impress June. I want to get the answer right. I've been reading with this deck for half my life. The answer is right there. Unless it's a trick question? Or—

"It's alright to take a guess. I asked what you think, not what you know. There's no wrong answer," June says gently.

I don't know about that. I can think something all I want, that doesn't make it *right*. But I know what June's trying to say.

"Do you… make some kind of oath with the book spirit? Some kind of exchange?"

I pull another card from the deck for further clarification. The Protagonist: a young woman who looks a lot like me (my great-grandmother, actually) stands between two rainbow shelves of books, her dress swirling and halos of golden magic hovering around her head. I scrunch my face up, running through all the possible interpretations. There are endless ways to combine four cards and apply them to a situation. Which one is right? Which one *feels* right?

"Do you put a piece of *yourself* in it?"

June's face is still blank, but there's a sparkle in eir blue eyes that suggests I'm on the right path. My chest fills with a warm, expansive sense of pride.

"That's just about right," e says. "No, that *is* right, in a way. When you make every part of an object and either arrange the type or write it all by hand, you certainly do put a piece of yourself in it."

"But? There's something else?" I ask, annoyed that I missed the mark.

"That process also instills a piece of the book within you," June continues. "It opens a pathway between book and Illuminator. We then intentionally create a spiritual connection between our deepest self and the book in the form of an etheric cord, which we ply with the physical thread that binds the book."

"Wow," I breathe. "How does *that* happen?"

"You'll learn, in time. Before we get to that, you have a lot of work to do," says June.

"What kind of work?" I say. If there's one thing I'm good at, it's work. I'll make a hundred books, a thousand, if that's what it takes to be ready.

June gestures to my Threadbound Oracle. "There are three suits in your deck, right?"

"Yeah. Paper, ink, and thread," I say.

"Can I see the Aces?"

I shuffle through and pluck out the Ace of each suit. The Ace of Paper shows a rolled up scroll tied with a green ribbon, laying on a bed of mulberry leaves, with tiny green sprouts popping up from underneath. The Ace of Ink shows a beautiful golden bottle with a sunrise etched on it, the cork popped off the top and ink pouring out in a wave; the ink changes color as it flows, from pink, to yellow, to blue. The Ace of Thread shows a drop spindle wound heavy with white thread, against a partly sunny sky and dandelion clocks blowing away in the wind.

"Though there are many, many elements to the making of a book, the first year of your apprenticeship will be split largely into these same categories. We'll start with paper, then move on to ink, and finally thread," says June, pointing at each card as e explains, "at which point, you'll be ready for the final secret, and can begin working on your own book, rather than just assisting me."

"So, I'll be making paper, and then inks, and then thread, before combining them all together?" I ask.

"Yes, but there's a more symbolic side to the progression, too," June says, "Much like in your cards. These really do make for a handy metaphor… I don't know why I'm surprised. They were created by an Illuminator, after all, weren't they?"

"Calliope Everberry," I blurt out, naming the deck's original creator. "Five hundred years ago. Back then, you had to make your own deck by hand, from scratch, and it was basically a part of you by the time you were done."

"Ah, I see," says June, and the tone of eir voice suggests there's an awful lot e *sees* about this fact, though e doesn't elaborate. "I'm sure you'll teach me a lot about these cards in the coming moons."

"If that's what you want!" I say, a tad too enthusiastically. The idea of teaching June about the Threadbound Oracle, and sharing my passion with em, gets my blood pumping.

"What I want is to help you grow into your best self, and to know who that self is," e says, "and if cartomancy can help us get there, then I welcome it into this studio."

E settles back in eir chair, fingers laced together in eir lap. E gazes down at me with a fondness that I must prove I'm worthy of. I pick up the Ace of Paper and study it carefully, though I've seen it thousands of time, and then hold it up to June.

"So, paper first?"

"Yes. What's the title on that card?"

"Pulp," I reply. Each of the suit cards has a title on it, relating to the process of making or using that thing. The suit of Paper goes: Pulp, Page, Fold, Signature, Cut, Glue, and Cover. It's a clear progression with a beginning and an end, a story told in seven parts. The seventh, final card represents achieving a deep sense of wholeness, beauty, and strength.

June gets up and crosses the room, where e opens a cabinet and starts pulling out canvas sacks of various sizes. "And what does the Pulp card represent?" e asks, sorting through them in search of something.

"Malleability. Being raw and in need of processing, not really having a form yet, but having potential because of it," I say. "You could become anything, depending on how you decide to shape yourself, or your story."

"Good, good, that's perfect."

June returns and hands me a medium-sized sack, gesturing that I should open it. I do, and on peering inside find that it's full of raw cotton. I run my fingers through it, catching bits of seed and leaf among the soft tufts.

"Up until this point, you've been like this cotton. Cotton is wonderful for papermaking, but not in this state. As your card suggests, it needs to be processed before we can use it for what we want. Or perhaps you're not cotton. Perhaps you're hemp, or abaca, or the inner bark of the mulberry tree. They're all different materials, from different places, whose natural properties make them good for different kinds of paper— different kinds of books. These are the questions we were asking during the selection process for the apprenticeship: where have you come from? What are your natural abilities? Are you right for our needs?"

I nod to show I understand. For once, I'm just as interested in listening as I am talking. June talks with a lyrical cadence, lilting up and down through eir monologue in a way that sounds natural, not forced or rehearsed. E has a lightness of being that makes it seem like e could drift off on the breeze at any moment, and so you'd best listen to em while you can.

"Now, could I see the Two of Paper? What is that one about?"

I pull the Two of Paper from the deck and hold it up. It shows two crossed scrolls surrounded by clouds, concentric rings rippling outward from the center where they meet.

"It's the Page card. It's about understanding all the possibilities, dreaming up the future, and making choices. Which side of the paper do you want to use? What can you put on it?" I explain.

June reaches over to a nearby counter to snag a piece of creamy, off-white paper, which e holds up for me to see. E tilts it in the sunlight from the window, so I can see the little flecks of silver sprinkled throughout.

"Right *now*, you're like this blank page," e says. "You've already made one choice, when you were asked to apprentice with me or with Aeronwy, and now you'll be facing many, many more. The most important one will be what you choose to write your own book about, starting at the end of your first year. That book will be your offering to the Library catalogue, in exchange for full initiation into the tradition of Illumination.

"For now, you have a different choice before you: which book you'd like to assist me in creating, while you learn the basics of the craft. I have a few commissions on the table at the moment. Would you like to see the manuscripts?"

***

A few hours later, I bounce into the temporary studio I share with Tabby. The space used to belong to an Illuminator named Mayumi but was completely cleared and cleansed after e retired. Eventually we'll have our own studios, but Aeronwy and June haven't had the heart to empty Rose's space yet. The grief is still too near.

Tabby is clearing out a corner by the windows and setting up what looks like a foldable foam mattress. A pile of worn, well-loved blankets sits on the counter nearby, along with a giant stack of books. It looks like Aeronwy has already given em homework to do.

I flop down on the cool wood floor. Even in the mild Casporan fall, the ninth floor Bindery gets hot and humid. I reach for one of my nearby boxes of supplies and pull a folded paper fan. Seeing this, Tabby opens one of the windows. A fresh breeze blows in off the mountains, which rise steeply beyond the campus below.

"Much better," I sigh, letting the fan clatter to the floor.

Tabby chuckles. "Doesn't it get much hotter than this in Aquanea?"

"Yes, but that doesn't mean I *like* being hot," I explain. "Plus, we have air conditioning."

"Fair enough."

I roll over onto my stomach and lean my chin on my hands. Tabby continues setting up the bed in the corner but keeps eir eyes on me. E looks cute today in dark jeans and a button-up shirt patterned with butterflies. Aeronwy and June were quick to assure us that there's no dress code in the Bindery since the work gets messy.

I rack my brain for a topic of conversation and cheer internally when I find a good one.

"Hey, Tabby?"

"Yes?"

"If I had a weird dream the other night, could you tell me what it meant?"

Tabby laughs and spreads a faded blue quilt over the bed. It's patterned with blue-green stars that look like they glow in the dark. E smoothes it down and then sits on the end of the bed, watching me with a smile. The dimples in eir cheeks are adorable, and I'm glad e's no longer anxious around me now that the testing period is over.

"Dream interpretation is such a personal thing," e says. "You're a cartomancer. Shouldn't interpreting your dreams be like interpreting your cards? Visual symbolism?"

"Yeah, but you're the dream expert. Maybe you'd notice something I missed," I say.

Tabby taps one finger to eir lips, thinking. E has full, pretty lips that are probably soft and nice to kiss. I'd probably have to stand on something to kiss Tabby, though. There's at least a foot of height difference between us.

"If I noticed anything you didn't, it would probably be because you're too close to the issue, and I'm outside of it, not because I know more about dreams," Tabby says.

"Oh. I see."

E must hear my disappointment because e adds brightly, "You can still tell me about it if you want, though! I love hearing about other people's dreams."

That's all the invitation I need. I launch into the recurring dream I've been having every other week or so since I got to Caspora. In it, I'm working at the Library, in the Bindery, only I'm apprenticed to Eirlys instead of June. I always find myself wandering the stacks behind my mentor, who pulls books off the shelf to explain what's expected of me in my craft. The dream is unusually vivid, and I marvel at the brilliant inks and shining gold leaf of the Illuminated manuscripts. I can practically feel the leather covers and smell the parchment. The beautiful books are inspiring, but I also feel a weight on my shoulders: how could I ever make something *this* beautiful?

The dream books I see change every time, but the ending doesn't. Eirlys takes me into the Bindery, which looks nothing like it does now. It's still at the top of a tower, but the walls are made of whitewashed stone, and the floors are covered with rich, woven rugs. My room is tiny and contains only a desk and a contraption the dream tells me is an ancient book press, but which looks nothing like anything that's existed in real life.

Eirlys sits me down and tells me that it's time to write my book, the one that I will present to the Library for initiation. The trouble is that all my knowledge of writing and making books suddenly feels inaccessible. I wonder if I forgot to prepare before actually coming here. Didn't I go to school for this? Or did I sign up but miss all the classes? Was Eirlys supposed to teach me more before this point?

Not knowing what I'm doing, I panic and wake up.

Tabby listens patiently, without interrupting. When I finish, e pats the space on the bed, inviting me. I peel myself off the floor, my skin sticky with sweat—not from the heat, but from exposing my subconscious fears—and sit down beside em. This close, e smells like lavender and lemons.

"I'm nervous about this job, too," Tabby says. "Every day I come in here, I can't believe I actually got selected for an apprenticeship. It feels like I don't really deserve it."

I've seen Tabby's books now, when the Stargroves gave us back the work we sent in for portfolio review, and I know that's not true. They were all beautiful and unusual, collaged artist books and glittering dream journals, even a fully illustrated children's book about the cycles of the moon. It made me understand just how close the choice was between the two of us. I'm going to need to step up my game.

"You do, though," I say.

"And so do you, I'm sure of it. I'm glad we're here together," Tabby replies.

The compliment is so genuine and warm that I'm not sure how to respond. My heart beats a little faster, and I quickly turn to look out the window, sure I've got a terrible, sappy look on my face.

"Also," Tabby says, "dreaming of Eirlys is considered an omen of good luck in love."

***

I video call my oldest sister that evening. There's a twelve-hour time difference in our locations, so it's late here, but mid-morning there. She picks up on the fifth ring and fumbles with her phone, flashing glimpses of her luxurious Aquanean apartment before settling on her wide, dark face. She's all made up for the day, in gold eye shadow and mauve lipstick that pops and makes her look like a radiant goddess. Her hair is shaved in a tight high-top style, the wrinkles on her forehead barely visible. Jiji is almost twenty years older than me, but she doesn't look it.

"Hello, my dear little bookworm!" she exclaims, waving her manicured fingers at the camera. "I don't have much time in between meetings, but how are things on the other side of the world?"

It's nice to hear her voice, the familiar warm tones of my native language from a familiar face. Because she was already an adult when I was born—our mothers decided they wanted another baby before biology quit on them—sometimes she feels like a third parent more than a sister. When I was little, she would sometimes take me with her to her university classes to expose me to 'all the great knowledge that Gildea has to offer, while your brain is still growing.'

"Things are great! I'm learning a lot! June and I decided on the first book we're going to make together today. It's a classic romance novel fictionalizing the relationship between Eirlys Starsower and Daryn Sunseeker, two of the Founders. It's a popular topic for novels here, but this one is the most well-known, and won a bunch of awards. One of them is a grant that pays for an etheric copy to be made. It's called *The Stories We Sing,* you've heard of it, right? Tomorrow we'll ask the book's spirit what kind of ingredients we'll need to make the paper—"

Jiji laughs, interrupting me. It's a specific laugh, one I heard all the time growing up, from many of my family members. It's the laugh they do when I start going on and on about something. My cheeks warm and I swallow the rest of my words, embarrassed that I started word-vomiting immediately, without even a proper hello.

"Sounds very exciting," says Jiji, "if slow. How many books a year do they actually produce that way? Starting from scratch?"

Of course, Jiji is a stickler for numbers and efficiency. She oversees printing operations and resources for the family business. A global business that published thousands of books last year and printed millions of those books across the board. She's always looking to improve. Our handmade, often handwritten, pace at the Bindery—one to three books a year, per Illuminator—makes us snails beside her cheetah.

"It depends," I say, instead of answering properly. "How are you? How are the Moms? And Abi?"

"The same as always. I never see any of them except at phase day dinner," she says, rolling her eyes. "Abi's taken over a lot of the cooking and that's definitely not an improvement. She's good, but not as good as Mama."

My mouth waters, thinking of all the phase-day dinners I've missed since I got here. Peanut soup and chicken yassa and souya, fish pepper hot sauce and thirteen kinds of pickles… the explosive sound of my family's laughter when they all get together and drink too much imported Fenian wine. Mama Ade and Jiji shooting numbers and publishing jargon across the table while Abeni and Mama Yewande one-up each other with horror stories about authors and editors they work with. Round-table discussions of books we all read and whether we think they should be best-sellers or thrown in the recycle bin.

Also, the ever-running competition. Over everything.

"Mama's been cooking for like fifty years, though," I remind her.

Jiji purses her lips and shrugs. "Doesn't make it less true. Are you eating okay over there? Do we need to ship you anything? Are you homesick?"

Classic Jiji, acting like a mom instead of a sister. "I still have all the pickles and hot sauce I brought with me, but there's also a Gildean specialty shop in the harbor market. There are so many different cuisines here because of all the immigrants. The local seafood is the best, though," I tell her.

"Not better than fish from Chinyere's, grilled right at the riverside," she insists.

"Well, true."

"I'll send you whatever you need, just ask," she says, glancing down, probably to make a note on her calendar. I wouldn't be surprised if she programmed a box to be sent to me every full moon, express shipped at great expense. I wouldn't exactly say no to that, honestly. Who doesn't like getting mail?

"Maybe I'll send you some Casporan jam and honey in exchange."

"Aw, that's nice, but save your money for going out with your friends," she says, flashing me another wide smile. "You are making friends?"

"Yeah! There's my housemates, who are from Gildea and Mwari, and then there's Rhiannon, who works in the Archives at the Library, and Tabby, who also got an apprenticeship in the Bindery—"

"I thought there was just one spot open?" Jiji interrupts me again, eyebrow raised.

I hesitate. I'd been avoiding letting anyone in my family know that I wasn't the only one who made it through the application process this time around. I already knew how they'd all react. I can't lie to Jiji, though. She's been reading my expressions since I was born.

"Well, there was, but things changed. They let two of us in," I say slowly. "I still got the apprenticeship with *June*, though. Tabby's working with someone *else*."

I don't mean to slight Aeronwy, who I'm sure is just as masterful an Illuminator as June, but it might appease Jiji—and the others, once they find out—if she thinks I still came out on top somehow. That I was the one they wanted most, and Tabby was an exception to the plan.

"I'm sure you're relieved," Jiji says. "I know how much you wanted this apprenticeship, and how much we all wanted it for you. I brag about you to all my friends, you know. Not only is my little sister an Illuminator, she's working at the Eternal Library itself with the masters!"

"I'm not an Illuminator *yet*," I say. "Not everyone finishes the apprenticeship. It's *hard* work."

Jiji grins. "Which is what you're best at. Ever since you were small, you've been unstoppable. Never tiring. A true inspiration."

"Not as big an inspiration as you," I say. Not only did Jiji work her way up through our family company—they required she start at the very bottom, an intern fetching coffee—she did it while going to school, helping to care for me, and building a side business as an interior designer. The latter was eventually bought off for a tidy sum of money, most of which she donated to charity.

"Aw, you're sweet. Just promise me one thing."

"What's that?"

She tilts her head and side-eyes me. "Promise me you won't convert to that weird book religion."

"Scriptivism is not weird! You *love* books, Jiji, they're your life, why do you think it's weird?"

"I love books, but it's weird to take it that far," she says.

"*I* think it's a beautiful faith."

Jiji laughs and waves a hand at me. "Ame, I don't want to argue right now. I'm mostly joking. I just want to know that you're happy and successful and still part of our family, even though you're halfway around the world," she says.

"Of course I am!" I say.

"Wonderful to hear, darling," Jiji says. She purses her lips and blows me a kiss. "I have to run now, but I'm glad we got to chat. Schedule another call soon?"

I return the blown kiss. "Yeah, I'll text you. And tell Abi to text me back if you see her. She's not answering again."

"She's been at a string of conferences lately. I'll bug her soon. I love you, Ame," says Jiji. She says the last bit in a syrupy, teasing sister voice.

"Love you too, Jeej."

I hang up the call and flop down face-first on my bed, exhausted rather than energized by the conversation. I love my family. They're amazing. But sometimes it's hard to keep up with them—and their expectations.

CHAPTER THIRTEEN
TABBY

I dread having lunch with my parents, but I don't have a choice whenever they're in town. I promised to meet them at our usual spot, the only cafe that serves food they both like and can agree is mostly edible. I call to reserve a table in the corner, where we'll be out of the way if Oran goes on one of eir rants.

If only I had to work, then I'd have an excuse to escape. I was happy to learn that Aeronwy prefers working afternoons, so I can sleep in, but today it's a bother. Dealing with my parents and the anxiety of a brand-new job is a lot to take at once. There are too many unknowns, too much anticipation knowing *anything* could happen and I have no idea what to *expect*.

Rhiannon is already at the Library when I get up. E left me texts saying e'll be deep in the Archives again where there isn't any cell service. The etheric cords laid through the astral plane to carry data between devices are sensitive, and the ley lines under the Library are like untethered live wires, scrambling signal and data.

My brain buzzes with anxiety as I walk into Cloudberry Cafe. It's a large, busy space with several a la carte dining options, a mixture of made-to-order menus and buffets that my parents can mine to their liking. No sending dishes back to the kitchen here. They can make salads consisting only of iceberg lettuce and bacon bits if they like, or watch the employee behind the counter cook their burger for exactly six minutes. An ideal world, in their opinion.

It's the middle of the lunch rush right now, and it takes me a while to politely make my way through the serving lines across the red-tiled room. The air smells like burnt garlic and vinegar. My parents already have full plates on the table when I find them, and a tray with silverware waiting for me.

Oran is in eir early sixties, tall and heavy like me. Unlike me, e uses eir size to intimidate. E has a thick head of blonde hair pulled back into a ponytail, which whips around as e catches sight of me and nods. Beside em, Lilja looks up and flashes me a wavering smile.

My other parent, the one that carried me, is also tall, but thin and perpetually hunched over, reading a book or the news on her phone. She's ten years younger than Oran but looks the same age because her face is lined with worry and displeasure.

"Seems like you beat me here," I say cheerfully as I approach and slide into the unoccupied chair. "How was your trip into the city?"

Lilja sighs and puts her fork down. "Terrible. The train was four minutes late and packed completely full."

"We would have caught an earlier train with less people on it if you hadn't been fussing around the house," Oran grumbles, through a mouth full of noodles.

Lilja's mouth stretches into a thin line, avoiding eye contact with either of us. "I can't leave a mess behind, especially in the kitchen. I'll be too tired tonight to clean, and that would be the start of a larger disaster. Maybe if *you* helped more, it would be done faster."

"Not my mess."

"I may have done the cooking, but you still created dirty dishes by *eating*—"

This is starting off poorly. I have to nip this argument in the bud. "At least we get to have lunch together now," I say, smiling reassuringly.

"If we didn't have to go so far to get here, it wouldn't be such a damn inconvenience," Oran says.

"Tabby's right, though," Lilja says, putting a hand over mine and returning my smile. "I love getting the chance to see you. Why don't you go get yourself some food, honey?"

It's a relief to get away. Only a few minutes into their visit, and things are already going wrong. I should have expected that. My appetite is nonexistent with my stomach in knots, but I head to the buffet and make myself an assortment of fresh salads and fruits. Things that will be easy to eat even if I don't want to. When I return to the table, they're both ignoring one another in favor of eating their lunches.

Lilja eyes my plate and then gives me a worried look. "Aren't you hungry, dear? Are you feeling all right?" she asks.

"I'm okay, I had a big breakfast," I lie. "Plus, I get free meals at the Library, so I can always eat more later."

"I'm just making sure," Lilja says, pointing her fork at me. "You know, you should try this new regimen I'm on. You only eat between certain hours of the day and drink red wine every night. Some Fenian studies show it could cure depression and anxiety, in addition to making you live longer."

"Let em eat whatever and whenever e wants," Oran says. "Those diets are bullshit."

Lilja shoots em a glare. "Well, excuse me for caring for our child's *health*."

"Are you implying I *don't* care?"

Heart racing, I grab my tray and stand up. I only have to deal with this for an hour at most, and then I'll be free again. At least for another few weeks. I really should have used the new job to get out of this lunch. I really should have put more substantial things on my plate, even if I wasn't going to eat them. Anything to keep them from fighting in public.

"Don't worry, Ren's right, I'll go get some more food," I say, and hurry off into the crowd.

***

For the first few weeks of my apprenticeship, there's not much for me to do except read from a list of assigned books about papermaking, its history, and the unusual materials employed by Illuminators—a much more in-depth study than I ever had available to me in school, and surprisingly technical. Aeronwy is finishing up a project that's too far along for me to help with, so that we can focus on our first one together.

Still, e asks me to come to the Bindery and sit in the studio with em while e works. I read on the black leather couch by the windows and watch what e's doing. We don't talk much. Aeronwy seems to prefer quiet or soft music on in the background while working, usually bluegrass or folk. At first, I felt I must be doing something wrong, but I've grown to like this space of calm and stillness.

Aeronwy's studio is a clue to eir personality and taste. The walls are a vibrant red with gold stripes, the furniture dark, and there are shiny things *everywhere*. Not so much a mess as a clutter, the statues, crystals, books, jars, sculptures, photographs, charms, and assorted knickknacks are purposefully arranged, but… numerous.

On a low altar table by the windows there's an ornate shrine to the fire goddex Cináed. I was surprised to see candles in the Library until I realized they were all electric. Aeronwy's studio faces due south and has an incredible view of the volcano which is said to be the goddex's home. The snowcapped peak of Mount Cináed rises high above the rest of the Bell Mountains, its cone shape distinctly threatening on the horizon. It's an *active* volcano. Cináed's cult of worship is older than Scriptivism, and heavy with indigenous tradition.

But Aeronwy doesn't just worship Cináed. E's a Flamekeeper, one of the goddex's consorts who carry within them a living Flame. I know nothing about the practice aside from the fact that Flamekeepers can breathe fire, and I'm too afraid to ask more. I'll have to do my own research, first.

Aeronwy moves through the cluttered space without a glance, as if it were an extension of emself. I've spent the last three weeks stepping cautiously, trying my best not to knock anything over or disturb the nest. Often, I feel like I'm on the dreamscape, with its distorted nature of time and space.

After lunch with my parents, I do some deep breathing exercises to stave off a sleep attack. Aeronwy and I talked briefly about my affliction during our first session; there was no hiding it after what happened at Rose's memorial service. I explained that it's a stress reaction, and usually I wake up within twenty minutes. Still, I don't want it to happen again. I don't want to be a burden.

Especially when I know e didn't plan to take on a new apprentice so soon. If not for the dreams, I'd worry that we weren't a good match. But I trust my dreams. If it means

Aeronwy could play an important role in my life, I want to give em a chance.

Aeronwy is a visual artist in addition to being an Illuminator, and there's a new drawing on the easel when I come in today. I take a closer look and freeze. It's my dream garden. It doesn't matter that I haven't seen it in ten years. Every leaf, every petal, every seed is etched into my heart, and now my heart is on this page. The drawing is a rough pencil sketch, full of approximate scribbles and gestural lines and negative space, but it has *presence*.

The kind that could provide a portal to the very world it depicts, an opening in the ether that my spirit body senses, and is drawn towards as if being sucked into a black hole—

A sharp *clink* snaps me out of my daze: Aeronwy setting a coffee cup down on the nearby glass illustration table. Startled, I turn to face em with a guilty smile. The drawing is in the open for anyone to look at, but I feel I've seen something secret. Even if that secret is my own.

"A bit of automatic drawing from last night," Aeronwy says, nodding at the easel.

"Automatic drawing? Like automatic writing?" I ask. In automatic writing, the writer allows words to pour through them without conscious thought, channeling a spirit or the subconscious. It makes sense to apply the same process to drawing, though I hadn't considered it before.

"Essentially," Aeronwy says. "I use it to channel my clairvoyance. The images appear in my mind only briefly, but once I set pencil to paper, they flow more readily. It's how I speak with the books."

"Was this from the books?" I ask, wondering if e knows where it came from. Surely e would have mentioned it to me if e did?

"No. However, I do hope you and I can speak to them today. I've finished the book I was working on, so we can finally choose one to begin together," Aeronwy says.

"Oh! Really?" The drawing slides to the back of my mind in light of this surprise.

"Again, I apologize for the wait. By the time we made the decision to take on both of you, I hadn't had much time to prepare," Aeronwy says.

We walk over to the windows, where the shrine has been cleared to make room for three manuscripts. They've been typed and printed on ordinary copy paper, held together by binder clips. One of them sits on top of a folder labeled "Photo references."

Aeronwy and I sit down on plush floor cushions laid out before the altar. The books feel like sleeping infants, waiting for us to wake them and help shape them into being.

"I currently have three books on commission," Aeronwy says, gesturing at the manuscripts. "I typically work on two at a time, and one of those will be done with your assistance."

"What kind of assistance?"

"We'll speak to the book together, discuss our interpretation of its needs, and then carry them out. The details vary from apprentice to apprentice, but the bulk of the work is this: you will make the paper, the ink, and the thread needed for this book. These processes can take time, as we'll be gathering as much raw material as we can ourselves and creating from the barest beginnings. I will do the actual writing or typesetting, and the illustration, though if you like you may find room to help with those as well."

"That does sound like it'll take a while," I say.

I've made paper before, but from purchased, pre-processed materials. Ink I've made a few times, rudimentary stuff from berry juice and the like. Thread I've never contemplated spinning on my own. The idea of delving into the roots of all three crafts is exciting. It lights a little flame deep in my chest.

"Yes, but if you're here, then I assume you enjoy that type of work," Aeronwy says.

"I—I like the processes themselves almost more than the finished object," I confess. "I love just getting lost in the work itself. It's meditative. And satisfying, to see things come together."

Most of the time, Aeronwy wears a passive, observant expression that gives away little emotion. I get anxious when I can't tell how a person is feeling, and so I've been watching em for clues. Already I've noticed subtle changes in posture that reveal whether e's feeling relaxed or stressed. The one I'm catching onto now is the quickest twitch of a smile when e's pleased with something.

"Good," e says warmly. "Now, the manuscripts."

I turn around to face the altar, back straight and hands in my lap, ready to hear the choices. Aeronwy picks up the one on the left and then holds it out. I hesitate before gently taking it into my own hands, my heart beating fast with excitement and curiosity.

"The first one is a guide to gardening with special care paid to the garden's effect and manifestation on the astral plane. As you can see, it's heavy with illustrations. A curious subject, but then, many of the books we receive are," Aeronwy says.

We spend some time leafing through it. The writing is a little dry, but it's fascinating information.

"Maybe this is the one," I say. "I love gardening, and I've spent a lot of time on the astral."

"We'll look at the other options before you decide," Aeronwy says gently, a glimmer of excitement in eir eyes.

E takes the manuscript back and hands me the one in the middle. I recognize the title from the Casporan Times bestsellers list, and many of the review blogs I follow. It's been on my to-be-read list for months. Tegan Lightscribe is one of the most acclaimed writers of the decade.

"This one is contemporary fiction. I'm sure you recognize the author. I've read it, and the characters are so real, it's difficult to believe they only exist in your mind. The prose is exquisite. But it is also quite tragic. The death of a beloved mentor informs most of the plot," Aeronwy says.

Rose's image swims into view in my mind. "Would that be difficult for you to work on right now? So soon after—" I pause, searching for words. "—after Rose?"

Aeronwy heaves a heavy sigh. "Actually, it might assist me in processing those feelings. I wouldn't put this one on offer if I wasn't in a place to work on it with you."

"Oh. Okay." Still, I can't imagine it won't bring up a lot of grief and pain. I place the book back on the altar myself. I often mirror the feelings of those around me. It makes it difficult to know which ones are actually mine sometimes.

Lastly, Aeronwy gestures to the manuscript on the right, which is directly in front of me. I lift it carefully into my lap. "This one is a book of Casporan folk tales from the coast, with a focus on the natural world," e says, "and the author has given me freedom with the illustrations, since it's a specialty of mine."

I recognize many of the story titles. 'The Wishing Star,' 'The Selkie's Sibling,' 'The Forest Beneath the Sea.,' and more. All wonderful tales I dreamed about frequently as a child. Before I could control my dreams or write well, I found comfort in reliving the ancient stories every night. The familiar opening lines tug at my heart.

"I love folk and fairytales," I say, flipping slowly through the manuscript. "Myths, fables, things like that."

"I do as well. Do you have a favorite story?" Aeronwy asks.

A small laugh escapes me. "That's a really hard question! Maybe, um, I've always loved 'The Circle of Swans' and 'The Wishing Star,' but I could name a dozen others."

"The binding you made of 'The Circle of Swans' for your graduate thesis was beautiful. It was one of the pieces that caught our eye during the portfolio review," Aeronwy says.

I feel myself blushing. "Thank you. You said folktales were a specialty of yours? Do you have a favorite?"

"That answer has changed over the years," Aeronwy says, with a far-off look. "At different stages of my life, I find myself relating to different stories. I've always been partial to 'The Changeling' and 'The Red Robes,' though."

"'The Red Robes?'" I echo, surprised. "That one always scared me when I was little."

"Likely because you read a later Scriptivist version," e explains. "'The Red Robes' is originally a Cináedite tale, and Cináed emself plays a large role in the story. Without that context, the story does become quite threatening."

"I'd love to hear the original sometime," I say. I glance down at the manuscript in my hands. "Sorry, we got a bit off track."

"It's fine. You have plenty of time to make a decision about the manuscript," Aeronwy says, "although I'd like to hear your initial thoughts, at the least."

"The first one is definitely in my wheelhouse of experience," I say slowly. "Maybe that would give me a stronger connection to the book. I'd definitely enjoy it. Or the second one could be good for you, you said, to help you with your feelings about Rose. You'll still be doing most of the work and I'm just assisting, after all."

"Which one do you *feel* most drawn to work with, though?" Aeronwy asks.

E watches me carefully. I know which book I'm drawn to, but I'm afraid to prioritize my desires. To reveal my wants to someone else, and potentially be rejected. And I'm afraid that revisiting my favorite childhood stories might unearth the dark memories I've been trying to escape.

"Tabby," says Aeronwy, "I'm going to work on all three of these books eventually. You'll end up helping me with all of them, but your involvement is far heavier with the first. I want it to be the one you'll enjoy most, because it's your first impression of the craft. It should be like a first love, or a first friend. Someone you immediately like for reasons you can't quite explain."

It's as if e knows exactly what I need to hear. A wave of gratitude washes away my anxiety, and my body feels softer in its wake. I realize I'm hugging the folktale manuscript to my chest.

"Then I'd like to work on the third one," I say, "please."

Another tiny smile. "Very good. Now we can let the book know our intentions and introduce ourselves."

Aeronwy reaches into the space beneath the altar and brings out a red leather-bound sketchbook. There's a golden flame embossed on the cover, and thick ivory paper on the inside. As e flips through it to a fresh page, I catch glimpses of charcoal scribblings of plants, stones, and mysterious abstract figures.

"I assume you'll want to use your dream magic to speak to the book, as you did during the testing?"

"Yes, that's the best way for me."

"Then let us get you more pillows. This could take a while."

***

Later that week, I find Amane stretched out on the yellow sofa with a large stack of books. She has a tome with a two-foot wingspan spread open in front of her, its pages adorned not with ink, but with thread. The pages themselves aren't paper, but fine silk. Every word is stitched on perfectly. I stand behind the couch and peer over at it, entranced by the sheer amount of time and skill it must have taken to make.

"What are you reading?"

Amane turns the page. The backstitching for the previous page is part of the front stitching for this one, and vice versa. It's a testament to thoughtfulness and innovation. I scan a few lines; the text itself seems to be about etheric cords—the spiritual bonds which hold all of us, and all the world, together.

"*The Thread That Binds*. It's the book June wrote and made for eir apprenticeship," Amane says, without looking up. "I've read a mundane copy of the text, but nothing compares to *this*."

"It's beautiful."

She nods solemnly in agreement, then gestures towards the stack beside her. "There're so many Illuminated books I want to read now that I have access to them. I don't think I'm going to sleep for weeks if I actually want to finish before they're due back! You're so lucky you've lived here for years."

"Yes, although I think I took it for granted," I say. "It's just always been here. Maybe that's why it took me so long to figure out this career was what I wanted."

I perch on the arm of the couch and follow along as she reads June's book. Amane glances up at me, a curious look on her face. Her makeup is bright today, strong shades of magenta and orange blended above her eyes and on her lips like a sunset. She's like a beautiful painting that changes every day.

"Did you do something else before?" she asks.

"I got a degree in astral tech first. They need dreamwalkers to keep the Astranet and cell cords clear and maintained on the astral," I tell her.

"That sounds cool, though! What made you change your mind?"

I hesitate, unsure if I should give her the sanitized answer, or the real one. Do we know each other well enough to share those sorts of things? Will she understand about my mental health struggles? I remember the stress dream that revealed her anxiety about not being good enough for the Bindery and decide to trust her the way she trusted me.

"My first few years at university were... a dark period in my life. My parents had approved of the astral tech career because it was practical, and it would have brought me back to my hometown to work—there's a major astranet hub there—but that idea made me even more miserable than I already was," I explain.

Amane gently closes *The Thread That Binds* and sets it on top of her stack. "How come?"

"I... have problems with anxiety, and sometimes depression," I admit. "I didn't have the easiest childhood. By which I mean, it was pretty awful. Part of why I moved cities to go to school was to get away from that. Plus, I wasn't doing well in my classes, and I was starting to *hate* sleeping."

"But you're a dream witch! You must *love* sleeping!" She sounds outraged on my behalf, which is sweet. My parents hadn't seen anything wrong with it. They said that's just how life was.

"You see the issue then," I say. "My parents warned me away from a career in writing or books because once it turned into work, they said I wouldn't enjoy it anymore. It'd be 'ruined.' But that's what happened with my dreaming."

Amane snorts and crosses her arms, a derisive look on her face. "I've heard that one, too. All that's happened to me is that I *love* my work! It totally depends on the person, and the thing they're doing."

"My parents always criticized the way I couldn't stick to one hobby," I say, "drawing, painting, papermaking, stamp carving, writing... they said I'd never be good enough at one of them to matter, if I kept splitting my time. But it turns out that made me a perfect candidate for Illumination."

Amane nods vigorously. "People have told me that, too! Except I was learning all of the different crafts on purpose, because I knew the requirements for this job. They're *all* so interesting, I don't think I could have picked just one or two even if I wanted to have a different career. Which I didn't."

"When did you know you wanted to be an Illuminator?" I ask, happy to turn the conversation away from myself.

Amane's face lights up. "Ever since I was a teenager! My parents gave me the Threadbound Oracle deck my Great-Grandren used to read with, and a copy of Calliope Everberry's *The Guide to the Threadbound Oracle* for my thirteenth birthday. That led me to researching the Eternal Library, which led me to June's work and lecture series. One of eir Illuminated books was in a museum exhibit we went to later that year. As soon as I saw it, I knew what I wanted to do with my life."

So that's why apprenticing with June was so important to her. I picture a very excited young Amane in my mind, and my heart warms for her, knowing she's achieved her dream.

"And here you are," I say.

"Here I am!" she says, bouncing her bare feet against the couch. She kicked her sandals off ages ago. She must feel comfortable here already, and the truth is that I do, too. The common area feels like a second living room, where I can relax. The Bindery requires a key code and ID badge to get into, which means I don't have to worry about strangers wandering in.

"Can I look at June's book with you for a bit?" I ask.

"Of course! I've been texting Rhee this whole time, but it's so hard to fit everything in a text with something like this," she says, "and it's also hard not to spam. June really should be the next Head Librarian, don't you think?"

She scoots over so I can join her on the couch and puts *The Thread That Binds* across both our laps. We take turns pointing out the genius of it, in both word and make, until we're giddy with creative inspiration. It's fun to talk to someone who understands, who I don't have to stop and explain things to. Such deep discussion of the art is incredibly satisfying.

June deserves all the acclaim e's received as an Illuminator and writer if this is what e made as a novice. I was introduced to eir name because eir research on etheric cords was instrumental in the creation of the Astranet. It was from that point my research had spiraled into Illumination, and a door opened in the darkness of my mind. One that led out into the light.

June makes sense as the next Head Librarian. I don't know how the position is filled, but it's only been two moons since Rose's death, so perhaps it's still too soon. I wonder if June wants the position; I assume it's a huge responsibility to bear. I don't think I could carry that weight on my shoulders.

I should look up Aeronwy in the Library catalog, to see what e's done. Every Illuminator writes at least one book in their lifetime as their initiation offering. Aeronwy gave me a reading list, but it didn't include any of eir own writing.

I pull the catalog up on my phone and find four results. Two of them are collections of traditional Casporan folk songs. One is on the spiritual ecology of the Library campus after the '86 fire, and the other is a book of Cináedite folk tales and mythology.

"Make sure you check to see if there's anything under eir birth surname. I almost missed this one," Amane says.

She holds up the cover of *The Thread That Binds* and taps it pointedly. The author is listed not as Juniper Stargrove, but Juniper Starstitch. I hadn't thought of it, but of course Stargrove is a handfasting name. They must have gotten married after June's apprenticeship ended.

I adjust my search, and a fifth book appears under Aeronwy Greengrove. It's called *On Flamekeeping,* published in 3986, thirty-two years ago. It must have been the book e wrote for eir apprenticeship, which is incredible, because it's listed as being five hundred pages long.

Amane watches over my shoulder. "Starstitch and Greengrove. Did they combine them to make Stargrove? Is that how it works here?"

"Yes. Traditionally, Casporan surnames are made up of two words, often an adjective and a noun. When people get handfasted, they usually pick one word from each person's name and re-combine them," I explain.

Amane taps her chin with her finger. Her nails are painted with bright pink glitter, and are so long I wonder how she works without them getting in the way. "But," she says, "Rhiannon has like four words in eir surname, and you're not—well, you don't look indigenous, but you have a Casporan surname?"

"Rhee has four parents, so there's four words. Rivergreen-Haybloom."

"Ohhh. Wait. Like, four parents because they handfasted and then divorced and remarried, or are they—" She hesitates, searching for a word, and looks annoyed when she can't find it. "Are they all together?"

"They're a quartet. Is polyamorous the word you wanted?"

"Yes, that! What about you?"

Startled by her boldness, I say, "Rhee and I are polyamorous, too. I'm gray-asexual but alloromantic, so I do like to date other people sometimes, in a romantic way."

"That's… not what I was asking, but good to know," Amane says, amusement spreading across her face.

I can feel myself blushing. "Sorry. You meant my surname."

"Yeah." She giggles, and I can't help but giggle a little, too.

"My surname is Casporan because my Renna's ancestors arrived here from Glykiági under the Authorist dictatorship of the Reclamation period. Back then, immigrants were required to take new Casporan surnames if they wanted citizenship," I say. "This was five hundred years ago, so I probably have indigenous Casporan ancestors somewhere in there, but I don't really know. My family doesn't talk about those things. On my Ren's side, my great-grandparents came here from Hrafnland back in the late 3800s. Ren had a traditional Hrafnlandian surname, but in her culture, it's customary to take the name of the older partner. So, she became Lilja Fairweaver when she married."

"Wow. That's, uh, complicated?" Amane says.

"These things usually are."

"That's true, I guess. But, so… if you and Rhee got handfasted, you have a lot of options for names," she says, giggling again.

I press my hands to my cheeks and look away, my face and heart warm with the thought of getting handfasted to Rhiannon. We've been together for so long, and I love em so much. I would love to take the formal vows to spend our life together and then find each other again in the next one. We've had a lot of passing conversations about what life will be like when we're older together, and such things, but we've never talked directly about being married.

"Er, sorry, do platonic partners not do handfastings?" Amane asks, misreading my embarrassment.

"Oh no, some do. Handfasting doesn't have to be romantic. It's just. You know," I say, shaking my head. I can feel myself grinning like a fool.

"Aw, cute! Are you thinking of asking?"

"Maybe one day," I say.

Unbidden, images of my parents appear in my mind's eye. Their constant bickering, the plates smashed against walls, the screaming, the crying. I know they love each other—they say they do—but they just can't seem to get along. As if that weren't the understatement of the year. I know their unhappy marriage isn't an indicator of what my own would be like, but I can't help but wonder. Handfasting creates a strong etheric bond, deepening your ability to sense one another's emotions, to have the same thought at the same time, to find each other again in the next life. But if everything changes for the worst... would you want to?

RHIANNON

The centuries pass like hours. For I am eternal, and what is a century in the eyes of eternity? Faces come and go. Librarians, researchers, nuns, historians, priestexes, artists—readers of every shape and size. Magic and science advance side by side. Around me, the Library grows, a tree with roots that wind through story and song. The earth shakes, and often come the flames, wind, and water. I survive them all, though many other books do not. I feel each Head Librarian's soul link with mine, and I feel each depart as they pass into the next life.

Though I cannot die, I think I am beginning to understand death.

Weeks pass. In my visions, days turn into decades, and decades into centuries. The amethyst room turbo boosts my scrying ability, and I push through history at a breakneck pace. There's a cot in the room now for when the migraines hit, and I need to lie down. Mairead brings me bitter medicinal tea, whispering that it will all be worthwhile. I chug it down and go home to Tabby, who takes care of me until I feel calm and present again.

When Rose's face finally appears in the scrying bowl, my concentration nearly breaks from excitement. I crumple the old catalog card in my hand and lean forward until my nose is an inch from the surface of the ink.

Chapter Fourteen

It's 3984, two years before the big fire. Catrina Rosefall, age fifty-one, is not yet Head Librarian. E's just under five feet tall and built like a hummingbird, but eir spirit is mighty. E stares down at me with a smile, and thanks the archivist who brought me out of the safe. Mairead Moonsea is twenty-eight, with long black hair and heavily lidded eyes. The scent of floral cigarettes hangs around em. I know eir hands well.

"Hello, beautiful," Rose says to me once the archivist leaves. "You've certainly seen some things, haven't you?"

If there is one truth about Librarians, it is that they all talk to the books. But not all of them can hear—or see—me like Rose can. The Bindery is different now, a lofty spire high in the air that's filled with light, but I recognize it. This is where I was born.

Rose flips slowly through my pages, admiring Calliope's work as a peer and colleague across the centuries. Sometimes, e tilts eir head and frowns. Eir eyes are soft and far-away, as if e's Seeing something beyond the ink and paper.

"You're a mysterious one," e says when e's at the end. "Good thing you'll be in my care for a while now. We have time to figure you out."

Normally, my visions end by fading out, leaving only the reflective surface of the scrying bowl. This time, the image doubles and the ink ripples furiously. The vision continues, but I can't see what's happening. My sense of time speeds up, as if we're fast-forwarding through history. When it finally clears, Rose isn't the only one in the picture.

"Opal is right, we can't use it," Rose says, frowning down at me. Eir shoulders are tense, mouth a thin red line. "It's too dangerous."

"But think of all the things you could change for the better," says someone standing behind em. Juniper Starstitch is a new Illuminator in eir early thirties, chubby with brilliantly red hair in a thick braid. Eir freckled face is red right now, too. E doesn't

agree with the others on what should be done with me. I do not understand why the argument is happening in the first place.

"That's the danger of it," says Rose. "It's too much power for one person alone."

"What if you changed the rules?"

Rose shakes eir head. "We don't even know if it can be restored."

Juniper looks beside em. Aeronwy Greengrove is Rose's apprentice and helped em make the translated copy of my text. I've seen eir face many times over the last two years. E likes to sing to me. I'm reminded of Calliope, though they look nothing alike. Aeronwy is tall, with intense golden eyes and curly hair that's already graying at thirty. But their spirits feel the same.

"You've hardly said anything, Aery. What do you think?" Juniper asks.

Aeronwy's eyes scan my pages. E reaches out and brushes a long finger against my spine. "I hate to say it, but I think Rose and Opal are correct. Imagine the mess it would cause simply by announcing what we know," e says. "Worse, think of what could happen to Opal or Rose, as it did to Head Librarians in the past."

Juniper is quiet for a moment. Then e says, "Then, what do we do with it? Just send it back to the Archives? It's been there long enough without anyone realizing what it is."

Rose shakes eir head. "I can't. I can't do that and not *worry about it constantly. But if I keep it, and I become Head Librarian, and someone finds out—"*

"Then I'll *keep it," says Aeronwy. E loves Rose fiercely, as Calliope loved Llewella. "June and I will hide it. Even you won't know where it is."*

"It can't leave the Library," Juniper says, arms crossed.

"It doesn't need to. It can stay right here, in the Bindery."

Soon after that, the fire comes.

***

"I know where it is!"

The heavy metal door to Mairead's office slams against the stone wall, and the two people inside stare at me as if I've lost my entire mind. Which is not far from the truth. My heart is pounding like crazy, and my internal clock is set to somewhere in the mid-80s, years before I was even born. I feel like I teleported here from the sub-basement room.

"Uh, sorry for interrupting," I say, backing up. I don't recognize the guest in the office, and for a second, I don't recognize Mairead, either. My mind expects em to look like e did in the vision, young and cool and self-satisfied.

Excitement flickers through Mairead's gray eyes, but e remains calm, hands folded in eir lap. E peers at me over eir glasses and says, "It's alright, Rhiannon, we were just chatting after we finished up with business. Come in, I wanted to introduce you to Dr. Elkspinner, anyway."

My brain edges back into the present. Slightly. "Dr. Elkspinner? Rhys Elkspinner, the author?"

"That's me!" says the stranger seated opposite Mairead. "You must be Mx. Rivergreen-Haybloom. Mairead was telling me about your potential contribution to the exhibit."

Rhys Elkspinner is short and round, with curly brown hair and light brown skin. E's draped in a huge woven shawl with tassels that brush the floor and is wearing unfashionably thick rectangular glasses. The beard on eir chin is sparse and reddish. Eir cheerful, open face reminds me of one of my parents. Not exactly how I pictured the former photojournalist for the Casporan Times and the country's preeminent scholar of Casporan political history.

Clutching my vision journal to my chest, I shut the door quietly behind me and sit down beside Dr. Elkspinner. Now my head feels wack for an entirely different reason than the visions. I resist the urge to lean over and whisper *I love your books please sign my forehead* with a crazed look on my face.

"Author *and* brand-new curator at the National History Museum. Rhys is overseeing the Reclamation special exhibit," Mairead says.

"And Mairead is consulting, of course," Rhys says. "I'm sure I don't have to tell *you* how amazing your boss is. Mairead's books on the Reclamation period have been essential in much of my own research, and e helped me find original sources here in the Archives many times. We're excited to have someone with such a rich résumé on the team."

Sometimes I forget that Mairead is an impressive figure in academic circles. E rose through the Library hierarchy in the wake of the '86 fire, spearheading efforts to catalog what had been lost and what could be restored. After that, e went on to write five books: biographies of Isylwyn Moonscryer and Ciarán Stonefeather, a hagiographical text on the Reclamation, and two popular Authorist self-help books which can be seen on the shelf of any Casporan bookstore.

As if eir academic credentials weren't enough, e's also an accomplished paper artist and witch—several of eir pieces are framed on the office walls. The delicate paper cuttings are spells for productivity and protection.

I nod, for once unable to speak. Do I even belong here? My achievements pale next to Rhys and Mairead's. I might be half Mairead's age, but Rhys is only in eir forties.

Mairead leans in toward us conspiratorially. Rhys and I lean in as well, drawn by eir natural magnetism. "I told Rhys about our little project. Is that what you came in here to talk about? Tell me it is," e demands.

I swallow against my dry throat. "Yep. It sure is."

Mairead clasps eir hands together and inclines eir head toward a statue of Isylwyn in the corner of the room. "I knew you wouldn't steer me wrong," e says. "We found it at last!"

"Well, probably," I say. "The last vision I got was from right before the '86 fire. It might have moved after that, but I don't think so. And if it has, the person who had it then can tell us."

"Who was it? I've been wanting to get my hands on the Illuminated version of *The Founding* for ages. It'd be amazing if we could have it for the exhibit. We have a whole section on Ciarán, Calliope, and Llewella," Rhys says.

Unease settles in my stomach. For some reason, I'm not sure I want to talk about this in front of Rhys. "It's in the Bindery," I say, instead of answering the question directly. Suspicion flashes through Mairead's eyes, brows furrowing for only a second before smoothing over with a beatific smile.

"Of course, that is where I brought it last. After the fire, Catrina Rosefall reported the book missing, but it could have been there all along," Mairead says. "I'm so proud of you, Rhiannon. You're really an incredible asset to the Archives and the Library as a whole."

My unease melts a bit. Being praised in front of Dr. Elkspinner is cool as shit. "Thanks, I do try, you know," I say. Mairead beams. "When I'm at work I always think of that one line from your book *Records of Some Objectivity*, Dr. Elkspinner—*Our thirst for knowledge should be as infinite as knowledge itself.* It keeps me going."

"I'm delighted to hear that!" says Rhys. "I'm always excited to meet rising stars in the field. When I come back for *The Founding,* we'll have to have tea, all three of us. I'd love to hear about your retrocognition—it sounds like something every historian wishes they had. A real window into the past."

"It is pretty amazing," I say, my head spinning with the thought of tea with one of my favorite authors. And not as a fan, but as a colleague. A *peer.*

Dr. Elkspinner pats my shoulder and stands up. "Unfortunately, I do have to go now. Let me know when you have the book in your possession! I'll be in touch," e says.

Once we've said our goodbyes, Mairead and I head back down to the amethyst scrying room, where we won't be overheard. I slump down in the chair, exhausted, while Mairead paces the room. The smile is gone from eir face, replaced by a determined frown.

"There's something you didn't want to say in front of Rhys, I could tell," e says in a low, sharp voice. "What is it? What did you See? And who *actually* had it last? Don't think I didn't notice you dodge the question."

"They hid it," I explain. "Rose figured out something about the book, something—this is gonna sound ridiculous, but they said it was *dangerous*."

"They?" Mairead says, one eyebrow raised.

"Rose and the Stargroves," I say, "and apparently Opaline Sweetfrond, although e wasn't in the vision. Whatever it is, they went to the current Head Librarian for advice. I think Aeronwy's the one who hid it, but June might have helped. I didn't See them doing it. I couldn't get any more visions out of it."

Mairead makes me recount the entire vision twice, going over as much detail as I can remember. Because of the strange gap between the first and second vision, we have no idea what they discovered about *The Founding*. The same distortion happened when I tried to See past the decision to hide the book.

"I've never seen anything like it," I say, "but I don't usually scry through time for missing objects using something adjacent, like the catalog card. I dunno. It might just be that."

Mairead stops in front of the geode in the wall, where we've set up a shrine to Isylwyn and Dáithí, the goddex of knowledge. Staring at the statue of the Founder, e murmurs, "I knew the exhibit wasn't the only reason you wanted me to find it. There's something deeper going on here. Something important. If only it wasn't *them*."

"You have a problem with June and Aeronwy?" I ask, remembering what Tabby and Amane said about their oath-swearing ceremonies. Neither had been able to get answers from the older Illuminators.

"Some betrayals cut deep," Mairead says. "I never liked Juniper to begin with, but without me, Aeronwy wouldn't be who e is today. I made em that way. And e repaid me with abandonment."

"You wanna tell me about it?" I say, knowing how much Mairead loves to talk about emself.

"It'd be easier to show you," e says.

Suddenly, Mairead whips around and reaches over the back of my chair for my hand. The scrying bowl in the desk swirls as Mairead creates a psychic link between us and projects a memory through it. Alarmed as I am, I can't pull away. I just watch.

In this memory, Mairead is even younger than before. No more than eighteen, smooth-skinned and lithe. Eir shoulder-length hair is dyed bright blue, with black roots creeping in at the center part. A pair of green heart-shaped sunglasses sit on top of eir head. It's 3974, and floral print jumpsuits are in. Mairead is sitting in one of the Library reading rooms, a thick book in eir hands.

Aeronwy is draped across the couch, head resting in Mairead's lap. Eir hair appears recently shorn. At this age e's still gangly, not yet grown into long limbs and large hands. Aeronwy's default expression is grumpy, but today e looks distraught, wide lips pulled into a scowl. E's wearing the black collared shirt and pants of a Library staff member—not a Librarian, but housekeeping, it says on the ID badge clipped to eir belt.

"Don't you like any of these? How about Tristan?" says Mairead, pointing to a line in the book. It's a book of Casporan baby names, according to the cover.

"No," says Aeronwy, flopping an arm across eir eyes.

"Seren?"

"No."

"Rhosyn?"

"Eh."

"Gwenllian?"

"Certainly not."

"Arianrhod?"

"Hmm," says Aeronwy, sounding slightly interested.

Mairead flips a page in the book and grows suddenly excited. "Oh, I know, it's this one—Aeronwy."

Aeronwy opens eir eyes and looks up at Mairead. "...I like that one."

They sit in silence for a moment, smiling at one another. "Aeronwy Silverdream," says Mairead. "It sounds important. Artistic. Authorial. It's perfect."

"I still don't know about that surname," says Aeronwy, who until this moment, apparently went by another name. Another glance at the ID badge reveals that it's Morwen Greengrove.

Mairead pats Aeronwy on the head affectionately. "You'll grow into it. You want to make sure they never find you, right? You have to pick something different, something they'd never suspect was you."

"I still want it to feel like me, though," says Aeronwy. E sits up and stretches, rubs eyes that are red-rimmed, perhaps from crying. Beside em on the table is a handwritten letter that looks like it's been crumpled in someone's fist.

"You're becoming an all new you. A better you," Mairead says. "I'll make sure of it. And if somehow your birth family does find you, I'll protect you. So stop worrying about it. You're going to be fine. Great, even, once I'm through making you over."

"Thank you," Aeronwy says, looking at em sheepishly. "Everything's so different here than it is in the mountains. I feel so awkward, and there aren't books on this type of thing. I don't know what I'd do if we hadn't met."

"It was fated that we would," says Mairead, spreading eir arms towards the heavens dramatically. They both laugh. "Now, let's go get you some new clothes."

The vision dissipates, leaving my head pounding. Mairead lets go of me, and I drop my head into my hands, massaging my temples. Thank the Author this room is so dimly lit. Even the amethyst light makes my eyes sting, halos dancing around every crystal point.

"Holy shit, I need a warning before you do something like that," I say through gritted teeth. "Could you *ask* next time?"

I hear Mairead take a step back. "Oh no, I'm so sorry, Rhiannon. I don't know what came over me. I just got so emotional, bringing up those old memories, I didn't think to stop."

I want to ask how the fuck someone in eir position isn't firm about personal psychic boundaries and etiquette. Did e miss the training sessions Human Resources makes us all take every year? But Mairead is my boss, and e sounds contrite, so I keep my thoughts to myself.

"Next time, then," I repeat, pain stabbing through my head with each word.

Mairead helps me over to the cot, where I lie face-down, practically huffing the rosemary-filled pillow there. "I really can't say how sorry I am. I'm so terrible, it's why all my Assistant Heads leave, and why Aeronwy left—I'm just too much for people," Mairead says miserably.

Too much. That I can relate to. Growing up as a 'child genius, ' as 'psychically gifted, ' with my 'special requirements' as a young teen at university, meant I wondered if I was *too much* for people to handle on a regular basis. Sometimes they even said I was—implicitly or explicitly.

"That sucks, I'm sorry," I say, and I mean it. "I don't think you're too much for making a mistake."

"Some people do. We were like siblings. Aeronwy and I," Mairead says softly. "Have you ever met someone and known instantly you were meant to be lifelong friends? We poured our souls out to each other for years, but in the end, I guess I was just… too much for em. My problems, my ideas, my feelings, my needs. Apparently, I hurt em somehow just by being myself."

I think about how Amane and I clicked, how once Tabby and I started talking, it was like we'd already known each other for years. The thought of either of them leaving me leaves an ache in my heart worse than the pain in my head. I sigh into the pillow, the scent of rosemary soothing my nerves.

"After all these years, you'd think it'd hurt less, but—"

"No, I get it," I say, rolling over onto my back. "Don't worry. I have a way into the Bindery, so you don't even have to worry about Aeronwy."

***

Later that week, I get my chance to ask. Tabby has brought home a copy of Aeronwy's first book and asks me to read passages aloud while e braids my hair. Egg curls up in my lap and purrs loudly. This is our end of the week ritual, and usually we choose short, light books to read from. *On Flamekeeping* is so thick it could kill someone if it fell off the shelf, and the prose is just as dense.

I've seen this book hundreds of times, but I never gave it a closer look. A first edition copy sits in a glass case in the Archives as part of a display about indigenous Casporan history. The book was controversial when it was released, as there was an unspoken taboo among Cináed's worshipers about writing down their beliefs and practices. They preferred to stick with an oral tradition, which caused a rift between them and the Scriptivists, whose life purpose it was to put *everything* in writing.

> "*The Sacred Flame carries with it an imprint of every soul with which it has merged, memories formed of ritual and song. A Flamekeeper need only light a candle from the Flame within, and gaze into its light to unlock this ancestral knowledge. With pyromancy, the wisdom of ages is passed on to leaders of the Hearth, who then pass it on to their families, ensuring the chain is never broken. This, indeed, is how I have come by much of the information in this book, not by careful research without, but by careful gazing within.*"

I read the passage aloud in a haughty, nasal tone of voice that makes Tabby giggle and nearly drop the complicated fishtail braid e's weaving. My waist-length hair gives em lots to play around with. Most of these styles are too complicated to wear day-to-day, which makes this time even more special.

"Aeronwy doesn't sound like that," Tabby says in between giggles. "E sounds kind of like you, but… more proper?"

"Hmm." I flip to the back of the book, where there's a short author bio, and discover something disturbing. "Well fuck me, e's from the same fuckin' small town I am."

Tabby, who's sitting on the couch behind me while I'm on the floor, leans over to see. "Really?"

"Fuckin' Verdant Valley. It says right here," I say, stabbing the page with my finger. Of all the backwater places to be born in, what are the chances we're from the same one? This feels like some kind of cosmic joke. Disturbed by my movements, Egg shoots me an annoyed look and presses a paw into my leg.

"Do you think… your parents are a bit younger, but could they have known each other?"

"Nah. I bet Aeronwy grew up in the Traditional Cináedite community out there. They *really* keep to themselves, and they've been there for, like, centuries," I explain, "but it's still the same area, and they have to interact with the rest of us *sometimes*, so of course we sound similar."

"Ah. Yes, e told me e grew up Traditional, and the book mentions it in the beginning," Tabby says, sitting back again.

I flip back to the front of the book, curious. It's one thing to be a Cináedite and work at the Library. It's another to be a *Flamekeeper* and also an *Illuminator*. I didn't even know they'd let a Flamekeeper into the *building*, given what it is they do. What they *are*.

> *"In the beginning, there was Fire. There has always been Fire. Whether the sun shining on us from above, or the molten rock deep beneath our feet, the spark that jumps from cloud to ground in a blinding flash, Fire has been here long before we have. Fire shaped the*

beginnings of humanity, the campfire and later the hearthfire being the foundation on which modern civilization rests.

And so, Fire is life. But it is also destruction. Our ancestors in Caspora have dealt always with the forest fires of summer, year after year, a natural but dangerous occurrence. Then there is the great volcano, Mount Cináed, which every few centuries graces us with an eruption that threatens our very existence.

Yet these cycles are crucial to the land on which we live. We are part of them, and so we do not leave. We tend to the earth as if it were our own bodies, and for this, the goddex Cináed has recognized us. Millennia ago, the great goddex of the Mountain offered six humans the chance to merge their souls with the very essence of Fire, to keep a flickering Flame within their bodies so that they might be better stewards of the earth.

The Six, as we refer to them simply amongst ourselves, were the first Flamekeepers. Cináed would produce more Flames for more Flamekeepers over the centuries, but they were the first to go through the excruciating miracle of spiritual rebirth that takes place when one accepts the Flame into their lungs. Make no mistake, this Flame is real fire, one that would burn any other person to touch it. The magic that allows our bodies to hold the Flame is ancient and complex, wielded by priestexes but activated only by the hand of Cináed Emself. To accept the Flame is to become consort to the goddex, little different from a handfasting, and the ensuing relationship ranges from platonic to romantic and even sexual in nature.

> *A Flamekeeper cannot be burned. We can breathe fire out or in, which is how we have become the shepherds of the yearly wildfires and ordinary housefires that endanger our human settlements. Fire is not the enemy. We do not fight it. We merely ensure that it lives harmoniously with humankind, especially given that many believe the purpose of our species is to record knowledge on vulnerable parchment and paper. Scriptivists often fear and resent us for daring to love the flame that could consume their sacred texts, but the truth is that we are here to help them in their quest.*
>
> *We do that by using the tongue fire favors most: song."*

Interesting. It still surprises me that Aeronwy could get a job in the Library with *a real live flame inside of em,* but the bit about actually wanting to help Scriptivists in the sacred duty of recording knowledge makes sense. Why all the fighting, then?

"So, how are things going with the old teach?" I ask Tabby. I thumb through the book, glancing at the illustrations. They're beautiful. I should check the Illuminated copy out sometime.

"Really good. We've started talking more while we work, now, telling each other stories about our lives and talking about authors and artists we like. I get nervous when e comes over to check my work and give feedback, but you know, it's always been helpful, even when it's hard to hear," Tabby muses. "Everything e does is so precise, and you know me, I kind of just like to wing it."

"E's not like, you know, too blunt? Short tempered? *Fiery*?"

Tabby sighs. "Really, *fiery*?"

"Hey, would I be me if I didn't go straight for the lowest hanging fruit?"

"No, but still," Tabby says, chuckling. "E's definitely very straightforward. I haven't really seen em angry, except when

Mairead showed up for our Charter Oath ceremonies. Did you ever find out about that?"

"Apparently they have some, uh, history," I say. "They used to be really close friends, but now they're not. Seems like Aeronwy did the dumping."

"I see. From some of the things you've told me about Mairead, I can see how that might have happened," Tabby says. "I don't like that e forced that vision on you without asking earlier this week. That's not good."

E continues braiding my hair, pulling the strands tightly into the weave in that almost-but-not-quite-painful way that's necessary for a good updo. When we first became partners, and I let Tabby braid my hair, every one was so loose that it fell apart within a few hours. I had to get em to trust that I would say something if e pulled too tight—that e wouldn't hurt me by doing it right. It took some time.

"It won't happen again, don't worry," I say, petting Egg absently.

"How are things going down there, by the way? I heard Camille is still sick. It must be really serious, should we go visit her in the hospital?" Tabby asks. It's a brave offer; Tabby hates hospitals, but e can't stand knowing someone is suffering. E's never even met Camille, but e's willing to take on those emotions anyway.

"I'll try to find out if she wants visitors. I sent a card and some flowers, and a bunch of texts, but she never answered back," I say. "I just got the same email from Marion in HR everyone else did, explaining the situation. Everyone's pretty messed up about it in the Archives, but I honestly don't know the details. I haven't exactly been hanging out with the group much lately."

"Right, it's just been you and Mairead," Tabby says, sounding sympathetic. "Have you found anything new about where that book went? Are you feeling okay having so many visions? You've been so tired lately."

That's damn well true. I sleep like a dead person every night, my brain too exhausted to dream. Tabby says that I must be dreaming at some point, and I don't remember, but I'm not so sure about that. I just close my eyes and black out, opening them what feels like minutes later to find nine or ten hours have passed. Disconcerting, but it's better than *not* sleeping because my brain doesn't know what time of day it is, much less what *year*. That happened for the first week I was at it with the catalog card, until my body got the gist and gave up fighting.

"It's rough, but I did find something out last week..." I say. I pause. "Wait. This week. That was this week. I think."

"Check your journal?"

"Eh, it doesn't matter."

Tabby finishes tying off the braid and lays it gently over my shoulder, so I can inspect eir work. It's a new pattern I haven't seen before, with six strands intertwined.

"June taught me that one the other day with yarn," Tabby says. "E says e misses braiding Aeronwy's hair since e cut it all off in mourning for Rose, so e's been making belts and handfasting bracelets instead."

"It's pretty, thanks Tabs," I say, playing with it. I imagine the Stargroves doing exactly what we are now, probably for the thousandth time over the decades they've been together. I wonder if Tabby and I will still do this when we're their age, provided we have enough hair between us.

Egg stretches and leaves my lap, sauntering off to do cat things in another room. I get up and flop back on the couch, which is much more comfortable than the floor. Our apartment's living area is small, but cozy. The living room and kitchen-dining area are all part of one big square with a hanging paper divider between them. The whole thing is a maze of purple furniture and plants. And books. Mostly books. They don't all fit on the shelves, and a lot of them belong to the Library anyway, so they live in piles on any and every open surface.

I hand *On Flamekeeping* to Tabby, who curls up on the couch with it clasped to eir chest. E looks over at me, and it feels like the book is looking, too. Like it could be spying for its author.

"What did you find out?"

Draping my arms casually across the back of the couch, I say, "I think it's somewhere in the Bindery."

Tabby tilts eir head at me, surprised. It's cute. Even though I'm familiar with all eir mannerisms by now, I never get tired of them.

"Oh really? But that's great! You could come up with me and ask about it," Tabby says. "I'm sure no one would mind. It belongs in the Archives, doesn't it?"

"Yeah…"

Tabby tilts eir head again, in the opposite direction, thick blonde eyebrows furrowing. "Yeah? But what? Is something wrong?"

I've been wanting to tell em about this all week. Everything rushes out of me in one excited river of words. "Aeronwy hid it somewhere. Rose didn't want anyone to find it, there's something hidden in it that could be 'dangerous in the wrong hands,' but e didn't want to be seen keeping it for some reason, and Aeronwy was eir apprentice at the time, actually, Aeronwy worked with it too, but—"

I take a deep breath. Tabby has leaned back now, eyes wide.

"—whatever Rose found in it, Mairead wants to know, really, *really* bad. But because Aeronwy has some beef with em from the past or whatever, e can't ask for it emself. I said I would ask you to try to get it, because you're Aeronwy's apprentice and maybe e'll trust *you* with the secret, since you work up there. Um, so I guess I'm asking," I say, "if you'd ask for it?"

Tabby's quiet for a long moment. E looks down at the book in eir arms, the one Aeronwy wrote when e was our age, and possibly still friends with Mairead. Or maybe whatever disaster happened between them had passed by then. I keep hearing Mairead's voice talking about being *too much*, and whatever Tabby's opinion on Aeronwy, it makes me distrust the older Illuminator.

"I would ask if it was just for *you*," Tabby says finally, in a voice that's almost too soft to hear. "But I really don't want to get in between Aeronwy and Mairead."

I sigh, a weight falling onto my heart. Tabby's been mediating for eir parents since e was a little kid, which is totally fucked up. It means e's great at resolving disagreements between friends, but when it comes to elders and authority figures…

"I'm sorry, Tabs, I shouldn't ask something like that of you. I don't want to put you in that position, either," I say. I scoot across the distance between us on the couch and flop down into Tabby's arms. I press my face into the softness of eir ample bosom, and e pats my hair.

"It's okay. Thank you, Rhee." I feel the tension leave eir body, and then I can relax, too.

"Can I still come up and see the Bindery, though? See where you and Amane are doing all your amazing work?" I ask, voice muffled by eir chest.

"Yeah, of course," Tabby says. "I can't wait to show you everything!"

"I can't wait to see it!"

We settle in for a night of watching funny videos on EtherTube and eating too much cheese. It's fun, but I feel distracted. I promised Mairead I could get *The Founding* from the Bindery for em, but I can't imagine Aeronwy will give it to me, knowing who I work with. Tabby can't get it for me, and I shouldn't ask Amane for the same reasons. What the fuck am I going to do about this book?

AMANE

The books were restless. Eirlys stroked their spines with soft fingers, but still their spirits would not settle. They knew about the fire in Skyward Dell. One of the books had been part of that collection and had passed the knowledge along. Now they buzzed sorrowfully, like bees who had been told their keeper died. The librarian at Skyward Dell had indeed perished. Eirlys had gone to eir funeral.

Unable to calm the books, Eirlys walked back to the monastery's bindery. The other nuns were at lunch now, and it was empty. Manuscripts in various states of finish lay on the desks, and Eirlys judged them with a keen eye as e walked. Normally, e would eat along with all the others, but they were expecting guests. Eirlys would sit with them, instead.

Considering who the main guest was, e didn't feel very hungry.

Someone tapped em on the shoulder then. Eirlys turned around, and the nun told her that Isylwyn had arrived. There would have been the trilling of silver flutes to announce eir arrival, but Eirlys could not hear them. E couldn't hear much of anything these days, communicating mainly through writing and lip reading. The nuns were learning sign language, but few of them were as proficient as Eirlys and found it hard to keep up.

In the foyer, Sovereign Isylwyn Moonscryer was waiting with eir retinue. E was fifty-one, only two years older than Eirlys, and many inches taller. Isylwyn was deviously handsome, with a strong jaw and glimmering gray eyes. Eir thick black hair was pulled into an elaborate knot, the better to show off the thick white streaks at either temple that had earned em the nickname "the Magpie," although there were other reasons for that, too. Eir robes were a costly shade of violet and covered with ornate silver embroidery depicting phases of the moon.

Eirlys bowed to the leader of Caspora and High Priestex of the entire Authorist faith. Isylwyn inclined eir head slightly in return, acknowledging Eirlys's status as Head Abbex of the Friends of the Library. This was what the followers of a new branch of Scriptivism called themselves; others called them Readerists.

"Abbex Starsower, a pleasure to see you," Isylwyn said, though both knew there was little pleasure in the visit. This was purely business.

"And you as well, Sovereign," Eirlys said politely. E had been born hearing and had learned to speak before the sense faded.

"I expect a meal has been prepared for our arrival? Let us not waste any time—we have much to talk about. And I have a favor to ask of you which was not in my letter," Isylwyn said.

"Yes?" said Eirlys, warily. A favor for Isylwyn would put em in debt, but refusing could be just as dangerous.

Isylwyn gestured to the stranger standing beside em. "This is Daryn Sunseeker, my cousin from the mountain valleys. E'll be joining us for lunch, and I hope joining you here at the monastery."

Daryn Sunseeker was incredibly beautiful. Perhaps thirty years old, tall and with great soft curves of hips and belly. Eir round face held a cheerful smile, framed by short brown hair which suggested foreign parentage on one side. E wore a golden wrap patterned green with woad, and golden rings sparkled on eir fingers.

"It's lovely to meet you, thank you for having me in your home," Daryn said and also signed.

"You're very welcome," Eirlys signed back excitedly. "I'm glad you'll be joining us for lunch. Where did you learn to sign?"

Daryn laughed, and some of it reached Eirlys's ears. A pretty sound. "I'm sorry, I don't know very much. When Izzy said you were hard of hearing, I set out to learn a bit."

Eirlys held back a snort at Daryn's nickname for Isylwyn. A twitch in Isylwyn's jaw betrayed eir annoyance. E clapped a hand on Daryn's broad shoulder and said, "Daryn is a prodigy of languages. I'm sure e'll be signing fluidly with you by the end of the day. Which is all for the better, because I would like em to come here to live and study with you for a year."

Eirlys knew immediately that Daryn was meant to be a spy. The Friends of the Library were growing. Any religion which threatened the hold Authorism had on the state would be dealt with swiftly. The Cináedites knew this and were withdrawing to the mountains rather than fight. Eirlys would be wise to do the same.

But Eirlys was proud, and even more than that, e believed in the message e preached. Daryn seemed charming. Perhaps e could be swayed.

Again, e bowed to Isylwyn. "I'd be happy to accept. Come this way, and we will discuss the plans while we eat."

Reading *The Stories We Sing* excites me just as much the fourth time through as the first. The novel June and I are working on is a classic of Casporan literature and has been translated into dozens of languages across the globe. Stories about the doomed romance between Eirlys Starsower and Daryn Sunseeker have been around for centuries, but this one exploded into pop culture back in the 70s, inspiring countless movies, tv series, and other books.

I'm surprised there isn't an Illuminated copy of it already, but thrilled I get to help create it. My Casporan reading skills have improved since I was first assigned the book at university, and I'm excited to dive into the depths of its symbolism and spirit.

The elevator dings down the hall, and June appears, wearing a straw sunhat.

"Good morning, Amane! I've just got to grab a few things from the studio, and then we're out on our adventure today! Do you mind lending me a hand?"

***

I didn't realize learning magic bookbinding meant going outside. As much as I rail against my family's horrified vision of me living like a nun in a tower, I rather like the idea. Going outside in Aquanea meant getting all hot and sweaty just walking down the street. Sometimes after the rainy season, there'd be great beautiful blooms of desert flowers to take pictures of me sitting in for Astragram, but I've never been one for outdoor exploration. I happily resigned myself to a life of sitting inside next to the air conditioning to read.

I figured the other Illuminators would feel the same, but I was wrong.

"Why can't we just pick from the Library greenhouses?" I ask as the four of us—myself, June, Tabby, and Aeronwy— head out under the autumn sun. Arriving during the beautiful, warm, cloud-free summer tricked me into thinking that's how things would be forever. Now it rains half the days. The air is chilly, and the sky dotted with huge puffs of white. The sun dips in and out of view above.

"Not everything we need grows in the greenhouses," June replies, "and even if it did, it's best to meet the spirits of the plants we use on their own terms, in their own homes."

We stop at the edge of the manicured gardens, which is lined with thick, rectangular hedges. I'm still not used to how *green* everything is here. Green is precious in Aquanea, which is built on a large oasis in the middle of an even larger desert. Irrigation provided from deep underground caverns full of water mean we can grow an abundance of foods and flowers, but we lack forests like these. The steep slopes rise high above us, sheathed in emerald evergreens. Beneath the canopy and beyond the hedge, tangles of briars and bushes and grasses fill every available space. I don't even know how we're supposed to move through it.

"Talking to spirits sounds right up your alley," Tabby says.

I look up at em. Tabby is dressed in sturdy hiking boots and cargo pants with dirt stains on the knees. The large backpack e's carrying has a tube coming out of it for water, and there's a red handkerchief tied around eir neck. E follows June cheerfully as we head up a small trail that cuts through the hedges and into the forest. Seems to me this is *Tabby's* alley, not mine.

"Right, right, of course," I say. "It's just, I might be good at talking to spirits, but I don't even know any of these plants' common names, since I'm not from here. Much less their *real* names. Or their stories. Their uses. Which ones are friendly and which are foes. That makes talking a bit tricky."

"Isn't it wonderful that you're here to learn those very things, then," Aeronwy drawls from behind us. "Imagine that."

I glance over my shoulder and catch the smirk on eir face, beneath the large sunglasses and wide-brimmed hat. Even Aeronwy is better dressed for this adventure than I am, surprisingly casual in an olive t-shirt and athletic pants, with matching jacket. They look crisply ironed, but it's practical… unlike my flat-soled sneakers and dress with stockings. When I'd pictured "a walk in the woods," I hadn't realized we'd be *climbing a mountain*.

"Aery, be nice," June calls back from the front of the line.

"I wasn't being *mean*. I remember what it was like to move to a new place, only to discover I lacked an incredible amount of information that everyone raised there thought was common sense and took for granted," Aeronwy says, still looking right at me. "There's no shame in admitting it."

Easy for em to say, but it doesn't make the feeling that I *should* already know go away. That's how I got ahead of the pack and got this apprenticeship in the first place—by knowing things no one else did, before we were supposed to know it. I taught myself more than my teachers ever did.

"Rhee and I have a garden at home, in our building's courtyard. I wish it were easier for me to hear what our plants are saying. I can identify a lot of plants, but I don't know much about talking to their spirits," says Tabby. "Maybe we can help each other out?"

I turn back to respond, but before I can, my toes catch against something hard and I go sprawling forward. I throw my arms out to catch myself, but a pair of strong, soft hands grab my shoulders and keep me from smashing my face into the dirt. Tabby hauls me back upright with a concerned laugh.

"Are you okay?"

"Fine! Thank you!" I squeak, smoothing down my dress and stepping over the offending tree root on the path. My toes are throbbing, but I'm not about to admit that. I'll just have to lift my feet higher as we go, because I don't want to stare at the ground the entire time like a rookie hiker, even though I am one.

If I fall, maybe Tabby can catch me again. I wouldn't mind that. I can still feel the warmth of eir hands on my shoulders.

"I think helping each other out sounds like a fine idea," June says, glancing back at us with a smile. "Play to each other's strengths, and you'll both come out stronger."

We continue through the woods, following the trail up the slope and away from the sounds of the city. The air smells so different here than in the desert. The earth smells darker, wetter, woodier, I suppose. There's no salt, but there is pine. I lack the proper vocabulary for what my senses are telling me. Small streams of water trickle across the path in some places, gurgling as they fall off into the underbrush. The land teems with spirit activity, but it doesn't overwhelm me like the Library does. The beings who live here have no concern for a little group of humans passing by. They feel like sunshine and raindrops and cool rock in my spirit senses.

June and Tabby name the plants for me as we pass them. They exclaim excitedly every few feet, listing off magical and mundane properties, until eventually they seem to be talking more to one another than to me. There are *so many* big green leafy things I worry I'll never be able to tell apart, and all the evergreen trees definitely look the same, no matter how many times I pull out my guidebook to compare them. At one point, as I'm squinting at a pine cone (fir cone?) to try to identify it, Aeronwy reaches over and closes the book in my hands.

"I'd suggest letting yourself take it all in without the guide, first. See what you notice on your own. Enjoy yourself, maybe," e says.

"But we're working," I say.

"And?"

"And I want to do it right."

"You'll do it wrong, first. That's how it goes," Aeronwy says.

"And I guess *you* got all this plant stuff wrong too, when you started your apprenticeship?" I ask, tapping the guidebook against eir chest. Aeronwy may be intimidating, but when people get sassy with me, I can't help but return the favor.

"No, not really. I was raised on a farm, deep in the mountains. I likely know the flora here best of the four of us," e says, and when I roll my eyes in exasperation, e adds, "but I had my own deficits of knowledge, to be sure. We all do. They take time to fill. You won't do it in a day."

It's unnerving how well e seems to know my personal thoughts, and how unafraid e is to call them out. Good thing Aeronwy isn't my mentor, because I don't know how well I'd do being poked and prodded every day. I give em a sour look and get a little half-smile in return as I shuffle off to stand beside June instead. I pull my phone out, surprised to find it actually has signal out here in the woods. I text Rhiannon and get an immediate ping back. E must be taking a break from vision work right now.

ME: I feel attacked

RHEE: lol why, what happened

ME: do you ever feel like you just have to be the best at everything you do, as fast as possible, because anything else isn't good enough and never will be

RHEE: did you mean my life
RHEE: because yes

ME: we're out looking at plants IN NATURE and I'm so lost, and they all know it, I hate it

RHEE: well you've only lived here for what, a season? i'm sure they understand
RHEE: tabby knows a shitton about plants, you should get em to tutor you

RHEE: OOH we could all go hiking together!!!

ME: not you TOO

RHEE: you don't like hiking?

ME: …..I don't know, I haven't really done it much….

RHEE: oh I see what's going on
RHEE: "I gotta be good at everything new IMMEDIATELY or else I feel like a failure and don't like it"

ME: wow why is everyone coming at me today, gODS, RHEE

RHEE: only say it because I know that feel
RHEE: easier said than done, but hey, cut yourself some slack

ME: what does that phrase mean exactly

RHEE: give yourself a break, be nice to yourself, etc etc

ME: ugh that's what I thought. I'll try.

RHEE: hell yeah, that's the spirit, you got thisssss *thumbs up*

Feeling validated, I hold my chin up higher (and watch for tree roots) as we venture farther into the wilderness. The trees have opened up to a steep slope of boulders and wildflowers, the path zig-zagging up it in a way that leaves me gasping for breath. I chug my water until there's nothing left and groan. I'll have to get one of those water backpacks if we keep making these trips.

Tabby offers me the handkerchief from around eir neck, and I use it to wipe the sweat from my brow. There's a lot of it. At least Tabby looks winded now, too, cheeks pink and pale skin glistening with perspiration. E's smiling broadly, as if e enjoys it. We watch Aeronwy and June continue up the slope without us, undeterred by the challenge. June starts singing a folk song about eloping with a pretty farm hand to the city, voice echoing off the mountainside. I can't imagine how e has enough breath to do that.

"How are they in better shape than us, they're *old*," I whine. I try to hand the handkerchief back to Tabby, then think better of it, and awkwardly draw my hand back. "Er, sorry, this is gross now."

"You can hold onto it," Tabby says, "and I think they do this all the time. Rhee and I go hiking sometimes, but mostly I just sit around reading… or sleeping… writing…"

Tabby wanders over to the side of the trail and grabs a big branch that's lying on the ground. E breaks part of it off with eir foot and then hands it to me. I stare at it, then at Tabby, then back at the stick, unsure what I'm supposed to do with it.

"It helps to have a walking stick to lean on and keep your balance. It's not as fancy as what June has, but it works just fine," e says, nodding at the figures higher on the slope—June has a metal pole in each hand, something I hadn't really thought much about.

"Thanks."

"Also…" Tabby wanders a back off the side of the trail, plucks a few things from a tree with low-hanging branches, and comes back holding four small, rosy apples. E hands one to me. It's not as big as the ones from the store, or as shiny, but it looks delicious. There's even a small stem and leaf still attached, like you'd see in a children's drawing.

"This is okay to eat?"

Tabby beams at me, cheeks dimpling. "Of course! It's the perfect time of year for them, so they should be good and ripe. Also, there's spring water trickling down the rocks back there. I can fill your water bottle if you want."

I shuffle the walking stick around so I can hand Tabby my water bottle, then rub the apple on my shirt and take a tiny bite.

It's a little sour, but delicious. I've never had anything this fresh, even from a farmer's market. I never imagined myself eating fruit off a tree in the woods or drinking from a mountain spring. There's something special about it. Our ancestors lived like this.

"Is the water safe?" I call after Tabby.

"In this case it most likely is," e calls back. "It's glacial melt seeping out from underground… the earth is like a natural filter. We're right at the source, it's flowing, and there are raccoon tracks nearby. They probably drink here, too."

Tabby returns and hands me my now-full water bottle. I take a cautious sip and find it tastes sweet and minerally. Surprisingly cold, almost like it had ice in it. Maybe I could get used to this hiking thing.

"We'd better catch up," Tabby says, shading eir eyes and looking up the slope again. "I think they're waiting for us."

Feeling refreshed, we climb the rest of the switchbacks to join Aeronwy and June. Tabby provides me with the name for the shape of the trail, which reminds me of the word switchblade; appropriate considering it feels like someone's driven a knife into my side whenever I climb too many at once. Tabby notices when I start flagging and suggests we take more breaks, but I decline. Pushing through the pain will make me stronger.

At the crest of the next hill, the trail finally levels out, to my intense relief. We walk through a small grove of trees and emerge into the sunlight. I gasp at the vista laid out before us.

At my feet lies a meadow filled with golden grasses, dotted with red, purple, and white flowers. In the center of the meadow, a circle of ancient standing stones. There's one in the Library gardens, too: giant monoliths of gray, towering alone or connected at the top by horizontal slabs. Beyond that, the land drops off in a sheer cliff overlooking a huge alpine lake. The lake sparkles like an aquamarine and is just as clear. The mountains rise around it in shades of gray stone, evergreen trees, and white patches of snow at their peaks.

"How is this *real*?" is the only thing I manage to say.

June sighs happily and walks into the meadow, towards the standing stones. I wade in after em, the grasses brushing against my waist and shoulders. I can hear bugs whirring and birds calling. The sun is warm, but the breeze blowing off the mountain peaks is cold. There's not a single sign of human habitation nearby, despite how close we are to the city. A hidden paradise.

The four of us eat lunch just outside the ring of standing stones without much talking because of how hungry we all are after the hike. Afterward, we comb through the meadow and surrounding trees for paper and ink ingredients. June takes the time to point out useful native plants for me, how to recognize them, and what sort of books to use them for. Lupines for happy endings. Wild carrot for tragedies. Sweetgrass for spiritual tomes. I write everything down as annotations in my guidebook.

For *The Stories We Sing*, we gather canary grass, moonwort, and elderberries. June has a special woven box with wearable straps. Inside there are compartments for safely storing materials, even a little section of glass bottles for delicate petals and tiny seeds. We thank the plant spirits for allowing us to pick them and leave offerings of our own hair in return. I like the strands June plucks out, which are white at the root and bright red at the bottom. My own hairs are long black spirals, and together they look like a pretty bundle of threads.

Once we're done collecting, June and I prepare to enter the ring for meditation.

"Have you been in a standing stone circle before, Amane?" e asks, taking eir shoes off.

"No, but I've been in other types of spirit hubs," I say, doing the same. The earth is damp between my toes. "Cenotes and crystal caves."

"So you know what it's like to stand in a gateway to the other world," June says. "Good, this shouldn't be too much of a shock. Let me know if you're feeling overwhelmed and need to step out."

"I will, I will."

We hold hands and walk in beneath the largest trilithon, which directly faces the meadow and the west. A sharp, full-body shiver hits me as the circle amplifies my spirit senses. Some spirits are pinpricks against my skin, others a gentle brush of a petal or wing, but the lake and the mountains themselves press up against me with the weight of ages. I feel them the way you might feel the bass booming from a loud concert in your bones.

I grasp June's hand tighter. I can feel the calluses on eir fingers from sewing and writing, and the weathered softness of age. Suddenly I'm six years old again and holding my Great-Grandmother's hand as she walks us through the family burial tomb. So many spirits reached out to me, eager to meet their adorable new descendant, but I wasn't ready. I'd cried until Gramma told me she could feel them too, and they meant us no harm.

June squeezes back. It's the reassurance I need. I take a deep breath.

We lie down in the center of the circle, which is covered in soft, thick moss. I stare up into the sky and feel the flow of life around me. Like clinging to a rock in the middle of a rushing river.

"Close your eyes and just breathe," June advises in a soothing voice. "Pull yourself into center. Then send roots into the earth as an anchor."

I do as e says, imagining roots of light growing out from my body and through the moss with every exhale. On the inhale, I draw energy from the earth and use it to awaken my spirit. The earth feels so different here than in Gildea. There even the stone is made of sand, dry and shifting, hot like lightning and ringing like glass. Here, the earth is rich and wet, volcanic and green, cool like spring water and dark like smoke.

We lie there and breathe for a while, sinking into ourselves and our surroundings. Trying to, in my case. No matter how many times I envision putting down roots, they just won't go deep enough. Or they draw back up into my spirit, and I have to do it again. I feel restless, and my mind keeps skipping around to unrelated topics, like texts Abeni sent me earlier or how I should have worn better shoes, because my feet hurt. And we've still got to go back *down* the mountain.

"How are you feeling?" June asks, after I shift my weight around for the hundredth time.

"Fine."

"It's okay if you're not fine."

"I can handle it."

"What you're feeling doesn't always need handling," June says. "Sometimes it just has to be."

I let that one sink in. It squirms around in my belly uncomfortably.

"I admire your drive," June continues. "You really do push on towards your goals no matter what, don't you?"

"If I didn't, I'd never achieve them."

"What if," June says, "you try your best, and things still don't work out the way you wanted?"

I don't even have to think about that one. "Then I wasn't trying my best."

"Hmm, interesting perspective." I can tell e has thoughts about this e's not sharing. I wonder what they are.

After a while, June leaves the stone circle and heads down to the lake with Tabby, to forage for aquatic plants. I know I'd never make it back up the steep path, so I stay where I am.

Aeronwy joins me in the circle, sitting with eir back against one of the stones. My skin warms as if seated by a lit fireplace; in this heightened space, I can sense Aeronwy's Flame. Or, Aeronwy emself? I focus my spirit sense. Aeronwy *is* the Flame, but the Flame is more than just Aeronwy. Two spirits merged together, one far older and larger than the other.

"You're staring," says Aeronwy, and I snap out of my daze.

"Sorry," I say. "Why didn't you go down to the water with Tabby and June?"

Aeronwy shifts uncomfortably and glances away. "I don't like being near the lake."

"Are you afraid of the water?" I ask.

"Yes. You would be, too, if you were me," e says.

"Can you swim?"

A shake of the head. "Don't you ever stop asking questions?"

"No," I say.

"That's good. You should ask questions. I see why June likes you," Aeronwy says. E settles back against the rock with a tiny smile. "I'm sorry for teasing you earlier. You seem like the sort who enjoys a bit of banter."

"You're not wrong, I just—well—I need to be able to tease you back!" I sputter.

"Tease away. I can take it," Aeronwy says, and the tiny smile widens. E knows I'm intimidated and wants to push me past my fears. It reminds me of my sisters, and my heart warms.

"I need to get to know you better, first."

Aeronwy gets up and sits on the moss directly in front of me. "In that case, I have an idea. Could I request an oracle reading from you?"

"Of course!"

I scramble to retrieve my cards and settle back in the circle. Aeronwy's long-fingered hands engulf mine when I hold them to attune our energies. The fireplace warmth on my skin intensifies, accompanied by a whisper of silk and flower petals. Aeronwy's energy signature is delicate where I was expecting roughness.

"Do you have a question you want to ask? A topic?" I say as I let go and start shuffling the cards.

Aeronwy leans eir chin on one hand. "I'm planning to run for Head Librarian. I would appreciate some advice on how to handle that."

"Will it be hard? Are you expecting tough opposition?" I ask.

"June will be competition enough," Aeronwy says warmly. "If e wins, I'll be delighted. I don't know who else will run yet, but there are other things I'm concerned about."

As I'm shuffling, a spirit appears. The stone circle amplifies their presence, filling my nose with the scent of smoke. "Someone's here to answer the question for you. I'm getting… mugwort smoke and ashes… fresh linen… and the letter 'N.' Does that mean anything to you?" I say.

Aeronwy blinks at me in surprise. "Neirin," e says. "My Great-Grandren, who I inherited my Flame from."

The spirit affirms this. Smiling, I lay out cards until I feel an indication to stop; Neirin has a lot to say, and there are ten cards to flip over. In the very center of the reading lies The Library card. It shows a rainbow of books swirling up through several floors of shelves, not unlike the architecture in the Spire.

"Here's confirmation of our central theme," I say, "becoming Head Librarian here at the Library."

I turn over the cards above and below that, next: The Stars and The Mountain. The Stars shows a depiction of Eirlys Starsower in a beautiful green gown, pulling thread between eir fingers until it turns into starbursts overhead. The Mountain looks eerily like Mt. Cináed in the distance, and I glance over my shoulder at it. I find the volcano spooky.

"There will definitely be challenges to weather," I say, pointing at The Mountain card, "but luck is on your side. You should have hope."

The three cards to the right of center make me blanch, though: The Antagonist, the Five of Paper: Cut, and The Book. The Antagonist shows a person hovering upside-down, their back to the viewer, between dark rows of monochromatic books. The Five of Paper shows a pair of scissors destroying a roll of paper, with lighting behind it. The Book isn't a scary card, the big tome sitting on its pedestal amid giant redwood trees, but it hardly counters the other two.

"Someone else will definitely be opposing you. Someone you've had significant troubles with," I say. "I'm not sure about The Book card here, but maybe someone who will throw doubt on who you are as a person, or your identity?"

"I was afraid of this," Aeronwy grumbles, covering eir mouth with one hand.

"Do you know who it is?" I ask, and after a moment's thought, "Is it Mairead?"

Aeronwy looks at me sharply. "How would you know about Mairead?"

Rhiannon has been telling me everything about eir visionary work with Mairead during our shared lunch breaks, but Aeronwy doesn't know that. "From what happened during our Charter Oath ceremonies?" I say innocently.

Aeronwy relaxes slightly. "Ah. Yes, it is Mairead I'm concerned about. In the past, e ran a campaign blaming me for the '86 fire, right when I finished my apprenticeship and my first book came out—when I revealed myself to the rest of the Library as a Flamekeeper. It was incredibly difficult, and I'm concerned it will come up again during the faculty and staff vote."

"Oh, I see," I say. Another piece to the puzzle. I file it away for later. Rhiannon will want to know this.

Getting back to the reading, I flip over the three cards to the left of center: The Weaver, The Dreamer, The Teacher. "These are either people who will help you, or roles you can take. I'm getting the sense that they're all people. The Weaver is probably June, and The Dreamer could be Tabby. Who do you think The Teacher is?"

"I would hope it's Rose," says Aeronwy. "I haven't heard from em yet, though e promised to haunt the Bindery after… after passing on."

I can tell the grief is still fresh. Rose may have accepted death and found peace in the end, but the people left behind have to live with their loss. I've channeled enough spirits for the loved ones of the deceased to know that.

"If you wanted, um, one day I could try to channel Rose. Either with my cards or—or the whole-body experience!" I say, throwing my arms wide.

Aeronwy gives me a sideways glance, and a ghost of a smile. "I was waiting for you to offer. Perhaps there's a reason e hasn't been in contact, though," e says.

"Sometimes people just get a little lost. I'm like a lighthouse on the astral," I explain.

"You're in rough seas at the Library, then," says Aeronwy, frowning in concern.

"Don't worry, I put wards on." I've had to double them in strength since starting work here, which is tiring, but not beyond my capabilities. I love walking into the Spire in the mornings and sensing the books against my spirit-skin, their stories sending shivers up my spine and energizing me for the day.

"Wards are good, but sometimes you need more than fortifications. Sometimes you need to *turn off*." Aeronwy insists. "There are beings in the Library older and more powerful than you or I can imagine."

My mind flashes back to the Charter Oath ceremony, when Mairead called our deities and spirits to be present. Not only had the entire Gildean pantheon and my ancestral spirits arrived in force, but beings had come for Tabby, as well. Unfamiliar deities of earth and sky and dreams… and three who felt like books but weren't.

The Founders had pressed in on me with blinding attention, which I would have caved under if Tabby hadn't taken hold of my hand at that exact moment.

"I can handle it," I reassure Aeronwy.

"Be sure that you do," e says.

CHAPTER SIXTEEN
TABBY

Oran calls one gray and gloomy morning during Cedar Moon, and my stomach clenches. Oran never calls me unless something's wrong with Lilja. I chip a mug I was washing in my haste to dry my hands and answer.

"Hello?"

"Tabby," says Oran in eir gruff voice, "have you heard from your Ren?"

Not so much as a 'how are you' or 'do you have a moment' or a 'hello, ' just straight to the point. That's how e always is.

"No, why? Should I have?" I ask, stomach clenching tighter.

"I thought maybe she went to stay with you. She left last night in a huff and hasn't come back yet," Oran says, exasperated.

It baffles me that e thinks Lilja's at my apartment. Neither of them is allowed to stay overnight after Lilja showed up several times unannounced, crying and asking to sleep on the couch. 'Just one night' always turned into three or four. Eventually Rhiannon put eir foot down because I was too scared to.

"No, she's not here. Have you called around? Checked with her friends?" I ask.

"None of them will answer when they see my number," Oran growls.

That's not surprising. They've been shouted at and threatened not just over the phone, but when e shows up at their doors to collect Lilja. They lie low so they won't have to call a community mediation officer… again. Oran has been detained more than once.

"Maybe she just needs some space. She'll be back after a few days like usual," I say, diplomatically.

"I don't like not knowing where she is," says Oran, putting emphasis on every word, as if I don't understand the situation.

"I know—"

"Lil doesn't know how to take care of herself. I need to be there for her!"

I bite my tongue. *I'm* the one who's always taken care of Lilja. Suddenly leaning against the kitchen table isn't enough support; I pull out a chair with shaking hands and sit down, bending over to rest my head on my knees. It doesn't quell the nausea or stop my heart from racing, but I won't fall and hurt myself if I pass out. I hear footsteps from the hallway; Rhee walks into the kitchen and pauses.

"Tabs?"

I raise my head and mouth *parents*. Rhiannon utters a disgruntled sigh and then yanks opens the refrigerator.

"Tabby? Are you there? You better not have hung up on me—"

"I'm here, I'm here. I'm sure everything is fine. Will you calm down if I promise to call around and figure out where e is?"

"I don't need to calm down," e says, in a dangerously sharp tone.

"I mean, will you feel better? Obviously, you're very worried about Lilja. That's what I meant," I correct myself before this turns into a fight. After thirty years, I wonder why I still make blunders like this. I should know better than to accuse Oran of being angry. It just makes things worse.

There's a pause. "Yeah, I'll feel better. Call me when you know."

The call ends. No hello, and no goodbye. Oran doesn't see the point in wasting breath on 'social niceties. ' I sigh and put my phone face-down on the table, taking a moment to collect myself before I start calling Lilja's friends.

Rhiannon sits down with a plate of cut veggies. E chews on a carrot stick doused in dressing and glances down at my phone, then back up at me questioningly.

"Renna's looking for Ren again. She left last night and didn't come back," I explain.

Rhiannon sighs. "What did they fight about this time?"

"I don't know. I'll ask Ren, I suppose. When I figure out where she is."

"Are you sure you're feeling up for that?" Rhee asks, gently. "Don't you have a lot of work to do today?"

"I don't really have a choice," I say. I rub my face with my hands. "I'll just think about it constantly until I find out, so I might as well do it now."

"You could call their community resource center to look for you," Rhee says. "Report em as a missing person in danger, which, uh, she kinda is."

"No, because then I'll have to report Renna again. That will only make things worse for Ren."

Rhee crunches loudly on a piece of celery. I can tell e's going to say something delicate by the look on eir face. "Why do you keep protecting Oran? Lilja, I can kinda understand. Even though she acts shitty to you, she's a victim, too. But why do you have to be the one to sort out their shit? It's not fair."

I shake my head. It's not fair, but I don't know what else to do.

I contact Lilja's friends. Lilja probably turned her phone off to avoid Oran's calls. She was terribly lonely until she found online crafting groups a few years ago. She can keep up with her friends even when Oran doesn't let her leave the house. I hope she's gone to stay with one of them.

The question is, who? Many of them haven't heard from Lilja in weeks; friends move in and out of Lilja's good graces quickly. She can turn from sweet to spiny in a second. Often people don't even know what they did wrong when she dumps them. I start to despair after so many unsuccessful messages and calls.

Finally, a friend named Corday answers on the first ring.

"Hi, Tabitha, how are you?" he says lightly. His tone of voice is a dead giveaway.

"I'm okay," I say as cheerfully as I can manage. "I was just wondering if Lilja, my Ren, was with you. I can't seem to reach em, and I was getting a little worried."

Corday hesitates. I can hear him putting his hand over the microphone before speaking to another person in the room. My shoulders relax. Lilja must be there with him.

"Here, I'll let Lil speak for herself," he says.

There are fumbling noises, and then Lilja says, "You're not going to tell Oran where I am, are you?"

I sigh. "No, of course not."

Lilja exhales deeply and sniffles. "I'm going to do it this time, I swear. I won't go back. You know how I had the flu last week? Oran kept telling me it couldn't be that bad and berating me for being in bed too long. Corday says I can stay with him."

"That's awful. I'm so glad Corday is there for you," I say.

"It took all my strength just to get to the train station. I would have called a private driver, but last time Oran saw them pull up and broke one of the car's headlights," e goes on.

"I know it's hard, but you're doing the right thing. Do you have clothes and things with you?"

More sniffling. "Yes, for now."

"Good."

"You'll help me get the rest of it later?"

"Of course. Or we can hire movers," I say, because I hate going back to that house. There are too many memories there.

I can practically hear Lilja frowning. "That's too expensive, and totally unnecessary. You're so strong, Tabby! Unless sitting at a desk all day has gotten to you, and you're not willing to put in a little extra effort for your Ren."

"We'll figure it out," I say. I look at the clock. "I have to go to work soon, is there anything else I can do?"

"Could you call Oran and tell em not to come looking for me?"

I balk at the suggestion. "Well, I, I don't know—"

"It's just, you're so good at handling eir moods…"

It's true, I do know how to keep Oran from exploding. Sometimes. It doesn't make me any less terrified, especially if it's a face-to-face situation. Rage gives em superpowers, like the time e knocked over the entire solid oak china cabinet like it was a feather. The only reason I have any control over Oran is e thinks I'm on eir side. I have to be careful, because if e thinks I've taken Lilja's side, I'll lose what little trust e has in me.

"I'm not sure that will work," I say.

Lilja starts crying. I can hear Corday in the background offering to do it, but Lilja turns em down. A spark of resentment flares in my chest, but I smother it immediately.

"Please? Please, Tabby, this is so hard on me right now. I'm trying to do the right thing and leave. Don't you love me enough to help me do it?" she begs between sobs.

My heart breaks along familiar fault lines. Ever since I was little, Lilja has put me between herself and Oran. Her living shield. For years I thought weathering the storm made me stronger, but all it's done is left cracks in my foundation. Lilja worms her way into them with ease.

"I *do* want to help, I *do* love you. I'll call em right when I get off the phone with you," I say, even though the thought makes my heart skip a beat.

Lilja cries harder, this time out of relief. I soothe her with gentle encouragements until she quiets down. We move on to everyday topics of conversation, like how my apprenticeship is going. The whiplash leaves me exhausted, but I stay on the phone.

"I wish I could have your life, Tabby," Lilja sighs. "I could have been a successful and famous artist if I'd focused on my crafts instead of being drawn into having a family. Don't ever have children—hold on to what you have now."

This isn't the first time Lilja has implied e regrets my birth, even though it wasn't an accidental pregnancy. It's a valid way to feel, but I still feel hurt and guilty. And unsure what to say. I always feel like I should be apologizing.

"Don't worry, I will," I say.

We say our goodbyes and I slump down on the table. Rhiannon pets my hair comfortingly. E finished eating a while ago but stayed to support me.

"You shouldn't have to be the one to call. It's dangerous for you, too," e says.

"She's my Ren though," I say. "I'm her child. She needs me."

"Yeah, but like, I dunno, it seems backwards somehow," Rhiannon says. "Like *you're* being the parent."

"I'm an adult. It's not like when I was little."

"Still. You could call community services."

I shake my head, and Rhee sighs. "Then at least let me be on the call with you?"

"Okay. I love you," I say, groping across the table for eir hand. My head feels too heavy to lift, as if I'm carrying Lilja's burdens along with my own.

"I love you, too," says Rhee. "And hey, guess what?"

"What?"

"You gotta look up."

I turn my head slightly, peeking over my folded arm. Rhiannon is making a ridiculous face, chin smushed back, lips pulled back in a buck-toothed grin, eyes crossed at the middle. A laugh escapes me, and I bury my face back in my arms.

"That's better," e says.

***

The Bindery is my favorite place to be these days. I thought it would be quiet since it's in a library, but I was wrong. Amane and June always have an amusing anecdote, fun fact, or long story to tell. They even manage to draw me into their endless conversation loop at times with questions that are easier to answer than to evade.

The Stargroves are very keen on music, and something's always playing in the background. Folk singers from the 60s and 70s seem to be their favorite, but there's also synth, grunge, bluegrass, and modern pop. Amane enthusiastically introduces us to Gildean pop music, which is full of driving drum lines. I don't know why she needs to drink three cups of coffee in the morning when those bass beats are so energizing.

June often sings along or by emself in a beautiful mezzo-soprano that carries through the walls. As a thread witch, of course e would sing. There are many catalysts for activating magic: song, dance, sigil, bodily fluids, cutting, burning, speech, anything that can cause a release or transfer of energy.

Chapter Sixteen

Some kinds of witchcraft work better with a particular method, and thread likes to be sung to.

According to *On Flamekeeping*, fire magic prefers song as well. I have yet to hear Aeronwy sing, though. E's so reserved, and I don't have the courage to ask about it. I can't even bring myself to read *On Flamekeeping* in front of em, for fear that it might be awkward. It's a fascinating book, and it intimidates me that e published it at the very age I am now.

I borrow the Illuminated copy and ask the book's spirit what it was made of. Unsurprisingly, there's a lot of ash involved. Cover boards cut from a tree struck by lightning. Vine black ink, made with charcoal. The endpapers are embedded with two large pink flower spikes, which turn out to be fireweed. I've seen it around town, but apparently it largely grows on disturbed soil out in the mountains, especially where there have been fires. The book calls it 'phoenix flower, ' and it's Cináed's favorite.

Making enough paper for a book that will be lettered and illustrated by hand is a lengthy task. Aeronwy scrutinizes every sheet and sets aside any that lack perfection to be sold or recycled. Half the time, I can't even tell what's gone wrong until Aeronwy points out a tiny flaw. Accidents happen in the inking stage, too, and so we have to have enough extra paper to account for future mistakes.

The process is slow, but I'm learning. I put the raw fibers through the beater, pick apart the petals of the flowers we gathered on our mountain hike, measure the pulp, mix the slurry, dip the giant mould and deckle, stack the sheets between the felts to dry. They're as delicate as newborn butterfly wings when wet.

Today, after talking to Lilja and Oran on the phone, I make more mistakes than usual. Most of the time I can let go and move on, but this time it builds into a storm cloud of frustration. This won't do. I leave the paper room a mess and head into the common area to take a break.

Aeronwy is sitting on the couch, legs stretched out across the cushions while e types on a laptop. June is swaying around the common area with a watering can, tending to the houseplants and singing along with the cheerful folk tune playing over the sound system.

Aeronwy glances at me over eir horn-rimmed reading glasses as I plop down in one of the armchairs with a sigh.

"Everything alright?" e asks.

"Just one of those days," I say, putting on a smile.

"Sometimes it's better not to force it," Aeronwy advises, and then goes back to the laptop. I never realized how much time is spent on administrative work instead of binding books.

June finishes singing to the houseplants and comes over to join us. "Would a cup of tea help? I can make some."

"Oh, thank you, you don't have to do that if you don't want to," I say, sinking lower into the chair.

"It's no trouble. Just be a few minutes," June says, and then disappears into the tiny kitchen down the hall.

I rest my eyes, focusing on my breathing to clear the frustration and anxiety. After a while, I hear June's returning footsteps and the clatter of the tea tray on the table. E's brought out the whole tea set, not just the casual mugs. E pours us each a cup and hands one to me first: a bright, soothing blend of chamomile and mint.

June plucks the laptop from Aeronwy's hands and sets it aside.

"You should take a break, too. I've been watching the line between your eyebrows get deeper all afternoon," June says, then plants a kiss on the very spot.

"It's the paperwork for the Head Librarian nominations," Aeronwy grumbles. E takes the reading glasses off and rubs eir forehead. "It's due soon."

"Not *so* soon. There's still a few weeks until Winter Solstice."

"Better to get it done—"

June sits down on Aeronwy's lap and leans against em comically.

"Sorry, now you can't, a bigger job has fallen into your lap."

Aeronwy rolls eir eyes but wraps eir arms around June and settles down, smiling. When I first started working here, I was surprised by their casual affection. I can't remember ever seeing my parents act like that.

Chapter Sixteen

The song changes to a sprightly waltz with a full string orchestra. One of those classical pieces everyone recognizes, but no one can name. June sits up straight, a huge smile brightening eir face. Aeronwy winces as eir weight shifts somewhere uncomfortable.

"I haven't heard this in years! Here, this is what you need," June says.

E gets up and pulls Aeronwy to eir feet. They fall easily into a stance for waltzing, hands on each other's waists.

"A dance break?" Aeronwy asks, as they start to step lightly to the music.

Instead of answering, June starts singing. The words ring sweetly through the room as the two of them pick up the pace.

"On dusty mountaintop, high above the plain
There stands my spirit, waiting, watching
For you to come home again."

They step apart, step together, spin in time. Aeronwy twirls June under one arm, June's long blue sweater billowing around em. There's a deep, comfortable ease in the way they mirror one another.

"Come on, love, join me. You're not still shy around Tabby, are you?" June pauses singing to ask.

"It's impossible to be shy with you around," Aeronwy says.

They pull in close, spin out to the sides, both smiling now. When June starts singing again, Aeronwy joins in.

"Taller than the tallest tree, older than the sky
My light will always guide you
Towards truth, away from lies

If you should feel alone and lost and broken
Just look and listen for my voice
My love for you will never lie unspoken."

The harmony sends shivers up my spine that burst into fireworks of joy at the end. Where June's voice is charming and full of character, Aeronwy has the clarity and depth of someone

172

with a lifetime of classical training. The words flow from eir mouth effortlessly, providing a rich counterpoint to June's sweet warbling.

"My child, I know that you are worn and weary
You fear that you won't last this night
But turn your eyes from shadows deep
Find your way home by my light."

If Aeronwy *was* feeling shy, it doesn't matter; they're too caught up in one another to remember I'm here. Their eyes, hands, and smiles are soft, trained on one another. They repeat the last verse, voices louder, steps stronger, even as the music slows. As it fades, Aeronwy hooks an arm around June's back and dips em low for a kiss.

It's like something out of a romance novel. Their love is palpable, and warms my heart. So why do I feel like crying?

I clap as they slowly straighten up. June seems a bit stuck. Seeing em wince, I jump up from my seat to lend a hand, supporting em as e makes eir way back into an upright position.

"Sorry, I forgot we're not quite as young as we once were," Aeronwy says. "We're in good shape, but there's no stopping the march of time."

June exhales in relief and shoots me a look of thanks. "I don't know what you're talking about. I'll be twenty-seven forever," e says.

"Have you been dancing since you were that age?" I ask.

"Just about! They have ballroom dancing at the Illuminator initiation galas, the one they throw to celebrate finishing your apprenticeship. I found out at the last minute." June leans in to whisper conspiratorially. "Had a bit of panic about it."

"Good thing you found someone to teach you," says Aeronwy with a grin.

"They don't do that anymore, though?" I ask, laughing nervously. "I've got two left feet, myself."

"They still do! But here, the basic steps are actually very easy," June says.

E clasps one of my hands and guides the other to eir waist, then looks down at our feet. Under June's rambling instructions, we shuffle around, narrowly avoiding stepping on one another. Ordinarily I'd feel foolish, but June is too earnest. Besides, it's funny how e keeps giving me the instructions backwards.

"This is because I never taught you how to lead," Aeronwy says, after watching us fumble back and forth for ten minutes. "May I?"

June steps away and gestures for Aeronwy to take eir place. E goes over to the stereo and puts the original waltz back on. We'd been trying to dance to something far too fast, a bluegrass song with fiddles going at lightning speed.

Aeronwy is a steady dance partner, in contrast to June's fluttery energy. A boulder around which the stream flows. E takes the lead so that e can guide my steps. I've gotten better at reading eir body language and micro-expressions. Right now, I'd say e's comfortable, affectionate, pleased.

After a few repeats of the song, I can do the basic waltz steps, and even rotate in place a little. At the end of the third play, Aeronwy raises eir arm and I twirl, which makes me feel young and giddy and free.

And sad. The tears threaten again, but I blink them back.

This is how it should have been. How it should be.

The thought flows in on a tide of loss. A longing for something I didn't know I was missing threatens to pull me under, and I have to turn away from Aeronwy and June before they see it on my face.

"I think a dance break was what everyone needed," I say. "I'm going to get a glass of water and get back to work."

"Me too," says Aeronwy.

I hear the pause after e speaks, and I know I didn't hide fast enough. I head quickly to the kitchen, and then slip into the paper room before e can ask what's going on. Luckily, e doesn't follow me.

This time, the methodical, repetitious task of making paper draws me away from my thoughts. The tide recedes for now. I rock the mould and deckle back and forth to distribute the pulp evenly, and it rocks me in return. A boat to ride the waves. A cradle for the child in my heart who needs a soothing hand.

Eventually my arms are too tired to continue. I retreat to the temporary studio space that Amane and I share when we're not working with the older Illuminators. It doesn't have the same personality of the other studios, having been cleansed, cleared, and repainted white after its previous owner retired. Still, we've done our best to make it homey.

Amane's side is decorated in scarves and paintings of brilliant colors, her workstation organized in labeled wooden boxes. She has an altar by the windows, on which are photographs and hand drawn portraits of her ancestors, along with a few of their belongings. A statue of Ledeya watches over them. She's the Gildean deity of rain and something that Amane translates as 'blossoming in adversity, ' though it has more nuance in her language.

My side is messier, but I know where everything is. I used the studio as an excuse to buy new plants, including a solstice cactus that's now covered in bright pink flower buds. In my window area, I set up a small foam mattress with some old blankets and pillows. I sit down on it and stare out into the dark, rainy evening. Now that it's nearly Fir Moon, the sun sets around four thirty. Not my favorite part of Caspora.

Without a distraction, the tide of my thoughts comes rushing back in. Lilja and Oran this morning. The favor Lilja's asked of me. All the ways that could go wrong. The possibility that e might not be leaving for good this time. The possibility that e actually *might* be. How angry that would make Oran. All the times e'd been that angry before. The fact that I can't remember them ever looking at one another the way Aeronwy and June do. We had happy moments as a family, we did. But the dark ones drown them out.

The raindrops on the window slide and swirl into a whirlpool, and I know I'm slipping into a sleep attack. I let myself fall into it.

Once upon a time, there was a wood. And in that wood, there was a cottage. No one quite knew where it lay; there were no maps of this forest, and even the most skilled hunters dared not venture into its deepest groves. Still, everyone knew it was there. Everyone knew that was where the flame witch lived.

Chapter Sixteen

Not since I was a child have I dreamed myself into a story. 'The Red Robes' was a fairytale I skipped if reading late at night; it was too scary. When I reread it recently in *Soil, Sea and Sky*, the book Aeronwy and I are working on, I still felt a quiver in my gut. The opening lines roll through my head like song lyrics.

I find myself standing in the flame witch's wood, the trees dark and menacing. There's no moon tonight. The torch in my hand casts the barest flickering light in a circle around my body. Just as the protagonist does at the beginning of the story.

Toal was the youngest weaver in the village—or e would be, once eir apprenticeship was complete. To pass and open eir own shop, e was required to craft a beautiful cloak for the village elder. On their visit for tea, the elder requested a garment of brilliant red, the color of scarlet sage and poppy beetles and the setting sun during wildfire season.

Toal tried, but none of the dyes e used produced a color that incredible. Not madder, not St. Ifan's wort, not even cochineal had turned out right. The elder was known for having only the highest of standards, and Toal desperately needed eir approval.

And so, e would journey to find the flame witch.

As in the story, I douse my torch to find the trail of glowing mushrooms that lead to the blood witch's cottage. The night air is cold on my skin, the basket of gifts for the witch heavy on my arm. Coyotes howl in the distance.

I find the cottage in a clearing ringed with cypress trees. It's a squat stone building with an arched doorway and a roof of cedar shingles. In the near darkness, they appear the color of dried blood. A fire is lit in the front yard, a cauldron hung over its embers. Behind it stands a dark shape.

Toal approached the flame witch with a pounding heart. It was said that the flame witch could kill with a single breath, lighting you on fire in an instant. The many layers of clothing draped over the figure revealed little, save the glimmer of eyes beneath a red hood. It was the red that Toal sought, and a spark of hope flared within eir chest. Gathering eir courage, e bowed and placed the basket of honey and fine handspun yarns at the witch's feet.

"I know who you are and what you seek," the witch said in a deep, melodious voice. "It is inside my home. Take your cloak and go inside. When you find what you want, you will know the price you must pay."

I do as I'm told, walking up the uneven stone steps on quaking legs. The doorknob is cold iron and studded with garnet. I turn it, my hands sweating, and push.

Beyond lies only darkness. I stand on the threshold and peer inside, my fear of what's beyond gripping me like claws from underneath the bed. As a child, I was afraid of the dark. Also, this isn't right. In the story, the cottage is lit by a roaring hearth, in which e must throw the cloak to magically turn it red as flame. The price is Toal's desire for control, as e must risk destroying the garment by throwing it into the fire.

Before I can step back and shut the door, the world flips. My stomach lurches like a drop on a rollercoaster, and suddenly I'm clinging to the doorframe, dangling above the darkness below. I try to pull myself up, but my hands are sweaty and slipping.

I fall.

I wake up.

I'm still dreaming.

I must be, because I'm in the mythical redwood cathedral again, the one I discovered while in the main ritual hall three moons ago. The treetops disappear into the clouds, the comforting golden sunshine I remember gone now. Shifting, iridescent fog covers the forest floor. The trees stand silent.

In the tree nearest to me, there is a door. On the door, a book is carved. On the book, a seven-pointed star. It takes me a moment to place, but it looks exactly like the doors to the Head Librarian's office. I approach it slowly, studying it, and then raise a hand to knock.

As my knuckles touch the wood, I wake again. This time it's for real. I know because I'm lying on my side, and my hip hurts. My eyes are crusted with sleep sand, which I rub out before sitting up. The lights are dim, and it's still dark outside.

Chapter Sixteen

There's no way to tell how much time has passed, as my phone is dead. I forgot my charger this morning. I hope Rhiannon isn't too worried.

A shifting noise to my left jolts me back into reality. After the events of the day, my startle reflex is on high, and I nearly jump out of my skin. My whole body is electrified and ready to run as I swivel around towards the sound.

"It's all right, Tabby, it's just me."

Aeronwy is seated on the little chair beside Amane's altar, which is far too small. Knees drawn up around eir ears, e looks ridiculous enough to halt my panic. I let out a sigh of relief before the prickling heat of embarrassment creeps into my face.

"What, um, why—"

"I was concerned. You seemed to be having a difficult time earlier," e says, calmly and without judgment. The red leather sketchbook lies open in eir lap, a pencil still in hand. The end of the pencil is chewed to bits, a habit I'd *never* associate with Aeronwy if e didn't then bite on it right in front of me.

I'm not sure how to respond. Aeronwy takes this as an opportunity to elaborate.

"You aren't the only one who watches people closely to see how they're feeling. I attempted to knock on the door to check on you, and when you didn't answer, I came in. I suspected you'd had one of your sleeping spells and couldn't wake you. Through Amane, I got to your partner Rhiannon. I promised I would keep an eye on you until e got off work. E said you had a rough morning," e says.

"Yes," I say. I fiddle with a loose thread on my skirt. The lace on the edge is coming undone. Finding details to focus on keeps the tide at bay. I can feel it behind my eyes, welling up.

A tense silence fills the room, and then Aeronwy says, "If you need to talk to someone, I'm here for you. Even if you only want to talk about this garden. I've been picking it up whenever you dream near me, and I believe it's yours."

Aeronwy holds up the sketchbook, which is full of colored pencil drawings of flowers. I'd recognize them anywhere, right down to the last pistil and petal.

"It is," I say, voice wavering, and then the dam breaks.

After crying for a long time, I explain the situation with my parents. Not just the way they put me in the middle of their current fight, but the long history of it as well. I explain that the dream garden is likely my heartscape. How it was my sanctuary until I moved out of my parents' house to go to college. Away from them, I hadn't needed it as much, and my astral tech studies left me too exhausted to dreamwalk.

"What inspired you to find it again?" Aeronwy asks.

"It was actually… submitting my application for this apprenticeship," I say. "When I was going through my portfolio to pick samples to send, I noticed how many of them involved flowers. I found old journals I'd made that mentioned the garden. I got curious. It just felt like… time to return."

"Do you still want to find it?"

"More than anything. I don't know why. It just, it feels important," I say.

"I think it's important, too. If you're going to bind Illuminated books, you need to know yourself very deeply. The final step requires that you embrace the very core of yourself, including the shadow parts, or it will fail," Aeronwy tells me.

"Oh, I see."

"More importantly, you deserve to be happy and free from all this distress," Aeronwy continues, "as much as that's possible. Can I ask you a personal question, Tabby?"

"Yes," I say, laughing because I've already poured my heart out in the most personal way. I feel touched by Aeronwy's concern for my happiness, and intrigued by the way e speaks as if e knows what I'm going through.

"Do you have a therapist?"

I'm not sure what I was expecting, but that wasn't it. "Not right now. I have in the past, but I reached a place where it didn't feel like I needed to go anymore. At least at the time," I explain.

"Do you think it would help if you returned now?"

"Is it… normal to do that? Go in and out of therapy?"

"If it would help you now, that's all the reason you need. I hadn't been in therapy for over a decade, but with Rose passing, I needed more help than June and the rest of our family could give me," Aeronwy says, "so I went. I'm still going. It was a good decision. I know, even when you know from experience that it helps, sometimes you question whether it will again."

Having regular therapy sessions would give me an outlet so I don't dump everything on Rhee, or on Aeronwy, for that matter. Both of them are offering support, but I never want to do what Lilja does to me. I never want to drown them in my deepest woes without considering what they can carry.

"I'll call sometime this week to make an appointment. And, um, I'm sorry about Rose, I can't imagine what it'd be like to lose someone you've known so long," I say.

Aeronwy sighs and spins the chewed-up pencil between eir fingers. "Rose was one of the most important people in my life. E gave me the trust and guidance I should have had from a parent, but never got. I didn't have a pleasant childhood, either, as it were. Those wounds run deep. You can't solve them alone."

For a moment, I feel only terror at the looming specter of facing my childhood trauma—or even acknowledging that's what it was—but then I understand what Aeronwy's implying. That I'm not alone. That e *knows* how huge that shadow is, and is willing to help me through it. Like Rose did for em.

I stare into the rain, at the dark sky and even darker shadow of the mountains. "Does it ever go away? All of it?"

"No. We can't be what we would have been, if these things never happened to us," Aeronwy says. E traces the end of the pencil over one of the flower drawings in the sketchbook. "But a garden can still bloom where fire has ravaged."

RHIANNON

"Rhiannon, can I speak with you for a moment?"

Mairead catches me just as I'm handing off a box of old film stills to a patron. I remind them to bring it back to me when they're done and turn to face my boss. 'Can I speak with you' rarely turns out well in the context of work and relationships.

"What's up?" I say, folding my arms to hide my suddenly sweaty palms.

"Come with me."

We head to the Head Archivist's office. I settle into the hard-backed chair with dread in my stomach. Mairead and I have been getting along so well—what could possibly have gone wrong?

Mairead crosses eir legs and folds eir hands together primly. Eir expression reminds me of my elementary school teachers when I disappointed them. You'd be surprised how much disappointment you face as a child genius. For all the adulation, you're still a child. And people's standards are high. Failure is part of the parcel.

That doesn't even cover what happens when you grow up and become, by all standards, a very average adult.

"So, you still haven't found the Illuminated copy of *The Founding*," e says.

"I haven't figured out a surefire way to get it yet," I say.

"I thought you had an in with your partner. The one who's Aeronwy's apprentice?" Mairead asks, eyebrow raised.

"I decided I don't want to involve Tabby. Office politics and all. We know Aeronwy doesn't like you. Tabby doesn't need to be mixed up in that," I say.

Mairead sighs, eyes dropping to the floor. My stomach drops, as well. I *hate* disappointing people.

"Can't you get Circulation or the administration involved?" I ask. "Make a formal complaint?"

"We don't have any hard evidence. Just your visions. I doubt that would go anywhere, and then the Stargroves would know we know about it," Mairead argues. "They're not going to give it up that easily if they've been hiding it for thirty years."

"You see my problem, then," I say.

Mairead side-eyes me. "Do you remember a little while ago, we had a conversation about how you need to prove you're worthy of being Assistant Head by challenging yourself? When I said that, I meant *overcoming* those challenges. We promised Rhys we'd have it for the exhibit. You don't want to back down on that promise, do you?"

No," I say, miserably. I remember that conversation, all right. *I'd hate for you to find out you've already hit your peak, and things are only downhill from here.*

"I didn't think so. I don't care how it happens, just find a way to get the book. Otherwise I might have to consider other candidates for your position."

I clutch the chair harder. I feel like I'm fourteen again, sitting in my first college class and feeling ashamed that I answered the professor's question wrong. Like everything rests on the edge of a knife, and one wrong step will sever me from my dreams forever.

"But," Mairead continues, voice lightening, "if you do find it, you'll be rewarded in ways you haven't even imagined."

I raise my head slightly. "What do you mean?"

"I haven't told anyone this yet. You're the first," Mairead says with a conspiratorial grin, "but I'm going to run for Head Librarian. And I'm going to win. When I do, I'll promote you to Head Archivist. You'll be the youngest person to hold the position in three hundred years. I checked."

I should feel relieved, but instead the pressure intensifies. On one edge of the knife: failure. On the other: everything I've ever wanted in my career. It's up to me to decide which way I fall.

***

I put my plan in action on the last day of Cedar Moon, during a party in the Bindery. Aeronwy and Amane's birthdays are only two days—and thirty-six years—apart, and today is the day in between. Tabby and I ride the elevator all the way up to the top of the Spire. My spirits rise as we do, knowing I might actually succeed in securing *The Founding* today.

We step off the creaky elevator and head down the hallway. A paper banner hangs over the common area declaring 'Happy Solar Return! ' in beautiful, curling script. The decor is cozy and modern, and there's cheerful music playing.

The only other guest to arrive before us is the Caoimhen nun who helped Tabby at Rose's funeral. Siobhan Heartseeker is an energy healer in the Library infirmary, and I've been in eir care plenty of times myself. Today e's dressed all in gold, eir headscarf braided and wrapped in a complicated pattern.

I guess e's close with Aeronwy because they look comfortable sitting together on the couch. Siobhan has eir bare feet propped up in Aeronwy's lap. The latter is wearing a thick cream-colored turtleneck sweater and matching slacks, which is a gutsy move for anyone who works around so much ink. Even though this is eir birthday party, e's frowning.

In the background, June flutters around in a sweatshirt and jeans, setting out plates of food and listing off important tasks to make sure they've been done.

"Decorations?"

"Done," says Siobhan, who is scrolling through eir phone without paying close attention.

"Gifts?"

"Done."

"Food?"

Siobhan glances at the table. "Everything but the cake."

"Done!" I proclaim, holding up the one Tabby and I baked as we enter their view.

Aeronwy claps slowly. "Bravo, a well-timed entrance if there ever was one. Now all we require is the guest of honor. Usually she's early to everything."

"Oh, she was already here, helping me set up. I sent her on an 'errand' to stop her from doing all the work," June says, flopping down over the back of the couch, so that eir arms are around Aeronwy's shoulders. "Also, it's your birthday, too."

"I thought we were only going to celebrate milestone birthdays for me from now on," Aeronwy grumbles, arms crossed.

"That was before Amane showed up. Now we might as well," June says.

E kisses Aeronwy on the cheek and then walks around to sit snuggly between em and Siobhan on the couch. June pats Siobhan's bare foot, and Siobhan shoots em a grin, wiggling eir painted toes. The scene reminds me of my parents, who tend to accumulate in cuddle piles whenever they're not herding kids or cousins or grandparents around the house.

I turn away and wander around the Bindery common room, scrutinizing the door carvings, the stained glass, the wallpaper, everything. I wonder where the book is hidden. Behind a panel in the wall? Beneath a floorboard? Tucked up under the eaves of the glass dome above? I feel eyes on me and turn to see Aeronwy watching.

Hands on hips, I stare back and say, "So, how old *are* you?"

"Sixty-two," says Aeronwy.

I purse my lips. "I didn't think you'd answer that."

"Why not?" The look on eir face is completely deadpan. It's not going to be easy getting secrets out of this one.

"Well, y'know, some people are sensitive about that kinda thing."

"Which is why you so *boldly* asked," says Aeronwy.

We might not know each other, but Aeronwy's already got me pinned. I suppose I can respect that.

"Rhee just likes to joke around," Tabby interjects. There's no real animosity in our words, but I'm sure Tabby wants us to get along. I might need to tell em this is what getting along looks like when you're both snarky bastards.

"It's perfectly fine. I can take a joke," Aeronwy says.

June and Siobhan act as if this is the funniest thing they've heard all week. Laughing, Siobhan shoves Aeronwy playfully with one foot while June buries eir face in Aeronwy's shoulder to muffle the giggles. Tabby claps a hand over eir mouth but can't hold back the laughs and is soon rolling around like the others.

I haven't heard Tabby laugh much since the recent shit with eir parents. One point for Aeronwy.

"Hey, I'm back!" Amane's voice rings out from the hallway. Her heels clack on the wooden floor and then come to a halt as she sees everyone laughing, bewilderment splashed across her face. "What did I miss? Am I late?"

"You can't be late to your own party," Aeronwy says.

Amane sticks her bottom lip out. "It's your party, too!"

"So I'm told."

Amane joins the rest of the group, taking the remaining armchair and sitting with her legs folded up in it. She explains that June sent her to retrieve a friend from the kitchens, but that her quest was unsuccessful. Someone put in an order wrong, and the Library received a hundred pounds of red beets, instead of ten. Then someone spilled a vat of soup. Meenah, the Library's Head Chef, was going to have to sit this one out.

"She sends her love, though, and *that*," Amane says, pointing to a small, beautiful golden cake covered with pistachios and candied rose petals. I can smell the saffron from here. The pumpkin cake Tabby and I made pales in comparison.

"All those beets. We're going to be eating borscht for weeks," Siobhan says mournfully.

"Everyone's poop will be so red," I add, in a thoughtful tone of voice. "They might need to send out an email about that so no one gets alarmed."

That sets everyone to laughing again, even Aeronwy this time. That's one point for me. Two if arriving with the cake counts. I snicker at my own work and go sit on the arm of Tabby's chair, bouncing my leg impatiently. It's hard for me to resist showing off for a good crowd, even though all I can think about is that book.

Aeronwy's gold eyes settle on me, and e says, "I'm pleased you could join us, Rhiannon. Strange how we can work in the same place for so many years, but hardly know each other. Except for what we've heard about you from Tabby."

"All good things, I hope," I say, prodding Tabby with my elbow.

Tabby turns pink and says proudly, "Nothing but! I was just telling June the other day about all your work digitizing the old photographs and etchings in the Archives. It's an incredible database, I used it all the time in university."

"I'm glad someone down there is embracing technology," June says.

"No doubt that's how you ascended to Assistant Head so quickly," says Aeronwy, and I can hear the challenge in eir voice.

"Maybe it is," I say.

The party gets lively soon enough, as more guests fill the room. Most of them come and go, but the core group remains. Siobhan is loud and bawdy, and June has a story and a half for every topic that comes up, which Aeronwy peppers with dry commentary. Amane cackles at all their jokes, especially the dirty ones Siobhan cracks. Anyone who thinks being a nun is about being prim and proper has never met one of Caoimhe's devotees.

Tabby slips into eir usual habits, making sure everyone has had something to eat and fetching more tea and coffee from the kitchen. I take the opportunity to pull Aeronwy aside and ask about the book.

"Hey, so, I've got something to ask you," I say, standing as tall as possible. I'm used to looking up at Tabby, but Aeronwy is much more intimidating.

"Yes?" e asks.

"I'll just get to the point," I say. "There's a book I'm looking for, and I think you have it. The original Illuminated copy of *The Founding* by Calliope Everberry. It was reported missing years ago, but I had a vision in which you decided to hide it for some reason. What's the deal?"

Without blinking, Aeronwy replies, "I'm afraid I don't know what you're talking about."

"Are you sure? I promise I won't tell anyone whatever the big secret is. But I promised to find it for an exhibit at the National History Museum. If you're trying to keep it safe or whatever, it'll be behind glass and all locked up with sensors there," I say, putting my hands on my hips.

Aeronwy's face remains impassive. Damn, but e's good at this.

"I know you and Mairead don't get along, but you can trust *me*. I'll take care of it. I'll even smuggle it back to you if you want," I insist.

Aeronwy shrugs. "Unfortunately, I can't help you. Rose reported that book missing, as you said, and it hasn't been seen since. Likely another casualty of the fire."

With that, e walks away to join another conversation. E didn't even bother to deny the damning evidence of my vision. Excellent poker face or not, I know I'm being lied to. My hopes dashed, I grow frustrated instead, and then angry. What else has e been lying about? Amane told me that Mairead accused Aeronwy of starting the '86 fire, which of course e denied. What if it had been a cover-up for hiding *The Founding* that got out of control?

I sulk over to Amane, who brightens and says, "Rhee! This is your first time in the Bindery, right? Do you want a tour while you're here?"

Her enthusiasm softens my bad mood. "*You* wanna give me a tour, don't you?"

She nods vigorously.

Amane takes me on a rambling tour through each of the Bindery's rooms, starting with the ones near the elevator and moving counterclockwise. The architecture is fascinating, and many of the presses and other equipment are over a hundred years old. With the advent of computers, some people have questioned the need to continue funding such an archaic craft, but I see the value and history etched into every corner.

Eventually, we reach June's studio. It's everything I'd expect: cheery, neat, and calming. June is seated at a large tapestry loom by the window, working on a piece patterned with ginkgo leaves.

"Oh, sorry, we didn't know anyone was in here!" Amane says.

June turns and beckons to us. E pulls off a pair of large headphones and says, "It's no trouble. I just needed a break from the crowd. Come on in."

We do. As we near the loom, I spy the headphones and realize they aren't connected to anything. Not for music, then, but noise reduction. There are spell sigils painted on the earpieces. June notices me looking.

"I get overwhelmed by too much noise. I'm very clairaudient, and the psychic chatter in a room full of very psychic people only makes it worse," e explains.

"I get it," I say, "my retrocognition is what gets me far at work, but it also gives me hella migraines."

"That's what got you interested in working in the Archives, right?" Amane asks.

"Oh yeah, for sure. I wanted to understand what it was I kept Seeing when I touched objects with a history. I realized during college that my visions really helped with cataloging and finding and stuff like that, so I became an archivist," I say.

June nods sagely. "Your visions are an incredible resource, I'm sure. Sounds like you're doing wonderful work down there."

"Thanks," I say, and an idea strikes me. I work to keep my voice casual. "You know, it's funny. Recently I've been looking for an Illuminated book called *The Founding,* the original of which has been missing for—well, quite a while, and I had a vision that, ah, suggested it might still be up here somewhere. You don't happen to know anything about that, do you?"

A look of surprise crosses June's face, which is then carefully made blank. E starts fiddling with a ring on eir hand.

"Oh, really?"

E knows. E definitely knows where it is. June is not as good at subterfuge as eir spouse.

Amane jumps in. "Do you, June? *The Founding* was written and bound by Calliope Everberry, who created the first Threadbound Oracle! It'd be so amazing if I could see more of eir original work in person!"

"I don't see why someone wouldn't have returned it to the Archives if it was up here for that long," June says, but e looks away while e says it, and fiddles even more with the ring. "It would have to be lost somewhere."

"Or hidden," I say. "The vision I had suggested there was something, um, different about the book. I understand if that part has to be kept secret, but Dr. Rhys Elkspinner wants it for the National History Museum, and I promised I would find it. Have you met Dr. Elkspinner? Or read eir books?"

"Hmm," says June. "I have. Rhys is a good person, it's just..."

"Please?" Amane says, clasping her hands and batting her eyelashes. "Rhee's my friend. You can trust em with this. I promise."

June's worried look softens. With a sigh, e throws up eir hands. "I suppose a *look* can't hurt, since you obviously already know it's here," e says. "We were going to tell Amane and Tabby eventually. I'm sorry, Rhiannon, I can't let it leave the Bindery, no matter who wants it. But I hope this satisfies your curiosity."

With that, e turns and walks over to the giant green loveseat by the windows. E sets aside the mountain of blankets and pillows on it, then the seat cushion, revealing a wooden panel base. June licks a finger and then draws a sigil on the panel. I can't feel the resulting discharge of magical energy, but everyone's hair stands on end, so it must be a strong one. On the underside is a complex charm woven with red thread.

In the compartment beneath, there's a book.

June takes it out and lays it on a clean sheet of paper on the workbench. Amane *oohs* in reverence, voicing my thoughts. It's an enormous book, several inches thick and over a foot tall, but there's something oddly weightless about it. I'd expect a book this old and large to have its own field of gravity. The covers are plain for an Illuminated text, brown leather with *The Founding* and *Calliope Everberry* stamped in simple gold letters. No ornamentation of any kind, save the raised cords on the spine.

I open it gently. My heart is beating so loud I'm afraid the others will hear it. So I clear my throat and start reading the title page aloud on Old Casporan. Amane raises an eyebrow and June nods appraisingly.

"That's right, Tabby did say you were an expert on past Casporan languages," e says when I pause to turn the page. "Did you ever study under Dr. Shellsong at CCU? E wrote the translation that Rose Illuminated back in the 80s. The good doctor commissioned the copy emself, wanted it to look just like the original, which is how it ended up here in the first place, so Rose could reference it."

"No, but I've read that translation, and I heard stories about em. Dr. Shellsong was a legend in the department."

I want to ask about what Rose did with the book while it was in eir care, how e noticed something was off, but a cheer goes up in the common room. A loud voice issues a dramatic proclamation I can't make out, followed by roaring laughter.

"Oh, Meenah's here after all," June says brightly. E glances back and forth between Amane and I. "Can I trust you two to return the book to its hiding place?"

"Of course!" Amane says.

"Of course," June repeats, and then leaves us alone in the studio.

Amane turns back to the book, starting up a discussion about the differences in narrative between *The Founding* and *The Stories We Sing,* asking me which events are backed up by scholarship and which were invented by the authors. Normally I'd be thrilled to gush about my topic of expertise, but instead I feel distracted and hollow. I keep thinking about how the book I've been searching for all these weeks is *right here, in my hands,* and I can't have it.

You can, though. This is your opportunity, a little voice says in the back of my mind. It sounds suspiciously like Mairead.

All my anger, frustration, and fear bubbles up inside, threating to overflow. Instead of listening to Amane's chatter, I watch scenes of possible futures in my head. Scenes where I don't bring Mairead the book and lose my promotion, humiliated in front of the entire department and unable to keep my promise to Dr. Elkspinner about the exhibit. Where I lose all credibility and never get anything published. Alternately, scenes where I *do* deliver the book, and all my dreams come true. Where whatever we discover about its secrets benefits the entire library and brings me the power to make momentous change. And because of that, Amane, Tabby, and the Stargroves forgive me for what I had to do to get it.

I know which of those two futures I prefer.

When Amane says she wants to rejoin the party, I tell her to go on ahead. I'll put the book back in its hiding spot and be with her in a minute. She agrees so readily that her trust feels like a dagger in my chest. I grin through the pain and watch her leave the room with my toes tapping impatiently.

Once I'm sure she's gone, I wrap *The Founding* in a sheath of paper to protect it and grab a blanket from the loveseat nearby. I throw it over my shoulders, wearing it like a cloak to disguise the book clasped to my chest beneath. Holding my breath, I peek out through the studio door, watching the ebb and flow of the crowd until I'm sure I can get to my messenger bag by the couch without being stopped. Luckily, everyone is distracted by the extra food Meenah brought up from the Library kitchens.

I manage to tiptoe across the room and slide the book into my bag, wincing as the paper around it rustles, before someone says my name.

"Rhee!" Tabby says, coming up behind me. I quickly snap my bag shut and spin around, clutching the blanket. "I saved you some of the mini quiches Meenah made. I know how much you like eggs with stuff in them. This one is goat cheese and peppers."

I look down at the little party plate in eir hands, my stomach twisting. "Thanks, but, I'm actually pretty full. You can have them."

Tabby's face falls. E eyes the blanket I'm wearing. "Are you sure? Are you feeling all right?"

"I'm *fine,*" I say, with more emphasis than necessary. I pull a ridiculous face that makes Tabby laugh. "Just full and cold. Or, I was cold, but now I'm warm thanks to this." I pat the blanket. I'm actually dripping with sweat right now, but it's not the blanket's fault. It's the fear.

"Okay, then," e says. "I just want you to have fun. I'm glad you finally got to come up here for a visit."

"Yeah, me too," I say, "me, too."

AMANE

"Tell me what you've seen."

Daryn sat across from Isylwyn at the table, a simple meal spread before them. Spruce tip tea lent a fresh fragrance to the air, which was damp with the rains of spring. Daryn spread huckleberry preserves on a salal cake and took a bite, savoring the taste and Isylwyn's impatience.

"The abbey is a wonderful place. Clean, airy, full of interesting people. The nuns are gracious, even when they bicker about chores and whose cooking is best," Daryn said, in between bites of cake and sips of tea. "They clearly love their work, and it shows in their manuscripts. I showed them a few new ink recipes, and they were so excited."

Isylwyn tapped a finger on the table. E hadn't touched any of the food, or even the vessel of clear spring water. "You said as much in your letters. But what did you discover that you couldn't write to me of? What is Starsower doing up there in that tower?"

"Making books," said Daryn.

Isylwyn's eyes narrowed. "And what is e teaching you?"

"Recently, I've been learning to use a spinning wheel," Daryn replied cheerfully. "I used a hand spindle back home, although with my station, I wasn't required to do it often. We used hemp, but Eirlys uses flax. E can spin thread so fine it's transparent like spider silk. The secret is, you tell it stories while you spin."

"I didn't send you to spin away the idle hours. I sent you to discover useful information. Threats. I know from other sources that Starsower has plans which rival my own. Surely, you've

192

infiltrated eir good graces enough to learn something, cousin. I know how easily people trust you," Isylwyn said.

Daryn spread preserves on another cake. It was true, people did trust em easily. Eirlys had been no exception, though e knew from the beginning that Daryn was a spy. The trouble was, Daryn was quite taken with Eirlys, and with eir message. The Readerist philosophy that the Author was reading to them the story of life, rather than controlling them with it, resonated. Eirlys was beautiful, skilled, and humble. It had not taken Daryn long to fall in love.

Isylwyn reached across the table and laid a hand on Daryn's arm. "Need I remind you how I took you in after your village perished in the eruption? I have done much for you, my dear Daryn, though my council is wary of having a follower of Cináed in our midst. Without me, you would have been turned to the streets as a child."

Isylwyn's voice was sweet, but eir grip was painful.

"I told you, e's making books," Daryn said.

"What kind of books?"

"Everlasting books," Daryn replied, voice tightening as Isylwyn's hand did. "Books which, though still vulnerable to water and flame, will never crumble with age."

"And has e succeeded?"

"Not yet, but e will."

A loud rustle startles me out of my reading trance. June pulls my stack of paper from the press and sets it on the workbench. I put *The Stories We Sing* aside and join em in examining it. The cockles and warping from the drying process are gone, each sheet now flat. I run a hand over one, feeling its rough texture. I made paper in university, but never in these quantities or from such raw ingredients. The results are different than what I'm used to.

"Here it is," June says. "If we need more later, we'll make some, but this should be sufficient for now."

I fidget with my acrylic nails. One of them is coming loose. "Do you think it's good enough?" I ask.

"You tell me. What do you think of your work?" June replies.

"Well," I say, eyes roaming over the stack, "it's a bit thicker than I wanted, and not entirely uniform. The petal pieces could be more evenly distributed. The texture is nice, but will you be able to write on it easily?"

June picks up a sheet and studies it. "I suspect you've heard this before, but you're a bit of a perfectionist, aren't you? Especially with your craft."

I shake my head. "I'm not a perfectionist, I just hold myself to high standards."

"Sometimes those are one in the same," June says with a laugh. E sorts through more sheets. "I think these are beautiful. They have a lovely weight. The scattered petals will create a lot of happy accidents. You shouldn't be so hard on yourself. Illuminated books aren't meant to be entirely uniform, like a mass-produced tome. The irregularities are what turn them into art."

"Even if that's true, there's always room for improvement," I say.

June nods. "I'll be sure to guide you in those efforts. In fact, I already see a difference between your first attempts and your most recent ones. I'd encourage you to be proud of what you made, even if in your improvement you see mistakes now."

"Okay, I'll try," I say, even though it doesn't make sense to me. How can I be proud and recognize flaws at the same time? How can I be proud and still desire growth? My sisters and mothers taught me from an early age never to be satisfied as motivation to keep moving forward.

"Good." June tucks the stack away in a drawer and retreats to the loveseat. "Now, let's talk about ink. What does the Ace of Ink stand for in your Threadbound Oracle?"

"The Ace of Ink is the Pigment card," I say, joining em. I drape myself in one of the many blankets there. "It's about experimentation, alchemy, and the processes we use to get what we want."

"How appropriate. As you've seen, we have dozens of powdered pigments in the storeroom. However, we're going to make our own this time. It's a chemical process that can't be fully controlled and varies based on the materials. There will be a lot of trial, error, and transformation. Are you ready for that?" June asks.

Having known June for a few moons now, I know e's not just talking about ink. I set my jaw in determination.

"I'm ready."

***

The Library is closed to patrons two days before Winter Solstice, but every Librarian and staff member is required to show up for a meeting. The seating is arranged by department. Ours is the smallest by far, just the four of us behind the priority seating for people with disabilities. Siobhan, in a wheelchair today, turns and waggles eir fingers in our direction. E's one of few people I recognize out of hundreds. Working in the Bindery can be isolating at times.

I'm on the end of our row, with June and Aeronwy in the middle and Tabby sitting on the other end. The Stargroves have been holding each other's hands tightly all morning. Aeronwy doesn't look nervous to me, sitting up straight as a board in eir seat and staring intently at the stage, but Tabby says it's true. June keeps humming and tapping out rhythms to songs with eir free hand. Whenever e smiles, there's a little twitch first, as if e's having trouble getting it going.

Also, the cardigan e's wearing is inside out. I can't decide if I should tell em or just leave it alone.

The meeting starts out with a summary of significant changes at the Library since the Summer Solstice. This includes a moment of silence for Rose's death, as well as an announcement about Tabby and I being hired. We stand up when our names are called, to polite applause. Rhiannon does the same when eir promotion is mentioned. The wider Library body claps less for em than they did for us, but Rhiannon's own department makes a ruckus, led by Mairead.

A few minutes later, my phone vibrates with a text.

RHEE: gods that was embarrassing

> **ME:** haha, you don't like applause and attention?

> **RHEE:** I do when I feel like I deserve it

> **ME:** huh? Don't be ridiculous, of course you deserve it. You earned that promotion.

> **RHEE:** right
> **RHEE:** hey, did you ever think more about those cards Calliope's spirit gave me when we first met?
> **RHEE:** you know, when you got possessed and all

I type a response, but don't get to hit send. I catch Aeronwy side-eyeing me and put my phone away instead. A new Librarian in a sharp blue suit takes the stage. The Casporan Sign Language interpreter who's been translating the meeting follows, speaking into the microphone while the Librarian signs.

"Good morning, I'm Marion Dreamcloud, head of Human Resources," Marion signs, and the translator says. "Today I'm honored to bring you the names of our nominees for the position of Head Librarian. Catrina Rosefall bore the mantle for over thirty years and left our Library richer for it. Now the mantle must pass to another."

Beside me, June draws in a sharp breath. Aeronwy puts an arm around eir shoulders. The auditorium goes silent all at once, as if someone muted the sound on a video.

"Our astrological department has informed me that the next Summer Solstice will be the date of the Head Librarian Trials. This has left us in a considerable gap without a Head Librarian, but such are the instructions left to us by the Founders: the door will only open on this day. In any case, it gives us plenty of time to consider our choices, as nominees are required to collect a number of signatures in their favor to proceed to the Trials," Marion continues.

Trials? I assumed the Head Librarian would be elected democratically, by vote. The signature gathering seems to cover that part, but the rest sounds… magical. *The door will only open on this day.* What door?

"The full rules for signature gathering and candidacy can be found on the internal Library Astranet. Print, audio, and Braille copies may also be obtained from myself in Human Resources, by anyone who wishes to read them. Copies have already been forwarded to the nominees, who have volunteered themselves for the position. The nominees for the 111th Head Librarian of the Eternal Library are as follows. Please stand when you hear your name called, if you are able."

There is a sound in the auditorium now: the sound of four hundred people collectively holding their breath. I reach over and give June's free hand a reassuring squeeze.

"Nominee number one: Magistrix Aeronwy Stargrove, Master Illuminator, Library employee for forty-four years," Marion says, "Flamekeeper in the Modern Cináedite tradition."

Aeronwy stands up, and a spotlight swings from the rafters to illuminate em. E looks about seven feet tall, head held high as e raises one elegant hand to the rest of the auditorium. The resulting applause is thunderous, although it's accompanied by a strong undercurrent of murmurs. I wonder if it has to do with Mairead's old accusation that Aeronwy started the '86 fire.

"Nominee number two: Magistrix Juniper Stargrove, Master Illuminator, Library employee for forty years, and thread witch."

The spotlight moves as June stands up, wobbling a little and waving to equally loud applause. I'm contributing to that of course. The clapping goes on for a while, until the interpreter asks people to be quiet. June is smiling so broadly that eir eyes are crinkled shut, and e pauses to wipe a tear from one of them.

I sneak my phone back out now that the interesting part is over and send my drafted response to Rhiannon.

> **ME:** Yeah, I did, actually. I think it was a warning, but…for something that already happened, now, sorry!!

> **ME:** You had The Seer, The Author, The
> Book, and The End. I think it was a message
> about how your and Mairead's search (you're
> The Seer and The Author respectively) for The
> Founding would end abruptly. You got to see
> it, but you didn't get a hold of it.
> **ME:** Does that make sense?

"Final nominee, number three," Marion says, the interpreter's voice ringing out across the once-again silent auditorium, "Authorist High Priestex Mairead Moonsea, Head Archivist, Library employee for thirty-seven years, and paper witch."

The audience's response is similar to Aeronwy's: loud, but with murmuring. The Archival department is the loudest, of course, some of them going as far as to leap from their seats and cheer with their arms raised. Mairead stands gracefully, waving a hand at them to be seated, and bows to the rest of the auditorium. Beside em, caught in the spotlight's glare, Rhiannon claps half-heartedly, slumped down as far in eir seat as possible.

The meeting moves on, but no one around me is paying attention. The Stargroves have their heads together, whispering fiercely. June has eir arms crossed uncomfortably, and Aeronwy is making sharp gestures, but I can't hear what they're saying. Tabby is frowning at eir phone and typing up a storm, I assume sending texts to Rhiannon. I do the same.

> **ME:** Oh my gods, did you know Mairead was
> going to run, too?

> **RHEE:** yeah, I was gonna tell y'all, but I've
> been kinda distracted with work
> **RHEE:** not like it would have changed
> anything, knowing in advance

> **ME:** everybody is upset over here

> **RHEE:** i bet

After the meeting, everyone packs into the main cafeteria, discussing the news. On our way there, dozens of people stop us to express their support. June thanks them all with a sweet smile and hugs, but Aeronwy is getting testy, and it shows. Tabby starts running interference on eir behalf, for which e looks grateful.

The cafeteria buzzes like a wasp nest. Luckily, we find a table on one of the balconies, in a corner near an exit. I look around for Rhiannon, but I can't find em anywhere, even with the purple hair.

> **ME:** Are you going to come sit with us?
>
> **RHEE:** I can't, the HL thing is a big deal, they expect me to celebrate
>
> **ME:** but you're celebrating with the wrong people, for the wrong person! Don't you think June would be a better HL than Mairead
>
> **RHEE:** yeah, but i can't tell THEM that
> **RHEE:** ugh i hate Library politics SO MUCH since i got promoted

I glance up at Tabby, who's returning from the line with our trays of food balanced two on each arm. We all got the cod fillet with preserved lemon rice and green bean salad, except Aeronwy, who has what smells like a spicy tofu stew. I must have missed that option on the RSVP form.

Tabby sets the food down, but nobody starts eating. Aeronwy stares angrily into the distance, arms crossed. Tabby watches em while biting on one thumbnail. June stirs rice around with eir fork but doesn't take a bite. If I just start digging in, they might think I'm being insensitive. So I wait. And wait. And wait.

But I'm too hungry, and I can't take the tension.

"So, what exactly is the deal with Mairead? Do you think e's going to bring up the fire thing again? Are you worried about signatures?" I ask, turning to Aeronwy.

Aeronwy is methodically shredding the paper napkin that came with the meal into long strips, and then twisting them together. It's the first time I've seen em fidget. Tabby glances between the two of us with eir hands folded in eir lap, and chews on eir bottom lip.

"That was my original concern, before I knew e would be a candidate. Now, there's a larger problem," Aeronwy says.

"Which is what?"

"Mairead is a staunch, fundamental Authorist. Rose and Opaline worked their entire lives to remove traces of the Authorist theocracy from the Library after the Revolution. As Head Librarian, Mairead could undo much of that," e replies.

"How much power does the Head Librarian have, though? I thought it was more of a ceremonial role these days." I say.

"The Head Librarian speaks for the books, when it comes to changing Library policies, or creating new ones. There are far more books in the Library than Librarians or staff. Ideally, the Head Librarian acts only as representative on the books' behalf, listening for their opinions and conveying them," Aeronwy explains, "however, there is some choice in what messages are passed along. Which books are listened to. The Head Librarian's views ultimately color the way the books' vote is registered."

"Besides, Mairead is a manipulative, compulsive liar," June says.

Tabby and I look at em in shock. I can't remember ever hearing June say a negative word about anybody. Usually e's the first to chime in with someone's better qualities. To hear such a plain accusation from eir mouth is startling.

Aeronwy frowns, but June crosses eir arms and says, "It's true! That's why you stopped being friends. Then you almost *died* saving the Library from the fire, and what does Mairead do? Wage a campaign of misinformation to get revenge and have you fired."

"Wait, you *stopped* the '86 fire?" I say. "You didn't mention that during the reading I did for you."

"I don't like to take credit for it," Aeronwy says. "That's not the way of Flamekeeping."

"But wouldn't it be easier to get signatures for your Head Librarian petition if you did?" I ask, shocked that e would keep such a thing secret. If it were me, I'd be shouting it from the rooftops.

"You would," says June pointedly.

Aeronwy sighs. "That the books know is enough for me, but fine. I will remind everyone of the fact."

"Can I ask what happened between you and Mairead?" Tabby says.

"Mairead was my first new family member at a time when I had no one," Aeronwy says. "We were incredibly close for about seven years. It was an intense, tempestuous relationship, but I was used to such things from my upbringing. Then, I went to therapy and did the shadow work necessitated by my Illumination apprenticeship. I learned what healthy relationships could look like when I met Siobhan, and June, and Rose."

June scoots over and slides an arm around Aeronwy's waist, listening sympathetically. This isn't just an old wound, it's a deep one.

"Mairead didn't like when I set boundaries or disagreed with em. I had to end our friendship because I couldn't handle the push and pull, the vitriol, the guilt trips whenever I didn't do exactly as e wanted. The troubling insistence on suffering as a virtue," Aeronwy says.

"Do you think e's still like that?" Tabby says, voice quiet. I'm sure e's worried about Rhiannon. I'm worried now, too.

Aeronwy shrugs. "It's difficult to say. From our limited interactions as colleagues—"

"And Library gossip," June interjects, "especially about the old Assistant Head Archivists."

"—I don't believe e's changed much, unfortunately."

"Really? Not at all?" I ask. "Isn't everyone always trying to work out their flaws and be a better person?"

Everyone turns to look at me now.

"If only that were true," says Aeronwy acidly.

"Some people are too hurt and afraid to face that difficult work," says June, more charitably.

"Not the way you do," Tabby says.

We all fall silent. The background noise swells back into my awareness, as does the scent of our lunch. My stomach rumbles audibly, and I press a hand over it in embarrassment. It breaks the tension, though. We all pick up our forks.

"How does the signature thing work? And what about the Trials? What's all that about?" I ask, through bites of fish and rice.

"Nominees have to get signatures from other faculty and staff to support them, to give everyone a voice in the matter. You can give signatures to as many nominees as you like. Any nominee who does not reach a certain threshold is eliminated." Aeronwy says.

"If you get enough signatures, you go on to the Trials," June says. "It's required by the magical law of the Library, as it was written in the Charter Book. They're a mysterious, ancient test used to pick the next Head Librarian. Or series of tests. Hard to say. Candidates who go through it are oathbound never to speak of the experience, so we have little to no idea what entails, aside from the fact that it's a spiritual test judged by the Founders."

"Where does it happen? Mx. Dreamcloud said something about a door," I say.

"That much we do know. It happens on the astral plane," says June "The door allows candidates to travel there with lucidity and clarity, no matter your personal journeying or dreamwalking ability. You're still tethered to your body, but that connection is vulnerable to being cut or damaged. Unlike in ordinary astral travel or dreamwalking, if harm befalls you in this state, it can have a greater impact on your mind and even physical body. Though the candidates can't explain, we've seen the effects afterward."

"That sounds dangerous," says Tabby, alarmed.

"Oh," says June, raising eir fork to eir mouth, "it is."

A shadow covers the table, and e pauses. Mairead is standing between us and the windows, blocking the light. There's a smile on eir lips, hands clasped peacefully at eir breast. E doesn't *look* like a manipulative, compulsive liar. E just looks like a librarian.

"Sorry to disturb your meal," e says. "Now that our nominations have all been announced, I wanted to wish you all good luck."

"Thank you, Mairead," says June.

Aeronwy says nothing. E shares a long stare with Mairead, who eventually blinks and looks away.

"I know we all have a long history together, not all of it pleasant," e says with a laugh, "but I'm hoping we can put all that aside now. We may be growing older, but it's never too late to start fresh."

"This is true. Good luck on your fresh start, then," Aeronwy says. "As for putting history aside, I've long accepted my part in what happened and moved on. Perhaps you can finally do the same."

PART THREE: INK
WINTER 4018

CHAPTER NINETEEN
TABBY

On the first day of Wet Moon, when the endless, drizzling Casporan rains are at their height, we sit down in front of the altar to ask the book about inks.

To Aeronwy's amusement, I've learned to sleep sitting up, head tilted down and chin against my chest. I settle myself onto the floor cushions and hold the manuscript in my lap, while Aeronwy sits beside me with the red sketchbook open. I center and ground myself, weaving roots into the wooden floor of the Bindery in my mind, before allowing myself to drift off into the dreamscape.

I emerge into a field of soft grass lit only by the stars. I built this entry space during my astral tech studies to avoid getting whisked off by images from my subconscious. Dreamspace is part of the ever-shifting, unpredictable astral plane. Even dreamwalkers don't have total control over their dreamscapes, though we try.

I stand in place and call upon the spirit of the manuscript by reciting lines from its pages in my mind. Books are always dreaming. The grass around me ripples and parts; the dark line of the horizon rushes up to meet me, and suddenly there's a line of hedges looming over my head. They're glossy and green, laden with bright red yew berries.

I press my hands against the hedges. Beyond lies the dreamscape created by the book.

"May I come in?"

The leaves shiver, and the berries chime like bells. Beneath my hands, the hedge parts, leaving a gap just wide enough for me to edge through. Beyond the gap lies a dark void. The space between spaces. It reminds me of the nightmare I had featuring "The Red Cloak." I pray I won't encounter something like that again.

Luckily, the book is dreaming a different story.

Once upon a time, there was a forest beneath the sea. In those days, the coast lay farther to the west, and much that is covered now by waves was dry land. People and animals lived there in harmony. Trees grew tall as mountains, and the ferns as tall as houses. Moss blanketed all in soft green, and there was always enough food to go around.

I find myself in a village in the trees. High above the ground, platforms have been built among the massive redwood limbs. On the platforms are wooden huts, their roofs alive with leather-leaf ferns. A pine marten scurries across my feet, and I jump back in surprise.

Before I can even worry about falling, someone catches me.

The people who lived in this paradise were kind, and they welcomed strangers. Those on their first visit to the village were always gifted with its wealth. Travelers began flocking to this place after hearing wondrous tales of generosity—and often driven by their own greed. But upon arriving, they would find none of the usual treasures.

"Not silver, not gold, nor gems or oil," I said, reciting the next line of the story.

The villager who caught me smiles and gestures that I should follow. We traverse the great tree limbs with ease, riding platforms lifted by pulleys higher and higher into the canopy. At each level, someone is waiting for me with a different gift.

The first gift is a basket of deep black elderberries.

The second is a bag full of fluffy archil lichen.

The third is a huge bracket of dyer's polypore mushrooms.

Redwood canopies often contain entire ecosystems of epiphytic plants, but these giants contain entire worlds. All three of these plants can be seen growing on the tree. I recognize them from my lessons with Aeronwy on dye plants and understand these are what we must make our ink from.

The final gift is the view from the top. I walk to the edge of the highest platform, marveling at how clear the air is. I can see the Sound, the Bell Mountains, and far to the distance, the looming shape of Mt. Cináed. Caspora City doesn't exist yet. This is how the land looked *before* humans transformed its color and shape.

A deep feeling of gratitude spreads through my body. I'm so lucky to have this apprenticeship. To get the chance to do work like this for a living. It feels like coming home.

I turn to my guide and bow my head. "I think I have what I need, now," I say. "Thank you so much for the gifts. I promise I'll use them well and return the favor."

My guide smiles in return. I wonder if e knows how the rest of the story goes. How outsiders become overwhelmed by their greed and move to the giant forest in droves, cutting down the beautiful trees and destroying the balance of nature. The act goes so far that it angers Nia, goddex of the sea, into covering the land with water, creating the coastline we know today.

I certainly won't be sticking around for that part of the tale.

Holding my treasures, I call upon my own spirit. My sense of self. My own thoughts, dreams, and desires. It's time to return to my own dreamscape, so I can wake up. An opening appears in the ferns growing on the trunk of the tree. I smile and step through them.

Instead of returning to my field of safety, I emerge into a thicket of briars. The thorns surrounding me are long, sharp, and red. This isn't where I meant to go. I try to will them away, but they move in closer. A hot breeze blows, pushing me down into the tunnel that I suspect leads to my dream garden. There's a strange glow in the air ahead, and the scent of smoke.

Frightened, I wake up.

Aeronwy is waiting with the sketchbook open to a page full of scribbles and spirals, with sharp red lines scattered throughout. The rough sketch would look abstract if I didn't know it was meant to be my dream briars.

"Everything go all right?" Aeronwy asks, tapping the drawing with a pencil. "The tone seemed different here at the end."

Aeronwy would respect my boundaries if I said I don't want to talk about it, but surprisingly, I do. I feel lost, and I need guidance. I tell em about the thorns, and how I think they're the gate to my dream garden.

"That's a change, isn't it? You've been searching for weeks, unable to find it, when suddenly it presents itself to you. What do you think that means?" Aeronwy says.

I look down at the manuscript in my lap. "I'm not sure."

"Why do you think your garden is surrounded by thorns?"

"Briars and thorns in a dream are usually about protecting something. Guarding," I say.

"So, your dream garden is a place your mind wants to protect," Aeronwy says.

"It was where I went to feel safe. It's me protecting myself," I reply.

Saying that out loud unlocks something in my heart. New thoughts and understanding bubble to the surface. Truths about the garden I couldn't have understood as a child.

Aeronwy nods. "That makes sense."

"It isn't just a safe space. It's a *part* of me. Because I didn't feel safe in my body, awake, I pushed that part of myself into the dreamscape," I say slowly, "I think I've had trouble getting back in because I'm afraid of facing the feelings I tucked away there. Maybe I'm ready, now?"

My voice shakes at the end. "Are you?" says Aeronwy, gently.

"Yes, but… it scares me a lot."

"Do you ever take companions with you when you dreamwalk?"

"Once in a while. Sometimes Rhee will come sleep in my room, and we'll dream together," I say.

"Would you feel better if you had someone with you, going into the garden?"

I watch Aeronwy's posture for clues to how e's feeling. The way e's sitting now, arms crossed, hunched forward slightly, reminds me of when e asked if I was *sure* I wanted to be eir apprentice. I remember the oath e took in our Binding ceremony. *Do you pledge yourself to the sacred role of the teacher, to impart knowledge, to offer support, to protect and guide the mind, heart, and spirit of your student in ways that are compassionate and effective?*

I do pledge.

Taking a chance, I say, "Would you come with me?"

Aeronwy smiles.

***

We decide to take the journey in two weeks' time, during the full moon. Dreamwalking is easiest for me on the new moon, but we can't wait that long. Now every time I'm on the dreamscape, the briars rise to greet me. I can't meet with the spirit of *Soil, Sea and Sky*, and even worse, I'm losing sleep at night. No matter what I do, my fear of what the garden might reveal wakes me up before I can reach the end of the thorns.

Lilja calls me the morning before the dream journey. I consider not answering it, knowing it could wreck my already delicate emotional state. This is the fifth call this week. She's moving into her own apartment, but retrieving her belongings from the family house is proving tricky.

"Next time you speak to Oran, tell em e can have the pots and pans, but e can't have my Grandren's tea set. No. Don't tell em that unless the tea set is already in your hands, e'll probably smash it otherwise," e says, after telling me how Corday and his spouse got thrown out of the house when they came to retrieve Lilja's clothes.

"Okay," I say, my stomach churning, "I'll go sometime when e's at work."

I'm terrified of Oran when e's angry. It doesn't matter that I'm nearly as big as em now. If e so much as scowls, I become a child cowering in the closet again. I hear eir voice in my head before e even starts yelling, accusing me of all sorts of ridiculous things. The accusations rarely make sense, but that's not the point. The point is to make us feel small and make em feel in control.

"You'll have to go when e's home," says Lilja. "E threatened to accuse anyone who removes my things from the house of stealing. If you go secretly, e might accuse Corday of breaking in, and things will get even messier than they already are. You'll have to reason with em. You're the only one who can."

I don't want to do this. I close my eyes and take a deep breath. Even when they're apart, I end up in between. Is that how it's always going to be?

"Tabby, please," Lilja says, "it's the least you could do after practically throwing away your astral tech degree and moving hours away from me. I thought we were going to stick together forever. I barely even got to see you this Solstice. I was so lonely."

"We invited you to come with us to Rhee's family's farm, but you said no," I remind her. "Didn't you end up spending the holiday with Corday?"

She sniffs disdainfully. "I was too upset, so I stayed in my room all night. Ever since you left home, it's been hard on me. I thought you'd be coming back to live and work in town, but then you got that job at the Eternal Library. As if you forgot all about me."

"I'm only two hours away, that's not so bad," I say. In truth, I wish it were more. "Besides, it's my dream job."

"Must be nice."

My guilt overwhelms me. "I'll try to stop by and get your things sometime soon. I'm not sure when exactly," I say. "I have… I have my own things going on."

"Oh? Are things with Rhiannon okay? Do you need to come stay with me in my new place? Do you need to vent?"

The assumption that I'm also having relationship troubles throws me off guard. I even feel offended, although I'm not sure I can say why.

"No, it's not like that. It's my sleep attacks. They've been getting worse. I decided to go back to therapy," I explain.

"Hmm. If only therapy had worked for your Renna and I. You'd swear we were hearing completely opposite advice from the same person, the way those sessions ended up," Lilja sighs, exasperated. "Never really worked for me, either. I couldn't find a good therapist who didn't leave me in tears every time. They all kept recommending the same impossible things."

Even when we talk about my life, Lilja finds a way to make it about hers.

"Right, well, I'm not you or Renna," I say.

The resentment slips out of my mouth before I can catch it. I hear the shocked silence on the other end of the line and grimace. It's too late now. Lilja knows what I'm really thinking.

"What do you mean by that?" she says.

"Therapy might not have worked for the two of you, but it works for me," I say, cautiously.

"I didn't say it wouldn't. I don't see why you needed to make a snide comment," Lilja says.

"It's just… I'm sorry, I didn't mean to snap, but I was hoping for more support. That maybe we could talk about my situation for a little while, instead of talking about you or Renna," I reply. I rub my forehead, the first pangs of a headache beginning to set in. I can't tell if I feel sleepy because I'm about to have an attack, or if it's from not sleeping the last two weeks.

"Of course, you can, Tabby, I never said you *couldn't*," Lilja says, as if this were obvious.

"Right. Right. Sorry," I say. "You're right, you didn't."

Often what Lilja *says* happened and what I *feel* happened are two entirely different things. By the end of the conversation, my headache is in full swing. This is not how I had planned to spend the day leading up to my big dreamwalking journey.

***

Rhiannon meets me at the Library when e's finished with work. We join up in the children's section, which is painted with cheery pastel murals and dotted with beanbag chairs. I catch sight of Rhiannon first; e looks tired, but as soon as e sees me, e brightens up. It warms my heart how happy e always is to see me.

"Hey, how's things?" Rhiannon asks as we hug.

"I'm holding it together, I guess," I say.

"You guess?"

"It was a rough morning. I'm hoping tonight will help, though."

Rhiannon nods. "Me, too. So, what're we doing in the kids' section?"

I start walking through the stacks, and Rhiannon follows. The shelves here are only a few feet high, made for much smaller readers. I have a vivid memory of a class trip to the Eternal Library when I was nine and having to reach for the top row.

"I'm looking for the books of fairytales and fables I read when I was little," I explain. "A lot of the same stories are in the book I'm making with Aeronwy, but they're different versions. I want to reread them the way I remember."

"I getcha. The history of a folktale over the years can be pretty interesting. Especially when you connect changes in the narrative with real life events of the time," Rhiannon says.

E pulls a slim chapbook from the shelf and holds it up. The cover is a painting of a green dragon with a young Noxian rider on it, eir long black hair blowing in the wind. The title is simply *Dragon Riders*.

"Did you ever read this series?" Rhiannon asks.

"Of course I did. I don't think I ever finished it, though," I say, taking another volume off the shelf. This cover has a red dragon on it, and a Gildean rider with short hair and glasses.

"It was my fu—my favorite series ever for years. Sorry, almost forgot I shouldn't curse here," Rhiannon says. E flips through *Dragon Riders* with a fond smile. "Who were your favorite rider/dragon pair?"

"Let me guess, yours was Uzochi and Cadoc," I say, pointing to the red dragon cover.

Rhiannon snorts. I guessed right. "I bet you liked Alice and Ceridwen."

Alice was the shy blonde of the group who rode a blue dragon and had water magic. "You know me," I say.

We put the books back and continue hunting for my childhood fables. I don't remember the actual titles or authors, but I do remember what they looked like. We chat about what we remember loving or hating from *Dragon Riders*, how the anti-war themes influenced us and how Uzochi inspired

Rhiannon to learn Gildean. I don't find the books I'm looking for, even with the children's Librarian's help, but I do find many other volumes of Casporan folklore. I check them out and tuck them into my bag for later.

"Rhee," I say as we ride the elevator up to the Bindery, "do you think I could write a good children's book?"

The elevator makes a worrisome grinding noise. Rhiannon thumps the wall, unbothered, but my stomach does a flip. "Shitty piece of junk, I bet they put this in forty years ago," e says, then turns to me excitedly. "Uh, do I think you could write a good kid's book? *Absolutely.* And you'd illustrate it, too, right?"

"That's the idea," I say, blushing from the compliment. "It's just, so many people think they can do it without truly valuing the craft. They think it must be so easy to do, compared to an adult novel. I don't want to be one of those people."

"I don't think you are. You just said you get how hard it is. Weren't you working on something like that way back when we met? I remember you showing me sketches in the café," Rhiannon says.

"That's right, I was."

"It was about astrology, right? Or at least about the stars?" Rhiannon says. "Was it based on 'The Wishing Star' folktale?"

"I can't believe you remember that."

Rhiannon places a hand on eir chest in mock offense. "*I* can't believe you think I'd forget!"

The elevator dings, and the doors open at our destination. Rhiannon has agreed to come sit with me while Aeronwy and I go on our dream journey. That way e'll be right by my side if I wake up needing support.

Aeronwy is already there, preparing the space. The cluttered studio has been neatened, and my futon is on the floor next to the couch. We walk in as e's drawing a salt circle around our sleeping space for protection. The electric candles on the altar are all aglow.

"Good evening," Aeronwy says when e sees us. "We'll be able to begin very soon. I'm glad you're both here."

Once everything is set, I lie down on the bed, and Aeronwy takes to the couch. E offers me a hand, which I take. Rhiannon sits off to the side with a pile of *Dragon Rider* books in eir lap. E flashes me a thumbs up.

"Are you ready?" Aeronwy asks.

I hope so.

"Yes. Let's go."

I slip into my dreamscape. I aim for my safe-space field, but find myself among the brambles, instead. Even though I expected that, the lack of control makes me uneasy. I sit down in the tunnel of thorns and wait. Aeronwy falls asleep quickly; I know it's happened when I sense another dreamscape brush up against mine.

I feel for the bond between us, the invisible thread around my wrist that smells like ink and smoke. A light tug causes a ripple in the dreamscape, and suddenly Aeronwy is sitting beside me.

Now it's my turn to say, "Are you ready?"

Like in my dream at Rose's memorial, there's a Flame flickering in eir chest. Aeronwy's dream-self has long, white and silver curls cascading down past eir shoulders. It's common for people's dream-selves to take a while to catch up to their physical image, especially if e had that hairstyle for many years.

Aeronwy looks at me and nods. Good, e appears to be lucid.

I lead us on the long crawl through the tunnel of thorns. The brambles shrink away from Aeronwy's Flame, as if they fear its burn. I'm grateful. The wider the space gets, the easier I can breathe.

"This reminds me of my own childhood," Aeronwy says as we continue crawling, "I spent so many hours in the woods, hoping I'd find Faerieland. I must have crawled through dozens of tunnels like this one."

"Oh really? Even though the legends say you'd never return?" I ask. Many families take precautions against the Good Neighbors. Even the smallest child is warned and charmed against following a beautiful stranger into the dark parts of the woods. No matter how sweetly they sing.

"That was the idea. It seemed the only way I could escape home," Aeronwy replies.

Dried leaves crackle beneath my hands and knees. The dirt is dry and hard-packed, like clay baked in a kiln. The air is oppressively hot. If I glance upward through the twisting canes, all I see is white and gray. It could be clouds, it could be nothingness, it could be smoke.

As soon as I think of smoke, I smell it. I feel it in my eyes, and blink against the sting.

While awake, I've never been brave enough to ask for details, but dream-me is far more courageous. "What happened at home?"

Similarly, dream-Aeronwy is more forthcoming than eir awake counterpart. Here, we're inside of our shells. Our hopes and fears swirl around us, surfacing from the places they were buried.

"I was raised to be an extension of someone else, instead of my own person. You can't love yourself when you have no sense of self. Especially when the person you're enmeshed with is alternately full of hate or unhealthy adoration for the both of you," Aeronwy says.

The smell of smoke intensifies. I glance over my shoulder. Aeronwy's Flame burns clear, without any indication of smoke. There's a look of bitter resignation on eir face, but e doesn't appear pained.

"One of your parents?"

"My only one. And no siblings."

Sometimes I wonder what would have happened if my parents had split up when I was a child. Lilja is not shy about explaining that they stayed together because they thought it would be better for me than making me choose. I'm glad only because I'm not sure I *could* have chosen. Yes, I'm terrified of Oran when e's angry, but e can also be funny, is a wonderful guitarist, and taught me to be independent. E has moods I can label clearly. Unlike Lilja, who seems sweet, but makes me feel confused and anxious.

I'd have rather left them both. I couldn't do that, though. I still can't do it. After all, they're my parents. Even if I don't like them, I have to love them, don't I?

I don't speak the words aloud, but I don't need to. We're on the dreamscape. Aeronwy catches my thoughts in the dream logic.

Chapter Nineteen

"You don't owe them for that," e says quietly. "Don't mistake feelings of obligation for love. Love has no obligation."

The thorns ripple around me, clattering as they peel back and the sky opens up. Smoke pours in, irritating my eyes and lungs. I sit back on my heels, trying to clear it away with my mind, but it won't dissipate. I dream up particle filter masks instead. I offer one to Aeronwy, but e shakes eir head, unperturbed. E already carries fire inside em.

Those words—*Love has no obligation*—were the key I've been missing all this time. I stand up and turn to face the open air before me. We've made it through the briars.

What lies ahead is a nightmare. I can see the shape of my garden in the landscape. There are familiar hills and valleys, landmark trees where their roots have always grown, the spiral of the cobblestone paths, and even the little house at the center. None of it is as it should be, though. All of it is on fire.

I sink to my knees. Why is it like this? I'd imagined overgrown plants, weed-choked plants, dead plants, all of which I could have nurtured back to health. I'd *hoped* it would be the green haven I remembered. But this? I can't do anything when it's like this. And even if the fire ever goes out, there'll be nothing left. I'll be left with *nothing*.

"I don't understand how this happened," I hear myself say. "I don't—"

The truth hits me like an arrow to the chest. The garden really *is* my heartscape, the center of my spiritual world. As a child I'd turned inward, nurturing myself when no one else would. It wasn't safe to be awake, so I pushed this part of me into my dreams. But the soul can only take so much when it feels alone and unloved. Even I abandoned this place— abandoned myself—eventually.

Aeronwy and I don't need to talk. We're still dreaming. E knows what I've discovered. E surveys the flaming landscape with an open expression of sorrow. The compassion radiating from em is the only thing keeping me from waking up in despair.

"I don't know what to *do*," I say.

Aeronwy crouches beside me and puts eir hands on my shoulders, turning me to face em.

"I can't fix this for you, but I can help. If I put out the fire, can you replant it?"

"I think so... but... are you sure? It's not too much?"

"I'm here to guide you spiritually as well as in the physical craft of Illumination," e says. "This is part of the apprenticeship process. I also care about you. I wouldn't offer to do more than I can handle. Please trust me on that."

The last few moons in the Bindery have been an oasis of calm and joy in my anxious life. I picture Aeronwy and June dancing, how in tune they were, and how kind when they invited me to join them. I'd been thinking of *what could have been*, if I'd had parents more like them, but I wonder if it's actually *what we could become*.

"I trust you," I say.

Aeronwy nods and stands back up. With fluid, confident strides, e walks into the garden, hands outstretched. The flames lean in, swirling around eir fingers. Then e starts to sing.

I've read enough of *On Flamekeeping* to know what comes next, but am entirely unprepared to witness it. No written description could do justice to the beauty of flame set to song. The fire quivers and flickers, arcs around Aeronwy in an impossible dance of smoke and light. With every note, it draws closer, coalescing into a tiny ball in Aeronwy's palm. It's like e's holding the sun.

When every spark has been gathered, and the landscape is left only in ashes, Aeronwy holds the tiny sun up to eir mouth and breathes it in.

RHIANNON

"Wait, what do you mean it's not going in the exhibit?"

I stare at Mairead. We're in the amethyst room again, this time with the real live original Illuminated copy of *The Founding*, which I can't believe I stole from June's studio. My whole memory of the party feels like a bad dream, but nope, it was reality.

"This book was hidden for a reason," Mairead says. "We can't let anyone know we have it until we know what that reason is. The Stargroves will almost certainly be at the exhibit opening—all the senior Library staff is invited. We need to have the upper hand before they realize we have it. I assume they don't know?"

I slump down in my chair. I hadn't *planned* to steal the book. But in the moment, I was consumed with anxiety about proving myself to Mairead and keeping my job. I was angry at Aeronwy for lying to me about it, and curious what was worth lying about. Obviously, I haven't told Tabby or Amane what I did. I don't know how to do that without hurting them.

"We promised Rhys, though," I say.

Mairead shrugs. "E doesn't have to know. We'll tell em we couldn't find it after all, or that it's away for repairs. Then, once we figure out its secrets, we'll go from there."

"I wanted my name on that plaque in the exhibit," I grumble.

"I have a feeling your reward will be much greater when we're through with this," says Mairead. "I can tell just by looking at *The Founding* that it's something incredible. And *you're* incredible for bringing it to me."

Most Illuminated books have a *weight* to them, a gravity that tugs on your sense of spiritual space-time. *The Founding* is the opposite. It feels insubstantial, despite being huge, with wooden covers and goat skin parchment pages. When I try to read it, the text slips through my mind like a stream of clear, cold water, leaving nothing behind. It's as if it doesn't want to be remembered.

"Don't thank me yet. I've been sitting with it for weeks, and I haven't Seen anything useful," I say.

"I know you'll get to it. After all, you've come this far," Mairead says, patting me on the shoulder. I've learned not to flinch away, even though I still don't like em touching me. Saying so hasn't made a difference. "Why don't you get back to work? Your visions will be the key to our success."

Once e leaves, I fill the inkwell and place my hand on *The Founding*. A prickle goes up my spine. Did I do the right thing, bringing it down here?

"Please tell me this is all worth it," I say. "Just show me the truth, would you?"

I lean over and peer into the bowl, and once again become the book.

I am being undone. With every scrape of the knife, ink is erased from my pages. Words, crumbling into dust.

"I'm sorry," says the binder scraping my parchment bare. Eir name is Calliope, and e was the child of Llewella, whose spirit passed one night ago. "Eirlys Starsower forgive me. You couldn't have known this is how things would be, even as you became the first victim to people's greed. I'm so sorry, but I have to make sure it never happens again."

I don't understand. How will I exist when no one can read me?

"I read about the experiments Mgx. Whitewillow did. I know the theories," Calliope whispers, as if e can hear me. But I know Calliope uses cartomancy to speak with the other books. E does not know my thoughts. "As long as I don't break your binding, your spirit will hold. Your words still live within the Library itself."

Chapter Twenty

But will I know myself? I feel myself fading with every lost letter. I cannot feel pain, but I do feel sorrow.

Calliope continues, *"I will change the leather of your covers and write you anew. A story of caution. A warning about how from the very beginning, there are those who would kill to receive your power. Only now, they won't be able to access it. They won't be rewarded for their crimes."*

A new story? Who will I be then?

"I will call you The Founding. *I'm sorry it has to be this way."*

***

"Well, don't you look wonderful! Very appropriate for the evening. I often wish people still dressed this way, don't you? It's so elegant."

I hand my coat to the concierge and turn back to Mairead, who's eying my outfit with approval. Whenever formal wear is required, I pull out a traditional Casporan wrap dress. It starts with a long, square piece of fabric draped over the shoulders like a poncho. Then another, longer piece is wrapped around the waist and chest to make it more form-fitting. The way it's wrapped and the pattern on the cloth depend on what region you're from. Mine is emerald green with fern fronds curling across its length. Mairead plucks at my sleeve to study it.

"This has been in your family a while, hasn't it? It's in wonderful shape," e says.

"My Great-Great Grandren's," I say, pulling my arm away. "Thanks."

Mairead is wearing traditional garb, too; e's all decked out in eir ceremonial High Priestex's robes. The soft gray dress and robe are embroidered with books and quill pens in silver thread that shimmers under the museum lights. The wide leather belt at eir waist has a prayer book, a pair of small scissors, and fountain pen strapped to it. Draped around eir shoulders is a chain of ornate paper cutouts, depicting scenes of The Author writing the universe into existence. It flutters around em as we walk down the hall, our heels clacking on the granite floor.

The Museum of Casporan History is a grand building with vaulted ceilings and skylights made from semiprecious stones. It's nighttime, and raining, but still they glitter high above us, lit by crystal chandeliers. I've been here thousands of times, but never for an opening night. Only the most preeminent scholars, thinkers, and creatives get invited to the lavish parties that the museum puts on to celebrate a new exhibit.

This one chronicles the history of dress in Caspora during the Reclamation period. Tensions built for decades between Authorists and Readerists as the Library—then the government as well—argued over how to treat a new influx of refugees. Fashion became, as it often does, a way for people to declare sides, in this case escalating to an art that could tell entire stories with just one garment.

Calliope Everberry lived during this time. E was the author and illustrator of *The Founding*... but not its binder. I haven't filled Mairead in on my latest visions yet. The ones that show *The Founding* is older than we thought. *Much* older, if I'm right about what I Saw.

"Look at this one—can you imagine wearing that headpiece in the stacks? You wouldn't have to dust the books on the top shelf anymore."

Mairead's voice draws me back into the present. We're standing before a sweeping yellow robe. It's embroidered with dandelion clocks held by slender brown hands, individual seeds blowing across the fabric. The puffy sleeves end in long white cuffs edged with gold and violet. The lace hem is patterned with more dandelions. According to the placard, this combination proclaimed the wearer was in favor of encouraging knowledge to 'bloom' wherever it desired to grow, a common Readerist value.

The trouble is the matching headdress, which is made of dyed yellow feathers arrayed like petals a good twelve inches out from the wearer's head.

I snort, imagining myself wearing it, and Mairead chuckles.

"It's very masterfully done, of course. The embroidery alone must have taken a year or more... but that's what there was to do when working at the Library meant becoming a nun and living in the cloisters. You couldn't hit reply all and send passive aggressive emails to everyone in the department when you were angry; you did this instead," e says. "You let it *simmer*."

"I didn't know you liked this kind of stuff," I say, "clothes, I mean. Or that you even knew there's a difference between reply and reply all."

"I *do* have a life, Rhiannon. Twice as much life as you, in fact. I also once strove to look as though I woke up beautiful and edgy and *cool* every morning," Mairead says.

I know this is true from seeing younger Mairead in my visions, particularly the memory e showed me with Aeronwy.

"You remind me of me at your age," e says. "I used to dye my hair blue and wear big glasses. I wore artfully ripped jeans and glared at strangers while smoking herbal cigarettes. I quit that last one once I started working at the Library, of course."

No smoking allowed on campus. No open flames. After hearing from Amane that Mairead accused Aeronwy of starting the '86 fire, I dug into the Archives. Old newspaper articles, department memos, Library meeting notes, photographs, arson investigation reports. Aeronwy had been severely injured while putting out the fire, which flared out of control in an instant due to drought and high winds that day. The firefighters who pulled em out of the collapsed building—also Flamekeepers, it should be noted—said that Aeronwy's quick action saved the whole campus from burning.

After all that, Mairead had done more than accuse Aeronwy of starting the blaze; e tried to ban Flamekeepers from working at the Library in any capacity. There was an unnerving amount of support from other Librarians, who were looking to blame someone for their grief, but the ban ultimately failed when investigators proved the cause to be a tossed cigarette in the gardens.

Herbal cigarettes… but no, I'm jumping to wild conclusions.

I disguise my unease with a joke. "Well, what happened, then? To you being cool?"

"I realized there were bigger things than me at hand. More important things. Great destinies to channel, people to urge towards their rightful narratives," Mairead says, gazing up at the ceiling, "after mine failed to have a happy ending."

"You're still alive, so how can you have an ending to your story?" I ask.

Mairead's gray eyes settle on me, contemplative. "We all go through chapters in our lives. There are many small endings before *The End* of death. You're old enough to have had a few—the end of childhood, the end of adolescence. As our age and experience changes, so do our roles in our stories."

"Yeah, well, I guess I didn't get those like most people did," I say. "I was Seeing the world through adults' eyes in my visions since I can remember. I didn't go to school the normal way, with people my age. I knew too much for how old I was, but I didn't know *anything* about living the life adults thought I was ready for."

Mairead nods solemnly. "I understand. I was also brought up under the burden of unreasonable expectations. My parents were utter perfectionists, and they expected even more of me. I was born on the same day, at the same hour, as our family ancestor, Isylwyn Moonscryer emself, and showed great psychic promise. Immediately, I was put through rigorous training and given duties at various temples. I wasn't allowed to be a child, either."

"Wow, that's rough. I had no idea," I say.

"Great gifts are always offset by great sorrows," Mairead says. "But, Rhiannon, you're a Protagonist—a hero. Your bad experiences were all in the service of your greater destiny. The people who hurt you are tiny and insignificant in comparison, and will have tiny, insignificant lives."

"How do you know I'm a 'Protagonist' and not a side character?" I ask.

"Isn't it obvious? The setup, the context, the tropes, it all fits," Mairead says, as if I'm being thick. "Anyone with basic reading comprehension and a little knowledge of your life could figure it out."

"And what does that make you? The old crone doling out wisdom along the side of the road?"

"Many old crones turn out to be deities in disguise," Mairead grins. "See, you do get it."

I cross my arms. "Cool, cool, but I don't believe in that stuff. Character roles, the Author's Narrative. There's a little something called *free will* and *equality* that gets in the way."

Mairead rolls eir eyes and laughs condescendingly. "Do you really want to have this argument now, with me? As if I haven't spent decades refuting it from Readerists far more spiritually educated than you?"

A retort rises hot and fast in my throat, but I bite my tongue. "No," I say.

"Sorry, is this a bad time?"

I look up and find Rhys Elkspinner standing next to us, along with a distinguished looking stranger. There's an awkward look on eir face suggesting e heard us arguing. All the blood drains out of my face.

"No, no," says Mairead. "Not at all. It's good to see you both. Rhys, you've met Rhiannon already. Faraji, this is my new Assistant Head of the Archives. Rhiannon, this is Mgx. Faraji Sayyid, Curator of works on paper at the National Art Museum. He used to be the dealer for my cut paper art before I recommended him for this much more prestigious job."

I shake hands with Faraji, who raises an eyebrow. "What happened to your last Assistant Head? What was it, Camille?"

Mairead grimaces. "You didn't hear? It's so sad. Camille has been bedridden with a mystery illness for half a year, now. The doctors think it's something long-term, perhaps even lifelong. I told her I'd only replace her temporarily until she could return to work, but she declined, and recommended Rhiannon for the job."

Faraji and Rhys shake their heads in sympathy. I can only stare, too stunned by Mairead's bold-faced lie to contradict em. Why even lie about that? Why not just say they couldn't get along? Because it makes em look bad?

"We're glad to have you among us, Rhiannon, even if it's under distraught circumstances," says Rhys. "Though I'm terribly sad your loan of *The Founding* fell through. Such a shame it needs such extensive repairs."

I swallow against my dry throat. "Yes," I say. Mairead never filled me in on what excuse e gave the others for the book. E'd just said e would 'take care of it.'

"Having an accident like that after so much effort to find it! Always best to keep those stray ink bottles tightly capped, you know," Rhys says, with the chiding look of a schoolteacher.

That takes me by surprise. "What—"

Mairead cuts me off with a laugh and a pat on the back. "I've always said the same. It's a difficult lesson to learn the hard way, and with such a priceless object, too."

They all nod in agreement, clearly embarrassed for me. Do they believe I… spilled ink on *The Founding*, like a kid playing around in their parent's office? I shoot Mairead a piercing look that I hope conveys the message, *What the* fuck *did you tell them?* Mairead only looks back at me mildly.

"I heard you're hoping to be the next Head Librarian," says Faraji. He toasts the wine glass he's holding towards Mairead. "Cheers, and good luck."

Mairead beams and smoothes the front of eir dress. "Thank you! I think it's about time we have a Speaker for the Books who isn't an Illuminator. I understand why so many of them end up in the job, but the rest of us love books, too. I have big plans," e says, winking.

Faraji chuckles. "I'm sure you do."

"Will you keep your current position, as well?" Rhys asks. "I know Rose kept Illuminating books for years after e became Head Librarian."

"Yes, and it distracted em from the job," says Mairead. "I won't be staying in the Archives. I have too much work to do returning the Library to its former glory."

"But who in the world could ever replace *you* in the Archives?" says Rhys.

I stand up straight, more than ready for some praise to make up for the story about spilling ink on *The Founding*. To be named as next Head Archivist in front of such influential people would be amazing.

"That's a good question," Mairead says wryly. "I don't know yet. The other department heads would likely have their own nomination they'd vote for, anyway. That's one of the things I plan on changing. Returning power back to a central source."

Rhys looks skeptical, but Faraji is nodding.

I, once again, am frozen. This time in anger.

Chapter Twenty

"I'm gonna go get a drink," I say, excusing myself from the conversation. I can't deal with this right now.

As I approach the refreshments table in the hall outside the exhibit, I run into three familiar faces. I halt in my tracks, intent on swerving in the other direction, but it's too late. June has already seen me and started waving. I wave back and plaster on an expression I *hope* is a smile, closing the distance between us.

"Rhiannon! I almost didn't recognize you with your hair all pinned up. It looks lovely," June says.

E has no idea I took the book. I breathe an inward sigh of relief and pat my hair, which is in an elaborate crown of braids. These damn exhibit openings are so *fancy*.

"Thanks. Tabby did it for me," I reply. "Yours looks nice, too."

June's white-and-red hair is rolled into a high bun with a circlet of orchids tucked around it. E's wearing a traditional Fenian apron dress with a puffy-sleeved white blouse beneath. The dress is sky blue and covered with a rainbow of intricate floral embroidery that rivals the stuff on display.

I'm not surprised to see June and Aeronwy here, but I forgot that, as a world-famous fashion designer, Inyene would be on the guest list, too. He's wearing another suit bright enough to make my eyes bleed: this one is lime green, ultramarine, and cyan, patterned in an abstract representation of peacock feathers. Amane would be beside herself right now. He flashes me a brilliantly white smile and a respectful nod.

Aeronwy is studying my wrap dress intently. Probably because e's wearing one wrapped in the same style. The cloth pattern is different, though. Black silk with charcoal colored clouds, their swirling edges sewn in silver. These stylized smoke clouds are a staple of Cináedite taste, but there's no denying the similarity.

"You're from the southern valleys," Aeronwy says, eyes coming up to mine.

"Yeah, yeah, we're from the same town," I say, and when all three of them look shocked, add, "Tabby's reading your big-ass book, *On Flamekeeping*. I read the bio in the back. And some bits here and there."

June and Inyene look satisfied by this explanation, but Aeronwy's brow furrows.

"What was your surname again?"

"Rivergreen-Haybloom."

"Hmm," says Aeronwy, brow furrowing further.

"I know what you're thinking, and I already thought of it. Your birth surname was Greengrove, right? We're not related. Lots of folks have 'green' in their surnames in Verdant Valley—it's called *Verdant* for a reason—and the Traditional Cináedite community out there just doesn't mix with the rest of us," I say.

"That boundary is more porous than you think," Aeronwy says.

"Eh. Still. Seems incredibly unlikely."

"What a funny coincidence," says June. "I suppose I shouldn't be surprised. These sorts of things always happen with our apprentices and their families."

"A sign from the All-Knowing Author?" I ask, sarcastically. They all laugh, even Aeronwy. I'm starting to think I misjudged em. Especially after e did that heartspace dreamwalking thing with Tabby.

"Just a bit of synchronicity," June says, "twining threads in the tapestry of life. Past life ties, that sort of thing."

"Oh yeah?" Of course June would be interested in past life ties. E's an expert on etheric cords, the spiritual bonds that follow us from one life to the next. I've never had mine read, but I'm curious.

"Certainly. Have you ever met someone you clicked with very easily? Feel as if you'd known one another for years despite it only being a few weeks, or days, or even hours?" June asks.

"Well, *yeah*," I say. "Amane and Tabby."

June smiles. "Amane told me all about your first meeting. How did you and Tabby meet? I don't think I've heard that one yet."

My guilt over stealing the book stabs me in the back every second I stand here, but if I ever want them to forgive me, I should be nice.

"You ever been to the café attached to the library at Caspora University?" I say. All three of them nod.

"We used to hang out there all the time," Inyene says, hitting Aeronwy on the arm playfully. "Is it really still open?"

"They changed the décor," says June.

"Yeah, anyway," I say, before they can start reminiscing, "you know how crowded it gets. If you go alone, you have to share a table with a stranger. Tabby and I always went at the same time, and we always sat at the same table, but we were always silent. One day I came in and my usual drink was already there. Tabby bought it for me as a Winter Solstice gift. Once we started talking, we couldn't stop."

"That's adorable," June says. "We often have past life ties with the important people in our lives, though not always. Amane and I have no previous life connections, for example, but of course I adore her, and she's already part of our Bindery family."

If only I could have recorded that and played it back for Amane. She'd probably faint dead away hearing that her idol thinks of her as family.

I don't get to ask if e has a past life connection to Tabby, because someone hooks a familiar arm through mine. I flash Mairead an annoyed look. E takes off eir tiny round glasses and polishes them, refusing to make eye contact.

"Rhiannon, dear, I've been looking all over for you." E speaks sweetly, but there's an edge to eir voice. "I wanted to introduce you to Celeste Mael before e leaves for the night. Never stays the full evening, that one, but you don't want to miss em."

"Um," I say, hesitating. Celeste Mael is one of my favorite authors, but I'm still mad at Mairead. I pull my arm away in a huff, but Mairead latches on again.

"Mairead, it's been a while," says Inyene civilly. "I remember you were very into Reclamation fashion back in the day, you must be enjoying the exhibit."

Mairead ignores em and looks imploringly at me. Are there *tears* in eir eyes? Did something happen? When I set my anger aside, I see that e's hunched over and tense.

"Celeste could leave any minute now," e says, nails digging into my arm.

What is going on here? "Uh, good seeing y'all, guess I gotta go," I say, then let Mairead lead me away.

I snag two flutes of champagne from the refreshments table as we take off down the hallway. We head not back into the exhibit, but into the shadowed recesses of the rest of the museum. It's not expressly off limits, but we probably shouldn't be here.

Mairead sits on a bench beneath a stained-glass window of Drust Windstoker, the last Head Librarian to be Sovereign of Caspora. When e refused to split the Library from the central government, an angry mob of underpaid, undervalued housekeepers and kitchen staff made sure Drust retired. By dying.

I hand Mairead a champagne flute, which e downs in one go. I sit and sip mine cautiously. The air beneath the window is cold, the patter of rain on the glass smoothing over the murmur of conversation from the rest of the gallery.

"Are we ah, meeting Celeste here, or—"

"What? No, it's too late, e already left," Mairead says, waving a hand at me. "That was just an excuse."

My anger roars back in full force. "Why do you keep lying about things tonight?"

Mairead pushes eir glasses up onto eir forehead and rubs eir eyes. "I'm sorry, I just wasn't expecting to have to collect you from a conversation with *them*. Seeing Aeronwy and Juniper just reminds me that I'll never be enough for some people."

"That doesn't explain the things you said in front of Rhys and Faraji," I say.

"Do you have any idea how hard it is to socialize with these people? These elite academics, who I'm supposed to be one of? If you're not perfect, or they can't benefit from being your friend, they dump you immediately," Mairead says, voice muffled by eir hands. "I said what I did to stay in their good graces. Connections are everything in this world."

Guilt rises in my chest like the bubbles in my champagne. "It just hurt, is all," I mutter. "I thought you wanted me to be the Head Archivist after you."

Mairead sits up with a sigh. "I do. It's just that you don't yet have the qualifications for the position, in their eyes. We have to wait until we figure out the secret of *The Founding*, and then, after you announce it to the community, they'll understand your worth. I thought you would have caught on to what I was doing."

I sip my drink instead of responding. Why hadn't I figured that out? And why does it still feel like bullshit?

"Honestly, I thought you were clever enough to understand I'm doing all this for you," Mairead says. "I was so upset when you ran off. I'm just trying to help. Like I said, connections are everything with these people, and *I'm* your only one right now. I have to look good, or you don't stand a chance of getting in."

"Sorry," I say.

"Sure you are," Mairead says, morosely.

We sit in silence. It's getting late, and people are leaving the party. I can hear their laughter from down the hall as they wander out into the night, drunk on champagne or conversation or the sheer beauty of preserved five-hundred-year-old clothing. Among them are the Stargroves, who for some reason have kept this ancient book hidden in a chair, rather than reveal it to the world. The rain drums harder on the window above.

I don't really want Mairead to become Head Librarian, but if e *does*, I want to be Head Archivist. It's the only thing that will make all this worth it.

"It's a palimpsest," I say.

Mairead looks at me sharply, lips parted.

I finish off my champagne, the bubbles tickling my throat as the truth echoes through the dark museum. "Calliope did a good job scraping the original text off the parchment. *Extremely good*. I had a vision of em doing it."

"Do you know what it used to be?" Mairead asks.

I shake my head. "These visions are always from the book's point of view and I can't see the pages, so I don't know for sure. We'll have to use multi-spectral imaging and hope it picks up on something."

Smiling broadly, Mairead stands and offers me a hand. There's pride glimmering in eir eyes.

"I knew I was right to choose you," e says. "You'll be the Protagonist with the happy ending I never got, I swear it. The

Author has big things in store for us, Rhiannon. Bigger than you can imagine."

CHAPTER TWENTY-ONE
AMANE

The Bindery storeroom is an artist's dream. The walls are lined with apothecary cabinets made from polished redwood, the tiny drawers labeled in many different hands. The shelves above them are laden with glass and crystal jars, some with ornate stoppers the color of the pigments inside. In the middle of the room, huge, antique barrels are clustered together, full of raw fiber for paper and thread. The windows are lined with racks of living plants; some of the vines have entirely taken over the frame and are making their way across the ceiling.

Tabby and I are helping the Stargroves take inventory, which is exactly the sort of tedious task I *love* doing. I balance my tablet on my arm and rotate between the three of them, entering the numbers they provide. Tabby is going through a rainbow of powdered pigments, weighing each on a scale and noting which ones are below half full.

"Viridian, jadeite, serpentine, zoistite... nearly all the greens are out," Tabby says, pulling the jars from the shelf.

"I illustrated a book on faery flowers last year. The text was green as well. My dear, I thought you were going to put a special order in for those," Aeronwy says, directing the last part at June.

"I *was*," says June, voice echoing strangely. I turn around to see e has eir head stuck down in one of the barrels. E straightens up with bits of flax stuck in eir hair. "I'm sorry, I kept thinking of it at inopportune times, and then forgetting later."

"I suspected," says Aeronwy, but fondly. E plucks some of the flax from June's hair as e shuffles past in the tight space.

"It's okay, you have me around now to keep track of these things," I say, tapping a nail on my tablet. Previously, inventory was recorded on a stack of printouts hanging by the door. The pages are yellowed with age, layered with correction fluid and illegible numbers. Not very efficient.

Tabby glances at my screen and says, "Ooh, it's color-coded."

"Good visuals are key to comprehensive data presentation," I say.

Tabby laughs, and the sound makes my heart swell. Two weeks ago, e did some difficult shadow work with Aeronwy that made em sad and weepy. It hurt to watch. Eir laughter is the sun emerging from behind a cloud.

"You'll have to show me how to do that. I've never been very organized," Tabby admits.

"I can email my templates to you!"

"Templates for what?" Aeronwy asks. E's going through a shelf full of painting mediums and dye chemicals. "We're nearly out of acacia gum, by the way, in all three forms. Having both of you making ink and paint at the same time has drained our stores faster than usual."

"Templates for *life*," I clarify, and mark those down.

Tabby sets a bottle of burnt umber on the scale and notes the weight. The way e leans down to peer at the numbers, brushing back strands of golden hair, is cute. Everything Tabby does is cute. I think I have a problem.

I lean one elbow on the shelf and say, "That one's the same color as your eyes."

Tabby turns and blinks at me with eir big, dark brown eyes, making my heart flutter. E smiles. My heart flutters more.

"You think so?"

I pick up the bottle and hold it next to eir face. It gives me an excuse to drink in the view: round, rosy cheeks, soft chin, full pink lips, small nose with a little bump on the bridge, and yes, burnt umber eyes. I make sure to squint and turn my head appraisingly, as if all I'm doing is comparing the color.

"I know so," I say, nodding and setting the bottle back on the shelf. "You should wear more green, it'd look good with your complexion."

"I'll remember that. You *are* the color expert, after all," Tabby says cheerfully. E turns back to the shelf of pigments but watches me from the corner of eir eye.

Flustered, I sputter, "I am? No, you're right, I am."

"We have seventeen ounces of aluminum sulfate and fifteen ounces of calcium carbonate," Aeronwy calls out. I glance over and see em watching us with careful consideration. E raises an eyebrow at me, as if e knows exactly what I'm doing. I look away before e can see the answer written all over my face.

We work methodically around the room until everything is neatly recorded in my spreadsheet. There are a lot of numbers in the red, indicating a need for refills. They usually stagger when apprentices start so they're not going through the same materials at the same time, but Tabby and I are an exception. June pulls up several online order forms, chatting with Aeronwy about how to rearrange their lesson plans to adjust for the issue.

Neither one of them seems to mind changing a plan, or allowing the other to take priority with a material need. It's weird to me, so used to my family's hyper-competitiveness. I always liked watching my Moms' eyes light up as they bantered over dinner, their voices wry and their wits sharp. I like the calm, considerate space Aeronwy and June make for one another, too.

"Amane and I will probably use the last of the liquid acacia gum today," June muses as we tidy up the room.

"Then I'll go down to the harbor now and acquire more. We can't wait for a shipment," Aeronwy replies.

"Could I come?" Tabby asks.

"Certainly," Aeronwy replies warmly, "I'll introduce you to Oriane. The shop e owns is much like this storeroom, only ten times as large. We've been partnered with their family for decades."

"And account for at least half their business," chuckles June.

"They deserve it. No one else in the city cares about our work the way they do. They'll search with us for months if that what it takes to find the best material for a book, no matter how strange or rare," Aeronwy says, glancing between Tabby and I.

"Only the best for the best," I say.

Aeronwy nods. "I know you understand, but it bears repeating."

I think that was a compliment. *I know you understand what it takes to be the best.* I feel myself grinning like a fool, even after Tabby and Aeronwy leave. I dance around the storeroom, gathering the materials June needs for our lesson and humming happily.

We'll be making our own watercolor paints today, which is exciting. We already made lake pigments by extracting dye from plants and precipitating the color out with alum. Then we strained, dried, and ground them with mortar and pestle. It felt like the adult equivalent of a science fair project.

I line up the pigments and mediums on the counter in June's studio in an aesthetically pleasing way and take a photo for Astragram. Powdered pigments, gum arabic, glycerin, honey, tiny plastic trays—this is the alchemy I was hoping to learn here in the Bindery. June picks up on the tune I was humming and sings the chorus out loud as e joins me, carrying a set of glass plates and something that looks like a glass pestle with a much wider base.

"This is a muller," June explains. "Even though the pigments are already ground, to make sure our paint does what we want, they need to be ground even further, after we wet them with our mediums. Fine ground for fine paints!"

I stare at the muller with trepidation. I have a repetitive stress injury from college and my wrist has been acting up lately. Between the mortar and pestle and practicing my lettering for hours on end, my tendons are not happy. Most Illuminated books are handwritten. Working with ink now means working with words. I've been secretly hoping that if my writing is absolutely perfect, June will allow me to letter part of *The Stories We Sing*. Maybe the titles, or the captions.

Grinding pigments by hand is sure to bring the pain to the surface. June has us do stretches first, though, and my wrist doesn't feel too bad. I'll do it and see how it goes. I can always stop if I absolutely must.

June puts some calm, happy instrumental music on and we sit down to work. The studio is cozy and warm, the crystal lamps soft and the space heater humming. Outside, the day is gray and drizzly, as it has been since Cedar Moon. I've never seen so much rain in my life. It never seems to pour here, unlike the deluges we get in Aquanea during the wet season. Instead it drips steadily for days on end. The mountains have disappeared, obscured by perpetual mist.

I love it. I'm happy to spend the winter with the world wrapped in a big, gray blanket.

"So," I say, as I combine a yellow buckthorn pigment and acacia gum with a palette knife, "were you and Aeronwy apprentices at the same time?"

"No, Aery started soon after I finished mine. I was Opal's last apprentice, and Aery took the spot left when e retired," June replies. Our voices are muffled by the filtration masks we wear while handling the dry pigments, but I can hear well enough.

"Is that how you met?"

June shakes eir head. "We met when I first moved back here from Fenia to test for and then start my apprenticeship. Siobhan roped Aery into giving me the big tour of the Library, as a way to introduce me to new people. Siobhan and I had unexpectedly reunited in the infirmary after being separated for ten years. We'd grown up together before I moved away."

E gives me some pointers on medium and pigment ratios. June's method doesn't use exact measurements, relying instead on the feel of the paint beneath the muller. The same pigment could use different amounts of medium depending on the batch. It's frustrating for me. I feel like there's no guaranteed outcome. No $A + B = $ success.

"What was Aeronwy doing at the Library if e wasn't an Illumination apprentice yet?" I ask.

"Oh, e worked in housekeeping for seven years," June says.

"*Housekeeping?* Aeronwy? Really?" I can't keep the disbelief from my voice, and June laughs again. Above the dust mask, eir blue eyes sparkle mischievously. It's hard for me to imagine Aeronwy in the plain black shirts and jeans I've seen people wearing while vacuuming, dusting, and scrubbing carpet stains around the Library. It's even harder to imagine em with dirt on eir hands.

"It really does shock people. But you know, Aery's always been a hard, humble worker and a tidy person. Cleaning was an easy fit for em," June explains.

"I guess that makes sense," I say. "So, were you already dating when Aeronwy joined you up here in the Bindery?"

"Yes, but not for very long. We didn't start dating until we'd known each other for a good three years." When I raise an eyebrow at this, June continues, "We didn't have romantic feelings for each other at first. I'm demiromantic and demisexual, and Aery is gray-aromantic. It takes me a long time and a deep emotional connection before romantic attraction is even possible, and it only happens to Aery very rarely, among other things."

"And it went well? Dating and working together?" I ask.

"It went well. We made mistakes, of course. It wasn't always easy. It still isn't, sometimes. Any long-term partnership is two parts love, two parts hard work, and one part luck."

"Luck? Really?" I ask, surprised.

"You never know how someone will change over the years. So much that happens to us is out of our control, and those things shape who we become. Aery and I are lucky that we've changed in ways that still fit together," says June. "Not everyone does. It's no one's fault."

"Doesn't that make you nervous?" I say. It makes me nervous. I forget about being careful with my wrist injury, anxiously repeating the grinding motion of the muller.

"At the beginning especially," June says, "but it's lessened greatly over time. I've learned to worry less about things I can't control. All relationships have an element of risk, after all."

I think about Tabby. How I haven't moved beyond flirting because I'm afraid of what could happen if I fail. I can't stand the thought of being rejected. It feels like 'not good enough' being stamped across my forehead.

"I think I'm finished with this one," I say, setting my muller aside.

June wets a paintbrush and touches it to my paint, then makes a swatch on a piece of paper. The color is a beautiful medium yellow, but there are obvious grains in it.

"Almost," e says. "Just a little longer, and you'll be good."

I try to hide my trepidation. My wrist is aching fiercely, but I can't stop now, when I'm so close.

"So, you and Aeronwy don't have any children, right? I've never heard you mention them if you do," I say, getting back to grinding.

"Raising children just wasn't in the cards for us," says June. "I always liked the idea myself, but when it came down to practical matters, I was far too engrossed in my work and my research to have time for parenting. With another partner, things might have turned out differently, but Aeronwy absolutely did not want to have children, so we didn't."

"Do you regret it?" I ask.

"Not at all," June says. "Our family here in Caspora City has been cobbled together from many places. We've helped out with some of our friends' children, most of whom are grown now. We also knew when we made the decision that we'd have apprentices down the road, and that some if not all of them would be very special to us."

I want to be someone special to June. I have to prove I'm worthy of that.

When June and I are done making paint, I retreat to the temporary studio to gather myself before heading home. I flop down on Tabby's bed (which e said I'm free to use whenever) and groan, holding my wrist close to my chest. I definitely overdid it.

I hear the elevator ding, followed by the sound of Aeronwy and Tabby's voices in the common room. I can't make out the words, but they sound happy. I should get up. I should take my things and go. It's just that even the *thought* of moving my right hand is painful, and knowing I made it that way is depressing. I press my face into the pillow and groan again.

I keep my face down when Tabby enters the studio, soft footsteps vibrating through the old wood floor. There's a slight rustle of bags and bottles; I wonder if e thinks I'm asleep.

"Amane?"

I guess not.

"What?" I say into the pillow.

"I'm not waking you, am I?"

"No," I say.

"I know you usually go home around now, I just wanted to give you something before you left."

I roll onto my side and look up at em. Tabby holds out a glass vial filled with fine, iridescent glitter. Pink, blue, yellow, white. It sparkles even in the low lamp light.

"I know how much you like glitter," e says, "and the Stoneroots shop was so amazing. I felt bad you weren't there with us, so I got you this."

Without thinking, I reach out with my bad arm to take the vial. Pain shoots through my wrist and all the way up to my elbow. My pinky finger tingles with pins and needles, and I fumble the vial as my grip weakens. Luckily, it lands softly on the bed and not on the hardwood floor. We'd be cleaning up glitter for *years* if it broke.

"Oh, sorry!" Tabby says.

"No, no, it's my fault," I say, and pick it up with my left hand instead. I draw my right wrist back against my body and hold the vial up to examine it. "This is so pretty! Thank you so much, really!"

Tabby beams, then glances at my wrist. "Is your hand okay?"

"It will be. Just overdid it a little today, you know how it is," I say, even though it feels like someone has stabbed a dagger through my wrist and poured iron into my thumb joint.

Tabby sits down on the bed beside me, face full of concern. "Repetitive stress injury?"

"Yeah. I had it really bad in college, but it got better. Sometimes it flares up again," I explain.

"Would you like a massage?"

"Eh?" The incredulous noise that escapes me is more a squeak than a word. Tabby blushes.

"A hand and wrist massage. To help with the pain."

"Oh! That—that sounds nice. Sure," I say. My cheeks feel hot. I look away, not wanting to appear *too* eager.

"Okay. Wait right here."

Tabby gets up and leaves the room. I wonder what e's doing? I play with the vial of glitter, tilting it back and forth so the grains tumble from one end to the other. Its shimmer is soothing. I picture Tabby in the shop, gazing at a rack full of sparkles and thinking of me. The thought makes my heart warm.

After a few minutes, Tabby returns with a large bowl of water and a small towel. E carries it gracefully to the bed and sets it on the floor before me, then goes back to retrieve more things: a bar of soap and a bottle of lotion.

I sit up, placing my feet on either side of the bowl. Steam rises from the surface in delicate white wisps.

"Are you sure this isn't too much trouble?" I ask.

"Of course not. When you're in pain, you should be taken care of. I'm happy to help," e says.

Tabby pulls up a floor cushion and seats emself across from me. E sets everything out neatly, within easy reach, and then holds eir hands out above the bowl. The smile on eir face is soft and encouraging. I feel suddenly shy, my heart fluttering like a little moth, as I join our hands together.

The soap Tabby brought smells of sage and rose, a warm memory of the desert gardens I grew up in. E works up a white, foamy lather in the hot water, and then slowly washes each of my hands with attention and care. The hot water soothes my aches. Tabby's touch soothes my soul.

I had no idea hand washing could feel so intimate. My racing thoughts quiet as I absorb the calm radiating from Tabby's presence. Tension I hadn't realized I felt runs from my body with the water e pours to rinse away the suds. We don't speak as e pulls the soft gray towel from eir shoulder and pats my hands dry. We don't need to.

Tabby breaks the silence as e pumps some lotion into eir palms. "Now for the actual massaging part. Let me know if it hurts too much and I'll be gentler," e says.

I nod, not trusting myself to speak right now. Tabby starts with my injured hand, working each finger with firm, circular motions. Everything is wonderful until e reaches my thumb; I wince and gasp as e presses into the soft flesh between it and my forefinger.

"Too much?"

We look up, and our eyes meet. A spark leaps between us like a shooting star streaking across the sky.

"…the pain is worse than I said earlier," I admit, "much worse."

"I'll be gentle, then."

As if Tabby could be anything but. Strong and gentle, my absolute weakness. I don't fear the risk of rejection anymore. I'm too busy dreaming of love.

***

"I like the 3995 movie version. Less focus on the romance, more historically accurate," Rhiannon says.

"Yeah, that one is good," I say, "but the original novel is still my favorite. You've read it, right?"

We're in the old tunnels under the Library, where Rhiannon wants to show me something secret. There's little to no light down here, so we have headlamps strapped to our foreheads. The darkness and sense of abandonment is both exciting and scary. Rhiannon clears the spider webs with a stick, but e can't move the cold spots left by the ghosts. I shiver every few steps, despite my wool sweater.

Rhiannon rolls eir eyes. "Can't go to school in Caspora without getting assigned *The Stories We Sing* at some point. Multiple points," e says.

"I first read it when I minored in Casporan at university," I say. "In Gildea, everyone has to read *The Pale Bloom of Fire*. Have you read it?"

"The original and the translation."

"What'd you think?"

"Honestly? Dry as fuck. I read the translation first, so I thought maybe it was the translator's fault, but I was wrong."

I laugh. The sound should echo in these halls, but instead it feels muffled. "That's what everyone thinks, even if they won't say it."

Rhiannon lifts a book from a haphazard pile and cracks it open. I can see the dust floating in the beam of eir headlamp. "Gods, that's the thing about publishing, right? People get to read your book! But then… *people get to read your book*. And have *opinions* on it. Hey, check this out, it's a mortuary manual from the 3800s."

"Blegh, no thank you," I say.

"You talk to dead people all the time, but you can't handle dead bodies?"

"Bodies are fine. What I don't like is seeing diagrams of them cut open."

"You're missing out, these drawings are *so* weird."

I pick up half a paperback with a werewolf on the cover, a swooning, half-naked beauty in its arms. I'm glad we have headlamps because my right hand is still in a brace. It would be hard to hold a book and a flashlight at the same time.

"Can I tell you a secret?" I say.

Rhiannon turns and angles eir headlamp to light up eir face in a spooky way. "That's what we're here for, isn't it? No one to hear us but the dead, who tell no tales. Usually. Fire away."

"I have no idea what I want to write for my apprenticeship book. The one I get to make myself after June and I are done with *The Stories We Sing*," I say.

"You still have plenty of time to think of something, don't you?" Rhiannon says, but I can tell e's surprised. I sigh.

"I've already thought of a thousand things! I've been dreaming of this job since I was thirteen years old. I planned every step of the way and then went for it. Now I'm here, and I'm at a loss," I say, sitting down on one of the book piles.

"How come?" says Rhiannon, sitting across from me.

"I don't feel good enough for any of them. It's my first Illuminated book, so it's not going to be my best. I don't want to use any of the ideas I have until I can do them justice," I explain.

"I get that. Perfectionism is rough," Rhiannon says with a grimace.

"Why does everyone keep calling it that?" I say.

"Because it is? The sooner you admit to it, the sooner you can quit doing it," Rhiannon says, "and start feeling a lot less shitty about yourself. Not that I've made much progress, myself."

My heart sinks. I look down at my wrist brace. Are they right about me? Are my standards too high? Admitting that feels like abandoning the work and mindset that got me here. My mothers and sisters have proven to me time and again that success only comes to those who earn it.

Then I remember what June said about relationships, and how part of it is all luck. What if that's true with careers, too? I don't like it because it means I don't have total control over my future.

Rhiannon continues, "If you ever wanna bounce ideas for your book around, I'd love to hear them. I bet they're all awesome and you'd do a great job at any of them."

"Thanks, Rhee. You can always tell me your secrets and book worries, too," I say. "You'll let me read that drafted article you have about puns and jokes in ancient Casporan texts, right?"

"I'll email it to you. And, actually, I do have something I want to tell you, aside from the secret room I wanted to show you down here. Or, well, they're related," Rhiannon says hesitantly. I can't see eir eyes in the glare of my headlamp on eir glasses, but e might even be scared.

"What is it?" I ask.

"It's—I—you'll be mad, but—"

Something loud clatters at the end of the hallway. I jump to my feet, scattering erotic novels everywhere. Rhiannon sits bolt upright, squinting into the darkness beyond.

"What was that?" I ask, heart pounding.

"Dunno. Pipes? A poltergeist? Been a while since we had one of those," e says.

A shiver runs up my spine. "Maybe we should go. I'm not in the mood to get possessed," I say.

But it's too late. The clatter comes again, this time much closer. Rhiannon takes a step forward, and in the glare of the headlamp I see books falling from the shelves and onto the floor. Single books, one at a time, as if someone were running towards us and pulling them off as they go.

I dig my feet into the stone and focus on my magical wards, but the spirit tunnels through them instantly. The sound of cards shuffling fills my ears, the feeling of a fine carved woodblock presses against my fingers, and my hair curls tighter as if trying to hold on to a precious secret.

"Damn it—" I curse, before the spirit takes over my body.

My vision whites out, and when it returns, I'm floating above myself, surveying the scene with eyes that can see in the dark. My body is slumped across the pile of scattered books, with Rhiannon hovering anxiously overhead.

"Amane? Amane, are you okay? Can you hear me?" e says, slapping my cheek lightly, as if that would work.

It does, in a way. My body sits up and the spirit uses my face to glare at Rhiannon. It uses my voice to say something angry in a language I don't know. I recognize it then as Calliope Everberry, who possessed me the very first day I met Rhiannon over *The Guide to the Threadbound Oracle*. I'd been secretly thrilled about that—lending my body to the author and artist of my favorite oracle system—but this time, I feel annoyed and frustrated. I'll be exhausted after this, as if the pain in my wrist wasn't already enough to keep me from getting back to work.

Last time Calliope possessed me, Rhiannon performed an exorcism. This time, e says something to the spirit in the same old language. By the tone of eir voice, it sounds like e's asking for forgiveness.

Calliope only frowns harder, sighs, and goes on a long monologue that has Rhiannon more slumped over with every sentence. When e finishes, there's only silence. I never realized how creepy my eyes look when I'm possessed, rolled back into my head with only the whites showing. The spooky lighting from the headlamps doesn't help.

Rhiannon says one more thing, and Calliope nods. I know e's exited my body because my vision flashes white again, and my physical senses return. One of them being a sense of leaden weight in all my aching limbs.

"Ughhh," I complain, sitting up and rubbing my forehead.

"You okay?" Rhiannon says.

All I can do is grumble. I'm suddenly so tired that my brain can't form the right words. Especially not in Casporan. Luckily, Rhiannon seems to understand enough of my half-sensical Gildean to scoop me up and help me walk back upstairs to the infirmary.

The infirmary is a soothing place with lots of windows and pastel-colored walls. Dark green plants hang from the ceiling, purifying the air and the magical energy circulating around us. Siobhan is on duty for emotional/spiritual first aid, which brightens my mood. E kindly leads us to a room where I can lie down and does some work on my spirit body. Rhiannon waits impatiently in a chair in the corner, checking social media on eir phone.

"What were you even talking about? It was Calliope again, right?" I ask once Siobhan leaves so I can get some rest. I'd rather get up and head home, but my legs won't let me.

Rhiannon startles and shoves eir phone into a pocket. "E was like, 'Well, I warned you, and you didn't listen,' you know, about those cards e showed me the first time you got possessed," e says, "which were about the original copy of *The Founding*."

"I see," I say, scrunching my face up. I feel like e didn't fully answer my question. Or that answer doesn't quite make sense. But it might just be that my brain feels like scrambled eggs right now. I replay the whole scene in my mind, though it already feels fuzzy, like a dream. "What were you going to say right before I got possessed? Didn't you want to tell me something? And show me something?"

"Oh, um," Rhiannon says, "The room wasn't important, we can go there later. I just wanted to say that I know you have a crush on Tabby."

"What?!"

"Unless I misread the situation, which I often do, but it has to be pretty obvious for me to pick up on it," Rhiannon says. "I realized that whenever I get confused watching a conversation with weird undertones I don't understand, people are usually flirting."

"No, you're right," I say. I snuggle down into the blankets Siobhan covered me with. They're incredibly soft, and I could almost fall asleep right here. I stifle a yawn. "How do you feel about that?"

Rhiannon shrugs. "It's cool with me. I'd much rather Tabby date one of my friends than a complete stranger. All three of us can hang out together."

"Who said anything about dating?"

"No one. But maybe you should say something about it to Tabby."

CHAPTER TWENTY-TWO
TABBY

Slowly, the charred landscape of my heart begins to heal. At first, it's a desolate place, all ash and coal. I sit on the blackened stoop of my little cottage and cry until I wake with real tears running down my face.

Aeronwy gives me a book about wildflowers that bloom after fire. It explains the ecology of post-fire growth and the spiritual significance of each flower with a poetic flair. Bits of folklore and magical correspondences are listed in a swirling script so beautiful it rivals the pictures.

I tuck it under my pillow at night, to take the knowledge with me. In the ruins of my heartscape, I dream new seeds into being and scatter them across the gray and black hillsides. Then I let myself cry and hope my tears will be the rain they need to bloom.

I stop taking calls from my parents, instead sending brief text messages with vague excuses for why I can't talk. When they get frantic with worry and anger, I let Rhee screen their texts and voicemails for me. What would I even say to them right now? I thought that when I moved out of their house at eighteen, I was free. I distanced myself. I went to therapy. I switched careers to pursue my dreams, rather than theirs.

And yet… the fire. Even with distance I'm still drawn between them, placed there as a buffer for the worst they're capable of inflicting on one another. Like a ship riding the tide, pulled from the ocean through a narrow strait between high, rocky cliffs. Where would they be without my mediation? I always thought I was protecting them, but did it delay a necessary breakup?

Chapter Twenty-Two

The flowers begin to sprout. First red spikes of fire lily, glowing against the colorless soil like tongues of flame returned. Then waving fronds of fireweed, which scatter thousands more seeds, painting the hills pink. I watch as orange fire poppy, yellow hillside monkey flower, and purple temple bells add to the palette. Scarlet larkspur, daisies, lupines, wild sweet pea, mariposa lilies, and even wild cucumber appear in greater profusion each night. A rainbow of growth I hardly knew I was capable of.

Wildflowers bloom bright but brief. This is just the first step of many if I want to heal this place—to heal myself. I have an idea of how to do that, but I'm not certain I'm ready. For now, I'll sit on the hill and breathe in the sweet scent of my soul in spring.

***

One weekend, Aeronwy and June invite us to their home for dinner. They live close to the Library in the northeast quarter of the city, where the land slopes steeply into the mountains. Rhiannon and I trek through the gray, cold drizzle, curious what we'll find.

The apartment building Rhiannon and I live in is very new, a colorful glass skyscraper outfitted with hanging courtyard gardens and smart technology to keep everything running efficiently. We know the neighbors on our floor and a few scattered others, but there are hundreds more. In this neighborhood, the houses are only one or two stories, made of stucco or cedar shingles. They sprawl together in strange shapes, like letters scrawled across the hillside. Each structure is painted a different color. The streets are lined with enormous fir and redwood trees of great age, and their thick canopies protect us from the rain.

The Stargroves live in a house of sky-blue stucco with white and lavender trim, halfway up one of the largest hills in the city. Rhiannon pants and moans dramatically as we climb to the front door, which is painted yellow beneath an arch of wisteria. There are no flowers now, but I can imagine how beautiful it is in the summer.

My heart hammers along with the brass doorknocker as I announce our arrival. I can hear voices inside; Amane is already here, as well as Siobhan. Their loud laughs and exclamations are unmistakable. There are approaching footsteps, and then the door opens.

"Hi!" Amane says brightly. She looks dazzling in a sweetheart dress patterned with rolling ocean waves. Her hair is pulled into twists that she's piled artfully onto her head. Even in the winter gloom, her dark brown skin is glowing and dusted with glitter. She never misses an opportunity to dress up.

"Come on in!"

June calls to us from farther inside. Amane widens the door so Rhiannon and I can step through. We take our shoes and coats off in the narrow front hallway before emerging into the warmth and light of the living area.

The first thing I notice is the fireplace. The enormous stone structure takes up a third of the eastern wall and has a roaring blaze inside. The mouth of the fireplace is a semi-circle rather than a square, like a sun rising over the horizon. The wide stone mantle that tops it carries an altar that puts the one in Aeronwy's studio to shame: huge pillar candles with dripping wax, hunks of shiny obsidian and rough pumice, earthenware jars painted with indigenous patterns, bundles of herbs for burning, golden bowls brimming with offerings, and a stunning glass statue of Cináed in firebird form.

The light from the hearth makes the firebird statue glow, as if lit from within. I tear my eyes away from it with difficulty. The room is painted a warm peach color, with sandy wood floors and a profusion of colorful handmade rugs. The furniture is mismatched and quirky. The wall opposite the fireplace is covered with books and a restrained number of knickknacks. Hooked around to the left, I can see the hint of a dining room, and at the far end, an open archway to the kitchen.

Amane crosses the room and plops down on the striped couch between Siobhan and June. The old healer has taken off eir headscarf, which shows e trusts us as friends and family. Not all Caoimhen nuns cover their heads and dress modestly, but for those who do, it's an important part of their devotion to their deity. Siobhan's hair lays across eir shoulder in an enormous braid, the end coiled up in eir lap. It's black at the end and fades up to gray at the roots.

Rhiannon wanders forward, cradling the pot of soup we brought and examining the house with brazen curiosity. "I got soup, where should I put this?"

"In the kitchen is fine, just through that arch," June says. Then e looks at me and gestures at the loveseat beside the couch. "Go on and join us, Tabby! Aeronwy and Meenah are still cooking. We were just chatting, as you do."

"As *you* do," Siobhan says, eyeing June and Amane with amusement. The two of them exchange an embarrassed glance.

I set my purse aside and sit down. The heat from the hearth settles into my bones, a relief after the chill outside.

"Thank you so much for having us over," I say, "your home is really beautiful."

"Thank you, dear. We really should have invited you sooner. We've been having these weekend dinners regularly for years, and our apprentices are always welcome. Tonight's a quiet one, sometimes we have a good twelve or fifteen people in over the course of the evening, between coworkers and neighbors and friends," June says.

I'm glad there aren't that many guests here now. I'd much rather our first visit be an intimate one—as much as it can be with seven people.

"This is the main crew," Siobhan says, "all we're missing is Inyene. Bastard only lives here about half the year now. I think he's off on a tropical beach somewhere debuting a resort collection."

"I still can't believe you're friends with someone so famous," Amane breathes, leaning her chin on her hands dreamily. "I mean, June's kind of famous, too, in an academic way, but—"

"I'm not a celebrity," June chuckles. "Aery and Inyene went to university together. Aery was looking for someone to tailor eir clothes—nothing is ever long enough on em—and Inyene needed someone to model for him in the student shows he was doing at the time. They hit it off. He wasn't famous yet."

Amane fixes June with an incredulous look. "Wait, *what*? Modeling?"

Siobhan cackles heartily, belly and beard shaking with glee. E nods.

Amane's eyes widen, and e throws me a look as well. "Are there *pictures*?"

"Oh sure," says June. "Just a moment."

June gets up and goes to the wall of books, stopping at a shelf that appears to be filled with matching spines. E pulls off a few large volumes and lugs them back to the couch. Curious, I come sit on the floor by Amane's feet. She flashes me an adorably excited smile as June lays one of the scrapbooks in her lap and cracks it open. The spine is embossed with the date 3974 - 3978, about forty-some years ago.

The scrapbook smells wonderfully of old paper with a touch of incense. The paper is thick, with deckled edges and flower petals sprinkled throughout. The artfully arranged photos are captioned by hand. Their colors have faded, and they have the slight haziness of photography from that time, but they're still fascinating.

Rhiannon reappears, leaning on the back of the couch and peering over Amane's shoulder.

"Eh, what's this, then?" e says, green eyes lighting up with interest. Rhiannon loves old photographs.

"Ancient history," Siobhan says.

"Holy shit, is that Aeronwy?" Rhiannon reaches out one arm and stabs a finger at the page.

It has to be. The person in the photos can't be older than eighteen, but there's no mistaking the sharp cheekbones and narrow gold eyes. Or the intensity in them. Young Aeronwy posing stiffly by the sound, drawing in an art classroom, smoking on an unfamiliar balcony. E wears nothing but black, matching the short black curls on eir head. One gray streak in the front is always stylishly arranged.

"This was a bit before I knew em," June says.

Siobhan reaches over and turns a few pages. "But it was around when I met em, so I should be in here soon."

Sure enough, Siobhan appears beside Aeronwy in many of the following photos, leaning rakishly on a cane inlaid with abalone or draped across Aeronwy's lap. E's already a nun, wearing the same colorful but modest clothing e does now. The patterns are much more 70s, including a series of incredible tie-dyed maxi dresses. Young Siobhan gazes at the camera with sultry, half-lidded eyes that bring a blush to my cheeks. Aeronwy looks a lot happier in these photos, arms around an obviously close friend.

"What about the modeling though," Amane whispers through her hands, which are pressed to either side of her face.

They flip farther through the book. Here's Aeronwy with a person I assume is Inyene, although he looks incredibly different. Not just younger, but softer, without any facial hair, and more obvious curves. They're in a fabric shop, standing before a wall of colors. Inyene has his arms spread wide, dramatically posed, while Aeronwy looks contemplative.

"This is before he…hm, I don't know how to explain it in Casporan," Amane says. "He changed genders."

I look at her questioningly.

"Some other cultures assign people genders when they're born," she explains, "usually, um, based on genitals, although in Gildea it's more complicated than that, there's some things about birth order, and astrology and….well, sometimes people realize that they don't identify with that gender and decide to change to another."

"Like how?" Rhiannon asks. Rhiannon has never understood gender, and I don't blame em. I have a better grasp since Lilja and most of my family on her side still identify with Hrafnlandian roles and use neo-pronouns in Casporan, but I'm still not entirely sure what Amane is talking about.

"Different hair, different clothes, different pronouns, a new name, in this case, maybe hormones?" Amane says, looking back at the picture.

"The word in Casporan is 'transgender,'" June offers. "And you're right. He started hormone replacement therapy not to long after this, I think. We used to talk about it a lot, because he liked working through his thoughts aloud and I was the only one in our friend group who had lived in a gendered culture long enough to understand."

"You have hormone therapy here in Caspora?" Amane asks.

"Even without gender, some people still feel dysphoric in their physical bodies," Siobhan says. "As a priestex of Caoimhe,

I counsel people on body image often, and with native Casporans it's rare but not unheard of. Besides, there have been transgender people here from other cultures, like Inyene, for centuries. We have options for them."

Amane nods her approval and then goes back to the book. She turns the page and then squeals something in Gildean that makes Rhiannon snort with laughter.

"What was that?" Siobhan asks.

Amane looks shifty-eyed and clears her throat, clearly embarrassed. Rhiannon grins and translates, "She thinks Aeronwy is hot in those modeling photos."

Amane shoots Rhee a death glare. "I said it in Gildean for a reason!"

"Well, you should have said it in a language I *don't* know!"

Siobhan laughs, too, and then calls towards the kitchen, "Aery! June's apprentice thinks you were a hot, young thing back in the day!"

Amane shrieks again, this time in indignation, and covers her face with her hands. Aeronwy appears in the kitchen archway, drying eir hands on a dishtowel, one eyebrow raised.

"Just back in the day? I'm offended," e says.

Everyone laughs except Amane, who sputters with embarrassment. I pat her knee consolingly, even as I'm holding back my own giggles. She peeks through her fingers at me and shakes her head, a smile slowly curling across her face.

She's right. Aeronwy was beautiful and still is. Inyene's early work is vibrant and elegant. Flowy jumpsuits, draped gowns, blouses with huge, lacy sleeves—Aeronwy wears them all with grace and subtle emotion. A sense of longing, of being poised on some edge, suffuses each photo.

Amane pores over them with glee, exchanging comments with Rhiannon about how Inyene's work has changed over the years, before settling down to flip through the rest of the scrapbook. Aeronwy emerges from the kitchen and stands beside Rhiannon, peering down at the album. E has a small bowl and spoon in one hand; the smell emanating from it is divine, warm with ginger and cardamom and a dozen other spices I can't name.

"Give this a taste?" e says to June, offering em the bowl. "I think it's missing something, but I disagree with Meenah on what."

Instead of taking the bowl, June tilts eir head up and opens eir mouth expectantly. Aeronwy scoops up a spoonful of what looks like a potato curry. Smiling, e feeds it to June in a tender way that makes my heart hurt with sweetness. It's such a small moment, but it's yet another thing I missed seeing between my parents.

June chews thoughtfully and then says, "More salt."

"You always say that," says Aeronwy.

"I told you!" Meenah's voice rings out from the kitchen.

"Your food always needs more salt, love," says June, not unkindly.

"I like it this way."

"That's because you're already full of salt," Siobhan snorts.

"Fair."

Amane interrupts them all with another squeak of delight. She taps the scrapbook and then turns to June with a huge grin.

"This is you, right? You're so cute!" she exclaims.

I peer over at photos of a camping trip. Amid the lodgepole pines and fir trees and a sparkling alpine lake, is a person who must be June. Square face unlined and heavily freckled, brilliant red hair floating around em in fluffy wisps, gold wire framed glasses perched on a large round nose. The smile is exactly the same, bright and wide, eyes nearly crinkled shut.

"Aw, thank you Amane," June says, blushing.

Aeronwy, Siobhan, and Inyene are in the photos as well, including one scandalous lakeside shot featuring Aeronwy in a thong swimsuit. E's stretched out on a towel with a book, giving the photographer the middle finger.

"I took that one," Siobhan says, waggling eir eyebrows. "It's my favorite from that trip. I still have a copy in a drawer at home."

Rhiannon makes a face, and Amane snickers. The looks Aeronwy and Siobhan are trading are embarrassing, so I look back at the album. Amane is studying a group shot on a cliff overlooking the lake. It shows a cloudless sunny day with the impressive peak of Mt. Cináed rising high behind them. There are five people in the photo instead of four. One of them wasn't in any of the preceding shots.

Amane points to the fifth figure in the photo. "Who's this?"

"Great fucking Author of the Universe, is that *Mairead?*" Rhiannon leans all the way over the back of the couch and adjusts eir glasses.

Young Mairead is the shortest of the group, standing dead center and flashing two peace signs at the camera. Eir figure is lithe and graceful, a powder blue sundress billowing around eir knees. Mairead's hair is in its familiar bob, but much thicker, with black roots and ends dyed red. The smirk on eir face is confident and cool, eyes wide behind a pair of rose-tinted sunglasses shaped like hearts.

"It is, yes," says June uneasily. "We used to have a lot of photos with Mairead in them, but after things fell apart, we put them away—"

"Or burned them," interjects Aeronwy.

"—yes, or that. I did save a few, mostly group shots, if you ever want to see them," June finishes.

"No, I'm good," says Rhiannon. E leans back and crosses eir arms uncomfortably. I try to catch eir eye, but e doesn't look at me. E doesn't look at anyone. "What happened, though? Y'all look happy here."

"We were," says Siobhan dryly, "when we weren't fighting. Mairead and I had some, hmm, theological bones to pick with each other. E wasn't a priestex yet, but e was going to an Authorist temple, getting mixed up in fascist ideologies that should have died with the Revolution, bringing them back to us…"

"Mostly I was just ignored," June says mildly.

"E thought you were boring, which I've never fucking understood, because it's not fucking true," Siobhan adds. "Also, we took Aery's attention away from em. That was the worst offense of all."

Aeronwy stares into the hearth fire and says, "Mairead was like a magnet; e repulsed some people and drew others instantly close. E was brash and snarky and confident. A talented artist with an iron vision. When someone like that approves of you, trusts you with their deepest secrets, *relies* on you, it makes you feel special. The trouble is, it was always transactional. If you didn't repay eir favors, you were shamed and guilted for it, screamed at or weeped upon in some cases, until you gave em what e wanted. Even if it was something you weren't willing to give."

Everyone is silent. Rhiannon's lips are pressed into a grim line. E looks troubled, and I wonder if maybe there are things I don't know about. Not that I'd expect Rhiannon to tell me every little moment of eir day at work, but e has been quiet about it lately.

"Yeah I can see that," e says.

"If you ever end up in a bind with Mairead, we can help," June offers gently. "You wouldn't be the first."

"Thanks," says Rhiannon.

Amane and I exchange a glance. It's not like Rhee to sound so morose.

"Supper is ready!" Meenah calls out joyfully as she joins us from the kitchen. She's in her mid-fifties, with a tangle of black hair streaked gray and golden skin. A little shorter than Rhee, with a round, soft body and dark eyes that sparkle as if they contain stars. She gazes around at all of us, tea towel slung over her shoulder, and raises her thick brows.

"Did I interrupt something?" she asks.

"Nope! Perfect timing! I'm starving, let's eat already," Rhiannon says, and is the first to march off towards the kitchen.

That, at least, is normal. I relax and get up to follow.

***

Dinner is amazing. Meenah and Aeronwy cover the huge, round table with so many steaming dishes, it's impossible to decide what to eat first. There's clear lemongrass soup, saffron rice with pomegranate and parsley, spicy potato and pea curry, salt-baked cod with preserved lemon, crispy flatbreads with various spreads, lamb meatballs in rich gravy, a potent herb salad with sweet dressing, and for dessert, a decadent almond flour cake drenched in mandarin syrup.

Before we start eating, I do the honors and set a plate with the first bite of each dish on the altar in the corner as an offering to the ancestors. Rose's photo is prominent on the table, beside one I recognize as Opaline Sweetfrond, June's mentor and previous Head Librarian. There are pale faces framed by the same red hair as June's, and a portrait of a stern, elderly person with Aeronwy's eyes.

Then it's time for food and conversation. I love the tales the Stargroves and their friends tell. I can only hope to be as storied when I'm their age. Amane joins in, enthusiastically recounting hijinks from her childhood and college years. I'm not surprised she was prone to sneaking out to go clubbing or sneaking around the art building after hours to pull all-nighters on projects. Her energy is contagious. When I'm around her, I feel like I'm floating in a glass of bubbly, sweet wine.

The dining room walls are hung with June's beautiful tapestries, scenes of Casporan nature woven in jewel-toned yarns. I can feel the magic radiating off them encouraging a peaceful, abundant home. A large painting of Rose's takes a place of honor among them: it's a watercolor split into three panels, one end a swirl of blooming blues, the other a vibrant lick of reds. In the center panel, they envelop one another in beautiful, soft rings.

Aeronwy notices me looking and turns to gaze at it as well. "That was our handfasting gift from Rose. It's how e saw our auras when we were together."

"It's beautiful. Rose seems like e was an incredible person."

"Irreplaceable. We'd stopped having these dinners for some time after e passed. It simply didn't feel right without em here," Aeronwy says.

"Does it feel all right now?" I ask.

Aeronwy's eyes flicker across the table, then back to me. "It does. I'm glad you're here. Rose was my companion in calm beside this noisy lot. It's nice to find that balance once more."

After dessert, Rhiannon breaks out the hard cider from eir parents' farm. They always send us home with more bottles than we can drink ourselves. Siobhan and Meenah latch onto it immediately, arguing over who gets the first pour. Amane raises her glass and suggests we move back to the living room, where it's warmer. Casporan winters are mild, but she's from the desert. She shivers and June drapes a shawl around her shoulders.

Instead of joining them, I help Aeronwy clear the table. While e packs away what little is left over, I wash the dishes. Aeronwy picks up a towel to dry them, and we clean in companionable silence while laughter rings out from the other room.

"Thank you for helping. I suspect you'll miss out on the alcohol," Aeronwy says.

"That's okay. I like cleaning more than being tipsy," I say. It was always easier growing up to do the dishes before Lilja and Oran could fight over whose turn it was. The habit has stuck with me, even when I'm not in my own home.

"I'd say the same, except I'm not sure if the one time I had alcohol counts as being tipsy, so I suppose I wouldn't know. Mostly I was horribly ill," says Aeronwy.

"Right, because of your Flame." *On Flamekeeping* had explained, in excruciating detail, what happens to Flamekeepers who drink alcohol. It seems silly, but apparently booze doesn't mix well with magical fire.

"Rhiannon mentioned you've been reading my book," Aeronwy says.

I feel myself blushing, and keep my eyes on the sink, hands plunged into the soapy water. "Yes, I'm almost finished now. It's fascinating. I never realized how much I didn't know about fire, and Cináed."

"You're my first apprentice to check it out on their own. Some of the others looked it over after asking what I made for my apprenticeship book, but I don't think any of them read it from cover to cover. It is a bit dry and intimidating, I'll admit," says Aeronwy.

"Well," I say, laughing, "intimidating, maybe. But I... I wanted to know."

Aeronwy doesn't say anything, but e doesn't need to. I can feel the approval radiating from em with the heat of eir Flame, which feels much like the comforting warmth of the hearth fire.

Is this what having a healthy family is like? Doing everyday things together with love and support? I've wondered the same while visiting Rhiannon's home time and again, but this feels different. I feel less an outsider who's visiting to escape the cold, and more like I've moved permanently into a space that was made just for me.

There are so many dishes to wash and surfaces to clean. When we finally rejoin the others, they've quieted down and split into small groups. Rhiannon and Meenah are seated by the hearth, talking about food. Siobhan is asleep in one of the armchairs, and June and Amane are on the couch, looking at more photo albums.

Aeronwy steps outside to get more wood for the fire. I sit down beside Amane, my thighs pressed up against hers. Sometimes when she naps on my bed in the studio, I think about how nice it would be to lie down and cuddle with her. As if she's read my mind, she flops back against me and tilts her head back with a smile.

"Taaaabby," she sings, clearly intoxicated, "you're so comfy. I'm glad you're still here."

"I didn't go anywhere," I say, laughing. She's solid and warm. I resist the urge to put my arms around her, glad the room is too dim for anyone to see me blushing.

"Good."

Aeronwy returns with an armful of logs, which e goes about setting onto the glowing coals of the fire. The hearth is hot, and the new logs go up immediately, dancing with yellow flames. Aeronwy does this without gloves, though there's a pair hanging nearby.

Amane gapes. "Oh my gods. You're just—doing that with the fire! It's really not burning you?"

As a response, Aeronwy sticks a hand directly in the flames, holds it there for an uncomfortably long time, and then pulls eir hand out. There's soot on eir fingers, but that's all.

"Damn," says Amane, "that's cool."

"Good to know I'm not out of touch with the youth," Aeronwy says. E plucks a candle from the altar above and lights it with a puff of breath, the way an ordinary person might blow *out* a flame.

Amane squints at this, then shuts her mouth and shakes her head. She pats my leg and turns back to the photo album sitting between her and June.

"Tabby. We're looking at more pictures. Look at this shit," she says, "this cute shit."

"Now I know you've had too much to drink, you're starting to sound like me," Rhiannon cuts in from across the room.

"That's why we're friends. I *am* like you."

I surreptitiously move Amane's glass of cider to a side table where she can't reach it, then look at the album. It's smaller than the volumes we looked at earlier, with only one photo per page. The photos are all taken at the same location, from the same angle: Aeronwy and June standing inside the stone circle they took us to in the hills above the Library, the lake as their backdrop. They have their arms wrapped around each other's waists, and June is leaning eir head on Aeronwy's shoulder. A year is written beneath each one.

"It's our tradition, every year on our handfasting anniversary," June says.

I flip through the album, watching as they age before my eyes. Watching the changes in style and fashion, the haircuts, the growth. Based on the date, they would have been about my age when they married. The last photo is from earlier this year, and there are dozens of blank pages waiting beyond that.

I've always found it difficult to imagine my own future. I'm still surprised to have made it to thirty. Soon I'll be thirty-one. Now, for the first time, I feel like I can see where I'm headed— and where I want to go.

CHAPTER TWENTY-THREE
RHIANNON

I've never had good posture, but the weight of guilt on my shoulders makes my slouch even worse. None of them know what I've done. The Stargroves invited me into their own home, treated me as warmly as their own family, while I've been sneaking around behind their backs and lying.

If you ever end up in a bind with Mairead, we can help. Is Mairead the only one who's bound me, though? Or did I help by abandoning my values for a job?

Tabby suspects something is wrong. Of course e does. Tabby learned how to read subtle body language at an early age to survive life with eir horrible parents. I can only hide so much with shit-eating grins and jokes. Even Amane, who's more trusting and less perceptive, picks up on it.

"Has everything been all right at work?" Tabby asks one day at lunch.

The three of us are eating in the Library cafeteria, beside a rain-splattered window. Amane and Tabby share a meaningful glance, as if they've planned this.

"Yeah, is everything all right?" Amane echoes.

I shrug. "Same shit, different day, why?"

"It's just, after talking with people who have known Mairead for so long, it worries me that you're spending so much time around em," Tabby says. E twirls eir hair around one finger repeatedly, and bites eir bottom lip.

"It hasn't been that bad," I say, and when I realize that's a lie, I add, "I can handle the rest. Mairead's been my boss for over eight years. This isn't new."

"You used to avoid em before," says Tabby.

"That was before I got promoted. Kind of impossible to, now."

Tabby sighs, hugging emself tightly. E knows how much I wanted the promotion.

"We're worried because you're so tired all the time," says Amane. "Don't think I haven't seen the dark circles under your eyes."

"You've been having more migraines lately," Tabby adds.

"And you get the date wrong a lot."

"Last week you didn't know what the microwave was because you thought you were living in a time before it was invented."

"What is this, an intervention?" I snap, alarmed by their prodding. "I said I can handle it."

Tabby looks ready to cry. Amane's brow is furrowed, lips pursed. I've gone too far. Not only by snapping at them, but in this whole quest with *The Founding*. I have to figure out how to fix this in a way that will hurt them the least.

"Sorry, I have been stressed out about work lately," I say. "Just give me some time to think before I talk about it, okay?"

***

I keep replaying the conversation I had with Calliope Everberry in my head, down in the sub-basement where e possessed Amane. Luckily, Amane had been too disoriented afterwards to ask much about it, or about the "secret room" we'd been down there to see in the first place. The amethyst room, where I'd planned to reveal everything to her before I chickened out.

"I warned you, and you didn't listen," Calliope hissed in Old Casporan. Hearing em use Amane's voice was super weird, because it both did and didn't sound like her at all.

I glanced around the dim hallway, but of course I couldn't see Amane's spirit floating nearby. She probably was, though, from what she'd told me about possession. She could still hear and see what was happening.

So, when I replied, I replied in the old language she wouldn't understand.

"It was a vague warning," I said. "Even Amane didn't figure it out! You could have just said I'd be in deep shit if I stole the book."

Calliope blew out an exasperated breath. "You don't even know what it is you've found, do you? I risked my life and my craft doing what I did, and I did it to protect people. Now because of you and that priestex, that protection is in danger of becoming undone," e said.

I shrunk in on myself as e continued. "What happened to Llewella, what happened to Eirlys, and countless others because of the book The Founding *once was—it can't ever happen again. Do you understand? I know the priestex won't listen. E's just like Ciaran and Isylwyn. It's up to you, now. You have to do what's right."*

Calliope didn't name the book *The Founding* used to be, but from eir words, a possibility occurred to me. A wonderful, terrible, *horrible* possibility. The thought swirls through my mind until I can't take it anymore. I have to find evidence of the truth.

Without Mairead's knowledge, I take *The Founding* back to the amethyst room for one more round of visions. After I told em it was a palimpsest, we began scanning for old traces of ink immediately. I didn't have time to probe deeper into the book's history. Rose figured out the book's secrets without fancy machinery. Maybe I can, too.

I'm not usually one to pray. Readerists don't pray to the Author the way Authorists do. My family makes tribute to deities of the land for the farm, but I've never heard the gods' voices or gone to a temple regularly. Today I clasp my hands together and stare at the ceiling, where above me sit millions of books.

"Founders, I call to you for help with my foolish bullshit. Please? Eirlys, Daryn? I could really use some guidance right now. Maybe not from you, Isylwyn, you're part of the reason I ended up here in the first place," I say. "Also, you're probably a murderer. Sorry."

I wince. That must have been the worst prayer in the universe. Shaking my head, I fill the scrying bowl with water and sacred ink. My bottles are running low. I'm definitely going to have another migraine after this. It's the price I'll have to pay.

I put my hand on the book and gaze into the scrying bowl.

***

Multi-spectral imaging is a time-consuming process involving the most expensive piece of machinery in the whole Library: the Spectre. Flawless gemstones laser-inscribed with complex sigils are used to project beams of light over an artifact, hopefully picking up minute traces of old ink and other chemical signatures. It then delivers the information to a high-powered computer. Those are processed into images and data charts, which we use for study.

I was here when the machine was purchased five years ago; it was a *huge* deal, firstly because… technology, and secondly because of what it allows us to do. Mairead might prefer paper memos to email, but e's not a fool. The Spectre lets us see into the past, through the ravages of time, and uncover secrets impossible for earlier Librarians to find. Like my visions, only much more scientific.

There's a huge waiting list to use the machine, but Mairead cleared the schedule and put us up first. My coworkers who got pushed aside haven't been too happy about that, even the ones who ordinarily back anything Mairead does. Caerwyn and Elísabet are hovering in the hallway outside, muttering angrily over their tea.

I find Mairead dancing around the machine and humming cheerfully. "Good morning, Rhiannon, I hope you're ready to see the very first scans of our book," Mairead says. "I, for one, couldn't sleep last night out of anticipation. I spent the early hours making a new shadowbox—a gift, for you."

Mairead glides over to a nearby desk and picks up a gift bag the size of a paperback book. Taking it feels like accepting a gift from a faery: it's dangerous and puts you in their debt. Mairead is watching me expectantly, so I reach in between the crinkling tissue paper and pull out a wooden box with a glass front. Inside, layers of delicate white paper cutouts are arranged to create a picture: a small figure holding a lantern, walking between towering bookshelves. The detail is incredible.

"Thanks, this is cool," I say.

"You deserve it for all the help you've given me on this project. I couldn't have done it without you," Mairead says.

"And you're gonna need my help with the Spectre data, too, I assume," I say.

Hands on hips, Mairead replies, "Not as much as you'd think. I *do* know how to use this machine and arrange the output. What I need are your language skills. I could write a novel in Old Casporan, but I admit my Ancient is rusty."

I tuck the shadowbox back in its bag and set it to the side with my things. I don't even know what I'm going to do with it.

"Why do you think the original book was in Ancient Casporan? You think it's *that* much older?" I ask.

The visions I received earlier this week suggested as much. I haven't told Mairead about those yet, and I'm not going to. If my suspicions are correct, I'm in deep shit. I thought about stealing the book back and returning it to the Stargroves, but what would I have told Mairead? Someone that good at lying would recognize more lies. It would have been my entire job on the line, not just my promotion to Assistant Head.

Those things are still on the line. But if this book is what I think it is, so is the very sanctity of the Library and the position of Head Librarian itself. It dawns on me that I may have a choice to make.

"I sent a parchment sample away for carbon dating. The estimate came back around the year 3000 or so," Mairead says gleefully. "Around a thousand years ago, around the time of the *actual* Founding. Isn't that time period your specialty?"

"Yep," I say, my voice squeaking. "Yep, it is."

Mairead is too excited to notice I'm nervous. "Another sign from the Author that this is *our* story."

The Spectre is humming away, scanning more pages of *The Founding*. The whole contraption is housed in a cast iron box the size of a dinner table, to keep ambient magic out and the machine's magic *inside*. Otherwise, it gives people headaches and hallucinations. Various panels open on the sides with heavy levers and screws, to allow access to the instruments or put a book inside. The whole thing is hooked up to a massive ley line. It's an unconventional and unreliable method of power, but the building's solar and wind grid can't handle the strain.

Beside the giant iron box is the most modern computer in the whole department. The huge crystal flatscreen is made for viewing the high-resolution images the Spectre software processes from raw magical data. A system of towers beneath the desk whir and blink as they open the files we've requested.

Mairead pulls up a chair, and I hover beside em, leaning on the desk. I feel like my insides are filled with bees. I tap my fingernails impatiently while Mairead clicks through a series of dialog boxes. A spinning wheel icon pops up, and we both lean forward, waiting.

The first image loads slowly, but even the first inch of text is a revelation. Mairead sits up straighter and adjusts eir glasses.

"…could it really be?" e says in a low voice.

I don't answer, too busy staring at the script on the screen. The script is surprisingly plain, made with legibility in mind rather than ornamentation, which is unusual for something in this age range. I recognize those opening words. Even someone who doesn't read Ancient Casporan would recognize those words—they're inscribed on the walls of the Library itself, most notably at the base of the Founders statues in the main lobby.

Mairead stares at the screen, mouthing something silently. Praying, I think. "Do you see this?" e says. "Read it out loud for me."

My tongue is a desert, my mind in a fog. I fumble through the words, which translate to:

> *"In the beginning, there was Story. In the present, there is Story. In the future, there will always be Story. By the light of the Sun, the Moon, and the Stars, this book is the warp on which we, the people of Caspora, weave our Library: the Eternal Library, record of all knowledge, house of narrative, and center of our world."*

Uncovering this book was a mistake. A glorious, horrible, wonderful mistake. I know that the instant I read the first lines aloud and see the fire lit in Mairead's eyes. We both know what this is. We don't say it out loud, but we know: the lost Charter Book. The one the Founders wrote, and Eirlys Starsower bound, crowning em the very first Head Librarian and Speaker for the Books. The magical basis of the Library's core purpose, its rules, its structures, codified as a magical oath to last beyond the bounds of time.

"So, this is why Isylwyn wanted me to find you," Mairead says to the screen, in a voice full of wonder. "Oh, the Author of our world is incredible. After so many years… it'll all be worthwhile. I should have known my time would come before the end."

Images of the following pages continue to load on the screen. Eirlys Starsower's own handwriting, all this time hidden beneath Calliope Everberry's clever facade.

"But only the Head Librarian can alter the Charter Book," I say slowly. "Calliope wasn't Head Librarian."

"Rhiannon," Mairead says, "clearly, anyone could *physically* alter the Charter Book. But none of those alterations would affect the *magical* foundation and Laws of the Library unless the editor was the Head Librarian. Calliope Everberry may be a criminal, but e was a brilliant one."

"A criminal?" I say, not bothering to hide my shock.

"E defaced our most ancient and holy relic," Mairead says, gesturing at the screen. "Aren't you enraged that we'll never see this cultural treasure the way our ancestors did?"

"I don't know about enraged. Disappointed, sure. Upset, sad, whatever. But Calliope had good reason to do what e did," I say. "Llewella Golddancer was murdered over this book—like many others, including *Eirlys Starsower* emself—and Ciarán Stonefeather would have never listened to pleas for change."

Mairead scowls. "It was never proven that Isylwyn murdered Eirlys. Don't believe that pop-culture garbage. Ciarán would have been right not to listen," Mairead continues. "The Head Librarian's role is meant to mirror that of the Author, giving em control over the fate of the Library. The Charter Book is the instrument through which that control happens. Tradition must be upheld, and that power must be reinstated now that we've found the book."

"So that you can use it when you become Head Librarian," I say. The horrifying reality opens before me like a black, bottomless pit.

Mairead takes my hands. E leans in close, grinning, and says, "What would you do if this power fell into your hands, Rhiannon? If you could right all the wrongs done to this wonderful institution, if you could restore the Library to its former glory, if you could return it to how it was meant to *be*, with just the stroke of a pen—and a lot of restoration work first, I admit— wouldn't you? *Won't you* help me do that? As our next Head Archivist?"

"No."

Mairead blinks, expression carefully blank. "Excuse me?"

I wrench my hands from eir grasp and back away, until I hit the desk behind me. The knot of dread in my stomach pulls tighter into a knot of anger.

"No, I won't help you do that. You're exactly the sort of person Calliope was trying to hide this book from," I say.

Mairead draws emself up, arms crossed and gaze steely. The room goes from cold to freezing. When e speaks, it's so quiet I can barely hear em.

"Then why have you been helping me all this time?"

E starts circling the desk I'm up against, keeping the distance between us but making it clear that e's the predator and I'm the prey. I resist the urge to spin around when e circles behind me, feeling my back exposed to eir fangs. Mairead stops in front of the computer and touches a hand to the screen. The pages are still piling up.

The look on eir face morphs from suspicion to rage to anguish. "Or did you think you were being sneaky? Did you think you were somehow cleverer than me, that you'd use me to discover the secrets of this book and then go running back to the Bindery with the news? Were you really planning to betray me like that?"

"No!" I say, confused by Mairead's emotional whiplash. "But if I'd known from the beginning what—"

Mairead cuts me off, lunging forward and slamming eir palms down on the desk between us. "If you knew what it was, you wouldn't have done it? I thought you trusted me. I trusted you. I promoted you to Assistant Head, even though you're clearly too young and inexperienced for the position," e spits. "I gave you guidance. I made your potential clear to other important minds. We were going to stand beside each other in greatness. Me, the restorer of the Eternal Library, and you, the Seer who brought it about. But here we are. The truth comes out."

The truth is that Mairead isn't the one I've betrayed. It's the Stargroves. Amane. Tabby. The entire Library. My values, my integrity. Myself.

"Or maybe you're scared by the weight of greatness, the history that we're about to make. An understandable reaction," Mairead says quietly. E straightens up, posture relaxing, and gestures at me curiously. "Maybe I've jumped to conclusions too quickly? Maybe you need time to take it all in, to understand your role in the Author's Narrative? Under all the bravado, I expect you're actually quite humble. It may be difficult to accept. I can help you with that."

"I'm done with your *help*," I snap.

Mairead closes eir eyes as if in defeat. "I hope you know this means that you are, effective immediately, suspended from your position as Assistant Head of the Archives."

All the blood drains from my face. I feel lightheaded. And furious. Mairead is shorter than me, but I feel like a child glaring up at em, ready to throw a tantrum.

"You can't just do that!"

"I can," e says. "Sadly, I don't have the power to fire you outright, but that will be one of my first edits to the Book as Head Librarian."

"What happened to my role as the Protagonist?" I say. "Doesn't that make you the villain right now?"

"Every villain is the hero of their own story," Mairead says, shaking eir head sadly. "I was wrong about you. The Author loves a good twist. I saw myself in you. I wanted to make you my protégé. Now I see that you were merely a pawn in greater service to *my* story."

"I was always a pawn to you," I say. My hands tremble at my sides and I clench them tightly to stop it. "Why are you *like* this?"

Mairead stares at me with tears in eir eyes. "I ask myself the same question every day. I'm like this because I'm hurt. Because people hurt me in the past and continue to do so today. I try so hard to protect myself, but trust someone just a little, and they use the opening to stick a knife in," e says bitterly.

I don't know what to say to that. In a weird way, I feel sorry for em.

Mairead turns away from me, face reddening. "You're dismissed. Leave the building and do not stop at your desk first. Your things will be returned to you pending the results of the investigation of your incompetence. They may be used as evidence."

My feet feel rooted to the spot. I glance at the Spectre, where the Charter Book is hidden behind the iron paneling. If it were in plain sight, I'd grab it and run. I start calculating how fast I could get it out of the machine without causing damage to either, or hells, at least to the book, but Mairead knows what I'm thinking. E places emself between me and the machine, arms crossed.

"Leave immediately, or I'll have you removed."

I plant my feet wider and cross my arms as well. "Fucking try me."

CHAPTER TWENTY-FOUR
AMANE

I hate taking the elevator to the Bindery. The Spire's elevator is abysmally slow, clunks at odd times, and doesn't always line up perfectly with the floor when the doors open. So, I hesitate before stepping inside with Tabby on our way back from lunch. The beet stew in my stomach plummets with the elevator car in my mind's eye. I have nightmares about it sometimes.

Tabby notices my apprehension and holds out a hand, smiling.

"If we're going to get stuck, at least you won't get stuck alone," e says.

"That's not *exactly* comforting," I groan, but I take eir hand and step inside anyway. There's no way I could climb the stairs when I'm this full of food.

"But it is a little?"

"If it's you I'd be stuck with," I say, because if one thing can take my mind off fear, it's flirting.

Blushing, Tabby swipes eir ID card and presses the button for the top floor. The doors to the elevator slide shut, and the whole thing trembles. Tabby squeezes my hand gently. I'm still wearing a brace after an entire moon.

"How's your wrist feeling?"

"Better. I want to take it off and get back to work, but Nurse Oakbrew said it needs another week. June said after that I should also keep it on while writing or drawing," I say, failing to keep the sullenness out of my voice.

"They just don't want you to re-injure yourself and have to spend another moon resting, or worse," Tabby replies, all too reasonably. "We don't have deadlines for our work. What's the rush?"

The rush is that I'd like to get out of this elevator. I stare up at the dial showing what floor we're on. First, second, third, fourth—

"I'm just trying to do my best."

—fifth, sixth, seventh—

"I know you are. You inspire me with all your hard work, you know, and how much you obviously love it," Tabby says.

"Really?"

—eighth—

"Really. Which is why I don't want you to keep getting hurt, so you can keep going."

We exchange warm smiles. Mine fades when I realize the elevator isn't moving anymore.

"Um," I say, "did we stop? Why aren't the doors opening?"

We both look up at the dial. The arrow is still, pointed directly between the eighth and ninth floor. I stare at it, willing it to move, but it doesn't. I feel like someone dumped a bucket of ice water over my head. Tabby presses the buttons, swipes the ID card, presses more buttons, but nothing happens. I feel myself getting dizzy and cling to Tabby's arm so I won't fall over.

Tabby presses the emergency call button, summoning an old-fashioned dial tone. It rings for an interminable minute, and then a voice on the other end says, "Hello? What's your emergency?"

"Hi, my name's Tabitha Fairweaver, myself and a coworker are stuck in the main Spire elevator between floors, at the Eternal Library? It doesn't seem to be moving at all."

"Okay, I just need a little more information from you, and we'll have a team out as soon as we can. It might be thirty minutes to an hour before we can get you moving again. No one's hurt or needs immediate medical attention?"

Tabby informs the operator that we're fine and gives them the information they need. I pull eir arm around me and press my face into eir side. I may act tough, but when I'm scared all I want is for someone big and comforting to hold me. Tabby rubs my back soothingly until the call is over.

Then e sighs and sits down on the floor of the elevator. I sit beside em as close as possible and tuck my face against my knees. Tabby keeps rubbing my back. I could enjoy it more if I wasn't terrified we might plummet to our deaths at any moment.

"I'm sorry I made that joke now," e says with a weak laugh.

All I can do is grumble wordlessly.

"Don't worry, someone will be here soon."

"Thirty minutes to an hour isn't soon! Anything could happen by then!" My voice cracks at the end of the sentence, and tears well up in my eyes. I bury my head deeper in my arms and sniffle.

Tabby sighs again. Eir hand stops moving against my back, and I feel em lean over towards me. "Would you feel better if you didn't really… *feel* like you were in the elevator?"

I raise my head up to squint at em. "What do you mean?"

"We could take a nap, and you could lucid dream with me on the Library dreamscape. I can use magic to help you fall asleep and take you along if you want," e says.

Part of me is terrified that being away from our bodies in this situation might be dangerous. Either we won't be awake to save ourselves from some impending doom, like the cables snapping, or we won't hear the rescuers calling, or my body will be vulnerable to possession. Another part glances around at the metal walls that seem to be closing in on us, and wants to be *anywhere* else, as much as possible. *Anywhere*.

I take a deep breath and say, "Okay."

***

The dream opens in a forest of redwood trees. Rhee and Tabby took me to a famous grove of them for a hike once, but these trees are easily five times as big. When I try to look up at the canopy, I feel dizzy and have to glance away.

I've never lucid dreamed before. Once in a while I'll realize I'm dreaming, but it always wakes me up. I've used ritual and entheogens to astral travel, but in those instances, I can still feel my body. As a dreamer, I'm here entirely. I feel soft and fluid, my edges undefined. My fears about the elevator fade, replaced by bubbling excitement.

Chapter Twenty-Four

Tabby stands beside me, still holding my hand. E looks radiant in a white pantsuit with two rows of gold buttons down the front, and a cloak with a matching gold lining. Eir blonde hair glows as if the sun's shining just behind eir head. Usually Tabby is slouched over, as if to appear smaller, but here e stands tall. I could just about swoon.

I look down at myself. I'm not wearing anything cool, just the same clothes I put on this morning.

Seeing my frown, Tabby says, "If you can dream it, you can change it."

On the astral proper, there are rules. You can't make something from nothing. Your soul has abilities and limitations just like your physical body. The dreamscape, however, is full of infinite possibilities. In a dream, you can be anything! The catch is that most of us don't have any control over our dreams.

Excited, I try to dream up a voluminous, shimmering gold ballgown. The images in my mind shift and slip through my grasp. Memories of old dresses pop up unexpectedly. A hemline here, a sleeve there, a pattern on the fabric. What comes out is beautiful but strange. This is harder than I thought. Tabby chuckles and tugs on my hand.

"You look wonderful. Let's go."

We set off through the trees. The forest floor is soft beneath our feet, thickly carpeted with red needles. Many of the trunks contain doorways with words carved into them, which Tabby says are the titles of centuries old folktales. They have names like 'The Red Robe, ' 'The Ringing in the Mountains, ' and 'The Bending of the Rainbow. '

"One time I saw a door that looked just like the ones to the Head Librarian's office. I didn't get to go inside," Tabby muses.

"What do you think is in there?" I ask.

Tabby pauses, thoughtful. "It could be anything. But… the Library is a living, spiritual being. I wonder if that's where its heartscape is."

We stop in a beam of sunlight. The air is golden and warm, Tabby's words floating among the dust motes and pollen. Nothing has changed, but suddenly I know for sure that Tabby is right. We've called the heart of the Library. It knows we're coming, and we know that's where we're going.

"I know what you're thinking. It's the dream logic, trying to herd us into a narrative," Tabby explains. E gazes into the distance, then turns back to me, cheeks flushed. "Can I put my arm around you?"

"Um—yeah, of course, that's fine!" My hair curls tighter at the prospect. I can feel it standing out around my face in cloudy poofs and swirls.

"We'll get there quicker this way, instead of doing what the dream wants," Tabby says. I can sense eir emotions like a scent on the breeze: flustered, excited, affectionate.

E hooks a strong arm around my waist, pulling me against eir side. The golden cloak wraps around us both, floating against all proper laws of physics. A surge of giddiness electrifies my body as Tabby literally and metaphorically sweeps me off my feet.

"Hold on tight!"

Tabby takes a deep breath and one step forward, poised as if to spring into the air. The forest around us shivers, and a flock of ivory butterflies flutters down from the canopy. Once they're directly in front of us, Tabby breaks into a run.

The swirl of butterflies explodes around us, soft wings brushing against my arms and face. There are words written on them, soft whispers of a story someone lost long ago. It only distracts me for a moment, but when I look ahead once more, we're beneath a completely different configuration of trees. The sun fades and the light turns blue, the shadow of the trees deep violet as twilight descends.

I cling as tightly to Tabby as I can. The dream narrative pulls at us, but Tabby defies it, deciding where and when we'll go. I can feel the strength of will this takes radiating from em, and I understand fully why e was chosen for an apprenticeship at the Eternal Library.

Tabby puts me back on the ground.

"How did you learn to do that?" I gasp, my heart still pounding with all the magic in the air. Magic of more than one kind.

A wry smile unfurls on eir face. "By desiring it with all my heart. I love it here. I love who I get to be when I'm here. But I don't know that I'd have pushed so hard to improve without the pain I was experiencing at home. Maybe pushing and pain are worth it sometimes," e says, gesturing at my wrist.

My chest warms with compassion, but also embarrassment. "You were making the best of a bad situation. I'm just ruining one that's already good. I do my best work when I've rested, when my head is clear and my heart is leading me. I don't know what I've been doing lately. I don't know why I push myself so hard. I mean, I do know… but I guess I don't want to know," I say.

"Trying to live up to your parents and siblings?" Tabby says.

I nod. I feel tears forming in the corners of my eyes and wipe them away with a laugh. "I'm sorry, I don't know why this is all suddenly coming out of me."

"It's the nature of a dream. Even while lucid, we're never fully in control. This is where our subconscious lives. Our secrets. I should have mentioned that before inviting you," Tabby says.

"I would have come anyway. I really like—I really like being around you," I say.

The truth sits on my tongue like a candy waiting to melt. I hold onto it for now.

"Me too," Tabby says, and laughing self-consciously, "I'm really happy we both get to be apprentices together."

E tucks a strand of hair behind one ear and then turns to look at our surroundings. The forest is quiet save for the whispering of the leaves high above. At least, I think it's leaves. Words float down amid the susurrus, bits of story sifting through my mind like from the butterflies' wings. From the corners of my eye I catch glimpses of scenes and places, characters. Is this how an entire library dreams?

Between the gaps in the canopy, there are brightly shining stars. I've never seen them so large and lit before, even though I grew up in the desert where the sky looks like black velvet coated in diamond dust. One of them appears to be drawing closer. We watch as it arcs toward us, landing directly in front of the closest tree-trunk door. In the light, I notice the doors look exactly like the ones on the Head Librarian's office.

My spirit senses tingle. That star isn't a star. It's a person. Someone with a presence bigger than the trees themselves.

The star dims, revealing Eirlys Starsower's calm, smiling face. E doesn't look much like the giant quartz statue in the lobby, slight and knobbly rather than shapely and graceful. All the same, our spirits recognize each other.

Eirlys raises eir hands and signs, "I'm sorry, but I can't let you through these doors. Another time, you might have that adventure, but for now the way is shut."

The dream logic grants us understanding of the ancient Casporan Sign Language Eirlys is using. Historical sources show e began losing eir hearing as a teenager and eventually became deaf. It's speculated that creating the Library to collect written knowledge was even more important to Eirlys because e understood the need for accessibility on a personal level.

"Can you tell us why?" Tabby asks aloud, although e also adds the modern hand sign for *why* at the end. The dream translates this for me, too.

"It must be important if you're here," I say.

"This is a time of transition. The heartscape is waiting for a new Head Librarian," Eirlys says, "as is its current occupant."

It occurs to me this might be the reason why Rose hasn't returned to haunt the Bindery or send messages to Aeronwy and June.

"Is Rose in there?" I blurt out, and Tabby looks at me in sudden understanding.

Eirlys just holds a finger to eir lips and smiles.

"It isn't quite fair for me to tell you these things, but Isylwyn has been helping one of the other candidates," Eirlys says, "by harassing Catrina Rosefall's spirit for information on the Charter Book's whereabouts. Rose resisted the best e could, but Isylwyn is strong. E's resting now."

"Rose knew where the Charter Book is?" Tabby asks, shocked. "But it hasn't been seen in over five hundred years!"

Eirlys's face falls. "I know. I did not understand the consequence of my actions when I first created it. I was glad when it disappeared. Now it has resurfaced."

"Where? How?" I ask, excited. Its history may be tainted by death, but it would be incredible to see in person.

Eirlys frowns. "I'm surprised you don't know. Either of you," e says, glancing between us.

Tabby and I glance at each other, confused. Neither of us knows what e means.

An owl hoots nearby, making me shiver. Eirlys holds a hand up, and an enormous brown bird swoops silently down from the treetops. Like Eirlys, this spirit is powerful and old. There's sunlight in its yellow eyes. Eirlys gazes at the owl affectionately, then turns back to us as it shuffles to sit on eir shoulder.

"If you don't know, it's not my place to say. However, I can share this with you: as apprentices, you may accompany your mentors in the Head Librarian Trials in order to assist them," Eirlys says.

"Really?" I ask.

Eirlys nods. "This rule has been largely forgotten. Illuminators are the only ones in the Library who still use the mentor-apprentice system and Binding ceremony. It used to be widespread in all departments."

"We can help make sure June or Aeronwy wins instead of Mairead," Tabby says.

"Hopefully. That is all I wanted to say. I'm sorry for interrupting your dream. Let us make up for it," e says.

Eirlys walks over to a nearby tree. There's a round red door set deeply into the trunk, on which I can barely make out the inscription: *The Stories We Sing*. The owl's head turns all the way around, watching us. I could swear it was smiling, if birds could smile.

"Look, it's the book you're working on with June," Tabby says as we approach the door.

"What happens when we go through?" I ask.

"We'll be inside the story," Tabby replies. "Shall we?"

Eirlys opens the door, beyond which there's nothing but swirling, colorful light. Tabby holds a hand out for me to take, and I do. It feels natural now.

As we walk past Eirlys, I narrow my own eyes at the owl. "You're not really a bird," I say.

The owl laughs and puffs up its feathers. "Who's to say what I am, when I am what I appear?" it says in an amused, melodious voice.

"Daryn," Eirlys chides the owl aloud, speaking the third Founder's name with affection.

I open my mouth to say something, but Tabby steps into the swirling vortex of light, pulling my arm inside as well. Tingles run through my body like I've just eaten a handful of crackling candy. The owl—Daryn—laughs again, and hoots ring out in my ears as I stumble through the door.

"See you in the Trials, lovelies," e says, and the world around me dissolves.

CHAPTER TWENTY-FIVE
TABBY

Eirlys Starsower put on eir best robes and headed to the standing stone circle on the hill, ready for both the end and the beginning.

The swirling light of the portal slowly fades, and the room around me comes into view: stone walls washed white, hung with fine tapestries and sparsely furnished with a bed, desk, and bookshelf. The books are large and bound with thick leather in natural hues, their spines ridged with heavy cords. I know these books as intimately as anyone can, for I'm the one who bound them.

So says the dream.

Amane is no longer beside me. I want to go look for her, but the story moves me along accordingly. I'm not frightened, just anxious about tonight. I pull on my ceremonial robes, which are deep indigo and dotted with silver stars. I spun, wove, dyed, and embroidered them myself. Unlike Isylwyn, who has 'support characters' for such tasks, I prefer to join my nuns in their chores and crafts.

I linger by the fireplace, enjoying its warmth before I rake the ashes over, quieting it to coals.

Eirlys's eyes strayed to the prayer to Cináed posted over the mantle, and the offering bowl of fireweed flowers. Scandalous proof that Daryn had been here. Eirlys hated keeping secrets, but Daryn feared Isylwyn's reaction, should e find out about their relationship. Considering Daryn feared little, Eirlys was apt to take such a thing very seriously.

It's been many years since I read *The Stories We Sing*, but the words come back to me as the dream provides them. I take the winding staircase down from the tower and step outside.

Though it was summer, the night was cool. There was no moon visible in the sky, only the constellations by which all people of the day charted their lives. The stars and planets were in alignment. Auspicious astrological weather for the birth of an institution.

I thought the ancient night would be impossibly dark, but my sight is clear. There is so little human-made light that the stars alone are enough to light the way, a marvel that lifts my spirits and my gaze to the sky. There are no wind turbines, no glass skyscrapers, no solar arrays, no Spire. Not yet. From the hill the Readerist abbey is built on, I can see the sprawl of wood and stone houses as they tumble down the slopes towards the Sound, here and there pierced by a temple tower. The vast silhouette of the Spiral Mountains on the peninsula is as familiar as ever.

Eirlys turned and followed the rocky path up the hill. The standing stones had been there as long as anyone could remember, constructed some said by ancient ancestors and others said by the gods themselves. Whoever built them had known about the lines of power running through the earth, and with careful calculation (or omnipresent knowledge) opened a gateway between this world and the invisible one.
This was where they would build the Library.

The forest path is dark but intimately familiar, thanks to the story. I know the place of every root and stone and step confidently around them.

The books in the abbey knew what was about to happen. Eirlys had told them, and now they were restless. Paper rustled and yellowed faster than was normal. Ink bottles overturned themselves at the lightest touch. Spools of thread unwound themselves in the night.

Eirlys knew it was a sign. The question was: a sign of faith, or a sign of doom?

Isylwyn would never agree to the terms Eirlys set for the Eternal Library's creation. That was why they were binding the book of laws tonight, under moon-dark secrecy. Curse their need for Isylwyn's money and resources. They were the only reason Eirlys allowed Daryn to report eir research to the Sovereign. It was telling that once the first Illuminated book had been successfully bound, Isylwyn had showed up, riches and demands in hand.

I hear the narration in my mind as I reach the top of the hill. It's crowned with a standing stone circle of massive size, easily a hundred feet in diameter, with stones twenty feet tall. In them, I can see the shape of the main ritual hall in the Library. They must now be part of the building itself.

Daryn was already at the stone circle to set up the ritual. A central fire illuminated the space, ringed by fragrant beeswax candles. A stone slab beside the fire would serve as a workbench. On it the completed manuscript sat waiting to be stitched together. Beside it, Daryn was placing a spindle of red thread.

As I walk into the circle of stones, I see her. For a moment, Amane isn't herself. Instead she's Daryn Sunseeker, a large, soft figure of rolls and curves silhouetted against the bonfire. Light brown skin, deep brown hair cut in a bob, and amber eyes often crinkled in mischief. Then the illusion drops, and Amane takes on her own familiar form.

She turns and catches sight of me. Her eyes go wide for a moment, and I wonder what she sees. Do I look like Eirlys? Does she hear the same narrative I do, or has the dream created one from Daryn's perspective?

Amane puts down the spindle and runs to meet me. I catch her in a tight hug.

"Are you ready?" she says, gazing up with the stars reflected in her eyes.

"Yes. Let's not waste any time," I say.

The dream supplies us with the dialogue from the story. I sense that I could deviate from it if I wanted, but to what end? I've always enjoyed this part of the book. A moment of happiness and triumph before the inevitable downfall between Eirlys and Isylwyn.

Hopefully, the dream won't take us that far.

Dawn would come soon. Eirlys took the thread from the spindle and wound it around eir fingers. Daryn added herbs and salts to the fire which flared in a shower of colorful sparks, purifying the space. E sat on a nearby stone and picked up a drum. Eirlys couldn't hear it, but e could feel the vibrations in eir bones. It sounded like a heartbeat.

Daryn's lips moved in song. Eirlys knew the words, and sang with eir hands, combining sign language with the rhythm of dance.

"If we were down on the water,
Your voice quiet on the evening,
The light of the stars wound round,
And drawn down to softest ground,

Would you stay with me?
Would you be true?
Would you listen to the sound of my heart,
As it sings out loud through you?

If we were deep in the valley,
Beneath the ancient trees that sleep,
All dark and green and grown,
Our secrets bared like flowers bloom,

Would you stay with me?
Would you be true?
Would you listen to the sound of my heart,
As it sings out loud through you?

If we were high on the mountain
With fires glowing red
And ember-swirling smoke
If soon we both be dead

Would you let me go?
Would you set me free?
Would you sing along, would you know our song,
As your heart sings out through me?"

I know these lyrics without the dream's assistance. Oran used to play the guitar and sing them to Lilja when I was little—one of the few times I saw my parents express affection for one another. I allow the story to guide my hands while I improvise the dance using Aeronwy's waltzing lesson. The energy of the song thrums through my body, connecting me with the earth below and the sky above.

Eirlys wove the song into the thread wrapped around eir fingers. It was spun from flax grown on the slopes of Mt. Cináed following the eruption eighteen years ago. Twined within were strands of Eirlys and Daryn's hair. Together forever, just as their spirits would be in death. There was not a lifetime in which they would not seek each other out, following the golden cord which stretched between them.

E gazed at Daryn, who had been the key to so many mysteries. Filled with love and inspiration, Eirlys dipped deep into eir own soul, spinning a cord of pure energy which would bind eir spirit and the words within the book. The eternal spark of divine light inside em would ensure that the pages never crumbled, the ink never faded, and the stitches never broke.

All Illuminators can trace the lineage of their craft back to Eirlys Starsower. How many but me can say they stood within Eirlys's shoes as e bound the Charter Book? This story may be a fictional account written a thousand years later, but it contains a core of truth.

I kneel before the stone workbench, needle in hand, and join Eirlys's essence with the book's. The work is tender, intimate, and frightening. Eirlys's memories flash before my eyes. These are not memories described in *The Stories We Sing*. The author couldn't know how Illumination truly works, the spinning of the thread of the soul: this part must be the real thing. Great joys and pains, sorrows and small delights. Like standing beneath a waterfall of emotions, each as strong as the moment it was originally felt.

I understand why I need to heal my heart before I do this myself.

It was finished as the sun rose. The fire was naught but coals, and the stars faded overhead. Exhausted, Eirlys lay eir head on Daryn's shoulder and watched the sky grow light beyond the mountains. Daryn was silent, twisting the rings on eir fingers in thought. They were all e had left from the Cináedite village e was born in, and e never took them off.

"There's no going back for me, now," Eirlys said, "but we don't have to tell Isylwyn you were here. Not if it would put you in undue danger."

Laying my head on Amane's shoulder proves far too awkward, so she leans on me, instead. Her hair smells like coconut oil and sweat from tending the fire. We may be role playing, but my heart beats faster, knowing where the story is headed.

Daryn shook eir head slowly. "Izzy will be furious, but..."

"...I believe in you. I don't want to hide anymore." Amane looks directly at me as she says the line. She doesn't sound like she's playing a role anymore.

Eirlys straightened up. "Do you mean support for my vision of the Library, or do you mean—do you mean the truth of our relationship?"

I hope she can hear that I'm not playing anymore, either. I cup a gentle hand around her face.

Daryn smiled. "Both, of course. My love for you cannot be denied. Not by anyone in the history of the world."

Amane looks like the sun in her golden dress, dawn come early between the mountain peaks. I know what I want, and I can feel her wanting, too. She closes her eyes as I lean in closer.

A flickering glance, parted lips, and then they were kissing under the faded stars. Spirits pressed together as well as mouths. There was nothing now that could tear them apart.

***

The elevator jolts to life, and we wake. Amane clings to my arm and screams, while I instinctively grab on to the handrail. The emergency call speaker crackles, and a voice lets us know that they've gotten things running again, and are we all right?

I crawl forward and press the answer button. "Just fine, thank you," I say shakily.

It takes seconds for us to reach the ninth floor. We step out of the elevator and stand in the hallway, blinking and confused after being yanked out of the dream-story. Particularly at that point in it. My chest warms with joy and my face with embarrassment.

Amane takes a deep breath and turns on her heel to face me.

"Tabby, I swear it wasn't just the dream, or the story, I actually really—I really like you!" she stammers. Her brows and mouth are determined, but the look in her eyes is vulnerable and searching.

Even though I was expecting her confession, I feel loopy and caught off guard. "Me too," I say, "I mean, I like you quite a lot, too."

The smile that lights up her face makes my heart melt. I bend down to kiss her in the waking world this time, but a voice calls out from the common area, interrupting us.

"Tabby? Amane? Is that both of you back there? Where the hell have you two been? Why haven't you answered my texts?"

We look up, and Rhiannon is standing at the end of the hallway. As if eir anxious tone of voice wasn't enough to signal something is wrong, e also looks incredibly disheveled. Clothes wrinkled, a fresh ink stain on one sleeve, hair frizzy, several small bandaids on one cheek.

Every good feeling in my body drops into the void. It's replaced by a cold emptiness, the stark clarity that comes just as the tower falls.

"Oh my gods, Rhee, we got stuck in the elevator! We didn't have any signal! For like, ever!" Amane laments, stomping dramatically down the hall. She pauses, looking up at Rhiannon, and adds, "What happened to *you*?"

Rhiannon stares at her miserably. E glances up at me, and then immediately away. "Just come sit down so I only have to say it once."

I'd ask what e means, but my mouth feels glued shut. June and Aeronwy are already sitting on the couch, looking just as lost. June is nervously plucking on the tassels of a throw pillow. Aeronwy has eir elbows propped up on eir knees, leaning forward with hands clasped together and a solemn look. E glances between Amane and I, but eir gaze returns to Rhiannon almost immediately.

"So, now are you going to let us know why you appeared at the top of the stairway, begging us to hide you from security?" e asks. Aeronwy is always a little rough around the edges, but eir voice cuts like a sharp pair of scissors.

I sit down in one of the armchairs, and Amane sits on the arm beside me. I can't feel anything. It's like I'm watching from outside my body, or on TV. Rhiannon stays standing, pacing in front of the coffee table, on which are several untouched cups of tea. June picks one up and holds it with both hands but doesn't drink from it. E is watching Rhiannon with concern.

Rhiannon paces a few more laps before throwing eir head back and dropping eir arms to the side. E opens eir mouth a few times, as if to start speaking, and then sighs. Everything in em deflates.

"I stole the book. At the party."

The words perplex me, but June fumbles the tea mug and Amane jumps to her feet.

"You did *what?*" she demands. "Please tell me you aren't talking about the book I think you are."

"The original Illuminated copy of *The Founding?* Yeah, that one. I took it," Rhiannon says listlessly.

June is as white as a sheet, hands shaking as e wipes up the spilled tea with a tissue. Amane turns to em, her expression pleading. "I swear I didn't know anything about this—"

Aeronwy cuts her off, standing up and walking over to Rhiannon. I've never seen em look so furious, and the way e towers over Rhee reminds me of Oran, towering over me and Lilja.

"Where is it?"

Rhiannon clenches eir fists and forces emself, with obvious effort, to look up at Aeronwy.

"Mairead has it."

Aeronwy stands completely still, arms crossed tightly. When e speaks next, a wisp of white smoke escapes eir mouth, along with the words. I can feel the intense heat of eir Flame from several feet away. It feels like the heat of a wildfire.

"Does Mairead know what it is?"

"Do you think I'd *be* here if e didn't?" Rhiannon exclaims.

"Are you saying you would have continued to deceive all of us if that weren't true?"

Rhiannon lets out a groan of frustration and turns around, head clasped in eir hands. "No! That isn't—I fucked up, okay? I didn't *plan* on taking the book, it just… happened. Mairead threatened my job if I didn't get a hold of it, and I knew Aeronwy was lying about it being here, and I wanted to know why, and I'd promised Rhys, and—once it happened, it happened. I thought I could… I thought I could… I don't know anymore."

From a long way away, I hear myself ask, "What is going on?"

"Remember that book I told you I had a vision of, that was hidden up here? The one Mairead and I had been searching for? Turns out it's actually the Charter Book. Now Mairead has it, and e's going to become Head Librarian and use it to rewrite the laws of Library. Then I got suspended—"

Amane, shocked: "You got—"

"E tried to have me kicked out of the building, but I fought back and escaped up here to, uh, ruin everyone's day I guess," Rhiannon says.

I've never seen em so miserable. E finally looks at me, eyes pleading and filled with tears. But my mouth is stuck shut again and all I can do is stare blankly back. I feel like I'm going to faint. The stripes on the walls are starting to move.

"Wait," says June, speaking up for the first time, "why did Mairead suspend you?"

"Because when we figured out what the damn book actually was, I told em I didn't want to play along anymore. E didn't exactly take that too well," says Rhiannon.

June starts to relax, a compassionate look on eir face, but before e can say anything, Aeronwy fixes em with a piercing glare.

"Why did you show them the book? And when were you going to let me know about that?" I've never heard Aeronwy speak so coldly to June, and it's shocking. Even more white smoke is escaping Aeronwy every time e speaks or breathes now, filling the room with the scent of burning wood.

"I-I thought I did," says June.

"You certainly didn't. I would remember being angry about it, because as far as I know, we promised never to show it to *anyone* without reaching a consensus on it first, and it doesn't seem like you did that."

June rubs at eir eyes, pushing eir glasses up on top of eir head. "I swear I—I definitely did say that we should talk about showing Amane and Tabby the book, which, well, we haven't exactly gotten around to yet, but that was when I was going to tell you about it, I just kept forgetting—"

"The birthday party was *three moons* ago. You left them alone in the room with it? What's in there now?"

"Nothing," Rhiannon drones. "I kept expecting one of you to check and figure it out, but I guess you never did, huh? Kinda makes me feel even worse, to be honest. All that trust."

"I didn't tell them what it *was*, I just let them see it. Amane was going to find out anyway, and she vouched for Rhiannon," June says firmly, looking at her but deliberately avoiding Rhiannon. "You might want to step outside, Aery, you're going to set off the sprinklers…"

Amane looks at the floor and mutters something in Gildean that makes Rhiannon wince.

"You broke your promise," Aeronwy says, eyes still fixed on June. "As a result, the exact sort of situation we were trying to prevent has happened."

June looks up at em beseechingly. "I'm sorry. I made a mistake."

Just a few minutes ago, it seemed all my dreams were coming true. Now, as the people I love and care about most in the world stand around me arguing about who's fault it is that the Library as we know it is in danger, I understand. This is how it will always be. I thought I'd escaped it, in coming here, in meeting Rhee, and Amane, in leaving my parents and (at least in my heart) adopting new ones, that my life would change.

I was wrong. Now as my trust in everything falls apart, so does the world around me. The stripes peel off the wall. The smoke hanging in the air twists into cyclones. The color drains out of my vision, and I circle the drain of consciousness along with it.

RHIANNON

As soon as Tabby's eyelids flutter, I know what's happening and rush to catch em before e hits the floor face-first. With help from Amane, I manage to push em back into the chair, head lolling unconsciously on one shoulder. Fast asleep, but not peacefully. The look on eir face is one of distress, and it kills me to know that's my fault.

I turn to Amane to thank her, but she quickly turns her back to me. *That's* my fault, too.

Behind me, Aeronwy huffs and approaches us, footsteps heavy on the wood floor. The room is starting to get hazy with the smoke e's breathing out.

"Of all the people to get their hands on that book—"

But before e can go on a rant, June stands up and points toward the balcony doors in exasperation.

"Aeronwy Stargrove, *go outside* before you set off the sprinklers and more things get ruined! *I* will take care of Tabby."

I'd never guess June could sound so commanding. Amane's eyebrows shoot up and we watch as Aeronwy immediately turns heel and stomps off down the hallway. Smoke trails behind em, followed by the sound of the balcony door slamming.

June slumps back down on the couch, then sighs and immediately gets back up to check on Tabby.

"Is e going to be all right? Should we do something?" e asks. Once again, e looks at Amane but not at me. It feels incredibly shitty to be ignored by someone who's usually a saint of compassion.

"E usually wakes up after a little while," Amane says.

"I don't know about this time," I say, voicing the churning pit of despair in my stomach. I may be a retrocognitive, but sometimes I can see the future plainly enough. "This is pretty bad."

She rounds on me with a smoldering glare. "Bad? You lied to all of us! I trusted you and you used me! Tabby trusted you and you went behind eir back! Now someone awful could use the Charter Book to ruin the Library? And you gave it to them? I don't think 'bad' covers it," she snaps.

"Okay, I deserve that."

The energy in the room drops somewhat. A simmer rather than a raging boil. She glances worriedly at Tabby and places a gentle hand on eir arm. June takes off eir glasses to clean them and clears eir throat.

"Rhiannon," e says, sounding pained, "am I at least correct in understanding that you've told us all this because you intend to apologize and set things right?"

June finally looks me in the face, which is actually worse because I can see how disappointed e is. Amane purses her lips and rolls her eyes. Tabby continues to sleep like the dead, completely unaware of my presence.

"Yes," I say, and my voice cracks.

The adrenaline that's been ricocheting through my body for the last hour drops off the face of the earth, leaving me exhausted. My chest feels hollow, my spark doused. Usually the Library is my refuge, but now it hurts to be here. It'll hurt even more to leave, knowing it could be my last full day here as an employee.

June watches me expectantly. Amane does so as well, at least from the corner of her eye.

"I'm so sorry," I say, as the tears start running down my face, fogging up my glasses. "I fucked up. Mairead made everything so—no, I won't make excuses. I was selfish, and I fucked up. I hope you all can forgive me eventually."

I turn to look at Tabby. I don't know if e can hear me where e's at, but I have to try.

"Especially you, Tabs. I'm sorry."

***

While June and Amane keep watch over Tabby, I slip outside for some air. It's not raining, but the dark clouds overhead look threatening. Aeronwy is leaning on the balcony railing, still exhaling smoke.

"So, does that happen every time you get even a little mad, or only when someone throws a can of emotional gasoline on the fire and burns the whole house down?" I ask, standing as near to em as I dare. Even five feet away, the metal railing is warm from the heat e's giving off.

"Do you ever stop making smart remarks, or is that the only way you have to cope with your part in the disaster you cause?" e responds, glaring.

I shrug. "Pretty much, yeah."

We gaze out over the city in awkward silence.

"I wanted to tell you I'm sorry," I say once I have the guts to do so. "I fucked up. I was only thinking of myself when I stole the book. I was… scared, if that makes sense."

"Scared of what?" Aeronwy asks.

"Losing my new promotion. Being unworthy. Disappointing important people," I say. I groan and dangle my head over the railing. "It sounds so ridiculous when I say it out loud, but I swear in the moment it was like—it felt like a panic for survival."

To my surprise, Aeronwy nods. "That sounds about right."

"What?"

"You were being manipulated by Mairead, I assume," e says.

"Maybe," I say. I think about the inconsistencies, the lying, the threats, the guilt trips. Is that what that was? "That doesn't excuse what I did."

"No, but it is important. Would you have stolen it if you discovered the book all on your own?" Aeronwy asks.

"No," I say. "I would have just, like, harassed you until you gave it up. Or maybe Tabby would have asked about it and found out honestly. I didn't want to put em in between, uh, whatever grudge match you and Mairead have going on. But without that…."

"So, you *were* considering how it would affect others, to a point."

"I guess. Why are you being so damn nice about this?" I demand. I wrap my arms around myself with a shiver. I left my coat in the Archives, and it's cold up here. Aeronwy has stopped smoking and is giving off less heat. E must have calmed down.

"Because I've been where you are, and we said we would help if you needed us," Aeronwy says, turning to look at me. E has golden eyes like my Grandren, and a gaze that sees right through my bullshit.

I drop my eyes to the ground nine stories below, pushing my glasses up my nose so they won't fall. "I don't know how to explain what happened. Sometimes e was so nice to me, and sometimes—if I try to describe it out loud, it doesn't sound like much, but there were always… weird undercurrents, shit that went unsaid. The implication that I *owed* em, and if I refused, I deserved to be punished. It got to me. I dunno, I can't believe I didn't see it," I say.

"That's how emotional manipulation works," Aeronwy says. "What are you going to do now?"

"Fuck if I know. I'd steal it a second time, but we keep the damn thing in one of the locked, alarmed, magically warded drawers only the Head and Assistant Head Archivist have access to. I uh, left my bag down there in the scuffle, so I'm sure they've confiscated my keys now," I say, grimacing. "If not that, then, uh… Well, if I tell HR the truth, will they believe me? And that means your secret will be out."

Aeronwy's face darkens. "I suppose that's inevitable now."

"What were you gonna do with it, anyway? Keep it hidden up here forever?" I ask, and when e doesn't answer, I continue. "You're running for Head Librarian. Don't tell me you haven't thought about using it if you win."

"Of course I have," Aeronwy says. "That's the danger of it. The power it grants a single individual is enormous. Even if we were to vote on how to edit the Charter Book democratically, that assumes the Head Librarian will act in good faith and comply. There's the fact that the title of Head Librarian is only passed on in death, which tempts some individuals to seize power through murder—the reason we're here. There's too much room for corruption."

"Why not just burn it?" I ask, because I'm feeling extra edgy today.

"I've thought about that, too," Aeronwy mutters, gazing out into the mists.

I stare. "I wasn't serious, but okay. What would happen to the Library if the Charter Book were destroyed?"

"You mean, will the very stone we stand on crumble beneath our feet as the entire collection spontaneously combusts in an act of sympathetic magic, as some academics have suggested?" Aeronwy says, voice dripping with sarcasm. "I suppose we can't rule it out."

"If only we had it back, we could study it more and figure out a solution," I say. "Maybe we don't destroy it. Maybe we restore it and heavily alter it. Make it so the Head Librarian can retire normally, instead of by dying. Change it so that a whole committee has the ability to edit, one that's fairly elected by the Library faculty and staff."

"Whoever's Head Librarian still needs to agree to make those edits," Aeronwy says. "They have to be willing to give up the power of the Book forever."

"You'd do it, wouldn't you?"

"In a heartbeat."

"And so would June?"

"I don't doubt it. I believe that's what e wanted back when we were deciding whether to hide it or not."

"So, we just have to make sure one of you wins," I say.

The door to the balcony opens then, interrupting our conversation. June peeks out at us nervously.

"I thought you should know, we've called for an ambulance," e says. "Siobhan came up and is very concerned by Tabby's energetic state. E's fine for the moment, but if it gets worse or this continues too long, it's better that e gets immediate care."

Hot tears well up behind my eyes. I take off my glasses and rub my face, not wanting to cry more in front of the Stargroves. "Thanks, I'll go with em when they get here," I croak.

"Take your time."

I hear the balcony door shut. Aeronwy sighs heavily. I hope the two of them make up. My relationships aren't the only ones I've strained.

I lean my back against the railing, exhausted. All my adrenaline is gone, leaving behind a black void where my soul should be. "I don't think this is what Eirlys wanted when e made the Book," I say.

"Can we ever know what the Founders truly wanted?" Aeronwy says.

"I Saw the creation of the Charter Book in my visions," I say. "I Saw a *lot* of things. Some things that we have written sources for, and others we don't. The Founders might be deities now, but back then they were as human as you or I. By which I mean, people make mistakes."

"Hmm," says Aeronwy, "I suppose you would know."

***

The Head of Human Resources stares me down from across the polished oak desk. The sign language interpreter glances between the two of us, waiting to see how Marion is going to respond to what, I don't deny, is an absolutely outrageous story. One I know doesn't match whatever tale Mairead spun for them.

Marion Dreamcloud looks like a middle-aged bodybuilder dressed up as a Librarian. The green collared dress e's wearing is sleeveless, revealing muscled arms covered in tattoos, mostly quotes from classic literature. Eir hair is pulled up in a tight bun, black and glossy. The beard covering the lower half of eir face is neat, with only a hint of gray.

The tension in the room draws to a point, like a rubber band being stretched over some kid's thumb in the back of the class. The only question is whose head it's going to hit.

Finally, Marion raises eir hands to sign, without taking eir eyes off me. Xavier Silva-Sweetgum, Marion's young, blue-haired interpreter, shifts in eir chair.

"If what you say is true, this incident is bigger than you and Prx. Moonsea," e says. "The Library hasn't had a scandal this big since the '86 fire—and somehow, it involves the same damn people. I didn't work here then, but I know about it."

Xavier only hesitates a little on the curse word. Marion's not one to curse at work. I raise an eyebrow, but Marion keeps a straight face.

"If I could, I would halt the Head Librarian Trials until this is straightened out," Marion continues. "All three candidates have acted questionably in this situation."

"Why can't you?" I ask.

"The laws of the Library, according to the Charter Book," Marion says with a wry smile. "The candidate's names have already been submitted in a ceremony to prepare for the Trials. I don't think it's possible to stop the Trials from happening, now."

"What about me, then?"

Marion leans back in eir chair and says, "I've been over Prx. Moonsea's personnel file more than once. You're aware you're not the first person to have issues with em."

"Yes," I say, remembering the fight between Mairead and Camille. Marion had questioned me about it last year. "Does that mean you believe me?"

Marion makes a face, lips pressed into a thin line. "I won't believe you've found the Charter Book until I see it for myself. Otherwise, yes. The problem is that Prx. Moonsea is talented at evading discipline. We never seem to have enough evidence to bring a case against em."

I sit up straighter in my chair. I came into this meeting with a sense of doom and a wicked stomachache. I haven't slept in days. I was sure I was about to be fired on the spot for some fabricated reason.

"When we talk to coworkers of Prx. Moonsea's accusers, they either claim they've never seen em act that way or are too scared to speak against em. Given what's happened to Ms. Dubois, I can see why," says Marion.

"What do you mean?" I ask. "Is Camille still in the hospital?"

Marion nods. "Ms. Dubois thinks that her illness may be the result of a curse by Prx. Moonsea. I'm inclined to agree. There's a disturbing trend of coworkers who have offended Prx. Moonsea falling ill with no clear explanation."

"Are you shitting me?" I exclaim, before I can stop myself. I definitely fall into the category of 'coworkers who have offended Prx. Moonsea' now.

Marion continues without acknowledging my outburst. "Unfortunately, we can't prove it. No one wants to take a stand, and we've never found hard evidence of cursing."

E stares at me meaningfully.

"Oh. You want me to—what do you want me to do?" I say. I grip the arms of my chair tightly.

Marion shrugs. "Be careful. You're still on suspension, but if you *find* anything, *tell me*," e says. "Get pictures. Or better, *bring it to me*."

I don't need the interpreter to see the emphasis in eir hands and expression. Or to read between the lines.

"I sure as hell will."

I leave feeling considerably lighter than before. Even though Tabby is still asleep, Amane still isn't talking to me, Mairead still has the Charter Book, and I might be the target of a nasty curse any day now, things could be worse. I suppress a manic chuckle at the thought.

Outside Marion's office, I run into Rhys Elkspinner sitting on a bench. Eir eyes widen, then flicker back to the book in eir hands.

"Hello, Dr. Elkspinner," I say loudly, emboldened by the success of my meeting.

Rhys sets the book in eir lap and clears eir throat. E's wearing a suit and waistcoat today, with a pocket watch chain dangling from the pocket. Looks vintage, maybe 3940s. The curls on eir head have been slicked back into a bun studded with brass pins. Dressing to impress?

"Hello, Rhiannon," e says. "Fancy meeting you here."

"Yeah, fancy that. Are you here to chat with Mx. Dreamcloud, too? About Mairead?" I ask.

Rhys fiddles with eir glasses. "These sorts of things are supposed to be confidential—"

"Are *you* scared of Mairead, too? What did e do to you?" I ask.

"Mairead is a respected colleague with a lot of pull in historical circles," Rhys says, avoiding my question and my eyes. "We may have differing political views, but e was kind enough to write a letter of recommendation for my appointment at the National History Museum."

Damn. Mairead's network of 'favors' goes farther than I knew. "What does that have to do with you being here, now?" I ask.

"E asked me to come speak about my interactions with the two of you," Rhys mutters. "Apparently e's afraid you might try to get em fired."

I can't stop the grin that spreads across my face. "That hadn't crossed my mind yet, but thanks for the idea! I'll be sure to write you a recommendation one day if your testimony helps them decide in my favor."

With that, I turn and stomp away, Rhys's gasp of indignation echoing behind me. I shouldn't be so mean; Rhys is probably acting in fear, just as I did when I stole *The Founding*.

Chapter Twenty-Six

My anger isn't so much for em as it is for what Mairead's done
to em. To so many of us.

I'm not going to back down this time.

CHAPTER TWENTY-SEVEN
AMANE

The Bindery has been quiet this week. It's strange. Tabby is the quietest of all of us, and yet eir absence is so loud. The days are filled not with laughter and singing, but sighing and the rustle of pages. Outside it continues to rain nearly every day. I liked it at first, but now I feel like I haven't seen the sun in five years, and it's not helping my mood. Sour, gloomy, depressed… still angry, a little.

I've tried to channel my feelings into my work, but there's so much and I'm afraid of overdoing it again with my wrist. The conversation Tabby and I had in the elevator keeps coming back to me. Everything that happened in the elevator—on the dreamscape—is forefront on my mind, like a wiggly tooth that just won't come out. I take a lot of naps on Tabby's studio bed. It still smells like em: lemons and lavender.

Today I'm painting illustrations for *The Stories We Sing*, but my heart's not in it. It feels like paint-by-numbers instead of a beautiful opportunity to collaborate with my idol. June's drawings are quirky and perfectly imperfect in a way I've never been able to achieve. The fact that e's letting me do the colors should have me over the moon, but the excitement is a small, small thing lost somewhere in my hollow chest.

June hasn't done much work, either. The stress made eir digestive illness flare up, leaving em in terrible pain on the couch or in the bathroom. Today e's been at the loom, slowly picking away at the ginkgo tapestry. E keeps clucking eir tongue and undoing bits.

I put my paintbrush down and lay my head on the desk with a thunk.

"Everything all right over there?"

"Yes," I say. I'd pick my head back up, but it's too heavy. "No."

I hear the scrape of a chair on the floor, followed by soft footsteps. June always wears socks in the studio. E places a gentle hand on my shoulder.

"Why don't we sit by the windows and have some tea?"

"What about the work?" I ask, turning my face to gaze blearily up at em.

"It'll get done eventually," e says. E looks just as tired as I feel.

I grumble, feeling guilty about stopping, but Tabby's words come back to me again. About how I don't need to push myself so hard. June's been telling me the same thing since we met, but I never listened. Now I feel like I have no other choice; if I keep going, I'll collapse. And we don't need more strife on top of what's already happening.

In just a few minutes we're both watching the rain fall outside, hot cups of chamomile tea in our hands. June sits in the loveseat while I lounge on the floor with pillows, wrapped up in a blanket. I glare at the armchair, which held the secret of Rhiannon's betrayal for weeks. Neither of us noticed. We were too busy being trusting fools.

"I think that's the first time you willingly stepped away from your work," June says.

"I'm tired," I say.

"Usually you just drink a pot of coffee when that happens."

I struggle to find the words to express myself in Casporan. "I'm tired in a different way. In my emotions. If that makes sense."

June nods and smiles wryly. "More than you know. Or as well as you could guess. It's been a difficult week for all of us."

"I'm sorry," I say for what must be the thousandth time.

"It's not your fault. It was my responsibility to hold my ground when it came to the book, and I failed to do that. Just as Rhiannon failed to cave in to pressure and desire that ultimately had… unwanted consequences," says June.

The little bit of anger bubbles up bigger inside me. "I guess so."

June traces a finger along the window, following the path of a water droplet. "You're still upset with Rhiannon, then."

"Of course I am!"

"You have every right to be. I was quite angry with em myself. But I've been friends with people Mairead manipulated before, watched them fall into those traps and make mistakes that hurt people—most of all themselves. That isn't to absolve Rhiannon entirely of blame, but e was a victim in this, too."

"Hmm," I grumble, noncommittally.

"Is that what's been bothering you?"

"Partly."

"Would you like to talk about the other things?"

I stare out the window. The wind chimes on the balcony are playing a mournful, magical tune. The mountains are wreathed in fog. The rain is a drizzle too light to see except in puddles, where dozens of ripples overlap one another in a constant rhythm.

"I miss Tabby. I'm worried about em," I say, and clamp my lips shut before more words get out. I haven't told anyone about what happened in the elevator. Tabby certainly hasn't told anyone, because e's still asleep.

"Oh, me too, dear," June says. "Should we go pay em a visit?"

***

Once we're out of the rain, I pull my hat off and jog down the hospital corridor ahead of June, eager to get to Tabby's room. My wet shoes slide to a halt on the tile with a squeak, and both the people already in the room look up at me. I freeze.

Aeronwy is sitting by the bed, which is fine, but Rhiannon is there, too. Our eyes meet for a second and then we both look away. I haven't spoken to em since everything went down.

June appears behind me and gives me a gentle push into the room. E must have known they would be here, because e doesn't look surprised. Aeronwy stands and they hug for a long time. This week, they avoided working the same hours in the Bindery. They must have talked and made up at home.

The only chair left is beside Rhiannon. I sit down in it and ignore em the best I can. E doesn't try to speak to me.

Tabby is so still that if I didn't know e was asleep, I'd think e was dead. I stare at em long enough to catch several long, slow breaths, just to make sure. The monitors show eir vital signs are steady, and there's an IV hooked up to one arm for hydration and nutrients. There's also a metal band around eir head to measure psychic activity. The readout looks like a series of jagged mountains and valleys, with a slower, rolling ocean wave underneath.

"Here we are, then," Aeronwy says, "all together again."

"Except Tabby," I say.

"E's in there somewhere," says June.

The room goes silent, save for the beep of the monitors. I thought seeing Tabby would make me feel better; instead all of my emotions are churning and bubbling within me, threatening to overflow. The cheerful yellow walls and bedsheets patterned with hearts seem to mock me. This room is the opposite of a happy place.

"How's Tabby doing?" I say, directing my question to the room in general, even though I know that as Tabby's partner, Rhiannon will have the answers.

"Last night the hospital energy healers had a dreamwalker try to go in and wake em up, but it didn't work. Tabby's mental defenses are too strong," Rhiannon says wearily. "They said e has to decide e wants to wake up."

I wring my hands in my lap. "But what if e feels too alone to do that? What if e doesn't know everything's going to be ok? What if e doesn't know how much I—we care for em?"

"I've been talking to em. I don't know if e can hear me," says Rhiannon.

"What if e doesn't *want* to hear from you?" I mutter in Gildean, and Rhiannon winces.

"I'm *trying* to *apologize*," e replies in the same, but Aeronwy cuts em off.

"If you're going to fight, don't do it here," e says sternly. When I gape at em, e adds, "I don't need to understand your words to know what you're saying. Do you think that will help Tabby feel safe? Take it elsewhere."

I cross my arms and glare at em, but e doesn't back down. I drop my eyes to the bed.

Rhiannon groans and says, "Look, I've been thinking. Maybe if someone Tabby really trusts tries dreamwalking in there, e'll let them in. Someone who's done it before."

"You mean me," says Aeronwy.

"Yes, you! And June," Rhiannon says. E sits up, arms wide in a pleading gesture. "I'm serious. You don't know what it's been like, dealing with eir parents through the years—through this. They're awful, but Tabby wouldn't let them go until recently. I think it has something to do with finally having someone safe to replace them."

E looks at Tabby with so much emotion—affection, longing, sorrow—that my heart softens, if only for a minute. I care about Tabby, might even be in love, but we haven't known each other that long. Rhiannon has been with em for years. Not once has Tabby said a bad word about em. I wonder if Rhiannon knows Tabby was planning to ask em about handfasting.

Sometimes people make mistakes, says a little voice in the back of my mind. *Even you.*

Aeronwy presses eir long fingers together. As usual they're covered in big, golden rings, today filled with black tourmaline and hematite, which absorb negativity and doubt. When I arrived, the older Illuminators seemed untouchable, like the Founders themselves. This week has shown me otherwise.

"Will you notify the hospital that we have your permission to do the ritual?" Aeronwy asks.

Rhiannon nods.

***

The next day, I text Rhiannon and ask em to meet me at a café near my place. It's tiny and warm, orange walls hung thick with local artwork. They serve Gildean coffee and vegetarian food, which I know Rhee likes. We've been here a dozen times. I arrive early and sit in a booth, rolling the memories between my fingers. I wish things would go back to the way they were.

I look up every time the bell rings on the door. I've already had two cups of coffee and my nerves are zinging. Eventually I can't sit still any longer and have to make a break for the bathroom. When I come back, Rhiannon is seated at the table with a new cup of coffee for em and a refill for me. E's wearing a Caspora City University hoodie with the hood pulled up, eyes just as red-rimmed as eir glasses.

"Hi," e says as I slide into the booth.

"Hi," I say, shortly.

I feel awkward. I understand why Tabby just wants to sleep; when everything breaks apart, putting it back into place is uncomfortable. It makes you confront parts of yourself you'd rather not think about. Sharp, gritty, hurting parts. I stare into my coffee cup. There's purple lipstick prints all the way around the rim.

Rhiannon clears eir throat. "Isn't that the same lip color and dress you were wearing when we met?"

"Yeah. I didn't do it on purpose," I say, and even I can hear how defensive I sound.

"Ah."

After a beat, I say, "Sorry. I guess it's probably some kind of meaningful coincidence."

"Yeah?" E sounds cautiously hopeful. "Synchronicity or whatever. But, you know, you don't have anything to say sorry for. That's on me. I'm sorry."

I let my reaction simmer. I brought us out in public so I'd think twice about shouting.

"I can't believe you took advantage of me like that," I say eventually, in Gildean. It's easier to express my feelings in my native tongue. "We could've figured out some way for you to study the book in the Bindery. We could've asked June more about why it was hidden! Explained the situation! I'd have done those things for you. Instead you waited until I was out of the room to take it, and then didn't say anything to anyone! After I vouched for you! Do you know what that feels like?"

"No," says Rhiannon. "I mean, I can imagine. It wasn't planned. I just… the opportunity came up, and I did it, and I didn't think about the full consequences until later. Which is just as bad, because it means I wasn't thinking about how it would affect you."

"You're lucky June doesn't blame me at all. I don't know what I'd do if—" I stop and bite my lip to hold back the tears. Just the thought of June being angry, disappointed, or losing trust in me is extremely upsetting. "You keep apologizing and saying you were wrong, you know it was wrong, so why did you do it?"

The baristas are eyeballing us from behind the counter. I'm sure they'll have a whole conversation about us later. One of them puts on a bright, innocent look as she brings our food over. I only ordered an appetizer of fried plantains and rice, to settle my nervous stomach. Rhiannon, on the other hand, receives a huge steaming bowl of lentil soup that's spicy enough to make *my* eyes water.

"I was trying to prove I hadn't peaked yet," Rhiannon says, switching back to Casporan. "Sorry, I don't know how to say that in Gildean."

"What does that mean exactly?" I say.

Rhiannon stirs the soup around absently, then picks up a piece of flatbread and rips it into pieces. "It's, like, is the best version of myself already in the past? Have I already hit my biggest achievement for my entire lifetime? Am I just condemned to mediocrity for the rest of my life? Is it just all downhill from here? I had to prove that none of that was true. I still have more in me. Better, bigger things."

"Oh." It's as if the words were read right out of my own diary.

"It seems totally ridiculous now, but Mairead just like… had a way of getting in my head… one minute saying all kinds of good shit about me, the next pressuring me to do things to 'prove' all the things e *just* said were true. It's really confusing. I thought I could get something I really wanted and no one would get hurt if I just did it exactly right, but I was wrong. Mairead was using me, and then I ended up using you, too."

Rhiannon dunks the flatbread into the stew and takes a bite every few words—eating never slows em down from talking— and immediately begins sweating from the spice. By the time e's finished speaking, I can't tell if e's crying because of all the emotion or because of the food. I hand em some napkins and e blows eir nose loudly. The baristas are staring again.

"I don't think you've peaked," I say, "but… I understand the fear. Um, are you going to be okay, eating all that?"

"Yes. I deserve this. I must be reborn in fire from the inside out," Rhiannon says in an entirely deadpan voice, then shovels another flatbread full of stew into eir mouth.

I can't help it. I cackle. Rhiannon grins through the pain. The baristas are giggling, too. One of them holds her hand over her mouth as she comes over to refill our waters, then leaves the whole pitcher on the table.

Rhiannon gulps down a glass, then sets it down with a sigh. "I get it if you hate me. I kind of hate me lately. But if it's at all possible, I'd still like to be friends. I know we haven't known each other that long, but it *feels* like we have. It makes me wonder how good of friends we could be when we *have* known each other forever."

"I don't hate you, Rhee," I say, poking my plantains around, "I'm just… really, really hurt."

Rhiannon nods solemnly. For everything that's happened, it's nice to have someone hear me out, to take my feelings seriously. My anger deflates; now I'm just tired.

"I do want to be friends still. I do want to forgive you. Will you give me a little time?" I say.

"Whatever you need."

"Thanks."

It's dark outside, but the lights inside the cafe are bright. The chatter of the other patrons fills our silence, a dozen other stories unfurling alongside ours. I wonder what they're going through.

One of the baristas brings over a plate with two dark molasses cookies.

"I'm glad you seem to have worked things out," she says in Gildean. "We were very nervous for you. This is on the house."

We thank her and her coworker behind the counter, embarrassed but pleased by their kindness. After eating the cookie, Rhiannon leans back against the book and closes eir eyes.

"Two down, two to go," e says.

"Eh?"

"I've apologized to Aeronwy, and I've apologized to you. Now I just have to talk to June, and," Rhee says, swallowing hard, "to Tabby."

***

As soon as I get home, my phone rings. I throw my purse on the bed and stare at it, wondering if I have the energy to answer. My nerves are frayed, and the ringtone is annoying, so I decide to silence it.

I change my mind when I see who's calling.

"Hi, Mom," I say, answering as brightly as possible. "Isn't it a bit late over there?"

"No, simply very early," says Yewande, in her low, no-nonsense voice. "The forecast was wrong and it's raining this morning, but I was already awake for my daily run. I thought I would use the time to call my youngest instead. It's been a while."

My stomach cramps with guilt—or perhaps that was all the coffee. I sit down on the edge of my bed and pick at my nails. I haven't had a manicure in a few weeks and it's all chipped, now, flakes of dark red polish dropping off like blood.

"Things have been..." I struggle to find the right word. "Busy? Over here."

There's no fooling her. I can practically see her piercing stare, light brown eyes laser-focused with so little blinking you'd swear she was a statue. The shaved gray stubble of her hair and her strong, proud shoulders. The expensive but utilitarian black tracksuit she wears for running.

"Are you in trouble, Ame?"

"No! It's not like that," I say.

"The way you say it makes me wonder," says Yewande dryly, "as well as your, hm, previous history? Especially when you were at school. Remember that time you signed up for two classes with overlapping time periods and tried to attend both via astral projection for several weeks?"

I laugh weakly, "Ha, yeah, that was an adventure."

Yewande laughs, too. "The doctors thought you might be stuck that way permanently. You could have left for Caspora and still been able to join us for brunch."

"Good thing those days are behind me. I'm older and wiser now," I say, while staring at my wrist brace. Painting earlier today made my injury flare up.

"It's difficult for me to believe, but you must be," she says. "I've been telling my marathon running group how proud I am that my baby is becoming a world-class Illuminator at the Eternal Library, with one of the great masters. When do we get to see your first Illuminated book?"

"The one I'm working on now is a collaboration with June, so I don't know if it counts as my first one," I say, "but definitely soon!"

"When do you get to work on one by yourself? Don't you get to publish your own work, too?" Yewande asks.

"Yeah, that comes next."

"What are you going to write about? You know we'll pick up your book for distribution here at home and give it a full promotional package," she says. "The sooner we know the details, the sooner I can get the marketing department working on it."

I flop down on my bed and curl up, keeping the phone against my ear. "I thought you didn't believe in nepotism in the publishing industry," I say, to avoid answering her first question. I still don't know the answer.

"I don't," she says with a chuckle, "but I know you'll be amazing, as you always are. My daughters are all brilliant writers—I made sure of that. If I publish your work, it's because of the latter, not the former."

"So, if my book was trash, you'd toss it out?"

"I would. But I know it won't be," she says, laughing.

I laugh, too. Her confidence in me should feel uplifting, but instead I sink deeper into the blankets under the expectation. I wrap myself in a fleece throw and take a deep breath. Time to change the subject.

"Are you training for another marathon this year? Which one?" I ask.

"The Mt. Cináed Marathon, of course! I can combine that trip with one to visit you," she says. "Your Mama will come, too, and your sisters. Abeni is running, too. She placed fourth in the Fjallborg Marathon last year, remember?" says Yewande.

"I remember. She sent me a copy of the article from the Aquanean Post. When is it?" I ask, twisting my fingers around the tassels on the blanket.

"Just after Summer Solstice. Not long to train for the high altitude, but I'm glad I get to see you and your new work sooner."

"Me, too," I say.

Yewande pauses. "You don't sound too excited. Are you sure you're doing all right?"

I bite my lip and roll onto my other side, so I'm facing the wall. It's covered with photographs of my friends and family in Gildea. The article on Abeni's marathon win is included, along with articles on Sol Publishing, my parents, and Jiji. I call it my inspiration wall, but right now all it inspires is a lump of dread in my stomach.

"One of my new friends is in the hospital," I say.

"Goddess! Why didn't you say so? What happened?" she exclaims.

"It's complicated. Kind of an emotional-spiritual coma."

Yewande clucks her tongue. "I'm so sorry to hear that. I know you, though. You'll be at their side through it all."

"I'm trying, but it doesn't feel like there's anything I can do," I say, tears gathering at the corners of my eyes.

"That's not true. You're a strong young woman. You'll figure it out, and everything will be fine," she says.

I wish I shared her confidence. I wipe my eyes and hold back a sniffle. "Thanks, Mom. If you say so."

Our chat exhausts me, and it's past midnight, but afterward I can't sleep. After tossing and turning for an hour, I get up and sit in front of my altar. At home, I don't need to wear magical wards. I sense my Great-Grandmother's spirit strongly when I pick up her Threadbound Oracle deck; she feels like warm hands on my shoulders and a silk scarf wrapped around my brow. Her presence beside me stretches through time, back to when I was a little girl.

"What am I supposed to do now?" I ask.

I shuffle the cards and lay them out: the Five of Ink: Solvent, The Mirror, and the Six of Ink: Calligraphy. The Five of Ink depicts five bottles spilling out liquid that erases the thorns and roses surrounding it. The Mirror shows its namesake surrounded by bright flowers, all completely symmetrical. The Six of Ink shows three bottles of ink pouring fluidly into another three bottles without spilling a drop.

Forgiveness, mistakes, truth, reflection, patience, fluidity.

"Is this about Rhiannon?" I ask.

I pull another card: The Protagonist. The message is about me.

Part Four: Thread

Spring 4019

CHAPTER TWENTY-EIGHT
TABBY

There's so much work to do in the garden. The wildflowers I planted after the fire have faded, their bodies decomposing into the ashes and building the soil anew. Now I can plant the perennials, the shrubs and saplings, the sweet-and-savory herbs that will restore my heart, if not to its original innocence, at least to its beauty.

I water the seedlings with tears until I run out. Dry-eyed, I find the well and peer down into its depths. The bottom is invisible, shrouded in darkness. I drop a rock inside and hear a loud *plook!* as it hits water. I dream up a new bucket and rope. The water it fetches is clear and cold and tastes like mountains.

Everything was going so well until now. The garden reflects that in its recovery. I should have guessed there was a lightning bolt coming, despite the blue skies.

I dig my hands into the dirt. I only use a shovel when I have to, preferring the feel of damp earth between my fingers and under my nails. I dream up seed after seed, sprout after sprout, start after start, and place them in the ground with a whispered prayer and a kiss. Soon, the entire field is scored with neat circles of mounds and valleys. Soon, everything is growing.

I pour everything I have into this garden. I keep my mind off the waking world. When night falls, I dream up a soft bed of grass and a flannel blanket. I don't sleep here, exactly, but I do rest. Above me, the stars chime lightly. The flowers murmur to one another when dawn comes, and a single ruby-colored bird sings me awake.

I get to work on the little house that once stood in the center of the garden. The foundation is all that remains. I want it to be strong and fire resistant, so I make mud bricks, patting each one together with my hands and leaving them to harden beneath the sun. I remember what it was like, during the good moments of my childhood, to find simple pleasure in getting dirty. And the even greater pleasure afterward of jumping into the pond naked to get clean.

The longer I spend here, the more natural it feels. The more real.

The wind blows off the sea, bringing rain. I dream up a bed, a stove, a bath, books. Safety. The garden continues to grow, until the plants are ankle high, knee high, waist high. A jungle of green tomatoes, curling vines of cucumbers, the cheerful faces of sunflowers the size of dinner plates, lavender blossoms full of honey bees, bluebells ringing beneath incense cedar boughs.

I know I'm running away, but I don't know what else to do. A desperate part of me hopes that when I wake, it'll all have been a bad dream. Or that everything will have been solved for me.

I know neither is likely.

One day—not that there are exactly days here, time being a nebulous concept in the garden—I wake not in my bed, but beside the well. The sun hasn't crested the hills yet, and the sky is a vivid pink and yellow painting. The dandelions and morning glories are open, their faces pointed towards me. There are poppy beetles crawling over my hands and through my hair. How did I end up out here?

The denizens of the garden are silent. No rustling leaves, no chirping birds, no buzzing insects. Dawn is one of the noisiest times of the day. Have they all gone? Or are they waiting for something? Listening?

I listen, too, and am startled to hear faint singing coming from the well.

"Sweet as rushing mountain stream
Bitter as medicine root and green
To find and lose you
To know and love you

Would that wandering through
I might find the wooded way
Where you've hidden yourself away

I asked the sun, the moon, the stars
How you could have gone so far
But they only say
I should have asked you first to stay."

There are two voices, one low, one high. Sometimes they sing alone, sometimes they intertwine. I recognize those voices. My heartbeat is a drum, my heartstrings pulled taught and plucked in accompaniment. Entranced, I pick myself up off the ground and walk up the steps into the wellhouse.

In front of me, a glimmer. Like a spider's web, but golden. The nearer I get to the well, the thicker the thread becomes, until I reach the very edge and see the inch-thick glowing cords coming out of my chest and disappearing into the darkness below.

The mouth of the well is much wider than before. Perhaps four feet in diameter, big enough for me to climb inside. Is that what I have to do? Is that what I'm being called for?

But the well is a portal, and the waking world might be on the other side.

Instead, I tug on the golden cords. They vibrate and hum like harp strings. The singing stops. A sound like a wine cork being popped pierces the air, and all the water drains from the well. I can see that it's dry as two shooting stars rush up from bottom, arcing over my shoulders and into the garden.

When I turn around, there they are. Their backs are to me.

"That's not the way we came in before," Aeronwy is saying with a full-body shiver.

"Well, you're here, and you're all right. You are all right?" June places a hand between Aeronwy's shoulder blades, where eir Flame is visible. It's flickering wildly, but brightly.

"There was no water. I'm all right."

I clear my throat, and the two of them turn around. To my surprise, they look twenty years younger, early to mid-forties instead of sixties. Their faces are smoother. June is thinner, and Aeronwy stronger. June's hair is entirely red still, shining in the morning sun. Aeronwy is all gray, long curls pulled back into a bun, but there's no white yet. Just a few threads of black. June is wearing the gold wire-rimmed glasses from the photo albums and has even more freckles than usual.

They also look taller, but they aren't. I'm shorter. I realize with embarrassment that I'm *also* twenty years younger. The purple overalls I'm wearing were a gift for my eleventh birthday. Is it too late to run and hide?

"Tabby!" June exclaims, adjusting eir glasses. "That is you, isn't it? It does look like you. This place feels like you."

"How did you get here?" I ask.

"You let us in," June says, gesturing at the well.

"Thank you for that," Aeronwy adds, quietly.

"I heard you singing," I say.

They smile. I glance back and forth between the two of them, trying to assess whether those smiles are real. They don't seem to be angry, with me or each other. Usually when I regress into a child body, it means a nightmare is on its way. One that's rooted in memories and crystallized in time.

June looks around curiously. "Is there somewhere we can sit and talk?"

I force my legs to walk down the steps towards them. Even at eleven I was nearly as tall as June. It feels strange to look em in the eye, and to look up much farther at Aeronwy.

"I was always tall for my age as well, as you can imagine," Aeronwy says as I lead them into the garden.

"It was hard," I say, unable to hide the truth while we're inside my own heart. "Everyone thought I was older than I was… and more adult."

"I know."

In the dream logic, I see a young Aeronwy head and shoulders above the other kids. E's gangly and thin, moving like a fawn on unsteady knees. Hardly the elegant, confident Librarian I've come to know. If I ever wake up again, maybe I can transform myself, too. Maybe I've already begun.

The patio sits between the cabin and the pond, shaded by the one mature tree that survived the fire. It's a lodgepole pine, and though its lower trunk is scorched, it's surrounded by saplings. The cones of the lodgepole pine are sealed shut with resin that only fire can open. I've closed myself off again, but the saplings are still growing.

There's a small wrought-iron table, painted white, in the tree's shadow. There are only two chairs, but I easily dream up another one. I gesture for them to sit and then hurry into the cabin to make tea. Tea may seem silly without physical bodies, but the ritual is what counts. As I crush the fresh herbs from the garden and add them to the boiling water, my nerves calm. Rosemary, mint, lemon balm, a touch of honey.

I carry the tray out to the table and serve everyone before taking my seat. The sunflowers planted along the sunny edge of the patio lean in to listen. Aeronwy tilts eir head back to look at them, unbothered by the bees zooming around eir face.

"You've done a lot of good work in here. I'm glad," e says warmly.

"Thanks to you," I say. I hold my teacup with both hands and drop my gaze.

"I only helped you restart. This is your own strength."

Is running away my strength? In my teacup, my reflection grimaces.

June leans forward, shadow falling over the table. "Tabby, how are you feeling?"

"I… I don't know." It's fine in here. In here I'm safe, happy among the flowers. But there are skeletons buried in the earth, and sometimes the well is salty, as if it were full of tears.

"I'm sorry you had to see us arguing like that. It doesn't happen very often, but, obviously there was reason for it to. I understand it probably brought up some bad memories for you," June continues.

A cold breeze blows through the garden, scattering leaves and petals everywhere.

"Some emotions must be expressed as soon as they are felt, so they don't fester. So that we can speak of them frankly and more gently afterward," Aeronwy says. "I also used to be afraid when people expressed their anger, but doing so is healthy. There are certainly people who take their anger too far, but we try not to be among them."

I glance between them. They're holding hands, their faces soft and their bodies angled towards me.

"We've made up," June says, interpreting my searching gaze correctly. "I broke a very important promise… but I've apologized, and we've talked through it. It's been difficult, but not impossible, given our long history."

"So quickly?" I ask.

June looks pained. "Honey, you've been asleep for ten days."

Ten days? I knew it had been a while, but time works differently in dreams, on the astral, in the heartspace. I assumed that when (if) I woke up, a day or two at most would have passed. Everyone must be out of their minds with worry, especially Rhee and Amane—both of whom I care for deeply, both of whom it hurts to think about—and my parents, there's no way my parents don't know—but I don't want them to, don't want to have to explain how much this has to do with *them*—

I press my face into my hands. The light seeping between my fingers dims as clouds roll in over the sun. I hear the scrape of a chair on brick, and then June wraps eir arms around me in a tight hug. E leans eir head against mine and strokes my hair. The scent of jasmine and spun wool envelops me like a weighted blanket.

"I don't know what to do," I choke out as the tears begin to fall. "I just want everything to be okay and not fall apart *again*."

"I know," says June soothingly.

In the magic of the dream, I see a young June, barely a teenager, on a boat leaving the Casporan coast. Yet it's also June as a young adult, moving in the other direction, away from Fenia and back towards Caspora City. Both versions of em are crying. Both versions are alone, having lost almost all the people e knew and loved, whether to death or distance. June is such a cheerful person, it never occurred to me that e's suffered great losses in eir life. Which is ironic, considering the way I'm always putting on a smile, always doing nice things for others in order to get away from the darkness of my own experiences.

I feel a warm hand on my back. Aeronwy has moved closer, the heat from eir Flame steady and comforting, like a hearth fire late at night. Overhead, the sun rapidly sets, the sky a kaleidoscope of colors. Clouds thicken, hiding away the stars before they can even appear. The night air is cold.

"Even if things do fall apart, you won't be alone this time," Aeronwy says. "I promise."

Slowly, I wipe the tears from my face and lower my hands. The tea is still hot, white wisps of steam disappearing into the darkness. The teapot is the same one Rhiannon bought me for making gem infusions, the same one e used when making me breakfast before testing for the apprenticeship at the Library. The amethyst in the infusion chamber is the same color as eir hair.

"What do you do when someone you love hurts you?" I ask.

"That depends. How did they do it? Has it happened before? How did they react? What do they do when you tell them how you feel? What do you think they'll do about it in the future? And how do you feel about it?" June says.

Scared. Terrified. Heartbroken. I shiver.

"Remember that Rhiannon and your parents are not the same people," Aeronwy cautions.

E's right. They're not. Aeronwy and June aren't Oran and Lilja, either. I'm always expecting everyone to act and react like my parents do, and yet I'm always surprised when my parents continue to act like themselves. I never fully realized how much power I've given them over my life.

My breathing eases, my shoulders slump. The warm sound of crickets and cicadas fills the air.

"I want to let it all go, but it's so *hard*," I say. "I don't want *this* to be my story again, but I feel stuck in it."

June releases me and leans against the edge of the table. "That's why you don't have to do it alone. That's why we came to find you, and let you know when you wake up, it's going to be all right. It might be hard for a while, but not forever," e says. "Can I show you something, Tabby?"

I nod. I dream up some candles to add to the light from Aeronwy's Flame.

June hovers one hand just above my heart, then makes a plucking gesture. I feel a curious *tug* on my soul, and rippling harp-like notes fill the air. Dozens of glowing threads appear, starting from my chest and disappearing out into the night.

They're all different sizes and colors, from the finest silk thread to thick ropes and cords. Two of the thickest ones are connected to Aeronwy and June, the same ones I used to pull them out of the well.

June puts a gentle hand on the cord connecting us, and it chimes softly. "This is how we found you in here. I usually avoid looking at my cord with someone until I've known them for at least a year, to keep it from influencing the beginning of our relationship in this lifetime, but when I was having trouble deciding between you and Amane for the apprenticeship, I peeked."

"And that went so well," Aeronwy chuckles.

"I think it did," June says defensively, "in retrospect. You see, Tabby, what I found was that you and I have known each other many times before, in very important ways, as I'm sure you can see. You know a bit about etheric cords, don't you? Having studied in AT and all. This could easily have been the tie-breaker, the sign that you should become an important person to me again. And yet…"

"Yet," says Aeronwy.

"Amane and I had no previous cords. Our souls have never met before this lifetime—oh, and the first meeting can be so exciting! There's no history, no baggage. You can make it what you want, you can set the stage for many more lifetimes of joy. So, it was still a tie," says June. E laughs and adjusts eir glasses self-consciously. "In the end, I'm getting to know both of you, which just proves we often have more choices than we realize."

"Sometimes you can use both sides of the paper," Aeronwy adds, and June beams.

"That's right, my love. Aery kept advocating for you in the apprenticeship, while Rose kept suggesting I choose Amane. Eventually Aery suggested taking you on instead. I hadn't looked at the cord between the two of you, but I could guess, since e felt so strongly about it," June says.

I look over at Aeronwy. "But you let us choose who we'd apprentice with. We could've picked the opposite of what you wanted."

"It only seemed fair to give you both a say," e replies, then pauses, finger resting against one elegant cheekbone in thought.

"Well, I wanted an external sign that it was the right decision. Then you decided so quickly and surely…"

"I had a dream," I blurt out, "that you were in, at Rose's memorial. So as soon as you offered, I knew."

I hadn't meant to tell em about that yet, but we're inside my own heart, and it's difficult to hide something so huge. Aeronwy doesn't ask what the dream was about, but does e really need to? The larger an etheric cord, the more emotion and thought can pass between two people. E smiles at me affectionately, a real smile, not the little twitch I've grown so accustomed to looking for. Behind em, the moonflowers open their pendulous blossoms, and the jasmine unfurls, scenting the night sweetly.

"When was the last time you had your cords read?" June asks.

"Years ago," I say. "They required it for AT studies."

"Did you have any cutting or clearing done?"

I shake my head. "Just a little. The thread witch I saw said that e would recommend cutting my parents' cords if they were anyone else but my parents. E said e'd do it if I wanted em to, but… e made it clear that was the wrong choice."

I glance down and find the two cords connecting me to my parents. They're about as thick as a child's marker, multicolored threads all spun together into an energetic tie between our spirits. Each bundle of threads in a cord is a lifetime. Some are thicker, some are thinner. There's a good bit of gold and silver, but several bundles are filled with black threads.

"May I?" June asks, holding a hand over one of the cords. I nod. When e touches it, a discordant note rings out through the air. Images of Oran float through my vision; Oran as I know em now in this life, and people whose physical forms I don't recognize, but whose souls I know are the same. Past lives. These come in tiny glimpses and fade from memory almost as soon as I've seen them.

"This is not uncommon, unfortunately," June says as e carefully thumbs through Oran's cord. "A beautiful beginning that becomes out of tune and toxic over time. We create these strong bonds in past lives, healthy and glowing at first, like two bells ringing in harmony. And so we meet these people when we're born again, and again. But we're all still walking our own paths, and life is unpredictable. People change. We get hurt. We hurt others. Harmony becomes disharmony. Two people who were once so right for each other become so wrong. Yet we can't let go. The hurt begins to make deeper connections than the health. It's a difficult cycle to break free from, but not impossible."

I've been slowly cutting my parents out of my waking life, but we're still connected. All the memories we share, in this life and previous, linking us no matter how far away I might run. It makes sense. I understand what I need to do, but I'm afraid to do it.

June says, "The thread witch you saw before was wrong. Wrong to judge you, I mean, not wrong that these cords should probably be cut."

"One of my parents just left an abusive relationship with the other," I say. "She's probably suffered far more than I have. Shouldn't I be there for her, at least?"

"Not if she's also causing you so much pain and confusion, and isn't making an effort to change," June says, as e thumbs through Lilja's cord. I wonder how much of our life e can see. "If you hurt someone else because you're hurting, does that make it all right? You can empathize and step away at the same time."

"But, they're my parents…" I say, as I've been saying over and over and over for years.

"Then they had even more responsibility to do better by you," says Aeronwy.

"I'm sure they did their best," I continue, aware that I'm treading the same path I always have, when everything in me longs to break free. But I need to be sure. *Really* sure.

"They probably did," says June, "but sometimes that's not enough."

A shift. Small at first, and then huge, cascading. The tears don't fall from my eyes, but they do fall from the sky, in great torrents. Lightning flashes and thunder rumbles. The wind whips the flowers into a frenzy, their petals blown into the sky. The paths all become rivers, and the well house is overflowing.

We hurry inside before my emotions drown us all.

The cabin is warm, the candles and crystal lamps already lit. All three of us sit on the bed, with piles of books at our feet. Stories I imagined, stories I wrote, either to imagine a better future or to rid myself of past pain. Worsening depression and anxiety caused me to stop. Recently I've been wanting to take another shot at it.

"Tabby," says June, "I can cut them for you, if you want. We can do it now, or we can do a proper cord cutting ritual later—"

"Do it now. Please." I clutch the two blackened cords in one fist. They vibrate unpleasantly.

June reaches inside the shirt e's wearing and retrieves a pair of silver scissors on a chain. The case is tiny and ornate, engraved with shining swirls and starbursts. The scissors themselves are plain, but powerful. I can feel the magic radiating from them.

"I brought these just in case. This won't feel good while it's happening. Just remember you're not alone," June says.

Aeronwy doesn't say anything, but takes my free hand. E went through this once, too. Let go of the parent who should have been there for em but wasn't. And that seems to have worked out well.

June starts singing in Fenian as e cuts the first cord. One thread at a time. My mind is flooded with memories: shame and blame, fights and sleepless nights, fear and the weight of the world on my shoulders, trying to be the glue between two people who, if they ever loved one another, have been eclipsed by their own pain and shadows.

Then, briefly: freedom. A darkness falls away, and I gasp, sitting bolt upright. June puts a hand on my back to steady me. The storm outside pauses; the eye of the hurricane.

"The other one, now. Let them go, Tabby, let it all go."

I do, I do. As best as I can, I do. The storm rages again as June cuts through the other cord, and this time I look each memory, each feeling in the face before it falls away. I'm not surprised when the last thread is cut. I'm ready.

I'm ready.

I wake up.

CHAPTER TWENTY-NINE
RHIANNON

"I'm coming with you."

I glance over my shoulder at Tabby. "Are you sure?"

Tabby nods and slowly rises from the couch, where e's been lying all day. Ironically, ten days straight of dreamwalking and bedrest left em fatigued. Without solid food, e lost weight and muscle mass. But after a week of hearty meals and sunshine, some of the color is back in eir cheeks.

"Could you bring my chair and some pillows?"

"Of course."

The outside of our apartment building is ringed with greenhouses and balcony gardens. Even though we live on the tenth floor, we can still grow vegetables in a raised bed enriched by communal compost. There's not much out here yet—spring only just arrived, the danger of frost barely past.

I set up a folding chair for Tabby, who wraps emself in a blanket and watches me work. My cousins make fun of me for being used to city life, but I haven't forgotten everything from my farmer's upbringing. Gardening was one of the things Tabby and I bonded over when we first met.

That Tabby wants to join me while I plant our new seedlings gives me hope. We talked about what happened for a long time after e woke up, and we'll be talking about it for a long time yet. I understand why it'll take a while to earn back eir trust. I'm just grateful for the second chance.

"I guess," Tabby said, pulling the hospital blankets up to eir chin, "I feel like you put your job ambitions before our relationship. I know how important your career is to you, I wouldn't want to take that away, but—"

I sighed. "No, I get it. There should be a certain, like, balance of those two things, and I threw it off. Way off."

"I wish you had talked to me about it more. I didn't want to get in between Mairead and Aeronwy, but I'd rather have asked em about it than go through what actually happened," Tabby said. "We could have figured something out."

All I could do was nod. These same thoughts went through my head a thousand times in the aftermath of the disaster I brought down on us. What felt impossible a few moons ago now felt obvious.

Tabby sighed and drew eir knees up, hugging them under the blankets. We sat in silence for a few minutes before e said, "Part of me can't stay too mad at you, though."

I lifted my head. "How come?"

"Because," e said, choking a little. E reached over and took my hand. "How Mairead treated you reminds me of my parents in a lot of ways. I think about how long I've let them manipulate me, and I feel like I understand why you didn't immediately back away from Mairead. E's not your Ren, but as your boss, e has a similar power over you."

The admission that eir parents were manipulators took me by surprise. Tabby had long made excuses for them, becoming uncomfortable when I called their bad behavior for what it was. I didn't know what Aeronwy and June did with em in the dream coma, but it must have been a powerful experience.

"Part of why I feel so terrible and embarrassed is I keep thinking I should have seen what was happening sooner," I replied. "I've been mad about your parents for years and frustrated when you stuck with them. It seemed so easy and obvious what I would do in your place, you know? But it's not the same as actually doing it. I'm sorry I didn't understand that until now."

Tabby squeezed my hand and smiled solemnly. "I'm sorry you do understand it now."

We sat smiling at each other, strengthening the connection between us that I feared was broken. To my relief, it was just stretched to its limit. Then I remembered the gift hiding away in my bag. I let go of Tabby's hand and pulled it out.

"You, um, missed your birthday while you were asleep," I said, handing over the small burlap sack. There was a green ribbon tied around the top, but other than that I hadn't bothered with wrapping. Things like that seemed trite these days. "I ordered these for you weeks ago."

Tabby opened the bag and pulled out its contents: paper packets full of heirloom seeds, their pictures colorfully embossed on each one: purple tomatoes, alpine strawberries, watermelon radishes, and sunflowers guaranteed to grow twelve feet tall.

"These are lovely, Rhee, thank you," e said, sounding touched. "I don't know if I'll be well in time to plant them, though. It's already a little late."

"I can get them started if you want," I said. "Then if you feel up to it, you can help me plant them outside later."

Tabby's face softened. "I'd like that."

Tabby's phone pings, drawing me back into the present. I pat the last seedling into place and reach for the watering can. The rainy season isn't over yet, but today the sun is shining in a bright blue sky.

"Rhee," says Tabby, "is it okay if Amane comes over tonight?"

"Yeah, I'll make some extra soup. Do you two want alone time, or could all three of us hang out? Play a game or something?" I ask, glancing over my shoulder.

When I first found out that Amane and Tabby had romantic crushes on each other, the thought of my partner and my new best friend dating was exciting. No awkward third-wheeling while I got to know a stranger Tabby met online or in papermaking class. We could all spend quality time together. I hope things can still be like that.

Tabby smiles and says, "That sounds nice. I could use time with both of you right now."

***

There's a brand-new wheelchair ramp outside Camille's house when I go to visit. The wood is raw and untarnished by the weather. I walk up and knock on the door, shifting the gift basket under my arm. A teenager with black hair and olive, freckled skin answers, solemn face shifting into a smile. I recognize em from the family photo Camille kept on her desk—the older of two kids.

E takes the basket, full of apple juice from my family's farm, to the kitchen and points down the hallway. I walk through the book-lined hall until I reach the living room, where Camille is seated beside a pair of sliding glass doors. One of them is open to let fresh air in from the courtyard beyond, but the cool breeze isn't what makes me shiver.

Camille looks like a completely different person. Her red hair is streaked with gray, her skin is waxy, and her face wrinkled in pain. She's wearing loose house clothes instead of the sharp blouses and slacks I'm used to from the Library. They make her look even skinnier, though I remember her as pleasantly plump.

She smiles wanly as I take a seat on the couch facing her.

"Glad to see you're out of the hospital," I say. Tabby and I visited her there several moons ago when her illness started. I stopped by last week, but she hadn't been able to talk. She listened, though, as I told her what happened between me and Mairead.

"Me, too," she says. "The pain in my stomach stopped. For now."

"Did they find out anything about what's happening to you? The doctors, I mean?"

"No, but a new energy healer *finally* confirmed there's a curse on me. It's very well hidden, e said," Camille tells me. "I hope you don't mind me getting right to the point. I'd love to have a friendly chat, but I only have so much energy each day."

I nod. "No problem. Tell me if you get too tired."

Camille sighs. "The healer couldn't tell me where the curse was coming from, but you and I both know, don't we?"

We'd texted a bit about our suspicions before I came over. "Pretty damn sure. I didn't know curses could be this bad," I say.

Ever since e fought with Mairead, Camille has been experiencing debilitating migraines, abdominal pains, extreme fatigue, weakness, poor memory, nausea, and a host of other troubling symptoms. They come and go in intensity, but never completely cease.

"It takes an exceedingly powerful and cunning witch to craft a curse this strong without implicating emself," says Camille. "You rarely see it because most curses of this level would give away their caster in a second. Like leaving your ID card and DNA at the scene of the crime. Even if you're good, it's risky. I've been studying the subject while in bed."

"Why do you think Mairead cursed you? To keep you from reporting eir abusive behavior to HR? Or just as retaliation for wanting to transfer departments away from em?" I ask.

"Both," Camille says with a shrug. "I wish I'd never taken the position. I knew that previous Assistant Heads rarely stayed at the job long, which should have been a sign. A high position like that should have good tenure. But no one warned me—not directly. And the manipulation didn't start right away. It grew slowly over time, until I was losing my mind trying to understand it."

"I could be lucky my stint was so short," I say with a dry laugh.

Camille doesn't look amused. "How are *you* feeling, Rhiannon?"

I rub my forehead. "Okay, I guess? I'm tired all the time, and I've had more migraines than usual, but there's a lot going on in my life."

"That's how it started for me, too. I thought it was just stress," Camille says. "You never gave Mairead something of yours, did you? Or had a small personal item go missing? A scarf, a glove, a pencil with bite marks on it?"

"Um," I say, too embarrassed to say I gave Mairead a piece of my hair for the spell on the secret scrying room door. Every witch knows to guard their hair, nail clippings, and other bodily castoffs—the best ingredients for cursing. I was so excited about the amethyst room that it hadn't even crossed my mind.

"It doesn't matter. These days, anyone can snap a photo with their smart phone and print it out at home. That would be enough," Camille says darkly.

"Did Mairead get something from you?" I ask. "Where do you think the physical part of the spell is being kept, if there even is one? Mx. Dreamcloud says we need hard evidence."

Mx. Dreamcloud had also informed me that my case with Mairead was on hold until after the Head Librarian Trials. Mairead invoked an ancient rule that claimed Head Librarian candidates can't be prosecuted or fired while in the period between official candidacy and the Trials. Which is bullshit, because there's no way to remove someone once they become Head Librarian except by killing them.

I assume that's the point. I can't wait for either Aeronwy or June to eviscerate the power of the Charter Book. It's time the rules were changed.

"I wish I knew. My memory and attention span are terrible these days. It could have happened any time in the last three years," Camille says. "What I can tell you is that it's probably paper magic of some kind. You've seen the cut paper art in Mairead's office—you know those are spells, don't you?"

"Someone told me about it at some point," I say. "I can't sense that kind of thing."

"I can. I'm very sensitive to magical energy, actually. The reason Mairead still uses paper memos in the Archives isn't because e doesn't like email, it's because e magicks them for understanding and compliance," she says.

"Excuse me? What?"

"I know. It's at such a subtle level, most people don't notice. Especially with all the other, more powerful energies swirling around the Library. But I did. It was one of the many things we fought over. I said it was unethical. Mairead said it was a benign necessity, to keep the department running smoothly."

A thought occurs to me. "Did e ever give *you* a piece of paper art? Like, a cutout? Or a shadowbox?"

Camille blinks. "I—I think so? E must have. I can see it in my mind, but I can't put the words together." She turns and calls down the hallway. "Naomi? Would you come here, please?"

The teenager who let me in reappears and talks with Camille about where e might have seen such a thing. I can tell it hurts Naomi to see eir Ren so confused and in pain. My shame about being manipulated morphs into anger at Mairead. How can e toy with people's lives like this? And for what? Eir own warped sense of security and justice?

After a short search of the house, Naomi returns with a shadowbox the same size and shape as the one I was given. The scene shows the moon rising over an intricate Caspora City skyline. Mairead's signature is penciled on the bottom left corner, dated nearly three years ago.

"It was in the back of the office closet," Naomi says, handing it to Camille.

"I completely forgot about this," Camille says. E takes the shadowbox and turns as white as the paper inside. "Mairead gave it to me shortly after I started the job. I thought it was a touching gift. There's definitely magic in this. It's faint, but it's there."

"Is that the curse?" Naomi asks, covering eir mouth in horror.

"I don't know. I'll have to call Mgx. Ravindra—"

I hold my hand out. "No, you don't. I've got this."

CHAPTER THIRTY
AMANE

"Close your eyes with me now. Send your roots down into the floor, your branches up towards the sky," June says in a soothing voice. "Focus on your breath."

I envision branches of light growing higher from my crown with each inhale, roots digging deeper from my tailbone with each exhale. With my spirit grounded, I pull my attention inward, finding my center as we always do during meditation. Seeking that space in my chest where my heart beats strong and everything I see, I see clearly. The space expands and contracts with every life-giving breath.

"Notice the way you inhabit your physical body. Feel the way your spirit fills up every inch of your blood and bones and flesh, this piece of earth that's animated by your presence."

June continues to guide me through each part of my body, from my toes all the way up to the top of my head. Each time I sense something outside myself or find my thoughts drifting, I pull myself back.

"Now bring your spirit deep, deep inside. Turn towards yourself. The core part of you which is aware, which watches, which is reborn each and every time your physical body experiences the inevitability of death. The part of you that is shining and eternal and without judgment," June says.

I sink into myself. I sense the spark of divinity that June describes… but also, a great weariness. Sadness. A fear of not being good enough. If I accept that at my core, I'm shining and eternal and without judgment, then what does all my hard work to 'improve' mean? Have I been punishing myself for nothing?

Is this what my cards were trying to talk to me about? Ever since the reading I did after visiting Tabby in the hospital a moon cycle ago, I've been pulling the same cards over and over again. If I try to read for anyone else, all I get is garbled nonsense. Cards that don't make sense. Nothing lines up with my intuition. Spirits I call on refuse to answer.

Forgiveness, mistakes, truth, reflection, patience, fluidity.

June rings a silver bell, the sweet sound creating ripples in my interior. Beside me, an essential oil diffuser fills the air with the scent of roses. Sunlight from the windows warms my back.

"What do you sense? How do you feel?"

I struggle to find an acceptable answer. This meditation is the key to Illumination. Through it, I should be able to pull a Thread of etheric energy from my soul and ply it with the physical thread I've spun. If I can't do this, I can't do my job. I can't finish my apprenticeship.

June rings the bell again.

"Who do you see looking back at you?"

"Um…"

"Can you describe them for me?"

I focus my mind's eye, breathing into the meditative state. "I see a child. She's thirteen years old. Short, round, with a big chest already that she's self-conscious of. Her hair is in cute little bantu knots and she just learned how to put lipstick on herself."

"And how do you think she's feeling right now?"

"She—she has a lot of energy," I say. "She's very excited all the time. She just wants to draw and paint and write and share it with people. She wants to make them happy."

"Make who happy?"

The words start coming faster now. The cloud of self-doubt and sadness envelops the image of younger me in my mind. "Everyone. Her parents and siblings especially. They're amazing. Everyone knows they're amazing. She wants to prove she can be like them. That she belongs with them."

"Does she feel like she doesn't belong?"

I open my mouth to answer, but all that comes out are tears. There's a clatter as June puts the bell down. E hands me a box of tissues and sits quietly while I get it all out. I blow my nose and wipe my eyes.

"I think," I say, "I need a break."

"I understand," June says. "This is the hardest part of the apprenticeship. Going deep within ourselves unearths a lot of buried emotions. We can always pick up again tomorrow."

The suggestion makes me bristle internally. I don't know if I *want* to pick up again tomorrow. I need a bigger break than that. But I bite my tongue and push my resentment down. I don't know how else to deal with it.

Forgiveness, mistakes, truth, reflection, patience, fluidity.

I wish I knew how to embody those things. I leave June's studio with the intention of going back to my own to practice my spinning—another daily frustration lately, as it never comes out how I want it to—but I notice the door to Rose's studio is open and the lights are on. I walk over and poke my head in.

Inside, Aeronwy is wiping down the shelves with a red cloth and spray bottle filled with water and herbs. The stereo in the corner is playing a hit Casporan pop song from fifteen years ago, which I heard even living in Gildea. Pop songs were a big way I learned to speak the language before studying it at university, and it strikes me with an unexpected wave of nostalgia. Hearing Aeronwy sing along (sounding better than the original, I admit) is a funny clash of past and present.

"You really know all the words to 'Underground Heart?'" I say. "I didn't think that was your style."

Aeronwy doesn't even look up. E waits for the bridge to finish and then says, "You'd be surprised what I consider 'my style.' In any case, I know it because Rose played it to death. It was eir favorite song towards the end of eir life."

I wander into the room. The three walls are painted in bright primary colors, the cabinets starkly white against them. Nearly all of Rose's belongings were cleared out last year, but there were some left behind. Aeronwy has piled them up beside the door: stacks of sketchbooks with pages warped by use, a scattered selection of books (mostly memoirs), cups full of colored pencils, and assorted unused art supplies. A watercolor painting of a hummingbird lies on the nearest workbench, beside a row of bookbinding tools. It's beautiful and delicate, with a looseness of style I could never replicate.

"You can have the painting if you like," Aeronwy says, continuing to clean. "The tools I plan to give to Tabby as a late birthday gift."

June joins us in the studio and stands with hands on eir hips, sighing. "You're really going ahead with it, then," e says wistfully. "I'm proud of you, my dear."

"Going ahead with what?" I ask, and then realizing what e means, "You're finally clearing it out for good? Cleansing it and everything?"

Aeronwy nods. "It's time. Rose was not a sentimental person. E would have laughed at us for leaving it this long."

"But—" I say, "but, a while ago you said you'd like it if I channeled Rose for you one day. If you clear everything out, it'll be harder for me to do."

Aeronwy pauses and looks up at me. "I hadn't thought of that," e says, looking contemplative.

"I could do it now, before you finish," I say, eagerly stepping forward. Thanks to Eirlys, I even know where Rose's spirit is. The Head Librarian's office is directly below the Bindery, which would give me the advantage of proximity.

"Are you sure you have the energy? We just did a lot of difficult inner work, and you did say you needed a break," June says.

"Yes, but this is important and urgent," I insist.

"We won't be upset if you can't do it."

I shrug and pick up the hummingbird painting. "I want to," I say. "I want to show you what I can do, and help you connect with someone you lost."

We gather some floor pillows and sit in a circle by the windows. I place my Oracle cards, the painting, and some of

Rose's tools in the center, where I can reach them easily. They're brimming with Rose's signature energy, the crackle that comes just before lightning strikes and the scent of turpentine. I settle into a comfortable position and sink into myself. The room falls quiet save for the sound of our breathing.

I open my spirit senses to the world. The Bindery is teeming with books—I can sense *The Stories We Sing* and *Soil, Sea and Sky* most potently, their pages rustling against my skin. There are imprints of Illuminators past, not their spirits but impressions left behind by strong memory and repetition. Rose is all over this room, sitting at the work bench, standing at an easel in the corner, working the press again and again for the last fifty years.

I draw those memories to me, spooling them the way fiber turns into yarn. With this thread, I can connect to Rose and show em where to find me. I never realized how similar this process is to what June was teaching me earlier. It gives me a huge confidence boost. If I can create an etheric cord this way, surely I can do it to bind an Illuminated book.

As I'm doing this, one of the imprints hanging around the Bindery comes to life, fleshing itself out into a full-fledged spirit. Usually it doesn't bother me, but in my tired state, it feels like someone turning on all the lights at three in the morning. I flinch and nearly drop my connection to Rose.

I'm unprepared for the way the spirit rushes toward me in a haze of anger and frustration. I slam the doors to my body shut against it, but I don't have enough strength to keep them closed. As the spirit pushes its way past my defenses, I recognize it. The sound of cards shuffling, the press of a brayer against a woodblock print, the quiver of a secret held for centuries.

"Calliope—" I gasp out loud, and then I no longer have control over my mouth.

In a burst of light, I find myself floating outside my body. My consciousness hovers over our little circle, looking down at Aeronwy and June's gray hair and my patterned headscarf. Both of them are sitting up straighter, looking at me with concern.

My head is bowed, hands splayed out over my Oracle cards, which have been scattered across the rug.

"Amane, are you all right?" June asks.

My body bolts upright, and Calliope Everberry starts ranting in a rush of Old Casporan that I don't understand a word of. Calliope spoke through me twice before, first on the day I met Rhiannon and second on our trip down into the Archives. E seems angrier than ever. E starts shuffling cards, laying them out and gesturing to them as e speaks, and pointing an accusing finger at the Stargroves.

"I see you're not Rose," says Aeronwy, who despite an even tone, looks properly shocked. "We can't understand you, you know. Hold your tongue for a moment."

E takes out eir phone and frowns at it, trying, from what I can tell hovering above, to get the camera to work. E's going about it all wrong, and if I had nails, I would bite them. After a moment too long, June takes it from em and gets the video recording with just a few taps, holding it up to record Calliope's screed.

"Someone should be able to translate this," Aeronwy says.

Rhiannon can do it, e did it before when Calliope possessed me, I say. I float over to hover beside June's ear. *Can you hear me?*

"Yes, I can hear you, Amane," June says. "Calliope? Is that what you said? Not Calliope Everberry?"

Yes, that Calliope, I say, and recognizing eir name, Calliope turns my body's gaze on us. The ranting picks up again as e glares at June and stabs a finger at the Five of Paper: Cut card.

"I suspect e's angry with us for losing the Charter Book," says Aeronwy.

"We're sorry," June says, spreading eir hands apologetically. "I know you had good reason to hide it, and so we kept it hidden, too. But it couldn't stay that way forever. This is probably better in the long run, that the truth comes out."

I don't know if Calliope understands em, but e huffs and stands up, starting to pace. The longer the possession goes on, the more e uses my body, the more exhausted I'll be when it's over. And I was already exhausted. Not just physically, but mentally and spiritually. Floating in the air now, disembodied and helpless, the reality of it hits me. I've gone *way* beyond what I can handle.

I guess I need to do the one thing I've always refused: ask for help.

June, I need my body back. I can't keep going like this, I say. *You have to convince em to leave. Or* make *em leave.*

"We'll try, Amane," June says. E turns to Aeronwy. "Amane needs her body back. I don't have the energy to exorcise Calliope right now. Would you…?"

Aeronwy stands up, rolling back eir sleeves, but before e can lay a hand on my body, something else happens. The thread I spun between myself and Rose thrums, tugging at my spirit as if someone were yanking on a lock of hair. I can *see* the static in the air as the hair on everyone's heads rises.

A lightning bolt of spiritual energy hits the crown of my body's head, and in this state I see Calliope thrown from my body like a ghostly afterimage of pale fire. E looks shocked, and then defeated, before dissolving, banished back to the astral plane. The sorrow on eir face moves me deeply, in a way I couldn't have expected.

My body jerks with the shock, surprising Aeronwy into taking a step back. My muscles sag for a moment, and then Rose straightens up, dusting off my dress with my hands. E smiles at June and Aeronwy.

"Don't worry, I took care of it. I know the apprenticeship can be hard on some, but usually things don't go *this* far," Rose says with my voice, in modern Casporan. It's weird hearing myself speak without an accent.

"Rose…?" says Aeronwy, disbelieving but hopeful.

"Yes, it's me. Hello to you, too. I can't stay long. Amane needs her body, and I need to get back before the Founders realize I broke out. I'm not supposed to leave the Library heartspace right now," e says. "I just had to tell you to take better care of your apprentices, or you won't have any left. And also, I love you."

"I love you, too," Aeronwy says, with more emotion in eir voice than I've ever heard from em.

"We miss you," says June, who's suddenly wiping tears from eir eyes.

"I know. But I'll be around when I can. And I'll see one of you soon enough," Rose says with a wink. E turns to look at me, hovering beside June, and adds, "I hope you've learned your lesson, Amane. You have a responsibility to look after yourself, too. I'm not going to come around and save you again."

I understand, I say, *and thank you. Thank you, thank you, thank you.*

Rose smiles. Even though it's my face, the expression is all eirs.

Rose's spirit exits my body, and it's as if the plug has been pulled on a giant drain. I feel myself sucked back inside with another flash of light, and then everything is full of pain.

***

"How could you?"

Isylwyn turned at the sound of Daryn's voice, which was hoarse and thick with tears.

"How could I what?" Isylwyn said, stepping away from the Charter Book. E blotted the quill e'd been writing with on a piece of scrap and set it down. E stood still and calm as a glassy pool.

Daryn eyed the red ink drying on the pages of the Charter Book with a scowl. It might as well have been blood. Eirlys's blood.

"And all so you could take control," e said. "I should have known. I thought murder was beneath you, but I forgot that you value control above all else. Even life."

Isylwyn crossed the room and put both hands on Daryn's shoulders, but Daryn wrenched away. Isylwyn frowned.

"You're not making sense. What are you talking about, cousin? What's made you so upset?" e asked.

Daryn backed away. The light from the fire reflected in eir eyes. Eir usually smiling face was full of grief and rage. "You're the one who killed Eirlys," e said, voice barely above a whisper.

Isylwyn was prepared for this. E didn't so much as blink at the accusation. Instead, e took a seat on the high-backed chair beside the Head Librarian's desk and spread eir hands in placation. There was red ink on them from editing the Book. It had taken a few tries to figure out how it was done, now that e was in charge. The spirits of the books all clamoring in eir ears hadn't helped. Some of them welcomed em. Others made the same accusation Daryn had.

"Now I see. You're grieving and looking for meaning in the death of one you cared for," Isylwyn said. "I'm glad you came to me. Eirlys's death, though it seemed an accident, was meant to be by the Author. Eir spirit has joined the books, strengthening the magical foundation of this place for eternity."

Daryn kept glaring. "You didn't deny you killed em."

"You're twisting my words. I didn't kill Eirlys," Isylwyn said. "As an artist, e worked with poisonous materials all the time. As do you. Unfortunately, sometimes there are tragic mix-ups, and death occurs."

"I Looked into the flames," Daryn said, "I Saw you."

Isylwyn stood, for the first time appearing affected by Daryn's words. Fists clenched, e said, "Your visions cannot prove anything. Especially not when they come from the fever dreams of a Cináedite. Accuse me of murder publicly, and you will never set foot in the Library again."

"You may have taken Eirlys from me, but I won't let you take the books, too," Daryn said, and stormed out of the room.

The book ends soon after this scene, leaving the reader on a dramatic note. In real life, Daryn stayed at the Library under Head Librarian Isylwyn, quietly undermining em and biding eir time until the Sovereign died of old age twenty years later.

Daryn fought with Isylwyn's heirs, but ultimately claimed the title of Head Librarian. Supposedly, the Trials that Aeronwy, June, and Mairead are going to face have their roots in that conflict.

"No wonder Calliope hid the Charter Book," I say.

"Calliope's situation was similar to Daryn's, wasn't it? Losing the person e loved most because of a grab for power?" Tabby replies.

We're lying in bed, doing two of my favorite things in the world: cuddling and reading. Tabby's cat, Egg, is cuddling with us, too, curled up against my thighs. We've been doing this a lot lately since I'm not working, and Tabby doesn't go in very often. After the possession incident, I was laid up sick for a couple weeks. My whole body hurt, and I caught something like the flu that had me throwing up every few hours. Even now, I still tire easily and have trouble keeping food down. It's absolutely awful, and it's all my fault.

Which is why I've decided to make a change. *Forgiveness, mistakes, truth, reflection, patience, fluidity.* It's time for me to slow down.

At least I have Tabby at my side. Whenever I get anxious about not being 'productive' or 'improving' myself, e just kisses me and makes me forget all about it. I snuggle closer to em tucking my head under eir chin. E's been helping to take care of me, and I'm letting em. It feels… nice. More than nice. It feels like it's nourishing my soul.

"I think it was," I say, "although no one's ever tried to tell that story. There are records of interactions between Calliope and Llewella and Ciarán, but no one but us knows about what Calliope did to the Charter Book. That changes everything."

As we suspected, the rant Calliope went on while possessing my body was about the Charter Book. E was angry that the Stargroves had let it slip from their grasp, and that it was now in the hands of an Authorist with beliefs not unlike Ciarán Stonefeather's. Someone who had a chance to become

Head Librarian. It was everything e was trying to prevent at risk of coming true.

"Do you think Mairead would try to murder June or Aeronwy if e loses the Head Librarian Trials?" I say.

Tabby shudders. "I hope not. After what happened to Camille and Rhee, I can't say I'd rule it out entirely."

Rhiannon is currently sleeping off another migraine. They've been happening daily for a few weeks now. June is working on a counter-curse woven with some of Mairead's hair ("I've had this for thirty years," e had said. "After e accused Aery of starting the '86 fire, I needed some security. Please don't ask how I got it."), but it has to be worked on certain moon phases, which takes time. Plus, Rhiannon insisted e make one for Camille first.

"Hey," I say, as I think more about the Trials, "did we ever tell Aeronwy and June what Eirlys said about bringing apprentices into the Trials? Remember, right before that dream where we kissed the first time?"

Tabby looks down at me thoughtfully. "I completely forgot about that with everything that happened afterward," e says.

"Let's tell them right now!" I say, grabbing my phone and hitting June's number on speed dial.

Tabby looks like e's about to stop me, but smiles and says, "All right. But only if you let me do most of the talking and don't tire yourself out. Promise?"

"I promise."

June picks up after two rings. I put em on speakerphone so Tabby can hear. "Hello, dear, how are you doing? I was just thinking about you," e says cheerfully. "How's your relaxation going?"

"Good," I say, "but Tabby and I just remembered something really important we need to tell you."

"What—" e stops talking, listening to someone in the background. "Aery, really!"

"What? What did e say?" I ask.

June makes a disgruntled noise and says, "E said, 'Is it that the two of you are dating, because we knew that already.'"

I feel my cheeks flush, and Tabby covers eir face with eir hands. We hadn't officially told the Stargroves about our change in relationship status, but we hadn't been hiding our behavior from them, either.

"It's not about that," I say, and June chuckles. Aeronwy says something in the background again, but I can't understand the words.

"It's about the Trials," Tabby says, leaning over my shoulder.

Silence. Fumbling noises.

Aeronwy's dry, deep voice comes over the phone: "Maybe we should meet up for afternoon tea to discuss this in person, then. Since it is a bit of a sensitive matter."

"Would you like to come over?" says June. They must have us on speaker, too.

"I'd love that, but we can't leave Rhiannon alone right now," Tabby says.

"Maybe you could come over here?" I say. I glance up at Tabby for permission, and after a second, e nods. E looks excited but worried. I have a feeling we'll be going on a cleaning spree as soon as we hang up the phone.

"Where's 'here?'" Aeronwy asks.

"My and Rhee's place," Tabby says. "I'll give you the address."

TABBY

It's raining today. Not the typical Casporan drizzle and mist, but really raining. It cascades down outside, streaking our windows with blurry tracks and turning the city into a series of waterfalls. I move my plants away from the edges of the balcony to keep them from drowning in their pots.

Our apartment tower has a keycode to enter the building, and I'm not expecting company, so at first, I don't realize someone is knocking at the door. I assume a neighbor is hanging something on the wall. But then the sound comes again, loud and insistent. Confused, I put down my sketchbook and go to peer through the peephole.

My heart drops into my stomach as I recognize my parents standing in the hallway, standing about a foot apart and looking harried. Why are they here? Did I forget something? Was there a warning in one of the many texts or voicemails I deleted before even reading or listening to? Rhiannon hasn't been able to screen them for me since e got sick.

But then, I should have expected it. If my parents have been consistent about one thing in my life, it's blindsiding me with crisis.

"Tabby, is that you?" Oran yells, disregarding the fact that we have neighbors. "I can hear someone on the other side of the door."

"It might be Rhiannon," Lilja mutters. "Rhiannon might not let us in. You know e doesn't like us."

Rhiannon is sleeping, and unlikely to wake up due to the strong pain medication e's on. E has enough to deal with without my parents bothering em.

Maybe this is it, this is the time to do it, says a quiet, calm voice in my mind. *When are you going to get a better opportunity?*

I take a deep breath, exhale, and then open the door.

Oran pushes eir way inside immediately, dropping a sopping wet umbrella next to the shoe rack and dripping water all over everything. I have to step back quickly to avoid the door knocking me in the face. Lilja follows slowly after, keeping at least a foot or two of distance between herself and Oran at all times. She's hunched over, hands in the pocket of her raincoat with the hood up, as if she doesn't want to be seen.

"Took you long enough," Oran says.

"Oh, I'm so glad you're home, Tabby! Is Rhiannon here?" Lilja asks, glancing nervously around the room.

For a split second, I think about lying. I don't want them to use Rhiannon's illness as ammo. On the other side of that second, I realize what that reveals about who and what I'm most afraid of, and that strengthens my resolve. I can't keep living like this.

"Yes, but e's sleeping because e's sick," I say, and Lilja visibly relaxes. "Please be quiet so you don't wake em up."

"I'll do as I please," says Oran.

Lilja hangs her coat up and then hurries up to me, cupping my face with her hands. They're ice-cold, and for once I don't hide my shock. I step away immediately, and Lilja wilts, wringing eir hands.

"We've—*I've* been so worried about you, Tabby. Why haven't you been answering my texts and calls? I even sent you an email last week. Is something wrong? Are you feeling alright after your time in the hospital?"

"Is Rhiannon keeping you away from us?" Oran asks. E looms beside the dining room table, large arms crossed over an even larger chest. There's a familiarly dangerous look in eir eyes. A steely one that threatens to ignite in a flash.

"What? No, why would you think that?" I say. Though Rhiannon helps screen my communications with them, it's because I asked em to. E listens to what I want and need over all, only passing eir own judgment when I ask for it.

I scoot past Oran into the kitchen and take a seat at the table, hoping they'll do the same. Lilja joins me, but Oran stays standing, watching us from the other end. E's grown a new mustache and beard since I last saw them. It's streaked with silver, barely visible against the blonde. I wonder when we all got so old.

"Because of how e acted when we visited you in the hospital. You were still asleep the first time," e says, "and e had us thrown out. Said e'd taken us off the visitor list until you woke up and decided if you wanted to see us. Absolutely ridiculous, why wouldn't you want to see us?"

I don't answer. I'm the one who told Rhiannon, long before I landed in the hospital, that if my sleeping spells got bad and I needed medical attention, not to allow my parents to visit. Not unless I personally requested it.

"It made me feel absolutely terrible, I don't understand why you haven't stopped em from treating us like that. Would you make us all some tea?" Lilja asks. I notice she won't look directly at Oran, and I don't blame her. She deserves to live her life without Oran's tyranny just as much as I do.

"I don't think so. I… This needs to be a very short visit," I say.

Lilja looks stricken, and my heart skips a beat. My hands and feet tingle, and a pins-and-needles feeling quickly sweeps through my body, followed by a rush of hot and cold. Lilja's anxiety still triggers my own. I prepare myself for the panic and doom that always follows.

But it doesn't come. The feeling doesn't intensify. Instead, it drops off, swallowed up by my determination and calm. *The cord cutting ceremony worked*, I think. How much of my anxiety around Lilja has been my own, and how much of it has been projected into me? This sense of separateness is a startling revelation.

"Rhiannon hasn't been stopping me from talking to you. It's because *I* don't want to talk to you. I only let you in because I needed to tell you that directly," I say.

The dismay on Lilja's face deepens, tears springing up in her brown eyes. It hurts to watch, but at the same time, I feel distanced from that hurt. I know it's not mine.

"Why—"

Oran slams two huge fists down on the table, rattling the empty mugs and knocking over a pile of books that lie on top of it. "That is unacceptable! How dare you be so rude to your own parents? We raised you better than this," e growls.

Lilja inhales sharply and flinches, curling inward on emself. I think of all the nights she would come curl around me in bed, crying and venting, as if I, a child, could protect and soothe her instead of the other way around. I keep my feet firmly on the floor and turn my eyes back to Oran.

"A-actually, *you* need to leave now," my voice breaks and I swallow against the dryness in my mouth.

I can tell I've caught em off-guard. I don't know if I've ever seen Oran shocked before, but it feels… satisfying, underneath the fear.

"Tabitha. I implore you to *think* about what you're saying. Because you obviously aren't," e says, voice low and threatening.

"Please leave, or I'm going to call Community Services to remove you instead. I don't want to see you or talk to you again," I say. The sense of calm has spread throughout my entire body now, along with a fiery anger I didn't know I was capable of. It wells up beneath the calm like hot water bubbling up beneath ice.

"Where is this *coming* from? It's either Rhiannon, or—" Oran stops. Slowly, e paces around the table towards me, squinting through eir thick square glasses. "You haven't been yourself since you started that gods-damned apprenticeship. What is it they're teaching you up there in that damn tower? That you're too smart for us? Too good for us?"

"They're teaching me how to be kind to myself. Something you never did. Now leave, or I really will call, like I should have all those times before," I say, picking up my phone and dialing the emergency number.

Oran stops six inches away from me, fists clenched, jaw clenched, taught as razor wire. Without another word, e turns and stomps away, heavy boots echoing on the wood floor. With the sweep of one large arm, e knocks everything from the table onto the floor. One of the mugs shatters. The books land awkwardly, pages fluttering, some of them bent.

But e does leave. The door slams hard enough behind him to rattle the paintings hung on the wall. Lilja jumps and then slumps down onto the table, head wrapped in her arms. She reaches one hand out to grasp my wrist.

"Thank you."

I pull my arm away. "I wish you would have done that years ago," I say, as gently as I can manage. It's difficult not to let the bitterness and grief seep into my voice. Now that Oran is gone, the adrenaline in my veins is fading and I'm ready to cry.

Lilja looks at me guiltily, tears already streaming down her face. "I had to stay. I did love em, and e did love me, even if things were bad. I had to try… Please, Tabby, please don't hate me for doing what I had to do."

"I don't—" I cut off the automatic response, because a part of me might actually hate her. Maybe I'll touch on that feeling later in therapy. For now, I set it to the side and breathe slowly. "I'm sorry. I'm sure you were doing the best you could. But it still wasn't enough."

"I don't understand?"

I've planned and practiced this conversation dozens, hundreds of times, but the words are all trying to flee. How can something feel so terrible and so relieving at the same time?

"I didn't really feel like you were my Ren," I say. "I felt like I was *your* parent. I didn't know what to do. It scared me. It still scares me."

"It scares you that I love you? That I wanted to be close to you, my only child?" Lilja's lower lip wobbles.

"It was… too close," I manage. "Being around you makes me feel confused and anxious, because I can't tell what you want or need or what I'm supposed to do, and it feels like I'm supposed to do *everything*. Sometimes you say things that make me feel awful about myself. I need space."

"What are you saying?" There's panic in her voice, but I keep myself safe from it, centered in my own core.

I only have so much strength, though. I can't hold her gaze, so I look down at my hands on the table. "I need space. I haven't been talking to you because I don't want to. And it's been… good for me. I'm sorry."

Lilja bursts into sobs, her thin frame shaking with the effort and emotion. "You don't love me… you don't love me… I don't understand, I finally left Oran… Right now is when I need you the most… I can't do this on my own… and you don't love me…" She gasps out the words in between sobs.

I get up and get a box of tissues from the living room, my head is spinning. The apartment feels as if it were someone else's home, not my own. I glance at the mirror that hangs by the front door and barely recognize myself. I feel like I'm floating. On a nearby painting, flower buds open and close, a sure sign of an impending sleep attack.

A sure sign I'm dissociating. Something I've always done, but rarely recognized until my new therapist brought it up. The sleep attacks are an extreme magical manifestation of the coping mechanism. I get a glass of water and sip it slowly, focusing on the physical sensation. I can get through this.

I'm certain I did love Lilja once, as all small children love their parents, but now I don't know. If there's still something there, it's buried beneath a mountain of hurt and I can't access it. All I can do is try to love myself and be as compassionate as possible. To both of us. Even if compassion looks like walking away.

Back at the table, I sit down and say, "I'm happy that you left Renna. You have your friends, and your own place, and your hobbies. You're going to be okay without me."

"No, I won't. I need you, Tabby," Lilja says. "Maybe if you hadn't moved away to go to school and leave me behind, I could have left Oran sooner. Or if you at least came back to work in AT like you were supposed to. How can you leave me when I'm on my own for the first time and need you more than ever?"

Even though I've heard these kind of words a million times before, they still hurt. This time, I let my hurt be known. "I was just living my own life. I can't let you make me feel guilty about living my own life anymore," I say.

"I'm not guilt-tripping…"

"You just blamed staying in your abusive marriage on my going away to college."

"That's not what I meant," she mumbles, rubbing her nose and refusing to look me in the eye. "I don't know what you're talking about."

An awkward silence falls, broken only by Lilja's sniffling. This time when I look around the apartment, it feels like home. It feels like mine. I can see the passage of all the years Rhiannon and I have spent here, all the laughs, all the stories, all the smiles and milestones. I can see all the tears, too, the illnesses and struggles. Our lives, intertwined but not competing. Not choking one another out.

Rhiannon may have damaged my trust in em, but e admits e was wrong and is making a change. I can't say the same about Lilja.

"If we had a better relationship, I would love to help you get settled in your new single life. But I can't. I can't be around you and heal from my own hurts. I can't stay only out of some obligation to be your nurse or your therapist. I'm sorry," I say.

Lilja's breath hitches as the sobs start up again. "But—"

"No. That's all I have to say. Please leave."

I watch her tamp down on the sobs, pressing her lips together and gazing at me with an agonized expression. Part of me wants to take it all back, to smooth things over, to make it all 'better' again. But I know from years and years of going through the same cycle that won't work. If things are going to be *better*, actually better, the cycle has to be broken.

For good.

Slowly, she gets up from her chair and walks to the door, glancing back at me every few steps. She puts eir raincoat on and stands in front of the door for a long moment, hands limp at her sides. Then, finally, she turns the doorknob and exits from my life.

I put my head in my hands and cry.

When the tears subside, I call my therapist to make an appointment for the next morning. E talks to me for a while, helping me end the dissociation and return to my body. I don't slip off into a dream. I lie down, but I don't take a nap. For the first time, I'm staying awake to feel what there is to feel.

***

The next day at work, I tell Aeronwy. I practice my spinning while e adds gold leaf to the story titles in *Soil, Sea and Sky*.

"I finally did it," I say. "I told them I don't want to see them again."

"How do you feel about it?" Aeronwy asks. E doesn't look up from the gilding, but I don't need em to. *Busy hands free the mind*, e's said many times. I know e's listening.

"Relieved, mostly. Ashamed, but I know that's the abuse talking," I say. My thread is getting better. It no longer breaks apart like it did when I first began. Now I can spin an entire bobbin on my own. It's not quite fine enough for our purposes, though.

"You have nothing to be ashamed of," Aeronwy says, brushing away extra gold leaf with a gentle hand. "I know that wasn't easy. I'm proud of you."

"Also, I decided I want to go with you," I say, "in the Trials."

When Amane and I told our mentors that they could bring us with them in the Head Librarian Trials, they had mixed feelings. They agreed it could give them an advantage over Mairead, but they were hesitant to ask us to face unknown dangers. They told us to take a few weeks to think it over, and that they would accept our decisions.

Aeronwy is silent for a moment. "You're certain?" e asks, looking up at me. "You don't have to do it. It won't change my opinion of you either way."

"I want to do it. Not because I feel obligated to help, but because I care about what happens to the Library, and I care about what happens to you," I say, feeling more vulnerable than ever. A difficult, but not unwelcome feeling.

Aeronwy nods and smiles. "Thank you, Tabby. In all honesty, I want you to be there too."

RHIANNON

It's gonna be okay, I repeat to myself for the thousandth time on my way to the Library. *It's gonna be okay, I'm not gonna fuck this up, I'm not gonna fuck this up, it's gonna be okay—*

I round the corner and the sight of the familiar buildings rising before me stops me dead in my tracks. A lifetime has passed since I last came to campus. The smooth stone paths are devoid of people. The windows are darkened or dimmed. I pull my jacket tighter around my shivering body. I'm definitely shivering from the chill night air and not from fear, yep, that sure is the case.

Aeronwy is waiting by a wall of thick, climbing ivy on the administrative services building. I'd say I almost don't recognize em without the usual makeup and fancy clothes, but that'd be a lie. Even in a simple black trenchcoat and jeans, e's too distinctive. I pull my beanie down further over my forehead and make sure my ass-length purple hair is all tucked up inside. I guess I'm kind of distinctive, too.

Aeronwy squints at me as I approach. "Are those new glasses?"

"They're old ones," I say, "and not the right prescription. I don't want anyone to recognize me."

"I see. June's counter-curse amulet is working well for you?" Aeronwy asks.

"I'm up and walking around and my head doesn't feel like it's being split open like a watermelon, so, yes," I say, fingering the woven bracelet around my wrist, which is protecting me from Mairead's curse. "Camille is doing better, too, although she's still weak from losing so much muscle mass."

Aeronwy nods. "June visited her the other day. I'm sorry it took so long to make them, but we had to be sure it would stand up to such a powerful curse."

I shrug. "Worth it."

Aeronwy stands up from the wall and stretches. "Come along, then. Please conduct yourself as if you're coming to work as usual, and not as if you're about to commit a criminal act."

I received a brain full of visions from the cut paper shadowboxes Mairead gave to me and Camille. In them, I watched Mairead make a copy of each shadow box and cast powerful health damaging magic on it. This was inside the Authorist Temple sanctuary, and afterward e hid the shadow copies in an office cabinet. I'm surprised either of us is still alive.

You used me for my psychic abilities, I think as Aeronwy and I walk around the back of the admin building. *Now I'll use them to take you down.*

There's a nondescript metal door hidden among the ivy-covered brick. Aeronwy uses eir badge to open it, warm yellow light and the scent of orange oil spilling out into the night. I follow em inside, eyes peeled for guards.

The hallway smells like fresh laundry and dirty mop water. We pass a few people on the nighttime cleaning crew, but most of them ignore us. One or two say hello to Aeronwy, but no one stops to chat. They're too busy filling carts with cleaning supplies or unloading broken chairs into a closet full of—what else—more broken chairs. Bless the intrepid folks who make sure the Library runs as smoothly as it does.

Aeronwy leads me through a maze of narrow hallways, back doors, and skybridges to what appears to be the most ancient freight elevator in the universe. It doesn't have proper walls, only a tarnished brass cage and a lever in the floor to take it up and down. Aeronwy unlocks it with an equally ancient key I'm sure e's not supposed to have.

"I used to use this to sneak up the Bindery at night to see June, before I was an apprentice," e says, and seeing the look on my face, adds, "We *do* occasionally still use this for equipment deliveries and other legitimate things."

"Suuuure."

"*You're* going down, though. Get in."

I eye the rickety floor distrustfully before stepping inside. "If I die here, I'll haunt you forever."

"Better than listening to your half-baked quips all evening."

Having thoroughly roasted me, Aeronwy reaches through the cage and pushes the lever all the way to the bottom. The elevator shudders, making me stumble, and descends slowly enough that I can at least get a good glare in before e disappears from view. E's smiling. It's all in good fun.

At least until one of us gets caught.

The Archives at night are spooky as shit. The hallways feel like they're full of hidden eyes. Just because I can't sense the ghosts and spirits doesn't mean they aren't *there*. It sure won't protect me from their mischief.

I have to fight the elevator cage door to get it to open once it hits bottom. It lets me off in a dusty sub-sub basement where the only light is a flickering glow from the crystal veins in the walls. The air is frigid and vaguely musty; a quick inspection of the books piled in the room reveal water-swollen tomes spotted with mildew. Victims of some past flood, probably put here with the intent to preserve them in the cool temperatures until they could be repaired. I guess no one ever got around to it.

"If I'm ever Head of the Archives, I'm going to clear all this out, get it in order, use some of Amane's *spreadsheets*, or something," I mutter, squeezing down the hallway through more piles of ruined books. I eye a particularly warped copy of *Fun and Fungus for Mountain Hikers*. "I swear to you, I swear on the Charter Book, if I get my job back, I'll do something about it."

There are pathways through the basements to the Temple. I don't know if I'll even be able to get in when I get there, or if it'll be empty, but I have to try. The windows are high off the ground and lit with spotlights, so I can't go in that way.

As I hurry through the darkened hallways, narrowly avoiding a book avalanche and climbing over a fallen crystal chandelier, I run one of the visions from the shadowbox through my head.

Once again, I join Mairead in the Library Authorist Temple, but this time it's brightly lit and full of people. I recognize several familiar faces from the Archives, along with a handful of other Librarians I didn't realize were Authorists. They chatter with one another with the ease that comes after a service has finished and everyone is ready for coffee and donuts in the basement.

Mairead feels a sense of excitement and pride, watching the flock. If only they knew about the Book, the treasure that the Author, through Isylwyn, has guided into eir hands. Every terrible thing, every disappointment, every tragedy in eir life has been worth it, now. Mairead's life is not a tragedy after all, but a parable on the value of pain. To experience great suffering often means one is destined to experience great joy. It's far more narratively satisfying that way.

A certain Knowing settles upon em, and e knows that Isylwyn is nearby, waiting. Mairead turns and walks through the circle of the congregation, pausing only briefly to wish people well, before slipping into one of the back rooms. This one is marked as private, made only for the High Priestex for meditation and receiving the Author's messages. Mairead locks the door behind em.

The room is small and decorated minimally. There is only one window, round and small and set high into the wall to let the light in. Crystal lamps glow softly on the altar across from the door. There are several open books laid between them, visionary works by previous High Priestexes which are used for stichomancy and divining the Narrative. Mairead knows them by heart.

A prickle rolls through our body, over our skin, and one of the books on the altar ruffles its pages. Mairead opens eir eyes and lays a finger on it, peering through eir bifocals to read the tiny type. E mouths the words silently, then frowns. I can feel the anger and pride and, of all things, fear welling up in our chest.

Chapter Thirty-Two

"They'll have help? From their apprentices? Is that your message?" Mairead says, I assume to Isylwyn. I can feel the Founder's presence in the room like an envelope of cold moonlight.

A book falls from a nearby shelf with a thud, then opens and flips to a page near the center. I've seen spirits move things before, but never with such ease. Isylwyn is pretty much a deity at this point. The mythology of the Library feeds em and the other Founders, makes them more powerful than they ever were in life.

In life, they were just people. But Mairead doesn't see it that way.

Mairead reads the page and scoffs. The book is a mundane copy of the Charter Book, translated into modern Casporan.

"Bringing the apprentices into the Trials won't help them. If anything, it will slow them down. I know how they are—they'll do anything to keep them safe. They won't be fully focused on the goal," Mairead says.

Another book falls from the shelf. This one is titled Riverend's Faerytales. *Mairead picks it up, running a hand across the yellowed pages. The fable it's opened to is 'The Day the Moon Died.' The page beside it is graced by an illustration of a young person standing on a sea cliff, with a huge full moon reflected in the water.*

"I understand. I will do what it takes to win, I swear to you," e says, and the vision ends.

Mairead knows Aeronwy and June will be bringing Tabby and Amane along with them in the Trials, but e was going to find that out eventually. It's the rest that both mystifies and worries me. I told the others about it, but they couldn't figure out what it meant either, beyond the implication that Mairead and Isylwyn were planning to cheat somehow. Aeronwy in particular was disturbed by the fable involved, but since we don't know what the Trials actually *are*, we have nothing to apply the story to.

As I'm slipping into the Temple basement through a service door that someone left mercifully propped open with a big rock, a string of texts come in on my phone, spaced a few minutes apart. I must be high up enough to have service now.

> **AERONWY:** I have arrived at the Temple exterior to keep watch. Unfortunately, it appears someone is here after all, despite the schedule we consulted. I'm afraid it may be Mairead, so do not enter the Temple until I have made sure. - A.S.
> **AERONWY:** Rhiannon, it is Mairead who is currently inside. E was always a night owl, and I doubt e'll be leaving any time soon. We should try another night. - A.S.

"You don't have to sign every text with your initials, I know it's you," I mutter. "Also—"

> **ME:** too late, i'm already inside the basement and if I don't do it now I'm gonna lose my nerve, can you give me a distraction?
> **ME:** I need to get to the h.p.'s private room, the door is right off the sanctuary in the back

The response comes back immediately.

> **AERONWY:** This is ill advised, but yes. Be quick. - A.S.

"Story of my life," I whisper to myself, then clamp my lips shut. I need to be quiet. My loud mouth has gotten me in trouble enough times.

I sneak up the stairs towards the sanctuary and peer out through the double doors. Thankfully, they don't creak, but they are heavy. I dig my fingers into the carvings of moon phases and squint in the bright light that falls through the crack.

Mairead is in the center of the sanctuary, dancing on the raised circular dais with eyes shining and arms raised towards the sky. Traditional Casporan harp music echoes against the high ceiling, overlaid by a voice singing in Old Casporan.

Mairead's fine gray dress floats around em as e twirls, lost in devotion to the sacred Narrative of the world.

You'd think that'd be distracting enough, but I'm on the opposite side of the sanctuary from the private room. I don't know that I can make it across the hall without being seen, much less open another door that might be locked and slip inside.

Luckily for me, Aeronwy enters the building at that moment. I watch em step inside the foyer and take a disgruntled look around. E clearly doesn't like being here, but e puts on a neutral face and moves forward into the sanctuary, boot heels clicking loudly on the polished wood floor.

"Welcome questing spirit, what brings you to the Temple so late—" Mairead begins with a warm welcome, pirouetting around on one foot to face the door. As soon as e sees who the visitor is, eir arms drop and all the warmth falls away, replaced with suspicion.

"I was hoping you'd be here," Aeronwy says, louder than necessary: alerting me that my time has started, and the clock is ticking.

"Really," says Mairead. E turns away and walks over to a nearby shelf, where there's a sound system playing the music.

This is my chance. I slip through the doors and scuttle between the last two rows of pews. If I stay on my hands and knees, I might be able to keep mostly out of sight. I crawl as quickly as I can.

The music cuts off, and suddenly I can hear myself shuffling along the floor. I halt, frozen, waiting for someone to speak before I put my hand down again.

"The Trials are approaching quickly. Midsummer will be here before we know it," Aeronwy says.

"And you wanted to do what? Wish me good luck?" Mairead says with a dark chuckle.

"I wanted to let you know that June and I will be bringing our apprentices with us in the Trials. Though no one has done so for many decades, it's an allowable practice," Aeronwy says. "Only fair you should be allowed to prepare your own response to that advantage."

Thank the gods for Aeronwy's verbosity. I'm halfway to the door now. A glance at the center of the room reveals Mairead looming over Aeronwy from the raised dais, eyes fixed directly on em and nowhere else. Aeronwy stares right back. The tension between them is so intense, it makes my hair staticky.

"I already knew about that. I have my own sources, as you obviously have yours," Mairead says with a derisive snort. "I'm sorry you feel like you need the help in order to have a fighting chance."

"I'm sorry you don't have your own apprentice to bring along. Whatever happened to Camille, or Rhiannon? The Assistant Head could be considered your apprentice, in a way. Since they're meant to take over your position eventually."

"I wouldn't take either of them with me even if they did still have the job. I prefer to work alone," Mairead says. Ouch. Not that I'd *want* to go, but ouch.

"Ah, yes, that's right. Have you been listening to the Library rumor mill, lately? I hear tales that you can't seem to keep an Assistant Head, and that, perhaps, you curse or poison the ones who don't do as you say—"

Mairead laughs loudly, the sound bouncing around the sanctuary like a bullet. I keep my head down. I've reached the end of the pews. It's time to cross the desert of open space between the back row and the hallway.

"I think that's one of the downsides of working with book-lovers. A little too much imagination. The reality is simpler: I have high standards. Some people fall ill. Not everyone can take the pressure of the position. They feel ashamed by that, so they disappear without explanations, and those who remain make up stories," says Mairead.

I'd love to stick around and hear the rest of this conversation, but there's no time. I throw myself across the gap, sliding on my belly most of the way and then wiggling into the shadows of the hallway. My shoes squeak a little as they scrabble against the floor. I don't dare glance back to see if they heard.

The door is mercifully unlocked. I slip inside and close it behind me, breathing a sigh of relief. We're halfway there.

Hopefully Aeronwy can keep Mairead distracted long enough. On my hands and knees, I lean over and peer through the dark little keyhole in the altar cabinet. Thank the Author I pinned my hair up for this. I pull a bobby pin out and get to work unlocking it. I've only ever read about people doing this in books, or seen it in movies, but it can't be *that* hard, right?

The first bobby pin breaks after just jiggling it around a bit in the keyhole. I curse and pull out another one. Gentler, now.

The second one breaks.

A third.

The fourth I stare at intently, trying to infuse it with good luck or strength of will or *something*. I'm bad at impromptu spells. I say a prayer in my head to every trickster deity I can think of, including Daryn Sunseeker, who some sources claim had a mischievous personality. If nothing else, maybe e'll help me against Isylwyn.

The fourth one works. With a soft click, the cabinet pops open. I shove the books aside and reach into the far back, searching by feel.

I pull out one shadowbox, and then another. It's a disturbing piece of art: layers of paper with my handwriting and Camille's have been dyed red and cut. The scene shows a bedbound figure being struck by lightning, a little open mouth of distress cut into its face. It's hard to see with my old glasses, but there appears to be a few strands of hair glued to the figure on each one. Familiar looping cursive spells out names on the beds: Camille Anne Dubois and Rhiannon Dilwyn Rivergreen-Haybloom.

I know a curse when I see one, have cast a few myself, but I've never seen it done exactly like *this*. This is diabolical. I tuck them into my backpack gingerly.

I head to the door and peer out. Aeronwy and Mairead are still talking, with Mairead's back to me. I text Aeronwy that I'm ready to leave, hoping e'll feel the vibration in eir pocket and know what it means. I see eir gaze flicker briefly in my direction before going straight back to Mairead. Mairead notices and starts to turn around, but Aeronwy moves sideways into eir view.

"Did you ever imagine it would turn out this way?" Aeronwy says.

I catch a glimpse of Mairead's frown before e turns back. "Not exactly. But then, that is the genius of the Author's Story. You can try to put the pieces together, you can follow the tropes, build expectations, but in the end, there is often a twist. We can never know the full extent of the Author's intentions for us, being inside the Narrative."

"That's not what I was asking."

The door of the room across from me is open. The curtains on the windows are rippling in the nighttime breeze, which means they're open. They may be high off the ground, but I'd prefer spraining an ankle to crossing the sanctuary again. I'll have to take the risk that someone might see me jumping out of them.

I can still hear the conversation, echoing through the eaves. Mairead replies, in a clipped tone, "No. I always thought you would be with me, not against me."

I tiptoe to the windows, relieved to see that they don't have screens. This building is too old. I peer out into the night to make sure no one's around.

"There was a time when I felt that as well. But I learned how to be my own person, and that person doesn't agree with the way you wish to do things. Goodnight, Mairead. Good luck in the Trials."

The coast clear, I clamber out through the window. The rose bushes surrounding the building are thorny, but what are a few scratches in the grand scheme of things? I fall into the bushes in the most undignified way possible, then roll onto the ground with a painful thump. I force myself to my feet and book it around the corner of the next building, a temple to Aislinn, goddex of dreams.

I text Aeronwy and e shows up a few minutes later on an adjacent path. We walk apart for a while, converging several buildings down.

"Were you successful?" Aeronwy asks, getting right to the point.

I swing my backpack around and pull one of the shadowboxes out. I touch it as little as possible. Aeronwy's expressions are hard to read, but when e lets out a breath, a wisp of white smoke escapes along with it. Sudden heat radiates from em. E's angry.

"Marion asked for hard evidence, and now I've got it. Because of the ridiculous rules, we can't do anything with it until after the Trials," I say. "That means it's your turn. Yours and June's. One of you *has* to become Head Librarian. Then we can get Mairead fired."

"It's been a long time coming," Aeronwy says.

CHAPTER THIRTY-THREE
AMANE

Midsummer arrives. I wake up with the dawn, vibrating and ready to go. Today the door opens. Today we face the Trials to see who will become the next Head Librarian.

The morning is cool and bright. I ride the train to the Library as I would any other day, though it's emptier than usual. Everyone else has the holiday off, getting ready to celebrate with parades and outdoor dinners and temple visits. I don't mind that I can't join them; after taking several weeks off work, I feel refreshed and ready to face whatever the Trials throw at me. It's a new and wonderful sensation.

The Library is shrouded in green and gold, the trees fully leafed and the flowers in full bloom. I try to see it the way I did a year ago, when I first arrived, but I can't. I love how familiar the curves of the shell-shaped buildings have become, how reassuring the lobby atrium, with its black marble columns and floor, is the second I step inside.

I head for the ritual preparation room, where we're all supposed to meet for the day. It's a bit like a locker room, only decorated to look and feel more soothing. Pink walls, white wooden cabinets, flowers blooming on every table and altars in every corner. I'm the first one here, of course, aside from the Head of Ceremony, who hands me a wrap dress the color of old paper and helps me get changed. The dress is soft in the way clothes get after being worn for years and years and years. It has little suns, moons, and stars embroidered on it in the same antique paper color, a bit frayed but still lovely.

As I settle myself into one of the meditation corners with my oracle cards, Mairead arrives. I've hardly ever spoken to the older Librarian, but eir presence makes my skin prickle. The Head of Ceremony helps em dress in the curtained area, then leaves us alone. Mairead stows eir clothing in one of the cabinets and pours a glass of spring water from a pitcher on a nearby table.

"Good morning, Ms. Sol," e says, tapping eir fingers on the glass in contemplation. The look e's giving me is thoughtful, scrutinizing. "Always good to be early for these things, isn't it?"

"I'm early to everything," I say.

"But in the grand scheme, you're too late," Mairead says, and smiles sweetly. The smile doesn't reach eir gray eyes, which are cold as a cloudy winter's day.

Before I can answer, e turns away and sits with eir back to me in front of an altar to the Founders, praying silently. *If you're so sure you're going to win, why the need to pray?* I think, annoyed. *If you're trying to intimidate me, it didn't work. I'm stronger than that.*

Fifteen minutes later, Aeronwy and June arrive together, with Tabby shortly on their heels. They all change and join me in my corner; Mairead doesn't even glance up from eir prayers. We only have enough time for a few short greetings before the Head of Ceremony returns to cleanse each of us with a purifying mist and spirit-opening tea. E leads us not into the main ritual hall, where Tabby and I took our apprenticeship oaths, but back to the Spire.

Since Rose's death last year, there's been a wide red ribbon tied across the door handles of the Head Librarian's office. The Head of Ceremony unravels the bow and leads us inside; the small round room is completely bare, devoid of its former personality. The wooden floor, which before had been covered with colorful shag carpet, is etched with a magical circle like the one in the ritual hall. The carving is deep and dark, a relic of a much older era.

A pair of assistants help the Head of Ceremony bring in long cushions for all of us to lie on. The Head Librarian Trials are known to go on for hours, sometimes days, so sitting isn't an option. They arrange the beds within the circle, heads pointed inward. From the skylight nine stories above, a beam of sunlight creeps slowly toward the center.

"A pair of guards will be posted at the doors. The doors will not be opened except in the case of grave emergency. Otherwise, none shall leave this room until the new Head Librarian has been chosen and returned to their body. Good luck to you all," the Head of Ceremony says.

We take our places. Mine is between June and Mairead; Tabby is on Mairead's other side. Without discussing it, we've already started protecting our mentors from their opponent.

This room is empty of more than just furniture. As the doors close behind us, my sense of the hundreds of Library spirits, and the books themselves, is cut off entirely. There is no sense of magical power in this room, save each of our own souls. No sounds, no scents. It's like being inside an egg before it hatches; the bright circle of sunlight is the yolk, ready to break over our foreheads at any moment.

June takes my hand and squeezes it. A peculiar weightlessness takes over my body, a tingle that starts in my feet and rises up to the crown of my head. The circle of sunlight is directly above now, its warmth glowing through my eyelids. The warmth spreads downward, turning the pins-and-needles into a powerful rush of energy. It breaks through the bounds of my physical body, freeing my spirit from its constraints, and for a moment I'm liquid, I'm light, I'm air, without boundary or form.

I feel the others flowing around and within me. For these few seconds we're all connected, all one, beings of blissful joy, and then the door opens.

***

I land on my hands and knees, a cushion of evergreen needles softening my fall. My head feels like someone put a rubber band around it, one that's just a little bit too small. I take a few deep breaths where I am, and slowly it clears. I open my eyes and look up to see if the others are experiencing the same thing.

At first, I don't see them. Instead I see, to my bewilderment and alarm, a large red fox watching me with intense amber eyes. And behind it, a hulking mass of golden-brown fur that appears to be some kind of bear. We don't have bears in Gildea. I've seen them in pictures and once in a zoo, from far away, but nothing prepared me for how *enormous* this creature is. I stay as still as stone.

The bear turns its head, and two oddly familiar, soft brown eyes meet mine.

"Interesting, so you get to be the human."

The bear doesn't open its mouth, but when I hear Tabby's voice, I understand, as you do in a dream, that's where it's coming from. *Oh.*

"What do you mean?" I ask.

"I suppose you don't recognize this cast of characters," the fox says in Aeronwy's voice. There's a little flame floating over eir head, and the white tip of eir tail dissolves into smoke. Whatever magic transformed em can't cover up Cináed's Flame.

A bright blue streak of feathers flits through the air between us and lands on my head. I can feel tiny bird feet on my scalp, and when I peer upwards, a little blue head gazes down.

"I believe we're in an old myth called 'The Stolen Sun'," says June, who I suppose is now a bluebird. "You may not be familiar, Amane, but it's a well-known Casporan story about how day and night came to exist."

Tabby looks around, slowly. "Where's Mairead?"

"Where's the wolf?" Aeronwy says cryptically, and I can feel the others' discomfort.

Around us stretches a great and ancient forest. The trees are tall, their branches thick, and they whisper constantly like leaves in the breeze, though there's no wind. Suddenly, the world goes dark. Not dark as if I've closed my eyes, but as if we were standing in a room and someone turned out the lights. I feel June's wings fluttering in surprise against my head. Tabby lets out a low growl, and Aeronwy gets to eir feet. For a moment all the illumination we have is the little flame above eir head, but then the moon appears.

Once upon a time,

They aren't so much words as a Knowing in the center of my soul. Like when Tabby and I acted out Eirlys and Daryn's love story. Like dream logic.

Once upon a time, a wolf stole the Sun from the sky. At first, the world was mystified as to why. Plunged suddenly into darkness, they waited to see if the Sun would return. For in these days, the Sun came and went as e pleased. In truth, e rarely left the sky, but there had been times before when e disappeared for a little while, only to return as bright and shining as ever.

This was not one of those times.

When the Sun did not return, and the night grew ever colder, the people turned to the Moon.

"Where has the Sun gone? When will e be back?" they asked.

"The Sun will not be back," the Moon replied. "It is only me, now."

For you see, the Moon was tired of sharing the sky with a twin who shone so brightly, it made em nearly invisible. Feeling unloved and uncared for, the Moon had arranged for eir friend, the wolf, to remove the Sun from the sky. There was no way, the two of them thought, the Sun would ever leave voluntarily, always citing obligations to the growing plants and trees and warmth of the creatures on the earth. The Moon deserved eir own time to shine, at least as many eons as the Sun had taken for emself.

For a while, the inhabitants of the world tried to live their lives only by moonlight. Sometimes only by starlight, for the Moon was fickle and also came and went as e pleased. Only this time, when e returned, e knew e would be the brightest being in the entire sky.

But moonlight was not bright enough for the growing of food, or of wood for the fires which the people now needed for warmth. The oceans were dark, and the good fish slept while strange, glowing creatures with fangs and tentacles appeared amid the waves. The forests fell under the domain of the owls, and few creatures dared venture out into the dark.

Chapter Thirty-Three

This was not a life to be lived. So the denizens of the world came together, and they selected four representatives to find the wolf who had stolen the sun. For there were reports of em whispered here and there, a creature that glowed so brightly from within it was almost impossible to look at. These representatives, the Bear, the Fox, the Bird, and the Human, would do whatever they could to find this wolf and return the sun to the sky.

The Narrative fades, releasing my attention back to the dark forest, and the others around me. June flutters over to sit on Aeronwy's back. They glance at one another, which is a funny thing to see a fox and a bird do.

"Off we go, Mx. Fox! I hope you do not mind if I ride upon your brow, for I am a creature of the day, and I cannot see very well at night. I fear the owls may devour me," says June.

The words sound different than the casual conversation we were having earlier. They feel like part of the Story, like the dream logic spoken aloud.

"It is of no consequence, and I promise that while we journey together, I shall not devour you either," says Aeronwy. There's a hint of humor to eir voice, as if e finds this funny. "With my keen night vision, I shall lead the way."

Night vision and a convenient source of light, as well. Aeronwy trots off between the trees, ears perked and tail trailing smoke behind em.

Tabby rises to eir feet. Even at the shoulder, e's taller than I am. Eir paws are the size of dinner platters and tipped with terrifyingly large claws. I shuffle over, squinting in the moonlight, and lay a hand on eir shaggy golden fur.

When I open my mouth, the words come out old-fashioned sounding and strange. "Mx. Bear, I don't mean to be a burden, but would you mind bearing me forward as well? I'm afraid I won't be able to keep the pace with such swift-legged beings," I say.

"It would be no burden at all, Little Human. And please call me Bear," says Tabby.

E lowers emself down as far as possible, and I clamber onto eir back. Through the thick fur, I can feel just how strong a bear's muscles are, just how much power is in this body. The Story chose our roles well, I think. Tabby may have a soft heart, but e's also strong. I dig my fingers into eir fur and hold on as tightly as I can as e trundles behind Aeronwy and June.

I don't like the woods at night. The moonlight pours through the trees in puddles and bars, not so much illuminating the ground as making the darkness even darker. Small shapes flit here and there, through the air, through the leaves. No matter how much I steel myself for it, every rustle and flutter sets my nerves on end. Instead of looking for the Wolf, I press myself tightly against Tabby's back.

"I can feel your heartbeat, Little Human," says Tabby. "Don't be afraid. I will protect you."

What if I want to protect you, for once? I think, and that more than the offered comfort makes me sit up straight and tall.

We continue through the deep, dark forest, the Narrative at our heels.

The four representatives searched high and low, for many days, looking for the Wolf. The Fox led the way. The Bluebird listened for news in the chatter of the treetops. The Bear foraged for them food and drink, so much as there was to be found. For without the light of the Sun, the forest was beginning to wither. The Human entertained them with song and story to strengthen their hearts.

Finally, one of the whispers led them to the foot of Mt. Cináed, which in those days was a place of fire and danger. Few trees grew this close to the mountain, whose sides were covered in barely cooled flows of lava and glass. Between these flows were the mouths of caves, which gaped open like glowing portals into the heart of the earth. It was here, among the warm light of the volcano, that the Wolf lived, when not out running beneath eir friend the Moon.

The representatives approached the caves cautiously. They knew not whether the Wolf would be friend or foe. Fox knew the Wolf well, for they were once close as siblings. Bird knew the Wolf well, but as snapping jaws and raking claws, a danger to be avoided. Bear did not know the Wolf, and did not care to, for their paths rarely crossed in a meaningful way.

Chapter Thirty-Three

Human thought she knew the Wolf. She knew the type, watched from a distance as their two packs hunted the same prey, or sat upon a ridge beneath the Moon and sang. She thought perhaps the Wolf was, like Humans, both beautiful and dangerous. And now she was, as all Humans are, curious to see if she was right.

I slide off Tabby's back and step into the cave. The ground is hard and sharp beneath the hide shoes on my feet. The air smells of sulfur and smoke. Sweat trickles down my back from the sheer heat of the volcano. Everything is so *real*. If you die on the astral while journeying, usually you just return to your body. But here… here I suspect you'd be lucky to ever wake up again.

We round a corner and the tunnel opens into an enormous cavern lined with sparkling crystals. It's as if we've stepped into the center of a geode. Points of every color glitter and glint in the light, which comes not from Aeronwy's Flame, but from a figure seated in the center of the room.

The Wolf is huge, nearly half the size of Tabby, and certainly larger than me. E sits on eir haunches, watching us approach with eyes that burn like white-hot coals. Eir fur is also white, blinding to look at for too long. I can hardly see more than an outline, but the outline of a wolf is, after all, hard to mistake for anything else.

"Why, if it isn't my keen hunters," says Mairead. "Long have I evaded your search, and longer still I may have done. I have let you find me, here in my home, for I grow curious. Why is it that you seek me?"

"I believe you know why, Wolf," says Aeronwy coolly.

Mairead throws eir head back and howls, which the Narrative translates as a laugh.

"You have stolen the Sun, which belongs to all creatures," says Tabby.

"Eaten it, more like," adds June, who is nestled in the fur between Tabby's ears.

"But why?"

The others turn to look at me. They know all they need to know, because a wolf is always a wolf. But I'm human, and *why* is built into my very bones.

Mairead smiles a toothy smile. "A Human of all creatures should know about the hunger of a Wolf. My friend, the Moon, wished to be free from the oppressive light of eir twin. I wished to be free from the hunger which keeps me always prowling, always hunting, rarely full. It was a mutually beneficial bargain."

"But what about the rest of the world? Without the Sun, how will they all live?" June asks.

"That is not my concern," Mairead responds, testily.

"Is it not?" says Tabby.

I press a hand into eir shaggy fur in thanks. I feel the Story welling up in me, offering me a choice: I can side with the Wolf, or stand against em. I don't know the original myth. I don't know what the human in that Narrative chooses. But I know what *I* would do.

I pull myself up tall and say, "When all the world is gone but you and the Moon and Stars, and the haunts beneath the sea, then shall you still feel so satisfied? Will you not feel lonely?"

"Is not 'a lone wolf' a phrase that Humans use often? I enjoy being alone," says Mairead. The glow within em pulses, refracting off the crystals and sending triangles of light dancing across the cavern.

"I spoke of *feeling lonely*, not being alone, which are not the same," I say.

Mairead rises to eir feet, teeth bared like molten daggers. "Get to the point," e says.

June flies to my shoulder and ruffles eir feathers against my neck. "Do not wolves hunt in packs? Where has all your family gone?" e says.

"They have gone to become like dogs to the Humans, but I refuse to be subservient," says Mairead. E takes a few steps forward, shoulders hunched menacingly. My basic instincts scream at me to run away, but I hold my ground.

"Still there are Wolves in the forests who would have you, though some choose to befriend the Humans," says Aeronwy.

"They will not," says Mairead. "I will not. They are all alike. I shall trust no one but myself in this world."

"Do you trust yourself, though?"

My words hang bright in the air, and then Mairead leaps. I flinch backwards, June fluttering from my shoulder in a panic, bracing for the blow. My eyes are shut tight against the light of the Sun as it flies at me like a comet, piercing my eyelids with its intensity.

A large shape eclipses the Sun. I open my eyes in the sudden shade and find that Tabby has stepped in front of me, raising a gargantuan paw to knock Mairead out of the way. The Wolf goes flying across the cavern, skidding to a halt on the stone floor amid a disco ball of dancing lights. E does not get up.

In the tense silence, Aeronwy trots across the cavern and sniffs at Mairead's face.

"E's not dead, simply unconscious."

We breathe a collective sigh of relief. But there's no time to wallow in it. The Story continues.

While the Wolf slept, the other creatures of the world formed a plan to retrieve the stolen Sun. On their journey together across the world, they had learned one another's strengths, and played to them now in their final hour. They returned to the Forest, where Bear took with long claw the inner bark from the trees. Fox slipped through the underbrush, and with keen eyes found berries of the deepest violet. Bird plucked from eir own tail a magnificent feather, and all three of these things were handed to the Human, whose strength alone lay in Words.

"With this spell we will retrieve the Sun," I say.

I mash the berries in the indent of a rock and dip the shaft of the feather in like a quill. The birch bark lays unfurled nearby, ready to be written on. I use my own native language, adding flourishes and artistry as best I can to write my intent.

"How will Words help us?" June asks.

"These Words are the Story made manifest," I reply, "with them we can create the world we wish to live in."

"The World may have other ideas," says Aeronwy.

"That's true, but these ideas are mine," I say.

We return to the cave cautiously, Aeronwy once again scoping out the danger. The light from the Flame above eir head casts rainbows when caught by the crystals. Mairead is where we left em, knocked out on the stone floor. One brilliant ear twitches, and then a paw. E's coming to.

Swiftly, my eyes shielded against the sunlight shining through eir body, I pull open the Wolf's jaws and stuff the birch bark scroll inside. Mairead wakes instantly and breaks free of my hands, but it's too late. E swallows the scroll.

The light inside the Wolf's belly flickers. The light emanating from every hair is no longer the bright, hot light of noon, but shifts through the full range of daylight as we know it: the pale gray light of dawn, the soft clear light of morning, the harshness of midday, the golden strength of afternoon, the indigo blanket of evening, and finally the last refuge of twilight, as the Sun comes forth from Mairead's mouth.

There's a blinding flash, and then it's gone. We run through the twisting tunnels of volcanic rock and emerge not into the endless night, but a beautiful red dawn.

For on the scroll was written:

We the People of the Earth
On leaf and wing and claw
Call forth the light, our Sun
And by our right we form the Law

Half the day we shall see light
By flaming fire of Sun
Half the day we shall have night
By misty mirror of Moon

And so shall we all be free
And so shall we all be seen
On Earth, in Sky, under Ocean
So it is, so it was, so it will be.

Chapter Thirty-Three

Thus were created the day and the night. The Sun, compelled by the spell at first, soon grew to enjoy this arrangement, and apologized to eir twin, the Moon. The Moon for eir part was sorry e had asked the Wolf to swallow the Sun, but e did not abandon eir friend. For now the night belonged to the Wolf, who forever more would howl at the bright white orb above in a song of kinship. So long as there was night, and the Moon, the Wolf would never be alone again.

I turn around in time to see Mairead limp up to the mouth of the cave. Eir fur is ordinary gray now, and there's a haggard look to em, but there's still light in eir eyes. They glow in the shadow of the cave, beyond which e doesn't seem capable of going, fixed directly on me.

In a very, very low growl, e says, "I see what you did, and so did the Founders. You had better hope they don't mind your… interpretation of the tale."

Does that mean I chose wrong? Did the human side with the wolf in the original story? What would have happened if I did, as well? Because right now, I feel victorious.

"I rather liked it," says a voice to my side, amused. One that's vaguely familiar.

Before all of us, in a beam of sunlight, stands Daryn Sunseeker. E's tall and large, like the ancient Goddess statues found in Gildean caves. Around em floats a beautiful golden gown with wide bell sleeves, the ends dripping with citrines, the bodice beaded with carnelian. A headpiece like the rays of the sun sits behind eir head, crowning Daryn with even more shining gold.

Everyone goes silent, looking to the Founder. Daryn smiles widely at us, and winks at Mairead. "Perhaps you should have made different choices yourself, Wolfie," e says, and chuckles. "But you played the part well."

Mairead bows eir head and says, "Thank you, Your Honor. Only, I wonder… can this Trial truly measure a Head Librarian candidate when an apprentice is the one driving the story, instead?"

A jolt of fear lances though my stomach, but Daryn shrugs.

"I think it can, personally, and this is my Trial to judge. You can tell a lot about a teacher by the methods and ways of their students," says Daryn. "In which case, I think June has been a good teacher, don't you?"

E turns to me, and I nod vigorously. Daryn beams.

"Good. You *all* pass. Beware, though, for my colleagues may have different criteria than I," e says.

Daryn steps away, gesturing gracefully to a cobalt blue door which has appeared behind em. It's narrow and twice the height of a normal door, framed in curling iron. The handle and knocker are shaped like cresting waves and radiate a strange cold. Inscribed on the door are the words, once again in the ancient script, *The Day the Moon Died* and the name *Isylwyn Moonscryer.*

We open the door and step into another Story.

This time we're on a grassy clifftop, overlooking the ocean. It's nighttime again, with a full moon directly overhead, larger than any moon I've ever seen. To the north, there's a cove with a town nestled inside. There are boats on the water, their lights bobbing as the rough sea tosses them around.

I walk to the edge of the cliff and peer over. Hundreds of feet below, the water swirls and froths furiously. As I stare, the distance grows and shrinks in a dizzying fashion.

"Stop that," Tabby says beside me, and the distance stabilizes.

"I almost felt like I was going to fall in there," I say, shaking my head to clear it. I take a step back from the edge.

Tabby nods. "I could tell," e says. "Also, you look like yourself again, instead of like the character from *The Stolen Sun*. I wonder if that means we aren't playing characters this time."

"I don't know, is that possible?" I say.

"Why should you be characters? You aren't Head Librarian candidates," says Mairead from behind us.

We turn around. Mairead is standing on the highest part of the cliff. E looks young, about my age, and is dressed all in white. Skin pale in the moonlight, hair black instead of gray. I don't see Aeronwy or June anywhere. Why aren't Tabby and I with them?

Chapter Thirty-Three

The Story begins without answering my question.

Once upon a time, the Moon was not fixed in the sky as E is now, following a most familiar path through the sky night after night, phase after phase. No, in the early days of the world, the Moon was as wild as fire on the mountainside, appearing how and when E pleased. This, as you might imagine, caused considerable chaos to poor fishermen trying to chart the tides, and to the calendar makers and bureaucrats, who could scarcely organize the year around such a flighty deity. Something would have to be done.

The land shifts beneath our feet. I grab Tabby's hand, afraid we'll be separated, and a second later, we're standing by the docks in the cove. The transition happens in the blink of an eye, but I have memories of us walking down the winding path from the cliff and through the narrow streets of the village. It's disorienting. Tabby, who must be used to this kind of thing as a dreamwalker, doesn't look bothered.

At the edge of the water there's an altar covered in candles and offerings. A large metal bowl set into the center has been filled with water, in which the reflection of the moon is visible. Around us is a huge crowd of adults and elders and children, possibly the entire town. They're wearing wrap dresses patterned with ocean waves, fish, and water lilies. They look worried and desperate.

The people begged the Moon for order, but the Moon only replied,

"There is no order in the night."

A glowing figure appears, standing on the surface of the cove. My heart leaps, because I recognize the Moon's voice before I see eir face: it's June. An ageless June, young and old at once. Eir hair is gray, floating around eir face in wisps, but eir face is unlined and clear. E's wearing a silver-blue dress with a long train that stretches out over the water, rippling with the waves.

I jump up and down, waving to get eir attention. Eir eyes flicker over me, but that's all. E doesn't acknowledge my presence.

"Remember, this is Isylwyn's Trial," Tabby whispers. "It won't be like Daryn's. They probably have to get the story exactly right, according to tradition."

I stop moving, filled with uncertainty. I don't know these stories. How will I be able to help, if at all? I expect to feel intensely anxious about not knowing the answer. But my time in the Bindery must have changed me, because I don't get my usual burst of panicked energy. I stand still and watch as the Narrative continues.

The people made offerings of honey and oil and cedar, but the Moon only smiled and said,

"A gift is only a gift when freely given, and so my gifts to you are given as freely as I please."

The people raged and yelled and threatened to cease worshiping the Moon, for it seemed to make no difference to their life on the sea whether they did or not.
But the Moon laughed and sang,

"The admiration of the stars is all I need to live, but it seems you shall always need me."

One of the villagers throws a rock into the reflecting bowl, and the spell breaks. June disappears from the water. My heart squeezes, wishing we could go with em, wherever that is.

Their pleas unheard, their needs unmet, it was decided, by the highest courts in the land, by the highest priestexes in the temples, by the highest minds in the libraries, that the Moon would have to die.

The words of the Narrative startle me. *The moon would have to die.* What does that mean for June? My heart skips a beat.

"They planned this," Tabby mutters. "If they're going where I think they are with it…"

As the crowd disperses, Mairead appears. E stands before the moon altar and refills the reflection bowl slowly, using part of a broken offering vessel to scoop water from the cove. From the cobbled ground e picks up the offerings which haven't been shattered and places them gently on the altar.

There was but one young person in the village who did not wish for the Moon to die. Eir name was Maighread Moonstone, and e was fated to become the village's next Grand Storyteller, the keeper of all tales and one of few elite scribes who knew the secret making of ink and paper. E knew that interfering with deities and higher powers rarely went well for humankind. For now e was only an apprentice, however, and eir voice was not considered important.

No plea e could make seemed to affect the decision, for it was final. The current Grand Storyteller convinced them all that this was the dawn of a new age, and that they would all become part of legend. They called on their friends in the mountains, who did not live by the Moon's wild sea, to assist them in their plans. For these were a people who made their own light, worshiping not the sky but what lie deep beneath the earth.

I turn to look towards the mountains, and at the head of a grand procession is Aeronwy. In this Story, e's young and handsome, hair still long and black save for a large curl of gray that falls across eir face. The wrap dress e's wearing is a brilliant red and open in the back, revealing an intricate tattoo of runes and circles covering eir skin. I've seen the magical Flamekeeper tattoo in the old photographs June showed me, but it's more stunning in person. In the very center of eir back there's a burn mark in the shape of a hand—the goddex Cináed's hand.

The Cináedites following are wearing gold and green and yellow, with tasseled headdresses and heavy ceramic jewelry that makes music as they walk. Aeronwy's eyes slide over us as the procession passes by, but like June, e doesn't do or say anything to confirm e recognizes us.

The procession meets with the villagers at the Moon altar. The officials and priestexes greet Aeronwy with respect and reverence.

In this time the followers of Cináed had in all the world the finest craftsmanship and knowledge of metals, particularly the magical metals of copper, silver, and gold. For their forges were lit from the fires of the Mountain, and their smiths held within them Flame hotter than any hearth. The people of the village offered to pay the young Flamekeeper handsomely in their own treasures: pearls and glass and violet murex dye, but e refused, saying that their currency would be story and song.

The Grand Storyteller was old and frail and could only proclaim for so long before eir voice gave way. Apprentice Mairead was pushed forward to continue the payment. Eir voice was young and strong, and the stories e told were sad and beautiful. This fed the heartfire of the young Flamekeeper, who imagined e saw in this coastal villager a kindred spirit.

By the time the night had ended, the Flamekeeper's heartfire was hot enough to begin the work: a great net woven from pure silver thread, the only substance which was capable of trapping the Moon Emself. They toiled for days, and weeks, and more weeks, until finally the great shimmering cloth was spread across the entire cove, its threads so fine as to be invisible unless glanced at from exactly the right angle.

Mairead and Aeronwy play out the scenes as the Story narrates them. Like in a dream, things transition strangely, with gaps that are filled only by the knowledge that they logically should have happened. Tabby and I watch from the sidelines, never given a chance to join in. I feel like we're being kept out of the way.

Once again the reflection bowl on the Moon altar was filled, and the Moon was called down from the sky. E came, appearing on the glassy surface of the cove as E always did, glowing and mysterious. The Moon took one look at the expectant faces of the village and realized that E had walked into a trap. But before E could escape, or say even a single word (for the song of the Moon could soothe any heart, lull the mind to sleep), the net was pulled tight by the boats of the harbor, ensnaring the luminary within.

A great weight was added to the net, and it was drawn by boat outside of the cove, into dangerous waters, and dropped into the deepest crack off the headlands to the south. The people of the cove watched as the light of the moon disappeared beneath the waves, fading away into the depths without a sound. And when they were sure that E would not return, they rejoiced.

I nearly cry out when they toss June into the ocean. What will happen to em now? For all that I've learned how to stand back and do nothing, that can't always be the answer. I turn to Tabby, my chest hot with rage.

"We have to do something," I say.

Tabby looks unwell. "I agree. I know this story. I know what Mairead and Isylwyn are doing. They're trying to get rid of Aeronwy—Mairead's never considered June a threat, and thinks after this e can beat em easily. I have an idea, but... it's risky."

"What is it?"

"You have to understand," Tabby says, "if this story plays out in the traditional way, June will be fine. But Aeronwy won't. Maybe if this were an ordinary dream, but—you've seen how eir Flame manifests in this realm. You can feel how *real* this place is. Aeronwy can't swim. If e dives into the water, as the character in the story does... that is, if e can even get past eir phobia enough to jump..."

Extinguished. Drowned. My heart skips a beat. "What do we do?"

"If this works, June will most likely be disqualified from the running, but Aeronwy won't. If I'm right about how Isylwyn will judge things," Tabby says.

"But—"

I stop myself. I love June. I'd love to be able to tell people I'm studying Illumination under the Head Librarian of the Eternal Library. *Then, I would be enough,* a part of me says. *Then, I would be the best.*

But this isn't about me. It's about the Library. It's about our family.

"Okay," I say. "Tell me the plan."

The Story continues while Tabby leans over to whisper in my ear.

Maighread wept for the loss of the moon and feared what was to come next. The Flamekeeper, who had decided to stay in the village, tried to comfort em with songs of earth and fire. For a while, it worked.

For a while, life became easier and more predictable, in such that the seas were exactly the same every single day. The fish were plentiful, the waves were gentle, the nights quiet and dark. But as time went on, the fish dwindled. Without the tides, the shellfish and other creatures which made their homes on the rocks of the cove had died. Wolves howled nearer and nearer on the outskirts of town, and fear crept into the villagers' hearts. They stayed inside, eating meager meals, and forgot the sight of the stars.

Yet they were too proud to admit that they were the ones at fault. And besides, they would say, was the chaos of before really all that much easier? So they stayed where they were, and talked idly of moving away to the mountains with the Cináedites. Some went, but most did not.

For in their hearts they still loved the sea. And to love the sea is to love the Moon, whether they wanted to acknowledge that or not.

Maighread understood this better than anyone else. One day the black grief that had enshrouded em snapped, and instead of sobbing and listening to songs, e marched out through the night to the highest cliff above the deepest depths. With only a small knife in hand, e leapt from the edge and into the inky waters below.

The young Flamekeeper by this time had grown fond of Maighread and the two considered themselves friends. But Maighread could not forget that the Flamekeeper had been the one to weave the very net that had captured the Moon, and so did not tell em about eir plan.

Chapter Thirty-Three

Nonetheless, the Flamekeeper noticed Mairead slip out that night, and quietly followed.

Mairead does what the Narration says, diving fearlessly from the cliff and into the sea. Aeronwy hurries up the hill after em, and stops at the edge of the cliff, fists clenched.

Not knowing Maighread's plan, the Flamekeeper believed e had given into despair and thrown emself to eir death. The belief that e had been such a huge part in eir friend's death fell onto eir shoulders like the weight of the entire world. E had only ever intended to help the people of the cove by capturing the Moon in the silver net, but now e realized that it had all been a terrible, unforgivable mistake.
There was only one way to set things right.

Aeronwy does not jump. E remains standing on the edge of the cliff, fists clenched and head bowed.
"Now," Tabby whispers, and we put our plan into action.

CHAPTER THIRTY-FOUR
TABBY

Without wasting any more time, I rush forward through the soft green grass and take Aeronwy's hand. E starts to glance at me in surprise, but stops emself, not wanting to throw off the Narrative.

"I know what to do. Do you trust me?" I say, my voice nearly carried away by a sudden gust of wind.

Amane runs past us and jumps from the cliff, determined to do her part. After a long moment, I hear her hit the water with a splash. Aeronwy keeps eir gaze on the ocean. I've never seen em like this before, body frozen tight, everything solid and tense except for eir face, which is openly fearful. E won't even walk over bridges in the Library gardens if they have water beneath. I can't imagine what standing beside the darkest, deepest ocean must feel like.

For the first time, I truly understand what Aeronwy told me all those moons ago, that I shouldn't mistake obligation for love. I knew what it was to feel obligated to my parents, to act out of fear and shame whenever I felt they needed me, but until this moment I hadn't understood what it would be like to do something dangerous purely out of love.

Aeronwy squeezes my hand. That's all I need. I toss an arm around eir shoulders and then throw both of us off the cliff.

This is not my dream, but I am a dreamer, and I can change it if I wish. I've done it millions of times before, opening my mind and molding the world as I see fit. Just before we hit the water, I wrap both of us in my gold-lined cloak. Rather than giving us an icy shock, the water ripples over the surface of the cloak and rejoins itself behind our heads, leaving a bubble of air for us to breathe in.

I can feel Aeronwy trembling, heart beating incredibly fast, but e doesn't falter. We continue to sink beneath the waves into darkness so complete, you'd think it was the very end of the world. I sense rather than see the shapes of monsters swimming around our little bubble, things with teeth and tentacles that ruled since before the world was made.

Then, at our feet there comes a light.

The story resumes.

Despite the possibly deadly consequences, the young Flamekeeper leapt from the cliff and descended beneath the waves, down, down, down, down... until finally, a soft glow could be found. Moonlight on water is one of the most beautiful sights the Author wrote into our world, but moonlight under water went far beyond beauty. Shimmering lights danced across the canyon walls and turned the strange plants and fish living within it to stained glass. The Moon lay, still tethered, in the deepest part, crying tears that fell around eir feet like shining diamonds.

The Moon was crying because although Maighread had reached em, no knife on earth was strong enough to cut through the silver net in time. Maighread had started sawing at the anchor line with vigor, but eir breath had nearly run out, and as the Flamekeeper approached, the knife fell from eir fingers onto the sandy floor.

What a strange and beautiful sight, to see June, ethereal and brilliant, crying while young Mairead's eyes flutter shut and e begins to drift away, hands over eir mouth. Underwater, their hair and clothes billow around them, lit with shades of blue and silver and white which never did and never will have names.

The Flamekeeper, without hesitating, used the hottest heartfire to melt the silver net. Even underwater, the Flame was like to that which pours from the core of the Earth, and cannot be easily extinguished.

In the original story, the Flamekeeper character, having traveled through so much water and used so hot a flame, is supposed to die at the bottom of the ocean. But not before asking the Moon to rescue eir friend, Maighread.

Here is where Amane comes in. She's floating beside June, having hopefully relayed the plan to em. She flashes me a thumbs up, and then rockets toward the surface of the ocean. My heart warms, my resolve strengthening.

We land on the seafloor. I let Aeronwy go, but maintain the bubble around us. It isn't easy. I can feel the Story pressing in on me from all sides, just as the dark water does here at the bottom of the ocean. I watch Aeronwy walk forward and stop in front of June, some of the fear melting from eir face. They press their hands up against the bubble wall briefly. Then Aeronwy takes a step back and breathes out a bright blue and colorless flame. It flows through the bubble wall and through the water like a lightning bolt, and the silver net around June glows red before going dull and falling away entirely.

"Beautiful Moon, please forgive me my transgressions, for I knew not what beauty and magic my work had pulled from the skies. Please, return my friend to the surface, and to life. E is the only one who never doubted you," Aeronwy says, kneeling before June and gesturing to Mairead's floating body.

While e talks, the Story keeps pressing in on my bubble. *Isylwyn* presses in. This is not a Narrative that's open to interpretation, and it wants to enforce the 'correct' reading on all of us. On me, especially. I'm an outsider here, not part of the cast. Earlier I thought of Amane and I as being 'watchers, ' but really, we're the readers here. Readers have power.

So does an Author who loves to assert their power over what they see as their world.

June gently leans through the wall of the bubble, miraculously dry instead of wet. The light e radiates bounces around the bubble, driving back the darkness of the underwater canyon. E takes Aeronwy's face in both hands and smiles.

"For your courage, I will return more than just your friend. For I also realize the error of my ways, the effect I have had on the people I am supposed to guide, and now it is my turn to put things right," e says.

Chapter Thirty-Four

June kisses Aeronwy on the forehead, and the bubble grows to the size of a room. I no longer feel Isylwyn pressing in on me, and fall to my knees on the seafloor, far more exhausted than I realized. Nearby, Mairead stirs and sits up. E surveys the scene with confusion—this is not how this is supposed to go—but says nothing, unwilling to participate in the rewrite.

June presses eir palms together and begins to sing. I don't recognize the language, but it sounds old and strange, with a lilting melody that fills my body with lightness and joy. Slowly at first, and then quickly, our bubble rises up from the sea floor and through the many depths, until it bursts from the water and hangs before the shining white cliffs, Amane watching us from the top with wide, laughing eyes.

Everyone is set down on the cliff, including Mairead, and June's song ends. Overhead, the Moon reappears in the sky.

The Moon walked with Maighread back to the village, who threw off their pretenses and greeted both with open arms. Among them they struck a bargain, that the Moon could still shift and change and take a day or two away in darkness, but it would be done with Order, in a cycle that would henceforth remain unbroken until the ends of time.

We remain on the clifftop, waiting with baited breath to see if this is it. The end of the Narrative doesn't acknowledge the changes we made to it, but it does omit parts of the original story that we've made impossible. New moons, when the moon does not appear in the sky, are supposed to be the Moon returning to the depths of the ocean to pay respects to the Flamekeeper who perished there, among other things. But Aeronwy's character did not die, and so here we are.

A heavy sigh comes from behind me. "You were doing so well up until the end," says a deep, weary voice.

Mairead stands excitedly, expectantly, and bows with praying hands. Everyone else simply turns to look at Isylwyn Moonscryer, who has appeared on the edge of the cliff from which we leapt earlier. The second Founder and Head Librarian of the Eternal Library is tall and straight-backed, wearing a robe patterned with moon phases and a long shimmering coat lined with white fur. Eir face is stern, with a thin nose and thick eyebrows furrowed close together. Two white stripes run through eir hair at the temples, pulled back into a high, intricate bun and braids.

"I never liked the end of that story anyway," June says, brightly but with an underlying note of sadness. My plan relied on em agreeing to be disqualified, to save Aeronwy. Having seen them together, I was certain e would.

"The sacrifice is important. It creates a greater depth of beauty and meaning," says Isylwyn. E speaks to June, but eir gaze wanders across all of us, most often to me. "There must always be great and terrible things at stake, and sometimes they must be lost. Such is the way of the world and how it was written. Such is how we can create greatness in our own tales."

"That's one way to look at it, yes," says June. E scoots closer to Aeronwy and they put an arm around each other's waists. The look Aeronwy shoots June is grateful, but knowing.

Isylwyn heaves another great sigh. "Juniper Stargrove, I'm sorry, but by my judgment you have not passed the second Trial. You and your apprentice will return to the Library immediately."

Beside June, a door appears. This one is simple and white, without adornment. It has no frame, save the blackness of the sky behind it. June eyes it with resignation and disappointment clear on eir face, and Aeronwy's shoulders sag. Amane looks resigned.

"It's all right, I knew what I was doing. I changed the story to make sure Aery was safe, and can continue on. *My* sacrifice will not be unimportant or meaningless to *this* story," e says, blue eyes glinting towards Isylwyn.

Aeronwy and June share a long kiss and a whispered conversation I can't hear. Amane appears beside me and gives me a tight hug.

"Thank you," I tell her, and she squeezes harder.

"Don't let em win," she says.

"We won't."

"I trust you," she says, and then, hesitantly, "Also, I love you."

I look down at her in surprise. I wasn't expecting this so soon, but here we are. "I love you, too."

I kiss her head, and then she leaves the Story with June. The white door closes behind them and blinks out of existence.

Mairead turns to Isylwyn with barely concealed fury. "Are you saying that Aeronwy passed, then?" e says in a voice that could cut diamonds. "Your *Honor*."

Isylwyn nods gravely. "Aeronwy Stargrove followed the proper Narrative up until the point it could no longer be salvaged," e says.

Mairead points an accusing finger at me. "Even though with this one's meddling, e didn't even come *close* to actually drowning?"

Aeronwy is watching Mairead now with an incredulous, wounded look, as if e didn't think e'd actually say what we were all thinking out loud.

"What happened is, unfortunately, not against the rules. The apprentice's actions assisted Aeronwy Stargrove, who if I'm not mistaken, is too thalassophobic to have jumped on eir own, in following the Narrative," Isylwyn says. "Unlike Juniper Stargrove, e in no way directly defied the story. And so, e passes this Trial. Are you so concerned? Do you not believe you will be the victor at the end of this trilogy?"

Isylwyn and Mairead share a long look. Things didn't go as they planned. For all that Mairead preaches about the Author, about following fate, and worshiping the wisdom of figures like Isylwyn, it seems that in the end e deals with a loss of control just as well as anyone else does. Badly, in other words.

"Mairead Moonsea and Aeronwy Stargrove, you have passed the second Trial. Only one remains. Only one of you may pass through the Heartspace doors and sign the Charter Book. Eirlys will decide who that is," says Isylwyn, and e disappears.

***

The door to Eirlys's trial is labeled *The Wishing Star*.

"Didn't you say this one is your favorite?" Aeronwy asks, standing beside me under a dusk sky the color of eggplant.

"You remembered."

"Of course."

Aeronwy looks sixty-two again. Unlike when e visited my heartspace, eir hair is cropped short as it is in real life. Both of us are dressed in traveler's clothes of wool and linen, with thick leather boots. From a deep valley we gaze up at craggy mountain lines. The distinctive outline of Mt. Cináed towers above every other peak.

Mairead is nowhere in sight.

"Tabby," Aeronwy says, "what you and Amane did back there… thank you. I don't know what I would have done otherwise."

"Well, thank you for trusting me," I reply. "After all, it was only your life in our hands."

Aeronwy looks upward with a smile. "I know."

Once upon a time.

Constellations speckle the deepening sky as the Story begins. I pick out their familiar shapes as they rotate as if in a time-lapse video. The Great Redwood Tree, Dáithi the Wise, Aislinn the Dreamer, The Bear, The Cub, Caoimhe's Bow, Cináed as the Firebird, and many more. These starry figures I memorized as a child, wishing I could escape into their boundless realm.

Before there was time. Before there was paper, ink, or thread. Before thought, speech, and movement was made manifest by the written hand—there were stories in the stars. Woven with dreams, around hearthfires and meals and festival days, the tales that humans told gave life to the glimmering light above.

In thanks for this sustenance, the gods decided to offer the humans a gift. They created the brightest star of all, Cináed's Eye, and placed it above the peak of the mountain, where those who proved their worth could pluck it from the heavens. Whoever completed the journey would be granted this: a single, precious wish.

Chapter Thirty-Four

As the Story narrates, the clouds clear from the top of the volcano, revealing an enormous red star, the 'eye' of the Firebird constellation. I feel its promise pulling at my heart, and Aeronwy takes a step forward. This must be our final Trial.

I have no doubt Mairead has the very same goal.

"We have to get there first," I say.

Aeronwy nods. "Then let's be off."

Many tried to claim this gift, but all so far had failed. For the way was long and paved with danger. But ever are there souls whose hearts burn with desire, and so ever would there be those who took the risk.

Aeronwy and I wade through meadow and over gurgling stream. The light of dawn is on us now, golden and clear. Dew coats our clothes, and the ground underfoot grows steadily softer. As we reach the base of the mountain, a great bog spreads out before us, fed by underground springs and glacial meltwater. The water looks deep and dark. Aeronwy stays well away from its edge.

The first obstacle the seekers did face was the Obsidian Bog, whose depths were said to reach the Underworld itself. All around the base of the mountain it stretched, without bridge or pause. In those days, giants of scale and fang were still seen in the black, black waters, and to swim in them meant becoming another creature's dinner.

I know this story by heart. I scan the grass around us until I find the nearest spider web, its gossamer lines glinting in the sun. I point it out to Aeronwy, who kneels in the mud beside the web. At the center is an enormous golden and black spider.

There was one being who did not fear the bog, and that was Spider the Weaver, who feasted on the many insects which called the muddy waters home. When Spider saw the travelers, e called out to them in welcome and warning:

"Hello my cousin humans,

What manner of friends be you?
If you wish to cross the bog,
You'll need a raft to guide you through!"

"We have not a raft, and we are in a great hurry," Aeronwy replies to Spider. "We humbly ask for your help in crossing the water. In return, we will pay you in the manner of our people—with song."

"A song about me?
I delightfully agree."

The toll paid, Spider the Weaver called for eir family, and together they wove a boat of silk broad enough for the travelers to sit in. The boat was light as air and would have floated above the surface of the water, had it not been weighed down by cargo. One of Spider the Weaver's many spouses took the helm, while Spider listened to the travelers sing.

Aeronwy elbows me as we climb into the boat. Eir face is ashen, eyes tight, but e manages a twitchy smile.

"That means you, too," e says.

"I'm not a very good singer," I protest, cheeks warming.

"If you won't do it for the story, would you do it for me? I need something to take my mind off the fact that—" e breaks off, unable to finish the sentence. E tilts eir head upward, staring anywhere but at the water surrounding us.

"All right."

Aeronwy starts singing a fast song about how the Spider is the greatest weaver in all the land, the one whose threads hold the world together. It's an old folk song, and I only know some of the words, but I catch on a few verses in. We don't sound terrible. I'm unsure if this is because Aeronwy's beautiful baritone makes up for my raspy alto, or if I'm not as bad as I thought.

Spider guides us expertly across the bog, through the maze of dead trees and reedy islands. Once or twice I think I see something large and slippery surface beside the boat, but we arrive at the other side untouched.

Aeronwy stumbles back onto land with a huge exhale of relief and leans against a tree while I talk to Spider.

"Thank you, cousin," I say. "We'll take our song far and wide, so all will know of you."

Spider's eyes glittered with pleasure as e replied,

"A better gift for which I could not ask,
Fair travels to you, good luck with your task!"

With that, Spider and eir family returned from whence they came. And so, the travelers arrived at the Mountain.

We hike upward through the dense forest. The fir trees tower above us, dripping with moss. On either side grow ferns twice my height. Everywhere there are mushrooms sprouting in shades of brown, red, and blue. There isn't a path, just bits of overgrown deer track here and there.

As real as this dream might be, without my body, I don't feel winded or sweaty like I would in the waking world. Instead, the climb takes a toll on my heart and mind. I begin the trek in good spirits, but the farther we go, the more doubt surfaces. We haven't seen hide or hair of Mairead. What if e's beating us? What if e's nearly there? What if I'm slowing Aeronwy down?

Our pace slows to a crawl. Aeronwy struggles, too, brow furrowed and eyes locked on the ground. I wonder what e's thinking. Was e embarrassed by my singing? Does e resent needing my help to complete the Trials? Does e even want to be Head Librarian?

In the Shadow of the Mountain, the travelers faltered. They felt as if the very weight of the earth were upon them, preventing them from moving forward. The Mountain knew of their quest, and had been instructed by the gods to weed out any unworthy of their gift. It pressed upon the travelers, unearthing their worst thoughts and memories.

I sit down on a rotting log, my head filled with visions of my parents and of the day Rhiannon revealed e stole the Charter

Book. Scenes from the past, replaying in vivid detail, in endless variation—what if I had acted differently? What would have happened then? What did I do wrong? What if it happens again in the future? What if I'll never truly be free?

Closing my eyes, I take a deep breath and imagine these questions flowing away on a river of thought. Floating through the sky like clouds on the wind. My mind momentarily quieted, I look around and see Aeronwy doing the same thing.

Then the opossum appears. A curious, catlike creature with a hairless tail, little hands, and babies on eir back.

"I heard you singing to Spider the Weaver,
I worried that you might not last
Under the Shadow of the Mountain.
Do you need help?"

"Yes, we do," Aeronwy says in a strained voice. A wisp of smoke escapes from eir mouth.

I nod. It's all I have the strength to do.

"Then climb onto my back,
I will bear you as far as I may,
I ask only that you serenade my children and I,
The way you did for Spider."

In the blink of an eye, Opossum grows to a huge size. The babies on eir back scoot over to allow Aeronwy and I on. When we don't have the will, Opossum picks us up with eir prehensile tail and deposits us behind eir head. I bury my face in the soft gray and white fur.

I don't leave it there for long. We have another song to sing, another story to tell. In this time without the written word, melody was what bore a tale into the world. Aeronwy makes this one up as e goes, and I catch on to the chorus. We sing about how Opossum, though e sometimes looks fearsome, is a kind and gentle creature. How eir pouch is like the womb from which we all came.

As we sing, my doubts subside. My sorrows lighten, and my voice grows louder. By the time we reach the treeline,

Chapter Thirty-Four

Aeronwy is sitting up straight with a determined light in eir eyes. The Flame in eir chest burns brightly.

At the edge of the forest, Opossum set the travelers down and returned to eir natural size. The babies were chattering and singing snatches of the song sung by the travelers, which would surely annoy their parent in time. For now, Opossum seemed pleased.

"I can take you no farther,
Farewell and take caution
For the most dangerous part of your journey
Still lies ahead."

Opossum disappears into the underbrush. Aeronwy and I turn to face the expanse of boulders, skree, and snow on the slope above us. We exchange a glance and set off.

I know this story like I know my own heart. I've read it dozens of times, in dozens of versions. Even drafted my own take, with illustrations. I'd been working on the children's book when I met Rhiannon, but never finished. I set the project aside and never returned to it, though I thought of it often. The feeling of longing the tale instilled in me was just too much to bear.

As we traverse the rough terrain of the mountain, I wonder if I might feel differently about it now.

Aeronwy and I are pulling ourselves up a sheer cliff of rock when I hear a shout. I turn towards it.

"What was that?"

Aeronwy is several feet above me, on another ledge. "There's someone stuck on the rocks. They just fell into an unfortunate spot and can't get back up," e says.

"Someone?"

When e doesn't answer, I realize it must be Mairead. I bite my lip. I should be glad, because if Mairead's stuck, then we have a free path to the end of the Trial. We can win.

But I gaze back the way we came, at the dizzying drop into the valley below. If diving into the ocean would have extinguished Aeronwy's Flame, what would falling off a mountain do in this heightened spiritual realm?

"I'm going to see if e's all right," I say.

Aeronwy just nods. "I'll wait."

I edge along the cliff face until I find a spot that's broken away. Peering over, I see Mairead trapped on a ledge lower down. E's covered with swamp mud and dead leaves and scratches. Eir glasses are cracked, hair a bird's nest. E scrambles at the cliff desperately, with reddened palms, but stops when e sees me.

"Are you okay?" I ask.

"What do you care?" e calls up, scowling.

"I don't like you, but I don't want something awful to happen," I say, shocking myself with my honesty. I don't think I've ever told someone that I don't like them before. It feels good. "Although, it looks like it already has."

Mairead spits over the ledge. "At least I got here all on my own."

I blink, taking that in. "*All* on your own? Without the help of the animals? Haven't you read this story before?"

"Of course I have," e says. "But I see how it is, now. I saw how you all triumphed by altering the last two stories, forcing your own interpretation on the Trial. Isylwyn told me that Eirlys would be set against me, would try to trick me. So, I've created my own version of *The Wishing Star*. I always thought the story was misguided, anyway. Clearly, the only way to prove myself worthy of the wish is to overcome the challenge *myself*."

I wait for em to finish eir monologue. "I see. But now you're in danger of falling to your death. Do you want help?"

I reach my hand out towards em, again surprising myself. Leaving Mairead on the ledge is a clear way to victory. E could take advantage of my kindness and pull me down with em. And yet, I can't just leave em there without trying. Everything in my heart stands against that.

Mairead stares at the hand I offer with disgust. "I'd call you a fool, but clearly this is a trick. Once I take your hand, you'll make *sure* I fall by letting go."

"Why in the world would I do that?" I ask.

Mairead sits down on the ledge, arms and legs crossed. E stares at the ground. "Because that's what's happened to me my whole life. And it's not ever going to change, so I have to hold my own. I have to be strong, and wily. Go away. I will do this myself and prove I'm worthy of being Head Librarian."

I watch em silently for a moment before withdrawing my hand. Once again, my mind is filled with questions. I get up and edge back over to where Aeronwy's waiting. E helps me climb farther up the cliff.

"I saw what happened," e says.

"I don't understand," I say.

"It's not my place to divulge the particulars, but Mairead had a childhood much like yours and mine," Aeronwy says. "Some of us are able to alchemize our hurt into kindness and trust. Others repeat the cycle, wielding their wounds as a weapon."

"I… I have a lot of thoughts and feelings about that."

"So do I. There's no easy answers, unfortunately."

"You're right about that," I murmur, and then we encounter the final phase of the story.

As the travelers neared the summit of the Mountain, farther than any before them yet had come, they saw before them a great beast with eir paw trapped beneath a rock. Few ever laid eyes on Mountain Lion the Strongest, a being made from grace and muscle. The big cat lay panting on the ground, fangs bared in pain. It called to the travelers as they approached.

"Little humans,
I am at your mercy.
Kill me or free me,
But do it quickly."

"We will free you," Aeronwy says, approaching Mountain Lion reverently. I can't help but compare the two; they have the same lean strength in their bones, the same pride in their raised heads.

"Do as you will,
Beware though,
For in my pain,

I may bite thee,
And you may be slain."

"Do not worry," I say, kneeling on the other side of the Lion. Gently, I take eir head in my hands. It's so huge, and I can feel the power in eir jaws. "We will sing you a song to ease your pain, and then you may not bite us."

I start this time, singing a lullaby Oran used to sing when I was very little. It tells the story of the Lion's strength as a metaphor for the bravery and power inside all of us. Aeronwy joins in, harmonizing while e slowly rolls the rock from Mountain Lion's back paw. My heart pounds and my voice quavers, but the Lion closes eir eyes and listens calmly.

Once freed, e stands and stares at us with intense golden eyes.

"My thanks you gain,
For you I shall
Clear the path ahead
For there is a wall
Which none can scale
Go beyond it, and you cannot fail."

And so, Mountain Lion the Strongest took them to a great wall of stone, which was the final test of the gods. Mountain Lion roared and the earth shook, the wall cracking and crumbling before them. With the swipe of one mighty paw, e cleared the path for the travelers. E turned and left without a word, for that is the way of Lions.

By now, the day has darkened into night. Aeronwy's Flame casts flickering shadows across the stone as we walk through the path carved by Mountain Lion, and emerge on the edge of a great caldera.

The wishing star hangs over our heads, its red light making the caldera look as if it were filled with lava. As we descend the slope, the star floats down to meet us. An aurora of indescribable colors blazes across the sky, and music of an unnamable instrument plays in our ears.

The star is the size of a fist, pulsing like a heart made of light. At the very center of the caldera, the ground hot beneath our feet, we stand before it in wonder. It hangs in the air, rotating slowly. Overhead, the constellations peer inside to watch us claim our prize.

Aeronwy turns to me and says, "When I escaped the place I grew up in, my greatest wish was to have a loving family of my own. I had little idea what that would mean, or what it would look like, but I knew I wanted it."

"I understand," I say. "That's what I always wanted, too."

"Over the years, that wish came true in ways both seen and unforeseen," Aeronwy says. "June and I knew that our apprentices could be part of our family, and most of them have been. But, I admit, it's different this time."

"It is?" I ask.

"I'm glad you'll be staying with us in the Library when your apprenticeship is over, because I'm certain you belong with us in a deep way we've only begun to understand. It turns out that my wish is still being granted," e says, "and you're a part of it."

Tears well up and spill down my cheeks. "Are you sure?" I say. "I feel like I haven't done nearly enough for you to feel that way. Especially before today."

"Tabby," Aeronwy says, "You don't need to *earn* the love of your family. Though I understand why you feel that way, as it was the same for me. Watching you grow and knowing that I helped is more than I could ever ask from you."

I don't know what to say, but words aren't necessary. We hug, and in the warmth of Aeronwy's Flame I feel safe and seen. I watch calmly, proudly, as e steps forward and takes the wishing star in eir hands.

"I wish to be the Head Librarian of the Eternal Library," e says.

The star flashes blindingly bright, and when my vision clears, Eirlys is standing with eir hands in Aeronwy's. E smiles at us and gestures to a door that's appeared behind em.

"Come with me," e signs, and the dream translates for us.

We step through the door and into the giant redwood forest I know from the Library's dreamspace. A few paces away is the tree with the doors to the Head Librarian's office in it. This time, e allows us inside.

The quiet hum of a library falls over us. Sunlight glances in through high windows. Arches filled with books line the perimeter, topped with a second-floor walkway reachable by ramp and stair. Everywhere there are warm wooden railings carved into fantastical shapes, and colorful tapestries cover the floor beneath our feet. The tables and reading lecterns are staffed by ghostly Librarians, all of whom wear the purple robes of Scriptivist nuns. The light refracts through them like amethysts, scattering rainbows across the pages of their books.

The center of the room is dominated by a large round desk that appears to be a single carved slice of redwood, the edges still lined thick with bark. A single book sits open on its surface, and a single figure sits behind it.

It takes me a moment to recognize Rose, forty years younger, but Aeronwy knows immediately. E takes a long stride past Eirlys and halts, glancing at em for permission to continue. Eirlys nods and Aeronwy is at the desk in an instant, Rose slipping out from behind it without the wheelchair e had used late in life. They embrace warmly, Rose nearly disappearing under Aeronwy's long arms.

"I knew it would be you," Rose says, pulling away. "Or maybe June. But this place was always your heart-home, in a deeper way, and the books know that."

"So, this is it then," Aeronwy says, as Eirlys and I join them by the desk.

"Yes. The Founders and the books have decided. If you'll accept the role, then you will be the next Head Librarian of the Eternal Library, Aeronwy Stargrove, until your death requires you pass the title to your successor," says Eirlys. E spreads eir arms wide. "This is the Library as it was at the Founding. With the binding of the Charter Book, the memory of this place was merged with my own heartspace. It is the heart of the Library, but it will be yours as well, as you are stitched into this unbroken chain of Storytellers."

"I would wish for nothing more," says Aeronwy, without hesitation. "I accept."

Eirlys reaches for the book that lies on the redwood desk, turning it to face us. It's enormous, with thick covers bound in yellow leather. The skyline of the Bell Mountains, including Mt. Cináed, is stamped there in gold, wreathed by common Casporan plants used to make paper, ink, and thread.

Aeronwy touches the First book with delicate fingers. "Even though it's been scraped and hidden and recovered in the physical world, it still exists here as it was made?"

"Yes," says Rose. "That's how I was able to See through the physical copy to what it really was."

"You can't edit it from here, or else you would have," Aeronwy says, "I'm assuming?"

"Editing the Charter Book and thus the foundational Laws of the Library require changes on both the physical and astral plane," Eirlys explains. A shadow falls over eir face. "The Head Librarian is the only person who has access to the astral form, and the position is only transferred after death. I understand why Calliope did what e did. To prevent more politically-motivated murder. Yet, it means that nothing of the Law has been changed in 500 years, as perhaps it should have."

"You should know, we plan to dismantle quite a lot of the Book, particularly those around the Head Librarianship," says Aeronwy. "We want to spread the power of the position around and ensure that everyone at the Library has a greater hand in deciding the laws. Hopefully, there will be no more murders."

"Good," says Eirlys. "I recognize my mistakes now, and I am glad you will be there to rectify them."

Eirlys opens the Book to the center pages. They're blank save for a seven-pointed star in a circle, which stretches across both leafs. In the center, Rose's name is signed in shimmering ink. The longer I gaze at it, the more I see other names instead. Opaline Sweetfrond, Llewella Golddancer, even Isylwyn Moonscryer, Daryn Sunseeker, and Eirlys Starsower themselves.

Rose hands Aeronwy a fine, old paintbrush. In Aeronwy's hand it becomes a glass dip pen, the nib already wet with the same shimmer as the signatures. Rose keeps eir hands clasped around Aeronwy's and gazes up at em for a moment.

"With my passing, I pass my title on to you. Your heart and mine were already linked, but now, our spirits, too. To be Speaker for the Books is a heavy weight, but a joyful one. Sign your name, and it will be done," says Rose, a smile playing on eir lips with the rhyme.

As Aeronwy steps up to sign the Book, Rose steps to my side and whispers, "Good luck to you, too, Tabitha. You're going to be a wonderful Illuminator. I'm glad to have you in my lineage."

"I'm glad, too," I whisper, "more than I can say."

CHAPTER THIRTY-FIVE
RHIANNON

"This is unacceptable! I won't tolerate this kind of slander!"

Mairead's voice carries through the wall. It's been getting steadily louder over the course of the last hour, as Marion presumably lays out the evidence and gives em the bad news. The sound makes my heart pound and my stomach clench. Being emotionally manipulated and then cursed does things to your fight or flight reflex.

Tabby and Amane are seated on either side of me for support. I squeeze their hands and stare at the holes in the ceiling tiles. *This will all be over soon,* I tell myself on repeat.

Suddenly, a door slams and heavy footsteps carry down the hall. Mairead bursts into our room, fury etched on eir face.

"How *dare* you—"

Amane jumps to her feet, and to my surprise, so does Tabby. They place their bodies between Mairead and I, arms crossed and fists clenched.

"You made your choice. Don't blame Rhiannon for what you did," Tabby says. I've never seen em stand up to someone like this. Cutting off contact with eir parents has done more good than I knew.

Mairead's eyes narrow. This is the first time I've seen em in several moons, and e doesn't look well. There are dark circles under eir eyes, and eir blouse is buttoned wrong. E looks like a sad stray instead of a graceful feline. Losing the Head Librarianship to Aeronwy hasn't done em any favors.

"I only follow the destiny that's been written for me," Mairead replies.

"Then why fight against this? Maybe it's your destiny after all," Amane says, raising an eyebrow.

"Someone like you could never understand," Mairead spits. "It isn't supposed to be this way. There's another answer, and I'm going to find it—"

Marion and Xavier join us in the room. Marion's expression is as calm as ever, but there's tension in eir muscled arms. Looking harried, Xavier takes a position where Marion can see em signing while e talks to us.

"There will be more inquiries, especially around the prior location and treatment of the Charter Book," e says, "but as we've stated, violently cursing your coworkers is grounds for instant termination. Multiple third party curseworkers have confirmed those shadowboxes were made by you, Priestex Moonsea. The decision is final."

I start and lean forward in my seat. "You mean you're really firing em? For real? It's happening?"

Mairead shoots me a death glare, but it's too full of desperation to sting.

"Yes, we are firing Prx. Moonsea," Xavier says/signs, and Marion nods.

Mairead plants eir feet firmly on the ground. "I've worked here for nearly forty years. I rebuilt the Archives with my own two hands after the fire in '86," e says. "I have many loyal supporters in every department, and in important positions around the country. If you want to remove me, you'll have to do it by force."

Xavier translates this, since Marion can't see Mairead's face to lipread. Marion's lips flatten into a grim line, and e says, "That can be arranged."

***

When we arrive in Verdant Valley, the apple trees have just begun to fruit. We round the bend at the foot of Mount Carys, and Haybloom Orchards and Rivergreen Brewery come into view. The Brewery stands out among the crowd, a huge ancient barn restored and painted bright yellow with white trim. The rest of the buildings are a hodgepodge of rustic charm. I hear

Amane's cry of delight before she sticks her head through the open truck window for a better look.

"You grew up *here*?" she yells over the crunch of tires on the gravel road.

"Sure did!"

They hear us coming from a mile away, so by the time we pull up to the main house, the whole family is assembled out in the yard. Along with the chickens, the goats, the cats, the dogs, and eccentric metal sculptures. My heart squeezes and leaps at the sight of my parents, and I'm on the ground running towards them before the truck has even come to a complete halt.

I'm not one for tearful reunions, but it's been a long year.

"We're so glad you're home, Rhee! We miss you so much," Nia coos, enveloping me in a gentle hug.

"Aw, I was just here a few moons ago."

"A whole season is forever in the life of a farm," says Idris with mock seriousness.

"You know you're always welcome home whenever."

"The fresh air and sunshine will do you good after spending all that time in a dusty basement!"

I surface from the pile of hugs and laughter to check on the others. Tabby is dutifully unloading our luggage and chatting with Aubeline, one of my siblings who lives on the farm with eir spouse and kids. Said kids are part of a ring of children surrounding Amane, peppering her with questions and trying to get her to hold one of the chickens. June is talking to Eirian, another one of my siblings, about the sculptures. Aeronwy is still sitting half inside the truck, petting the dogs and glancing at the crowd of people with amusement.

"Hey! Hey, everyone! C'mere!"

I holler, and my Library family—I guess that's what they are by now—lines up to meet my birth family. I introduce them to my parents. Gladys, who's tough and strong; Nia, who's round and soulful; Idris, who's built like a barn and has a laugh you can hear for miles; and of course Gwen, who's dyed the gray streaks in eir hair pink and always has a no-nonsense twinkle in eir eye.

They're all in their late forties and early fifties, a generation younger than the Stargroves, but they greet one another like old school friends. We're ushered into the house along with our things, which are quickly deposited in various bedrooms where the knickknacks have all been dusted and the pillows fluffed for our arrival. There are huge pots bubbling on the stove in the kitchen, piles of early summer greens waiting to be chopped, and a whole leg of goat in the oven, roasting to perfection.

Books are medicine for the soul, but so is this.

We've got our own library here, scattered as it is throughout the house. I don't think there's a single room without a bookshelf. Even the kitchen has a billion cookbooks in it, some of them over a hundred years old. How do you keep a family of sixteen entertained when all the chores are done (although honestly, the chores are *never* done), and there's only one television? I run my fingers across the cracked and fading spines of young adult novels, chapbooks, picture books whose words I and all my siblings know by heart. These books are worth more to me than the rarest of volumes in the Eternal Library.

Which, as it turns out, I've held in my own two hands. When I told my parents what had happened, at first they didn't believe me. The Charter Book is one of our culture's most enduring legends, lost over five hundred years ago. But once I'd convinced them, they were weirdly proud. Angry, at Mairead, frustrated, with me, and worried, but proud and enchanted by the idea that their own progeny had touched something so incredible.

As if e's read my mind, Gwen appears at my side, eyeing me. E has the same green eyes I do, bright against eir brown skin. There are new laugh lines etched in eir face. When did my parents start getting old? When did *I*?

"So, kiddo, what's up? You look spooked," e says, crossing eir arms and leaning against the bookshelf.

I clear my throat. "A lot's happened this year," I say, "and it's not letting up anytime soon. The discussions about the restoration and editing of the Charter Book are getting really heated. I know you've been reading all the damn newspaper articles about it, because Renna emails me every one."

"Well, that's why you're here, so you can rest up and get away from it all," says Gwen.

"Yeah. Thanks for letting the others come along. They've been through it, too."

Gwen places a hand over eir heart and pretends to swoon. "We should be *honored* to have the Head Librarian of the Eternal Library, eir spouse, and their apprentices visit our quaint little town. I'll break out the good silverware and fine china," e says in a faux-aristocratic accent.

"Now I see where I get my sense of humor from," I say, leaning against em with a snort. "It's good to be home."

***

After a dinner of epic proportions, we shuffle outside to burp and sit around the fire. A proper bonfire out in the field, not a little one in the patio pit. They've been clearing all the deadfall around the orchard, and now there are apple limbs blazing merrily ten feet into the night. The sparks flicker through the cool air like shooting stars.

Then Idris and Gwen come out with the instruments. A few people clap excitedly in anticipation, and they grin and bow. Tonight, Idris has the mandolin, Gwen has the fiddle, and Aubeline and Eirian have the guitars. They tune my nerves as they tune the strings, bringing my mood to a more harmonious chord.

They know all my favorite songs and strike one up immediately. The music is lively, fast-paced and chock full of life in the valley. Everything I miss about the place that raised me. For now, I can melt back into that role, and forget about the mess back at the Library. I don't have to be Rhiannon, former child genius, co-finder of the lost Charter Book, expert on the Founding of the Library, or noted visionary expected to Do Great Things. Instead I'm the eldest Rivergreen-Haybloom child, head director of storytime, helper in the kitchen, terrible dancer who's drunk enough on cider not to give a shit who's watching.

The fire continues to roar while I twirl around with Amane, trying to teach her the music of my people. We keep tripping over each other's feet and nearly fall headlong into the pyre.

"Would you back away from that? Even I can't save you from burning to a cinder if you're determined to do so," Aeronwy shouts at us.

Amane scuttles back dutifully. I plop down on the ground a few feet away and blow a raspberry at em.

Idris laughs, plucking out an absent melody on the mandolin. "Say, Aeronwy, you sing, don't you? Being a Flamekeeper and all. Could your hosts trouble you for a tune?"

Aeronwy looks like e's about to decline, but June elbows em in the side.

"Of course you can! Do you mind if I join?" June asks, clearly excited. E's been at the cider, too, and eir cheeks are rosy with good cheer.

"The more the merrier!" Idris exclaims. "What do you have in mind? I actually know quite a few old Cináedite tunes from around here. Gwen's Ren taught them to me."

That's news to me. I didn't know that Grandren Gwynedd, who lives down the way with one of my siblings, knew any Cináedite songs. Did I grow up hearing them, without realizing?

"How about 'Sound of my Heart?'"

"I was just thinking of that one," says Idris, starting up the tune. "You must be psychic."

"A bit," says Aeronwy dryly. "Everyone ought to take a step back from the fire. It may behave a little strangely."

I've only heard the Stargroves sing once, when they were preparing to find Tabby on the dreamscape. I'd been there to watch and wake them up in case anything went wrong, a job I was shocked they trusted me with so soon after my betrayal. On the very first note they sang, all the hair on the back of my neck stood up and goosebumps went cascading down my arms and legs. If nothing else they're true weavers of magic and melody.

'Sound of my Heart' *is* one of my favorite childhood songs. Grandren Gwynedd used to sing it to me when I was having a visionary episode and wasn't sure when or where or who I was. The tune is energetic and dark, solemn and hopeful at the same time.

"If we were down on the water,
Your voice quiet on the evening,

The light of the stars wound round,
And drawn down to softest ground,

Would you stay with me?
Would you be true?
Would you listen to the sound of my heart,
As it sings out loud through you?

If we were deep in the valley,
Beneath the ancient trees that sleep,
All dark and green and grown,
Our secrets bared like flowers bloom,

Would you stay with me?
Would you be true?
Would you listen to the sound of my heart,
As it sings out loud through you?

If we were high on the mountain
With fires glowing red
And ember-swirling smoke
If soon we both be dead

Would you let me go?
Would you set me free?
Would you sing along, would you know our song,
As your heart sings out through me?"

Silence falls within the circle as everyone turns to listen. I mouth the words along with the song, not daring to ruin the beautiful harmony Aeronwy and June are weaving together in each verse. Beside me, Amane and Tabby are making dreamy eyes at one another, lost in the music.

The fire goes still and tall, like a candle flame, as if it's listening, too. Then it begins to sway to the music, leaning this way and that, sending people scuttling out of its reach. Aeronwy leans forward and holds eir hands out; long tendrils of flame unfurl into eir palms, grasping at eir hands like an excited grandchild. June watches calmly from eir side, unbothered by the proximity of danger or else so trusting of Aeronwy that e doesn't need to move an inch.

Everyone applauds and cheers when the song ends and the fire returns to normal.

"Damn, I didn't know that was originally a Cináedite song," I say. "Where did Grandren Gwynedd pick that up?"

"Rhee," says Gwen, "e doesn't like to talk about it, so we never did, but Grandren Gwynedd was raised in a Traditional Cináedite family. But something happened, and the Hearth they were part of dissolved. Some folks joined other Hearths, but Gwynedd left entirely and married a non-Cináedite."

"Excuse me," I say, as a smug look spreads across Aeronwy's face, "but what. The fuck?"

Aeronwy turns to Gwen and says, "Do you have a family genealogy on your shelves, by any chance? I happened to bring mine, since I was wondering whether there's a link between us. It happens often enough in these parts."

"I've had too much to drink to read all that tiny print now," Gwen says, chuckling, "but sure, let's give it a look tomorrow!"

***

The next afternoon I come in from reading under the trees, shucking my muddy boots off in the doorway and thinking only of a hot shower, when I hear Gwen calling me from the living room.

"Rhee! Rhee, is that you? Get in here for a minute!"

I could pretend I didn't hear em, but since I have to pass by the open door anyway, I poke my head in. E's sitting on the couch with Aeronwy and Nia. There are several large, heavy books on their laps.

"Alright, don't drag it out. What's the verdict?"

Aeronwy looks up from the tome e's holding with an expression I'm sure is supposed to be deadpan, but there's too much *I told you so* in eir eyes.

"You and I are second cousins, once removed," e says. "Gwen and I share a pair of great-grandparents, who are thus *your* great-great grandparents."

"So, related by blood then," I pout, because Gwen was the parent who carried and birthed me.

"Yep!" exclaims Nia. E stabs a finger at the book on Aeronwy's lap. "Neirin Greensleep, who married Iwan Quickbough and became the Greenboughs. Their children, Alis and Bleddyn, went on to have Maeve and Gwynedd, who in turn had Aeronwy and Gwen. And then Gwen had you, Rhee!"

"But I've read our family genealogy a hundred times, and I never saw an Aeronwy in there," I say, pointing to one of the big books. The other one is unfamiliar to me—the book Aeronwy mentioned bringing from eir own library.

"That's because I changed my name when I moved to Caspora City, to hide from my relatives," Aeronwy says. E points to a name in each of the books. "This is me right here, but you wouldn't have known that."

I lean over to read it. "Oh shit, that's right, your name was Morwen."

"You say that like you already knew," Aeronwy says, suspicious.

"Mairead," I say, and e rolls eir eyes, "showed me a memory in a vision. But, like, I didn't know that the last time I looked through these books, and it didn't occur to me to look again…"

"I see. For a while, I also changed my surname, but when I finished my apprenticeship and published my first book, I reclaimed Greengrove. Then, of course, when June and I married, it changed to Stargrove. But I kept my new first name," Aeronwy explains.

I plop down on the floor in front of them. "Well, this sure is a development."

Aeronwy laughs. "I inherited my Flame from our mutual ancestor, Neirin Greenbough, who was a very famous Flamekeeper, and the only member of my family who was truly kind to me. It's a lineage you can find pride in, despite its other flaws."

"Does that mean *I* could inherit your Flame?" I ask, intrigued by the prospect.

"No," Aeronwy says with a snort, "you're too old and uneducated in the culture. But perhaps one day you could inherit something else from me, when the time comes."

"What's that?"

"You could be Head Librarian."

I stare at em incredulously. "Where did *that* come from? What makes you think I'd *want* to be Head Librarian, much less be *good* at it?"

Aeronwy shrugs, a smile twitching at the corner of eir mouth. "It's just a feeling. You have plenty of time to think on it."

"I'd better. Don't go dying until we've finished restoring that damn Book," I say, pointing a finger at em.

"It almost sounds like you care about me."

"Hey," I say with a shrug, "that's what family's for, right?"

CHAPTER THIRTY-SIX
AMANE

ONE YEAR LATER

I sit in my studio and breathe in the rainbow light. The stained glass hanging in the floor-to-ceiling windows casts a full spectrum of hues across the spool of thread resting in my hands. I soften my gaze until the world melds into fuzzy circles of color, and turn inward.

June's tree meditation is lovely, but I'm a desert flower. I send my roots wide instead of deep, pulling in all the energy I can until it's stored inside me, ready to burst. Then I exhale it all into a beautiful bloom at the crown of my head, opening my spirit to the universe.

When I look into the mirror it offers to me, I still see my younger self. She still has her doubts but is curious about them instead of fearful. Instead of feeling angry and ashamed, instead of worrying, I put my arms around her and tell her over and over just how worthy she is. How all her dreams will come true, and *then*, she'll have *new* dreams to follow.

My younger self smiles. She pulls a hair from her head and offers it to me. When I take it, the hair stretches longer and longer, glowing a faint gold. It stays connected to her head—to my heart—as I open my eyes and get to my feet.

I've never forgotten how Tabby, playing the role of Eirlys, danced in that first dream we shared. I twirl around the studio, winding the physical and spiritual threads together with my fingers. The thread which comes from my heart isn't visible, but

416

I can feel it thrumming in my hands. The very essence of my soul, which if I'm successful, I'll use to bind my first Illuminated book one day.

My mind drifts off with the thought. The partial first draft of my historical novel about Calliope Everberry is sitting open on my laptop, waiting for me to finish it. There are still so many plot points I need to get in order. Research that needs to be done on the technology and food of the period. Character traits that need ironing out.

The thread in my fingers breaks with my concentration, and I lose my connection to my younger self. My vision comes back into focus. The music playing in the background fades and forwards to a new song. I look down at the spool in my hands.

I almost had it. I very nearly did.

Putting the spool down on the altar, I gather up my Threadbound Oracle and do a quick shuffle. Even with protective wards on, I sense my Great-Grandma in the cards, like a warm leathery hand in mine. Rose is here, too, raising the hair on the back of my neck like an oncoming thunderstorm. I pull a card for each of them.

The Six of Thread: Stitch and The Festival. The Six of Thread shows a ring of colored threads atop detailed, repeating embroidery patterns. The Festival shows a trio of friends browsing brightly colored stalls, a huge tree filled with lanterns rising above them. They want me to keep practicing, to keep repeating the meditation until I do actually succeed—but they also think I should celebrate.

I thank them and leave my studio, skipping across the common area to knock on Tabby's door. We don't share a space anymore, since we all helped clear out Rose's studio, which I moved into. The low counters made for someone short and the bright colors of the walls made me feel right at home. I added my own touch with suncatchers and Gildean-woven rugs, neatly labeled tool racks and floor cushions for relaxing. Though there is also a coffee brewing station for when I need a boost.

Chapter Thirty-Six

Tabby's studio is a place of peace. The walls are soft periwinkle blue, the cabinets the color of the ocean at midnight. A large daybed occupies the space by the windows, perfect for dreamwalking, reading, tea, or naps. There are plants everywhere, and herbs blooming in the sunlight. The room smells like mint and pencil shavings.

I bounce over to where e's sitting at eir illustration desk. "I almost did it!"

"Did what?" Tabby says, turning to me with a smile.

I lean my arms on eir shoulder. "I almost plied my Thread. I was *this* close, and then I got distracted. But I think that means I'll be able to do it next time!"

Tabby's smile grows wider. E swivels eir chair and pulls me into a hug and a quick kiss. "That's amazing!"

"Thanks," I say. I glance at the desk to see what e's working on. There are pictures of opossums taped to the desk around eir sketchbook. "More animal studies?"

"When I decided on this project, I didn't think the fact that I'd never learned to draw animals would be a problem," Tabby confesses sheepishly. "I'm getting better, but my drawings aren't where I need them to be yet for the book."

"I'm sure it'll be great. I can't wait to read it," I say, kissing em on the cheek. "I wish I could have been there in the third Trial to experience the story in person, but your take on it will be even better."

Tabby's phone pings, and e picks it up to read a text message.

"Rhee says e's too tired to cook tonight, can we go out to dinner instead?" e says.

"Sure! I know just the place."

***

The three of us meet up at the café where a year and a half ago, Rhiannon and I started mending our broken trust. We've been there dozens of times since, sanding the sharp edges from those painful memories. Rhiannon is waiting at our favorite patio table, shaded from the evening summer sun by an umbrella that matches eir short turquoise hair.

"What's up? I already ordered some appetizers. Sorry, but I'm, like, starving," e says as we sit down. E gestures to a plate of flatbreads and spreads, a basket of yucca fries, and deep fried mandazi. "Five thousand million meetings about that damn Book, and not one of them catered. No one cares enough about snack time."

"Has anyone agreed to anything yet?" I ask, grabbing a fry.

"Yes, thank the Author," Rhiannon says, rolling eir eyes and popping a pastry into eir mouth. "Camille an' Aeronshfy jus' haff to finish reshtoring the damb thing."

"How long will that take?"

"You'd know better than me, you're the one who handwrites books for a living," Rhiannon replies, swallowing and reaching for some fries before Tabby and I can eat them all. Something looks different about eir wrist, and I give a start.

"Your engagement bracelet fell off!" I say.

"Yeah, that means I'm gonna die first," Rhiannon says, and Tabby shoots em a look.

"That's just a superstition," says Tabby. E plays with the woven bracelet on eir own wrist.

I take hold of Tabby's wrist and examine the bracelet. It looks a little worse for wear, but not like it's going to fall off anytime soon. "What if you have to have the wedding while my parents are visiting? Can they come? What if I'll be away with them at Mt. Cináed? I can't miss you getting handfasted!" I exclaim.

Tabby laughs. "You won't. We don't have to have the wedding *right* when both bracelets have fallen off. We can have it any time after that," e says.

"Oh. That makes more sense," I say, feeling silly. "Have you picked a handfasted name yet?"

"We're trying to decide between Greenweaver and Fairgreen," Tabby says.

"I thought you were going with Bloomweaver?" I ask. Out of the sixteen possible ways to combine their surnames, I think that one's the prettiest. If Tabby and *I* ever get married, it might become part of my name, too, so I have a vested interest.

"Bloomweaver is a little too froofy for me," says Rhiannon. "Plus, we wanna keep the 'green' from my name."

"Because it's from the family line you share with Aeronwy," I say, guessing the reason. Rhiannon shrugs and Tabby blushes in confirmation.

Our server appears then to take our orders. I'm trying to decide whether I want okra or papaya salad as a side when a familiar voice calls out behind me.

"Look who it is! If it isn't our favorite little trio."

I turn and see Inyene approaching our table with Aeronwy, June, and Siobhan in tow.

"Hi!" I squeak. Even though I've met him several times now, I still feel starstruck in the presence of my favorite fashion designer. "What're you doing here?"

"Having dinner, obviously," Aeronwy says. E's wearing an impeccable black dress and boots, eir shoulder-length curls without a hint of frizz. A few other patrons turn to look at em. I can't tell if it's because of how amazing e looks, or because they recognize em as Head Librarian.

"After you recommended this place to me, I've been back a dozen times," Inyene tells me. "You were right, it tastes just like home!"

Seeing the impatient glances exchanged by the servers, June steps forward and says, "If it's no trouble, why don't we all eat together? I'm sure we can fit if we move things around a bit."

We do just that. Rhiannon grumbles because e has to wait longer while the newcomers decide what to order, but e quiets down when more appetizers arrive. Probably because eir mouth is too full to talk, though that doesn't always stop em. Inyene and I recommend the best dishes to the others, and everyone falls into comfortable conversation.

I turn to June, who wasn't at work today, and say, "By the way, I almost plied a Thread this afternoon! I got really close."

"You're making wonderful progress," June says, setting eir fork down and beaming at me. E's been growing eir hair out naturally, the dyed red ends finally trimmed off. It's all gray now, wrapped around eir head in braids. "How goes the novel?"

"That's what distracted me. I was thinking about all the work I need to do on it," I say.

"You've picked an ambitious subject."

"Good thing you have me to help with the historical research," Rhiannon says, winking. Not only has e helped me find sources on Calliope's life in the Archives, but we've looked back in time with eir visions a few times as well. I haven't let em possess me again, though. Three times was more than enough. We stick to card-based conversations with eir spirit.

"Should we have another brainstorm session tomorrow?" June asks. "I know it helps when you talk it out."

"Let's do that," I say with a determined nod. "I'd like to finish this draft before my family comes to visit in a few moons. They all want to read it so we can talk about it in person."

"That sounds terrifying," Rhiannon says, adding far too many pickles to eir dish. "I've only met one sibling and one parent on a video call, and they were hella intimidating."

"I'm not worried," I say. "I know it'll be good, whatever they have to say about it."

After dinner, we part ways with the older crowd and take a walk along the Sound. The sun is a blazing red ball on the horizon, the sky streaked with pink and gold clouds. The wind whips the surface of the water into white-capped waves and blows our hair about. I hold hands with Tabby while Rhiannon wanders farther ahead, hunting for treasure among the rocks. The scent of seaweed fills our noses, and the wet sand is cool beneath my toes.

"Do you ever wonder what your life would be like if you didn't get the apprenticeship?" I ask Tabby.

"Fairly often," e replies with a pained laugh. "It's still hard for me to believe all this happened, and that I deserve it, sometimes."

I gaze out at the water. "Do you think we still would have been friends? Became partners? If just one of us got it, or neither of us?"

Tabby is quiet for a long moment. E squeezes my hand. "I like to think so. There's just something about you that draws me in. Just like with Rhee, or Aeronwy and June. Even if everything else was different, I feel like that part would still be the same."

"I think so, too."

Up ahead, Rhiannon waves and yells, eir words nearly carried away by the wind. "Y'all! Catch up already and come see this thing I just found! I think it's some kind of ancient stone tablet with writing etched in it. Or it could just be a piece of concrete from the old pier, but you never know. Unless you're me and you can use ink scrying to find out."

"Remember the last time you tried scrying on the beach!" Tabby calls back. "Do you want me to have to carry you home a second time?"

"Why do you even have scrying ink on you?" I yell. "I'm proud of you for being prepared and all, but really?"

We break into a jog until we reach where e's standing. Rhiannon holds up a flat piece of rock about the size of a fist. There are scratches on it that *might* be writing. Or not. "I don't, but I have you two, and you can make ink out of practically anything, right?" e says.

I look around us for potential dye sources. "Probably…"

"Why don't we just take it home and see?" Tabby says, reasonably.

Rhiannon pockets the stone and flashes us a toothy grin. "That sounds good. Let's all go home together."

Thank you for reading!

Book Two now available:

The Tale That Twines

Forty years before THE THREAD THAT BINDS, Juniper Starstitch returns to Caspora City young and hopeful. Chosen to be Head Librarian Opaline Sweetfrond's last apprentice, June arrives at the Eternal Library looking to discover the magical manuscript art of Illumination—and to recover the memories lost to the trauma of the massive earthquake that killed one of eir parents a decade earlier.

June quickly discovers that these memories can be recovered through the ancient art of reading etheric Threads, the spiritual cords that link the world together. But remembering can be painful, and living in the past means missing out on the present. Even to the point that June's beloved apprenticeship is threatened by eir inability to let go.

It will take the help of friends both old and new for June to untangle the knotted threads of time, including the mysterious and stern Aeronwy Greengrove, who June may or may not be falling in love with, one song at a time.

More info and buy links at:
numinousspiritpress.com/thetalethattwines

Are you a Tarot/oracle reader like Amane? Would you like to
become one?

Now available in the Numinous Spirit Press shop:

THE THREADBOUND ORACLE

The cards Amane uses in are a real deck, created and
illustrated by me, Cedar McCloud! This 50-card oracle deck
features the characters from the novel and can be used for
divination, self-exploration, writing prompts, and more.

Beginner friendly! Comes in a beautiful book-shaped box with
a 104-page guidebook that explains how to use the deck and
gives suggested interpretations for each card.

<u>Check out the full card gallery & shop link at:</u>

numinousspiritpress.com/threadboundoracle

Friends of the Eternal Library

This edition of this book was made possible in part by the following ultra-generous benefactors via the 2023 Kickstarter for *The Tale That Twines*. The Author and the Library thank you from the bottom of their hearts for your support!

Franki Berliner
Brenna Greenfield
Gabriela
@jitterbookperfume (Lorna Doone)
Donna Newton
Chad Tillner
Anonymous
Scott Casey
Chad Bowden
Catalina Hackney
Nikki K
Charlie Grayson
Jesse Ahern
Baba Bee
Joy Vernon
E. Bolhafner
Puck Malamud

Acknowledgments

First of all, thank you to *you*, the reader, for taking the time to read this book all the way through! It makes my heart so happy to know that I get to share my story with others out in the world. I hope you enjoyed it, and that perhaps you were able to relate to the message in some way.

The biggest thanks in the world goes out to my partner, Shamus, for supporting and encouraging me while I was writing this. And also to my BFF Gabby, who I was dating in 2015 when I first started working on this concept, and who would hear much about the evolution of the story over the years. Gabby came up with the name "Caspora," which was much better than anything I had at the time.

Huge thanks to my editor S.L. Dove for your insight and expertise. You helped me polish this story to a shine, and with such kindness that I lost a lot of my fear of criticism and not feeling good enough.

Thanks to my writing buddy Sid, who has always been an amazing cheerleader and sounding board. Our promise to have books on the shelf next to each other is close to being fulfilled!

To all my wonderful friends all over the country, and especially in Seattle, who have taught me what family and community really mean, especially when many of us are no longer supported by our families of origin (and were even harmed by them).

Thanks to all my main therapists over the years: Brad, Amy, and Lori, I couldn't have done this work without your wisdom and guidance on my healing path.

To my Nana Rae Heimpel, in spirit, who was the one kind family member I could trust growing up, and who was a huge inspiration for June's personality. I can feel you with me still.

And to everyone on queer indie writer Twitter who I met over the last few years; even though I'm not using Twitter now, finding that community while I was just coming back to prose writing after ignoring it for five years was something I really needed. Y'all are the best!

Love, Cedar